AMONG THE FALLEN

"*Silent Hall* is very nearly a perfect novel. I wish my first book had been anywhere near as inventive and challenging to the norm."
    James A Moore, *author of* Seven Forges *and* The Last Sacrifice

"Love this story."
    H D Lynn, *author of* The Corner Store Witch

"This is a very special debut novel. The quality of writing takes this tale way beyond a simple fantasy adventure."
    Strange Alliances

"What a lush world of magics and peoples, gods, and dragons. What's more, the author set it all in a patriarchal world, yet delivers some rather feminist notions in a very organic way. Likewise, there are nuggets about racism and even domestic violence, but done so subtly and woven in so smoothly that they don't stand out as such. They just blend in to make a much rounder story that has a lot more to say than the typical medieval-patriarchy fantasy. A delightful surprise, and cleverly done."
    Women of Badassery

"If you are a reader of fantasy, I highly recommend *Silent Hall*, the first in Dolkart's new series. Read it because you like a comfort read. Read it because you like to read about close friends succeeding together. Read it because you appreciate the value of ethical interaction that is so lost in most of the fantasy literature coming out today. Read it for its cleverness, read it for its endearing Talmud like study of a fantastical theology... Read it because it's raining outside. Whatever. Read it!"
    Dirty Little Bookworm

"I believe any fan of epic fantasy, or anyone who just like a well written, focused character driven story, will enjoy this book."
    The Bookwyrm Speaks

BY THE SAME AUTHOR

Silent Hall

N S DOLKART

Among the Fallen

GODSERFS BOOK II

ANGRY
ROBOT

ANGRY ROBOT
An imprint of Watkins Media Ltd

20 Fletcher Gate,
Nottingham,
NG1 2FZ
UK

angryrobotbooks.com
twitter.com/angryrobotbooks
Ride the Chariots of Laarna

An Angry Robot paperback original 2017

Cover by Andreas Rocha
Set in Meridien by Epub Services

Distributed in the United States by Penguin Random House, Inc.,
New York.

ISBN 978 0 85766 570 6
EBook ISBN 978 0 85766 571 3

Printed in the United States of America

9 8 7 6 5 4 3 2 1

*In memory of Gretchen Therrien,
Tom DePeter and Bob Mitchell*

PROLOGUE

"Your dress is torn." Mother scrunched her lips together. "You've been climbing again."

"No, I–"

"Don't lie to me," Mother snapped. "You know what happens to girls who lie."

Dessa bowed her head while Mother inspected her hands. "I'm sorry."

Mother sighed and took up her needle. "Just be careful, all right? And don't ruin the wedding. We don't want the Highservants to think they've made a mistake."

"I saw a dragon today," Dessa said. "It was flying so high in the sky..." She lifted her arms to indicate how high.

"Stand still," Mother said, "and don't tell stories." When she was done sewing the tear in the dress, she sat back and smiled. "You'll make a lovely bride."

"I'm not even a woman yet," Dessa grumbled.

"Nor should you be," Mother answered. "We've waited too long with you as it is! Any longer and the villagers might start noticing you! What if one of *them* wanted you? What could we say?"

"It's not fair," Dessa complained. "They get to marry

whoever they want, and wait as long as they want."

Mother shook her head. "Life isn't fair," she said. "Go ask your Grandma if she wants some soup."

Grandma was out weeding in the garden, tugging indiscriminately at weed and herb alike and gathering them all in her left hand. Dessa ran up to her and gave her a kiss.

"Sweet child," Grandma said, her face wrinkling with pleasure. "Where is your husband?"

"I don't have one yet," Dessa said.

"You must tell him to be careful," Grandma warned, dropping her pile of plants and taking Dessa by the shoulders. "I saw his doom today."

"I don't have a husband, Grandma," Dessa said soothingly.

Grandma's eyes flashed, and she did not let go. "They will be the end of him," she insisted. "The black dragon and the she-wolf. I saw them, Iona! They will be the end of him!"

"Grandma, I'm Dessa. Iona is my mother. Come inside and have some soup."

Dessa took her grandmother by the elbow and led her indoors. The old woman calmed down the moment she saw Mother. "Oh, Iona, there you are. We were looking everywhere for you."

"What were you telling Dessa?" Mother asked, guiding Grandma into a chair and bringing her a bowl of soup.

"She was telling me not to marry," Dessa said.

Mother shot her a warning glance. "Nonsense, Dessa. Don't tell lies. Mother, I think you'd better stay here indoors with me."

Grandma nodded. "Of course, dear, I would never leave you alone. I have to take care of you, don't I, now that your husband is gone?"

"Belkos isn't gone, Mother. He's just having the nag re-shod today, that's all. He'll be back by suppertime."

Grandma lifted the bowl of soup to her lips and slurped at it tentatively. "Enjoy him while you can, dear."

Mother sighed. "I think you'd better stay inside for the rest of the day. You look tired."

Grandma seemed surprised. "Do I?"

Mother lowered her voice. "I'm worried something will happen."

"You worry too much."

"I have to now," Mother said, exasperated. "You don't anymore. And Dessa's hopeless. You don't know what I have to put up with, Mother. Do you know she was climbing trees?"

Grandma's placid demeanor vanished. "Where? Did anyone see her?"

"No, Grandma," Dessa insisted. "And I did it the hard way. I promise!"

"Let's see your hands."

Dessa hesitated, but Grandma snatched up one of her wrists and turned her palms up. Then she slapped her. "Your skin is torn, you little liar!"

Mother rushed forward, crying, "Mother, stop! Torn skin is good, remember? It means she was telling the truth."

Grandma let go and Dessa scurried away from her, sobbing. "The truth?" Grandma asked confusedly.

"The truth, Mother. Dessa's a good girl. You shouldn't hit her."

"I didn't hit anyone," Grandma said.

"The red priest take you," Dessa muttered.

"What did you just say?"

Why did Grandma's hearing have to be so sharp?

"Nothing."

Grandma's eyes flashed again and she advanced on Dessa. "I'm sorry, I'm sorry," Dessa cried, cowering against the wall.

"Stop, stop!" Mother said, holding Grandma back. "I'll take care of it, Mother, I promise I will."

At last, Grandma relented and went back to her soup. Mother was shaking.

"Wait until your father comes home," she warned Dessa. "Honestly, can't either of you control yourselves? How will we survive if neither of you can keep out of trouble? I'm going to have to keep your grandmother indoors after this, Dessa, but what am I supposed to do with you? You should know better."

Dessa bowed her head, ashamed. She had been afraid – she hadn't been thinking.

"I'm sorry, Mother," she said, and turned her claws back into hands.

I

CRITON

The room was already spinning when he opened his eyes. Criton groaned, trying to focus on a single spot to slow the world down. It had been like this for the last two weeks, ever since the red priest of Ardis had robbed him of flight and watched him plummet to earth. Every time he woke, it felt like a struggle to come back from the dead. His vision blurred, his head felt heavy, and the spinning – well, maybe it was slowing down a little.

He sat up slowly, still trying to focus on that spot in the thatching. When he dared to look down, he found Bandu sitting across from him, nursing Goodweather.

"It still hurts," she said, concerned for him.

"It doesn't exactly hurt," Criton tried to explain, "and it's definitely better than it was, but…"

"But still bad."

"Yes, it's still bad."

Bandu sighed. "Rest is good for me too. You can take her soon?"

Criton began to nod, but stopped. Nodding brought the dizziness back. "Give me a few minutes," he said, "but I'll take her."

He sat there, getting his bearings, until Bandu rose and handed Goodweather over to him. "I sleep now," she said.

Goodweather had fallen asleep while nursing, thank God Most High, and she did not wake up when Bandu transferred her to Criton. Criton held her at his shoulder, rubbing her back absentmindedly with his scaly palm. He needed water, and he needed to relieve himself, but in what order? He stumbled out of the hut, carrying his daughter in his arms. He found Narky already at the well, pulling up a bucket of water.

"How are you feeling today?" Narky asked. "Good enough to travel?"

"What's the hurry?" Criton said, trying not to groan. "We have what we need here, and for once nobody's trying to kill us. Except my head."

Narky frowned and lifted the bucket onto the stones. "We should be moving already. I feel it here." He tapped at his chest.

Criton looked around, trying to open his eyes all the way. The abandoned village had suited their needs perfectly these last two weeks – did they really have to leave so soon? They had stayed here once to give Narky time to heal, back before the villagers had left for the dubious protection of a wizard's fortress. The villagers hadn't bothered taking the straw mattresses when they left, and some of the thatched roofs would easily last another ten years. It was a perfect place to rest – why should Narky, of all people, spoil that?

"My head's not all better," Criton said obstinately. "Could you hold Goodweather a minute? I need a drink."

Narky looked like he might refuse, but Criton didn't give him an opportunity. He placed his daughter in Narky's unwilling arms and took a long gulp of water straight from the bucket. Goodweather stirred a little, and Narky's eyes widened in panic.

"Don't worry," Criton said. "I'll be right back." And over Narky's whispered protests, he went to find a place to piss.

When his head had cleared, he found that he was still rocking from side to side as if Goodweather remained in his arms. That was what it was like now – taking care of his daughter had become a reflex. A sweet, happy reflex.

He couldn't stop thinking about her. Goodweather was growing so beautifully, and not just in size. She had begun to smile too, the briefest of smiles that filled him with joy one moment and disappeared the next. He had no knowledge of babies besides what few stories Ma had told him about himself as an infant, and he had not known to expect these tiny fleeting expressions. He wondered which would grow faster – her little body or her little smiles.

"Take her, take her," Narky insisted when Criton returned. "She won't hold her head up; I don't want to break her neck accidentally."

Criton took Goodweather back, holding her head against his shoulder and bouncing gently from side to side. "I'd have thought you knew about these things better than I did," he said. "You watched animals give birth and everything, didn't you?"

"And helped them, sometimes," Narky confirmed. "Lambs aren't so damned helpless, though. She's more than a month old already – a sheep would be running around by now!"

Criton shrugged, and Goodweather stirred. A little wave of heat met his shoulder and died away again, returning every few seconds in a steady rhythm. Hiccups.

"Where would we go?" Criton asked after a while.

Narky scratched at his chest. "Wherever your God takes us. It's generous of Him to let us rest for a while, but do you honestly think he could be done with us already? He's bound to show us the way soon enough."

"Do you count yourself among the servants of God Most High, then? I thought your theory was that Ravennis still lived."

"He does," Narky said. "He must. Until that last Oracle turns up dead, I won't believe He's really gone. So of course I'm His servant first, but what's that got to do with anything? People worship more than one God all the time."

Criton shook his head. "Not with God Most High. His worshippers follow Him alone."

"According to who?" Narky asked pointedly. "What's-his-name who wrote that scroll Psander gave you? He also told you Dragon Touched were monsters who should be wiped off the face of the earth. And you almost killed me when I said he could have been right about *something*."

Goodweather stirred. "I didn't almost kill you," Criton muttered.

"You're not the one to judge that."

Luckily, Hunter spared Criton the need to answer by arriving just then, carrying a saddle over one forearm and a sack in his other hand. "Take this," he said to Narky, handing over the sack. "It's all the food I could find that's still good."

"Why did you bring back a saddle?" Narky asked. "We haven't got any horses."

"Phaedra asked me to bring her any leather I could find," Hunter said. "There wasn't much left but this."

Criton sighed. "She's going to try leather now? That'll be a good deal heavier than the tree bark."

"But it won't fall apart," Hunter pointed out.

Phaedra had become obsessed with writing down what they had learned in their travels, but her attempts at creating makeshift books had met with abject failure.

Narky peeked inside the sack and grimaced. "This won't last us more than a day or two."

"Most of what wasn't burned has been picked clean by now," Hunter said. "And the battlefield is already overrun with vines. Between the scavengers and the Yarek, we're lucky I found this much."

Narky looked knowingly at Criton. "We should leave tomorrow, whether we have your God's guidance or not."

"Phaedra won't be happy about it," Hunter commented, "but I can tell her we're leaving soon. Where are we going?"

Goodweather began to cry.

"That depends on Criton and his God."

Criton went to bed that night hoping for a vision from his God, but it was not God Most High who spoke to him as he slept. Instead, the prophet Salemis appeared to him. The great dragon was flying so high above the clouds that his shadow seemed to span half the world. The air was thin and cold, but Salemis seemed to have no trouble staying aloft. When he saw Criton, still somehow lying in bed so far below, he almost smiled.

"Are you feeling better?" he asked.

"I'll be fine," Criton said, still asleep beside Bandu. "Are you visiting the heavens?"

"I will be returning soon," the dragon answered. "Are you well enough to travel?"

"I think so."

"Then gather your friends and go north. I will meet you in my old home, by the mountains of Ardis."

2

PHAEDRA

Hunter's dagger was not the best tool for this kind of work, but Phaedra considered herself an expert in perseverance. She carefully slid the blade back and forth, back and forth, working at the space between the saddle's seat and its frame. Slowly, painstakingly, the top layer of leather began to part from its base, and with each stroke, Phaedra moved the dagger more easily. When she finally dropped her tool and held up the single, pliable piece of leather in her hands, she found that it was still too thick to easily roll up like a proper scroll. But makeshift parchment was better than none; with a steel nail or a sharp rock, it would mark easily enough.

They ate what Hunter had brought with him from the ruined camp. Phaedra spent the meal lost in thought, composing her first words. When she had finished eating, she took a flint shard off the ground, settled the leather in her lap, and scratched into it: *I am Phaedra Merchantsdaughter, of the once-great island of Tarphae. Here is what befell my people, both those who perished and those few who remain beside me.*

I must begin my account with the circumstances under

16

which we left Tarphae behind. In the year before the plague, I had developed a youthful obsession with Atel the Messenger God, and I was eager to visit the Atellan abbey known as Crossroads on a pilgrimage. On the eve of Karassa's summer festival, I booked passage for myself and my nursemaid Kelina on a fishing boat headed for Atuna. Four others joined us there: Hunter of House Tavener, Criton of the Dragon Touched, Bandu of the woods, and Narky.

Unbeknownst to the rest of us, or indeed to the fisherman who had promised us passage, Bandu brought with her the wolf Four-foot, concealed under a blanket. Shortly after we left the harbor at Karsanye, this wolf escaped from its hiding place. In the chaos that ensued, my poor Kelina fell out of the boat and was drowned. Bandu was eventually able to calm Four-foot, but not before the fisherman gave him a long cut with his knife – a cut that would eventually become infected and mean the animal's doom.

On and on Phaedra wrote, her lettering growing smaller and smaller as she grew more practiced with the flint. When she next looked up from her work, the sun had nearly set. She let out a sigh of contentment and got up to stretch her uneven legs. *I've barely even begun,* she thought happily.

She slept well that night, better than she had slept in ages. In her dreams she was dancing with the carefree joy that she had lost the day her nursemaid Kelina had drowned. Her feet glided along effortlessly and the music went on and on, though the musicians were nowhere to be seen among the crowd that surrounded her, watching her glorious performance. They had never seen anything like it before, she knew. They would go home and tell all the world what they had seen.

In the morning, Phaedra did her best to roll up her makeshift scroll, and joined her friends as they prepared to leave. She had woken late, and seemed to have missed the morning's argument.

"Where are we going?" she asked Narky.

"Ardis," Narky told her, looking somewhat ill.

"The Dragon Knight's Tomb, really," Hunter explained. "It came to Criton in a dream. It's awfully close to Ardis, either way. I think we should ignore it, but I've been overruled."

"We can't go around ignoring the Gods," Narky said. "Certainly not now, and certainly not this one."

Phaedra nodded, noting how different both Narky and Hunter sounded from the young men she had met last year. They seemed to have taken up each other's sides of the argument.

"You don't believe in Criton's vision?" Phaedra asked Hunter.

"I do believe him," he said. "But going near Ardis means death, either for us or for a lot of Ardismen. I don't want to be a part of it."

"We may not need your sword, with Salemis there," Criton said hopefully.

"My sword broke," Hunter reminded him. "I don't plan on taking another."

The others all stared. They stared, but Phaedra was proud. The last time she had spoken to Hunter about his calling, he had been full of despair. His place as the islanders' protector was a constant burden on him, and yet when Phaedra had said that one day he might be able to lay down his sword, he had responded, "But I don't know how to *do* anything else!"

Now that despair was gone. He had made the decision to build himself a new life, and whatever it might turn out to be, he already looked happier for it.

"The army the red priest raised is gone," Criton

pointed out. "There'll be no scouts to watch for us when we near Ardis, and nobody who sees will dare confront us. They'll have heard stories by now."

"That's true," Phaedra said, weighing in. "As long as we don't go through Ardis itself, we may well be safe. Especially if Salemis meets us there."

"We can go," Hunter said. "Just don't expect any more killing out of me."

There had been a time when Phaedra loved to travel. Now her ruined ankle turned her pleasure sour; made her legs uneven, her hips disjointed, her back stiff and achy. She wished they still had a horse, and felt selfish just thinking it. They all still had their lives, didn't they?

They spent weeks slogging northwards in the dry heat, sleeping in the open with only clothes for pillows: the straw mattresses were too hard to carry, and all the tents that had gone up around Silent Hall had been burned when the dragon Salemis came to the islanders' rescue. They did not bother asking for shelter at the houses they passed along the way, for these were the families whose menfolk had died in the fire. It was a miserable journey in more ways than one.

They chose to give wide berth to the city of Anardis, a move that was as necessary as it was disappointing. Phaedra desperately wanted to know whether the Great Temple of Elkinar still stood, and how its high priestess had fared in the months since they had last seen her, but Anardis too had citizens who would blame the islanders for their misfortunes. In fact, the entire region of Hagardis had cause to hate them. Phaedra dearly wished Criton were leading them somewhere else.

They were deep in the territory that had belonged to the God Magor – but was it still His? Phaedra wondered whether the loss of the red priest's army had been enough to break Magor's power in the region. If so, who would benefit? Magor's worshippers respected power, and His defeat had been the work of God Most High, yet it seemed highly unlikely that the people of Hagardis would turn to the dragons' God. There was too much bad blood.

There was no doubt the islanders were getting noticed as they traveled north, but it seemed no one dared confront them. They foraged as they went – stealing, really – but nobody who saw them did anything but stare. It made Phaedra feel like they were somehow not a part of the world they traveled through.

When they reached the southern outskirts of Ardis, the people's reactions to them grew stranger still. Men and women gasped, and children pointed. "O see, the prophet speaks truth!" one woman cried.

It was not the reaction they had expected.

They grew bolder. At the next tributary village, they stopped and asked for food. Far from the aggression they had dreaded, the people there treated them as exalted guests, fed them a feast of lamb and dates and sweet wine, and offered them lodging in the house of an elder.

"The prophet spoke of your arrival," the elder explained. "Whether you're angels or men, you're welcome here."

"Thank you," Phaedra said, leaving the half-asked question unanswered. "When did you see this prophet?"

"Ten days ago. She appeared out of a cloud of dust, black of hair and white of skin, and said that you would be coming from the south to herald the beginning of a new age. A one-eyed man, she said, with skin black as night and four companions as dark as himself, speaking words of truth. Have you any words for us?"

The islanders looked at each other. Whoever this prophet was, it was not Salemis.

"The dragon Salemis has been freed," Criton said, "and God Most High has defeated Magor in battle. As the Oracle of Laarna said, the Gods Themselves will be judged in the coming days."

The elder and all the other villagers nodded meekly and asked no more questions. Phaedra wondered who this mysterious prophet might be, and why she had singled out Narky, but she did not have to wonder long. When the islanders left the village the next morning, their walk took them past a Temple of Magor, closed and abandoned. Some vandal had chalked an enormous sigil on the wall beside the door, an artless pictograph of a bird in flight.

A symbol of Ravennis.

3
NARKY

"It's the Oracle."

Only two of the three priestesses that had made up the famed Oracle of Ravennis had been executed when Laarna fell to the Ardisian army. The Graceful Servant, the one in the middle, had survived somehow. Now she had resurfaced, and was being hailed as a prophet. Narky had been right: Ravennis still lived. But in what form?

The battlefield outside Laarna had been riddled with the bodies of crows. They had believed Ravennis dead, or whatever passed for dead among the Gods. Was it possible He had recovered already? His servant was certainly wasting no time converting the men of Hagardis to her religion. How quickly Magor's triumph had been erased!

The next town they came to treated them just as well as the first. After the Oracle's visit, their very arrival seemed to prove her God's power to them, and even the most devout of Magor's worshippers began to doubt their own God's might. After all, wasn't Magor supposed to have defeated Ravennis for good? If Ravennis remained and Magor's high priest did not, who could argue that the God of the Wild was as strong as ever?

When Narky asked, nobody knew exactly where the Graceful Servant had gone. North, many thought, but to where? At the next town, however, the people pointed Narky west, to Ardis.

"The prophet said that the one-eyed man would follow her to Ardis while his companions traveled on," an elderly woman told him. "She said her God had marked you as His."

Narky nodded. "She's right," he said.

It was Phaedra who objected the most. "I don't understand," she said that night. "I'm as curious as you are about Ravennis, but don't you think we should stick together? We know now, from both Salemis and the fairies, that God Most High really is supreme among the Gods. He's been our protector more than Ravennis has – Salemis is the servant who really saved us, and he said to meet him at the Dragon Knight's Tomb. Bestillos might be gone, but Ardis is still the city of our enemies. Why don't you stay with us, at least for now?"

Her argument was weak, and she knew it. He could see the pleading in her eyes. The five of them had been together for over a year now, the lone Tarphaeans in a sea of pale angry faces, and parting had begun to feel unnatural – that, and inherently dangerous. He understood, and he felt the same way, but his God had spoken.

"Criton's God might be the biggest and the strongest," he said, "but Ravennis owns me. His mark is on my chest, Phaedra. If He says I ought to go into Ardis alone, that's what I'm going to do."

"We may never see you again."

The truth of her words struck him hard. She was afraid of losing him for good.

"The Dragon Knight's Tomb isn't far from Ardis," he said, but it was a feeble answer. He looked at his friends, friends he had never thought he would have, and his heart ached. When he had first met them all, he could hardly wait for them to part ways. But parting had been impossible – first Ravennis had held them together, and then Psander, and now the others felt like a part of him. Yes, they had separated before, but always with a plan to regroup afterwards, and Narky had never been truly alone since he'd first stepped into that fishing boat in Karsanye, hoping to escape justice. This time was different. This time his God wanted him alone.

What awaited him in that city? He couldn't pretend he wasn't terrified of being away from the others, of being at the mercy of his enemies, *in Ardis*. Could Ravennis even protect him there? He hadn't protected the Youthful Servant or the Venerable one.

But he had no choice. He dared not defy his God. Ravennis had spared him from His wrath once, but that had been for an honest mistake. Or a dishonest one, really, but a mistake nonetheless. In any case, Narky doubted his God would forgive open defiance.

He said his goodbyes the next morning and set off at a brisk pace, afraid that if he didn't hurry it would give his fears the chance to paralyze him. He tried not to wonder what the God of Fate had in store for him. He wondered instead what it meant to be the God of Fate when another God, the dragons' God, reigned supreme in the heavens. The fairies had convinced Narky well enough that God Most High really did live up to His name, so what was Ravennis' role? Did He not command fate, but instead guard it somehow; watch over it; decide what to reveal and what to keep hidden? To what purpose had Ravennis angered Magor, if He knew that His Oracle's words would lead to the destruction of His city of Laarna? Had it been some kind of trick?

He should have discussed it with Phaedra when he had the chance. Even when she didn't have answers, discussions with her were always clarifying. He hoped she didn't waste too much time writing the islanders' story – her talents were wasted on recording the past. He wondered what she would make of herself. He hoped he didn't die before he saw her again.

But back to Ravennis. After seeming to lose to the God of the Wild, He had instead outflanked Magor and was now stealing His followers. Narky had always thought himself unworthy of his God's favor, but these new developments presented another possibility: perhaps Ravennis had chosen him *because* he wasn't righteous; because he was the sort of man who shot his enemies in the back. Did his refusal to fight fair make him a more suitable tool for the God of Fate?

He hoped it was not too blasphemous a thought, but whatever this maneuver against Magor had entailed, it was devious. Surely the Keeper of Fates had an unfair advantage over the other Gods, even if it was only greater knowledge and not actual control. After this trick, what would be his God's next move?

Whatever it was, he was now a part of it.

Ardis rose in front of him, walled and imposing. Was he even going to be able to get in? If the guards at the gate were less reverent than the villagers in the outskirts, his journey was about to come to a sudden and disappointing – if not at all unexpected – end.

Two guards stood rigidly outside the gates of Ardis, their short spears and shields at the ready. Narky wished his friends were still beside him. It wouldn't have made him any safer, but it would have made him *feel* safer.

It was hard to breathe. If he didn't do this now, his panic would take hold of him. With a silent prayer to Ravennis, he walked up to the nearest guard and forced himself to speak.

"Um," he said. "I assume you know who I am. Can I enter, then?"

The guards stared at him silently. They probably couldn't believe that he had delivered himself like this. A few seconds dragged by, and Narky couldn't bring himself to meet their eyes. What was taking them so long? Were they dumb? Were they trying to decide what to do with him? Maybe they just liked to see him squirm.

Or maybe they hadn't heard of him. "My name is Narky," he said. "I'm one of the Tarphaean islanders who fought against Ardis at Silent Hall – that is, at the wizard's fortress. I'm sure you heard what happened there, or maybe even saw…"

Even at the gates of Ardis, the towering Yarek was just visible on the horizon. Narky waved his arm in that direction and kept right on talking, letting his nervousness spill across his tongue.

"The prophet of Ravennis left a message for me to follow her here," he said.

The guards still did not move, and when he looked up, he saw the fear in their eyes now. Terror, even. Something was very wrong here – were these men even alive? They seemed incapable of motion, besides the frightened little movements of their eyes.

"They're paralyzed," said a voice from up ahead, and a plump middle-aged woman strode toward him. Her hair was as black as his, though there were many gray strands mixed in, and her skin was as white as any mountain clanswoman.

"Not to worry," she said, "it's only temporary. Many

of the Ardismen have not yet converted, but Ravennis guides and we follow. In the case of these men, He guided me to poison the wine they drank with their noonday meal."

Narky stared much as the guards were doing. "You're the Graceful Servant," he said dumbly.

The woman smiled. "Welcome to Ardis."

4

Bandu

Things got quiet after Narky left. The pack had lost a member, and everyone was too sad to speak. It was not like when Four-foot had died. Then the others had closed around Bandu out of sympathy, but they had hardly known her and had seen Four-foot only as people had always seen him: a wolf, a wild animal, a monster with teeth. Losing Narky was more shocking to them, even though he wasn't dead.

Not yet, anyway. Maybe his God would protect him, maybe not. Bandu had a low opinion of Gods. Even Criton's God Most High did not impress her as He did the others. So, He had created the world. So, He was more powerful than all the other Gods. So what? Was He kinder than They were? The fate of the dragons spoke otherwise. So what if He had defeated the Yarek, built the mesh that separated the heavens from the earth, made a world that could sustain her existence for a time? It had to all be *for* something, and if it was not for kindness then it was no good. Bandu did not worship things just because they were big.

She wondered if Criton really understood how she

felt about his God; how she hated the way it consumed his thoughts. But then, it was wrong to blame the God for that: Criton was the sort of man who could only really care about one thing at a time. That wasn't his God's fault.

It was Criton's fault. He hardly knew a thing about this God of his, but now it was all that mattered because the God *belonged* to him, to the part of his family that he wanted to call his own. That was what really bothered her.

She knew he loved her, of course, and that he loved Goodweather too. Just not enough. If he lost them he would tear his hair and mourn, but he would heal one day and do his best to replace them, just the way he had replaced his father with a dragon half the size of a mountain.

Maybe that was forgivable. After all, she had tried to replace Four-foot too. But she had failed, she realized now. Criton was no replacement for Four-foot. The wolf had wanted only to live and to be with her; Criton was more complicated.

She still missed Four-foot terribly. The wizard Psander had offered to help Bandu tear her way into the underworld to retrieve him, but she had not done anything about it for months, and now she was gone. She had moved her fortress into the world of the elves and left the islanders to their troubles. Bandu almost hoped the Kindly Folk would eat her.

They traveled northward in subdued silence, all but Goodweather. Goodweather still cried, still scratched when nursing, still breathed sparks when she hiccupped. Bandu tried binding her hands so that she wouldn't scratch so hard at least, but the girl had a way of wriggling out of the bindings and finding flesh to press her razor-sharp claws against. Bandu had wanted the pregnancy, and wanted Goodweather still, but she had to admit that she hadn't really considered those tiny claws when she and Criton had mated.

At last they came to the foot of the mountain in which Salemis had once lived, in a cave now called the Dragon Knight's Tomb. The climb was not hard – at least, it was far easier than it had been when Bandu was still pregnant. Yet as they came nearer the cave, they began to hear voices up ahead.

"Who could that be?" Hunter asked, automatically reaching for a sword that wasn't there. He frowned at his empty hand for a moment and put it behind his back. "It sounds like a whole crowd."

"This is where Salemis said to meet him," Criton said stubbornly. "There's nothing for us to fear up there."

Nobody responded. They were all quiet, feeling the emptiness where Narky's voice should have been. Bandu did not know what he would have said – she had found some time ago that she could ignore him half the time without missing anything important. Still, his absence felt wrong.

They trudged the rest of the way up to the mouth of the cave, listening to the sounds that drifted down to them. Whatever the argument was about, it ceased when they reached the entrance to the Dragon Knight's Tomb, as those inside turned to look at them and fell into silence.

There were some thirty people in the cave, and they were all Dragon Touched. They were disguised as Criton so often disguised himself, but Bandu could see through such things. Their pale continental skin melted into golden scales beneath her gaze, and their frightened eyes turned an almost radiant yellow. Even outnumbering the islanders more than seven to one, they could not conceal their terror. How long had they hidden in the shadows of Ardis? Did they expect the islanders to turn them in?

Criton stepped forward, and Bandu was suddenly afraid. Her mate was not the last of his kind after all. Would he abandon her for this new family?

He cleared his throat and let his hands turn back into claws. "My name is Criton, the son of Galanea. We are here to meet Salemis."

A murmur went through the crowd. "It's true, then?" one of the women said. "My daughter thought she'd seen a dragon a few weeks ago."

"The Ardismen who fought in the south have been saying for weeks that they were attacked by a dragon," said one of the younger men. "I told you all then, but you wouldn't believe me!"

"The Dragons' Prisoner is free, then?" a gray-haired elder asked.

"He is," Phaedra said. "We freed him from his prison beneath the world of the elves, and he rescued us from the armies of Magor and Mayar. He told Criton he would meet us here."

It was hard for Bandu to tell whether the Dragon Touched were more excited or more afraid to hear that the dragon would be coming to meet them in this place.

Goodweather made some very upset noises, but those had less to do with Salemis than they did with her wet bottom. Bandu gave her to Criton. She wanted him to remember that he had a *real* family to worry about.

He knelt on the cave's floor and began to unbind the baby's clothes, but was unable to keep his mind on the task at hand. "If you didn't know Salemis was coming," he asked, looking up, "why are you all here?"

"I called the meeting," the elder said. "Even with Bestillos gone, turmoil is dangerous for our people. Who knows who may rise to take his place?"

"You come here to worship too, don't you?" Phaedra asked her suddenly. "We found a goblet here once..."

The elder nodded. "It is a site holy to God Most High."

Criton looked up again, though he was still not finished changing Goodweather's swaddling clothes. "You still worship God Most High," he breathed. "I – we – we are servants of God Most High too, but we know nothing of his worship. My mother did not teach me of our people's God."

Hunter made a noise of sudden understanding. "You're Dragon Touched," he said to the crowd.

"Yes," the elder said, and for a moment she too dropped the disguise. But only for a moment. "Bestillos' purge was not complete. Some of us managed to hide ourselves. As long as we kept out of the red priest's sight, no one else could see our true forms. We have been hiding for a generation now – I have been the midwife to every child born in our community. We teach our children to hide their heritage before we let them leave our homes, and we marry them to each other while they are still young so that no outsider can know of us. It has kept us alive so far."

"How many are there?" Criton asked.

"Each family has sent one person to this meeting," the midwife answered. "There were only thirty-eight who survived the purge, but we are nearly two hundred now."

Criton stood up. "Salemis is free, and God Most High has arisen. We should not need to hide any longer."

There was a murmur of approval from the younger generation of Dragon Touched, but the elder answered coldly, "That is not a decision to be made hastily. If Salemis is indeed alive and free and coming to meet us here, we can decide that together after he arrives. You have risked our lives once already, Criton, son of Galanea. After years of quiet, your appearance drove the red priest half insane searching for the remnants of the Dragon Touched. How many times have the Ardismen nearly discovered us? Now here you are, telling us to openly announce our presence!"

"I'm sorry my being here brought danger upon you," Criton said, "but I'm not sorry for what I've done. I'm not sorry I came here, and I'm not sorry that Salemis is free, and with God Most High protecting us, I'd be glad never to disguise myself again."

Half the Dragon Touched seemed ready to cheer, but they did not, out of respect for their elder. "I wish I could agree with you," the woman said, "but I was here during the purge. If the Dragons' Prisoner himself comes here and tells us to follow your advice, then I will trust that it is the will of God Most High. Until then, you are only a dangerous young man."

"We can wait," said Hunter, putting a hand on Criton's shoulder. "We only came here to meet Salemis."

"Are you *all* worshippers of God Most High?" asked the same young man who had spoken before. "Even the... even the rest of you?"

Bandu shook her head, but Phaedra answered for them. "We know little of God Most High," she said, "but Criton is our countryman, and the Goddess of our homeland has abandoned our people. We hope to find favor in your God's eyes."

The crowd nodded along, and even the elder looked pleased. Phaedra always knew how to talk to people.

They waited there together, talking, for more than

an hour, and still the dragon did not come. Criton and Phaedra passed the time asking questions and getting acquainted with the Dragon Touched, learning their ways, and telling them about themselves. Bandu knew she should join them – it was important to Criton, and he was bound to want to stay with these people for a long time – but for now she stayed back, holding Goodweather and trying not to panic. There were too many people here, too many eyes looking at her. It was agonizing.

Hunter seemed to feel similarly, but he at least could listen to the others without getting tired of it. Bandu couldn't bring herself to listen to Phaedra telling their story – her story – to these people, or to join Criton in caring about how the Dragon Touched worshipped their God. She just wanted to go somewhere quiet and hide.

"May I see the baby?" one of the women asked, and Bandu clutched Goodweather closer to her. "What's his name?"

"She is Goodweather," Bandu said, and the woman apologized for guessing wrong, as if Bandu cared.

After another hour, the crowd began to grow smaller as people went home to their families, afraid of what might happen if their neighbors noticed them gone for too long. Hour after hour went by, until only the elderly midwife remained with them, standing in the mouth of the cave and looking for Salemis in the darkening sky. Apparently her name was Hessina, and she was the matriarch of a family called the Highservants.

"The Highservants are the priestly line of the Dragon Touched," Hessina told them. "My father was High Priest before the purge, before the worshippers of Magor tortured him to death and tore the temple down. I thought I would never see it rebuilt, but if Salemis comes to fight for our cause, how can we lose? We may not have believed every rumor that came our way, but there's no denying that very few soldiers came back from the battle in the south. If Salemis was there, I can see why. What happened exactly?"

Phaedra repeated the story of the battle at Silent Hall, with even more detail than before, and also gave Hessina the leather she had been scratching on all these weeks. "I wrote it all down here," she said. "Please, keep it."

Bandu sighed. If these dead animal skins with the words on them were so wonderful, why did Phaedra have to repeat herself too?

Goodweather had fallen asleep in Bandu's arms, so she laid the baby down on their empty sack of food and stretched her weary muscles. She ought to make Criton do more of the carrying.

By this time they had waited so long that the sun had set. Hessina stood and stretched. "Salemis will not come tonight. We can return tomorrow morning."

It was an invitation, and Criton looked tempted, but Bandu shook her head. After all this, Goodweather was finally sleeping, and Bandu had no intention of waking her. "We stay tonight," she said.

Hessina nodded and made to leave them. "May I escort you?" Hunter asked. "It's almost dark; the climb will be treacherous."

"I know my way."

They settled down in the cave and tried to sleep. It was no good, and not because the ground was so hard. Criton kept her awake with excited chatter about how wonderful it was not to be the only Dragon Touched, and how much he looked forward to learning even more about their ways.

"You were not only the one before," Bandu pointed

out, gesturing to Goodweather between them.

"You know what I meant," Criton said. "I don't just have a child now; I have a people."

"You have people before too," she answered. "Us."

Criton growled in frustration and said, "Bandu, stop. You know what I'm saying. Stop misunderstanding me on purpose."

Bandu did not answer. It was useless. Maybe tomorrow he would realize that he was the one who was doing his best not to understand, ignoring her because he didn't want to admit that she was right. He didn't want to talk about the way the search for his 'real' family kept him from making one – kept him from giving Bandu and their daughter the attention they deserved.

She slept fitfully, as she so often did now – Goodweather kept waking up wet and hungry, and though the baby soon fell asleep again, it always took Bandu longer than it ought to. The last time Goodweather woke her was around dawn, and Bandu looked around the cave trying to decide whether to rise or to try to squeeze in another hour or two of sleep before her companions awoke. She thought she could hear wing beats in the distance, but she couldn't quite decide if they were real or if it was her imagination.

Then the ground shook, and she heard the dragon's claws scraping against the stones outside. Not her imagination, then. Salemis was here.

5

SALEMIS

It hurt to leave his mate; it always had, and it always would. There was no feeling that could compare with the touch of Eramia's divine presence in the world above, without a mesh of sky to come between them. What a reward God Most High had prepared for him, to open the heavens at his arrival! To leave now was pain itself.

But he had to leave, at least for a short time. His Dragon Children were waiting for him. If he did not return, who knew what they might think in his absence? What they might do? They needed his leadership, even if only for a moment, to set them on the path that his God intended for them.

So he left his God and his love and returned to the world that had hatched him, the world that now belonged to humanity. He arrived just as dawn was breaking, landing outside his former home for what must surely be the last time. That was all right – he would not miss it here. Now that he had seen his love's home in the heavens, this mountain struck him as unspeakably dismal.

But it was nice to breathe proper air again, to feel the satisfying way it filled his lungs as he called his

descendants to him. His voice rang off the mountains
that had once been his enemy Caladoris, echoing in the
valley between until he was sure all of Hagardis must
have heard him. But his words were intended for his
descendants alone, and only they would know what
they were hearing.

The islanders who had rescued him, children of
Tarphae, stumbled out of the cave that had once been
his home, and was now a tomb.

"You're here!" the dragon child Criton exclaimed.

"I am here," Salemis agreed.

"Have you come to lead us?"

He had known they would ask this. Of course they
would, poor things.

"No," he said. "I have not come to lead you."

The boy looked crestfallen. "Do not worry," Salemis
told him. "God Most High is with you. This world is not
for me anymore, but that does not mean the heavens
have abandoned you. Lead your people well, and our
God will watch over you."

Criton had been nodding sadly until he heard this last
piece of encouragement. *"What?"* he cried. *"I* can't lead
the Dragon Touched – I only just found out they exist!"

"I understand," Salemis answered. "You have
nonetheless been chosen."

"But I *can't!*"

Salemis dismissed his objection with a hiss. "It is
decided," he said. "God Most High has chosen you to
lead His people. Will you defy His wishes?"

Criton's eyes widened, and he shook his head. "But
why me?" he asked.

"I am a prophet," Salemis told him, "but I am not God
Most High. Only He knows why He has chosen you."

"But why would He keep something like that from

us?" Phaedra asked. "Shouldn't Criton know what's expected of him?"

Salemis looked down at them with sympathy. "Our God created the elves' world Himself," he said. "More than that – He watched the elves explore the world He had made for them; He taught them to sing and to pray and to write poetry; He guided their growth and gave them their castles as gifts. But still they wanted to live in the heavens, to join the Lower Gods or to replace Them, and when He told them they could not, they threatened to rebel. He and the Lower Gods had to create a new world to protect those creations that were salvageable. The first dragons were among these.

"God Most High no longer guides His creations as closely as He once did. Even when He intervenes on your behalf, He will not speak to you of it. It was partly His attentions that drove the elves to madness."

The islanders looked sullenly at each other, but he knew they understood. They had seen the madness of the elves first hand, and would not deny that the younger world was better without the risk of succumbing to it.

Salemis gazed down upon the valley, where groups of his descendants were now streaming toward the mountain, a few of them already beginning to climb it.

"It is almost time," he said. "Soon I will give the Dragon Children my message, and then I shall return to the heavens, possibly forever."

"Please," Phaedra said, "tell us about the heavens before you go."

Salemis had to turn his head away lest he laugh too hard and incinerate them all. "The heavens are indescribable. I would not know where to start."

"Then just tell me, was the sage Katinaras right about the Gods? Are They genderless? Do They have no families? Are They all equally ageless?"

"These are too many questions to answer at once," Salemis told her. "The Gods are genderless if They choose to be so; They have no bodies that we would recognize, and do not reproduce the same way that we animals do. They sometimes take on masculine or feminine aspects, but that is entirely by choice, and is not immutable. They are not ruled by physicality, which makes Them very flexible. Those that tie Themselves to your world can be greatly affected by the actions that Their followers take. Even God Most High has changed since I last flew these skies."

The islanders gasped. "How?" Criton asked.

"He has grown more forgiving."

The Dragon Children had gathered sufficiently by then, so Salemis turned to face them, raising his voice so that all could hear. "I am Salemis," he said. "I am the one you have known as the Dragons' Prisoner, the prophet of God Most High. I have returned to you for a time so that you will know the words of the God Above All. Listen to these words, for the age of petty gods is coming to an end.

"God Most High has told me that the Dragon Touched will rise to become a great people, but I will not be leading you. My place is in the heavens now. Our God knows that you have followed His ways even in hiding, and has told me to elevate His servant Hessina as His High Priestess. Heed her in all matters of ritual and worship, as it will please your God.

"As for your leadership in matters of war and peace, God Most High has sent His servant Criton, the son of Galanea and a son of Tarphae, to lead your army and show you your path. Respect him, and you respect your God.

"My time here is at an end. Trust in God Most High and follow His path, and you cannot fail."

With that, Salemis leapt from the mountain, gliding for a time on the warm summer air before beating his wings and rising up toward the heavens. If he missed anything, he thought it would be the good, fragrant air of this world. Perhaps if his God allowed him to, he would return sometimes, just to feel it in his lungs. But then, he didn't want to weaken the mesh by visiting too frequently.

Besides, his love awaited him. Why should he ever leave again?

6

Narky

The Graceful Servant led him through streets and alleys, twisting and turning through Ardis until she finally unlocked the door to a small house and let him in. It was dark inside, dark enough that Narky stood helplessly for a minute while he waited for his eye to adjust. It was a long wait.

"Most of the Ardismen do not know what I look like," the Graceful Servant said.

"You do sort of blend in," Narky said. Besides her distinctly Laarnese coloration, her features were not particularly memorable. In the dark, Narky found that he was already forgetting them.

"I have been spreading my teachings carefully," she said. "Those who would learn more come here, where none can see each other. If one or more is captured, they will not be able to identify each other."

"Fair enough," Narky said, "but won't they be able to lead people here?"

"Could you?"

"No, but I don't live here. If I'd lived in Ardis all my life–"

"–then you would find your memories escaping you even as I led you here." The Oracle's voice was almost smug. "There is nothing to fear. We will not be found until we are ready, and besides, we will be ready very soon."

That sounded pretty ominous. "Ready for what?"

"Ready for the open. Ready to convert thousands to the worship of Ravennis, Keeper of Fates and God of the Underworld."

"God of the Underworld?" Narky repeated. "I thought there was no God of the Underworld."

Laughter in the darkness. "You were right, but things have changed. There were too many Gods in the heavens, and nobody to watch the dead. The Keeper of Fates decided to seize that role, for all fates must end in death. You helped Him, you know, by burying my sisters at the foot of His temple. That is why He brought you to Laarna: not to prevent the city's destruction, but to witness it."

Narky felt sick. A city full of people. A city that Ravennis had essentially sacrificed to Himself. Narky hoped its citizens were being rewarded in the afterlife. It was the least their God could do.

"What was your part in this maneuver?" he asked.

"Just like yours, mine was to stay alive; to keep a thread of His power tied to this world while He established His kingdom in the world below. But that is nearly done. Soon He will require us to join Him, to sacrifice ourselves in His name and cement His place not only in the underworld, but in this world as well."

Perhaps Narky was going to throw up after all. His stomach seemed to be plunging down further into his abdomen – it was only a matter of time before it came back up.

"That's what we're preparing for?"

"That is what we are preparing the world for," the Graceful Servant replied, sounding almost giddy. "Our fearless deaths will inspire the people to entrust their souls to Ravennis. All the people of the world will pay Him tribute, in life as in death."

"But how about God Most High?" Narky asked desperately. "I've spoken to fairies, and to the dragon Salemis, and they both say that God Most High is supreme among the Gods. Ravennis owns me and I am His servant in all things, – *whether I like it or not*" – but is this plan realistic? How could Ravennis or His new followers stand up to God Most High?"

The Graceful Servant laughed again, a high carefree sound that was more terrifying for its levity than any more malevolent laugh could have been. "How many generations has it been since God Most High was active in the world? How many more before He withdraws His attentions again? There will come a time when the world has forgotten God Most High, but they shall never forget Ravennis, king of the world below. One day, when you and I are both long dead, the world may come to believe that Ravennis *is* God Most High."

Narky thought of Criton, his anger and his determination. "Not among the Dragon Touched," he said. "They're not completely gone – my friend is one, and he has a child already. They'll never abandon their God."

"The *Dragon Touched*," the Oracle scoffed. "How many of *them* will there be? Not enough to convince the world that we're wrong. God Most High may reign supreme in the heavens, boy, but Ravennis will have the earth."

Why did Narky find this all so horrifying? Ravennis *was* his God, after all. Why shouldn't his God cheat and

manipulate His way into power, especially when power
and survival were synonymous as far as the Gods were
concerned? And yet... the implications bothered him.
For all that he had come to terms with his own tendency
to take advantage whenever possible, he wasn't that way
on purpose. He had been trying his hardest to leave that
part of him behind. Was it really possible that the God
who had rescued him from himself now wanted him to
embrace that side of his personality?

This woman was a zealot, there was no doubt about
that. Even the thought of sacrificing herself to her God's
ambitions seemed to fill her with nothing less than
delight. Had the destruction of Laarna driven her mad,
perhaps? He didn't want to believe that she was right
about *everything*.

For one thing, he didn't want to die. Certainly not
soon. He hoped that Ravennis would settle for just one
holy martyr and leave Narky out of it. The fact was that
at this point he had little choice but to do whatever
Ravennis wanted of him, even if that meant dying
painfully in the near future. It seemed so wrong that
his God's survival should make him feel worse off, but
there it was. It had been bad enough when all Narky
had to fear from disobedience was becoming crow
food; that had been before Ravennis took charge of the
underworld. Now Narky could be absolutely certain that
sooner or later, his God would get him. If Ravennis did
find cause to punish him for disobedience, Narky might
spend eternity being torn apart by holy birds every day,
or every hour. He was trapped.

The door opened and a man's silhouette became
briefly visible before whoever it was stepped inside and
the door shut again, plunging them back into darkness.

"Teacher?" the man called. His voice cracked a bit.

"Are you here?"

"I am here," the Oracle said.

"The priests of Magor are asking for you. They want... a confrontation."

The Graceful Servant chuckled. "Let them wait. First with apprehension, then with anger. Then with desperation, and then with resignation. By the time I appear before them, they will have given up hope."

"But Teacher, they will call you a coward!"

"Death does not come when you call it," she replied calmly. "But it comes."

"Yes, Teacher."

The door opened again, and the man stepped out. When they were alone once more, the Graceful Servant opened a door on the other side of the room and ushered Narky through it into a dimly lit bedroom. There was a cot here, and a window that had been bricked shut and now served mostly as a shelf for candles. The bricks were not mortared, and were spaced far enough apart that some small amount of light slipped in through the cracks.

"You can stay here for a time," the Graceful Servant said. "We will bring you what food you need, and there is a chamber pot beneath the bed. The man who killed Bestillos must not be known to the masses, not yet. Rumors of your presence will spread as it is; the gate guards saw you, after all, even if they could not move. When you go with me to the meeting with Magor's priests, they will quake at the sight of you."

"So I'm a monster for frightening crowds now," Narky said, sitting heavily on the bed, "and until you're ready to use me, you're going to keep me locked up."

The woman looked at him curiously. "Do you prefer it that way? To be an imprisoned monster, to take no responsibility for the role Ravennis has given you? Our God has chosen you above all others, has placed His mark upon your chest! Will you take no pride in His favor? When you slew the champion of Magor, the man who brought fire and slaughter past the gates of Laarna, did you not glory in the task Ravennis set before you?"

Narky stared at her in the dim light. "You amaze me!" the Oracle cried. "Have you not done these deeds by choice?"

"I chose not to let my friends die," Narky snapped. "I don't know about you, but Ravennis hasn't ever told me what He's up to. He showed me mercy, and gave me a second chance. He saved me. But He's never explained Himself. I've just been doing what seemed right to me, trying to stay alive and follow whatever signs Ravennis sends me, and be… better. Better than I am."

He lapsed into silence, surprised and ashamed at how quickly his defiance had turned to confession. When the Graceful Servant spoke, her tone was softer.

"You may not deserve your redemption," she said, "but Ravennis is more merciful than the Gods above. Nobody in this world is good enough to join Them in the heavens, but Ravennis became Lord Among the Fallen so that we could share His mercy in the world below. Only through His love can we find kindness in the afterlife."

Narky's eyes widened as he began to understand. "That's what Ravennis told you?"

The Oracle nodded.

"And what happens to those who don't find favor in His eyes? What's the afterlife like for them?"

This time she only shrugged, a smile creeping across her lips.

"Gods above," Narky breathed. "Gods above and Ravennis below. It's not for His sake that you're trying to convince people to worship Him, is it? It's for their own sakes."

Another nod. The Graceful Servant's eyes shone with the power of her belief, and as he looked into them with his own single eye, he began to feel that same strength growing within him.

"We have to succeed," he said. "Life in this world is short, but the afterlife doesn't end! People have to know that only Ravennis can reward them in a way that lasts. My friends who worship God Most High are making a mistake – they're only thinking about this life and not the next! I have to tell them. We have to make them understand that the favor of other Gods is meaningless! We have to spread the word!"

"Yes, we do," said the Graceful Servant, and her eyes twinkled in the dim light. "Welcome to the brotherhood of Ravennis. We are truly glad to have you."

7

CRITON

When Salemis had disappeared among the clouds, Criton and his companions began their climb down toward his people. It took some effort – a part of him wanted to crawl away and hide. What would be worse: for his kin to reject his leadership, or accept it? He didn't feel at all prepared to lead the Dragon Touched, but he still wanted their respect. What would he do if they laughed at him, or gently listened to his words without giving them any weight? If Salemis said he was ready for this, he thought the Dragon Touched ought to accept that. But would they? After all, he couldn't quite accept it himself.

They were in sight now, all climbing toward him. His chest tightened in panic, and his breathing became heavy. How could Salemis have done this to him? How could his God? He had been so hopeful that Salemis would tell him what to do when he got here. Now he'd been abandoned.

Bandu was at his elbow. "I am here. They don't hurt you."

Criton looked down at her. "You'll protect me?" he asked, smiling weakly.

49

Bandu nodded, still looking down the mountain at the approaching crowd. Her face remained serious. "I always protect you."

They faced the descendants of Salemis together, while Hunter and Phaedra stayed a short distance behind. The Dragon Touched arrived not long afterwards.

"Are you Criton?" the first asked, a big solid man in his thirties, with long brown hair that reminded Criton of his Ma.

Criton nodded.

The man regarded him seriously. "My uncle was named Criton, and he had a daughter named Galanea, who fled her home as a girl before the purge. Can it be that you are my cousin?"

Criton nodded, stunned. "This is my family," he said, by way of hasty introduction. "My wife Bandu, our daughter, our friends Hunter and Phaedra and – and that's all of us."

"Who are you?" Bandu asked defiantly, pulling the top of her dress down so she could nurse Goodweather. Criton could hear Phaedra wincing at Bandu's immodesty, and hoped she wasn't shocking them too badly. He desperately wanted to make a good impression.

"I am Belkos," the man said. "My daughter is engaged to Hessina's grandson."

"Really?" Phaedra asked. "How old is she?" Hessina had said the Dragon Touched married their children to each other early, but Belkos still seemed a bit too young to have a daughter of marrying age.

"Eleven," Belkos answered. "Letting them wait longer is too dangerous. If even one of us intermarried…"

He broke off, eyes widening as he realized what he had said. Obviously Criton's mother had intermarried. She had been pale like Belkos, her hair brown and wavy.

Criton… was different.

His feelings about his mother's choice were more complicated now than he had even realized, and far too complicated to talk about in front of this crowd. Only Bandu would understand. She had a way of cutting through all the subtleties of a thing and plucking out its beating core.

But Bandu! Criton had intermarried as well; maybe *that* was why Belkos had broken off so awkwardly. Did the Dragon Touched already disapprove of his marriage?

"I understand," Criton said, hoping to reduce the tension. "Your community might have been discovered."

"Anyway," a tall woman said, "there will be no more hiding now."

"Right," Criton agreed. "Salemis says God Most High is with us. As long as He's with us, we have nothing to fear."

They continued the descent together and were soon surrounded by Criton's kin. Criton had to admit that it felt strange to suddenly be one among many, to have a whole community where his scales and claws and fire breath were the norm. And yet… he still didn't fit in. The Dragon Touched clearly saw him as a foreigner: exotic and unreliable. His darker skin put a greater distance between him and them than his scales and claws had ever put between him and Bandu.

Being named as their leader only made things worse. They would never have chosen him of their own volition. Even as a decree handed down straight from God Most High, it was pretty presumptuous. How could he possibly lead these people? He hadn't suffered with them; hadn't had to hide like them; had never lived among them. It took imagination and focus for him to relate to their struggles, and they surely understood him even less.

Why had God Most High chosen him? Was it some kind of misguided reward for freeing Salemis? In Ma's stories, the hero was often rewarded with the throne of a far-off kingdom. Sometimes he achieved this by marrying a princess; sometimes he turned out to be the long-lost heir to the throne. Would she have been proud to see Criton living one of these stories? Maybe. But it didn't feel like a reward now that he had it.

Hessina was at the center of those who had not climbed up to meet them, but people made room for Criton and his friends to get by. "So," Hessina said when she saw them. "Here is the boy who is meant to lead us. Come, Criton. Let us confer about the fate of your people."

There was an edge to her voice, though Criton could tell that she was doing her best to be civil. Naturally. She had led her people thus far, and was now being relegated to high priestess when before she had been everything. Criton sighed.

"We haven't got much time," he said. "I don't know if the Ardismen heard or understood Salemis, but plenty of them will have seen him, and seen us. How long do you think it'll take them to raise a new army?"

"I'm no strategist, but surely a week or two at least," Belkos said, "and longer if they want a big one. But they're dangerous to us even in total disarray. We have, what, sixty, seventy men and boys old enough to fight? A mob tonight could come close to wiping us out."

"Do we have weapons?" Criton asked. "Can we defend ourselves?"

Hessina shook her head. "We lost all these things in the purge. Our neighbors have spears and armor, those who came back from the south alive and those who never left. In this season they tend their fields in the day, and at dusk they set their fires and spear-dance until the light dies. It is a rite of Magor."

"Then we should take their weapons now, before they can prepare themselves."

"It cannot be done," Hessina said. "If you would attack now, they would raise an alarm. We would lose half our number before we were armed. The Ardisian women fight as fiercely as the men, and can wield a spear as well. Attack one house and the spears of the whole village will be set against you."

Phaedra made a noise. The islanders knew better. "I didn't say we should attack," Criton said. "I said we should take their weapons. You know your neighbors well enough, don't you? You know the way they look, the way they speak. What's to stop you?"

His new kin looked at him in confusion. He would have to show them. So he made his hair grow longer and straighter. He lightened it and his skin, reworked his face, shortened and broadened his body as well as he could without tearing his clothes, and, with a touch of Psander's illusion, made those clothes look more like those he saw around him. When he was done, he could easily have been Belkos' twin.

He clapped his cousin on the shoulder and surveyed the awed faces that surrounded him. "Don't tell me you've never done this?" he said. "You've been hiding your dragon blood for ages now, making yourselves look more like your neighbors, and you've never tried *being* your neighbors?"

"We've been *hiding*," Hessina snapped, "not practicing transformations or playing dangerous tricks on our oppressors."

Still, Criton could see that she was impressed – she and the rest of the community.

"Cousin!" Belkos cried. "That's ingenious. We can simply walk into our neighbors' houses and take their weapons and armor while their families look on!"

"But what will we say to them?" a younger man asked. "What excuse can we give for taking up their arms?"

"We will say," Criton answered, "that the Dragon Touched have returned."

8
PHAEDRA

"This isn't our fight," Hunter said. They were standing on the outskirts of the crowd while Criton discussed strategy with his cousin and the other Dragon Touched. "The Dragon Touched don't even want us here, Phaedra. And I love Criton like a brother, but I won't kill for him again. Not for him, not for anyone. The lives of the men I've killed are already too heavy for me to bear."

Phaedra nodded absently. There would be war, and soon. For all that she did not want to leave Criton and Bandu, she did not belong in a war either. They had already left Narky to his fate in Ardis – did Bandu and Criton matter more than he did, that she should abandon one and not the others?

The trouble was that Bandu needed her. As hard as it was to be human among the Dragon Touched, it would be so much worse to be the *only* human among the Dragon Touched. Bandu was suspect for being black, suspect for being human, suspect for being Criton's wife. *Criton* was more suspect for being married to her. It would be a very difficult time for her, and Phaedra felt wretched for wanting to leave.

And yet... she had things she wanted to do, things to learn that she could never learn from the Dragon Touched. The elves and dragons, Psander had said, grew their magic like a muscle of the body that could be exercised or neglected, but would grow naturally without any effort. Wizardry was not like that – it was a form of knowledge. With enough discipline and instruction anyone could learn it, and Phaedra meant to.

In the heyday of academic wizardry, Phaedra could have found any number of wizards to teach her the basics; now the only living wizard was trapped in another world. Phaedra's hope was that there were still other sources from which to learn: lesser magicians, or books that Psander had failed to gather in her library. With their natural magic, the Dragon Touched would be of no use in that regard.

"You want to leave Hagardis?" Phaedra asked.

"Yes," Hunter said. "This is no place for me now. It's no place for anyone who refuses to fight."

"Where do you plan on going?"

Hunter looked embarrassed. "I didn't have any particular place in mind. I thought maybe I'd take a ship to one of the outer islands where I can actually blend in, and try to learn a trade. But I don't know where exactly, or even what trade I ought to take up." He hesitated. "Would you go with me?"

"To take up a trade and start an ordinary life?" Phaedra asked. "No. We've escaped the lives we were supposed to have, Hunter. We have the chance to insist on something meaningful. I mean to try piecing together what remains of academic wizardry. I think God Most High might allow it, since He let us rescue Psander from the other Gods."

Hunter looked skeptical. "You want to be another Psander?"

Phaedra shook her head. "Psander did what she did to *preserve* knowledge. It's too late for that here. Most of the writings that weren't destroyed are in her library. I'm not going to reach her level of knowledge or power even if I work at it my whole life. But the Gods created a world full of magic, and I want to know how it works. I want to know *why* it works."

"So where will you go when you leave here?"

Phaedra thought about that. "I don't know. But I think I would have to start in Atuna, because of all the trade that goes through it. You can buy ink and parchment there, instead of having to make it yourself or to scratch your thoughts on heavy leather. After that, I guess I'll have to seek magic wherever I can find it."

Hunter studied her face with a look of profound gravity. "That sounds dangerous, Phaedra."

She smiled at him. "And what's so new about that?"

"There were five of us before. Now there will only be two."

"You're coming with me, then?"

"Do I have a choice?"

"Of course you do."

Hunter didn't answer, and they fell into silence. After a time, Phaedra said, "We're not traveling as a group anymore. Criton and Bandu are staying here; Narky's gone already. You don't have to stay with me. You can find an island to live on, stop wandering, stop protecting us all and think about yourself for once. You hate traveling. You hate fighting and killing. I don't want you to give up on finding a new life for yourself."

Hunter sighed. "I don't hate fighting. I love it, really. It feels natural to me. It's living with what I've done afterwards that I hate."

Phaedra felt for him, but what could she say? She could not guarantee that if he came with her, he would not have to kill again. Nor could she guarantee that she would survive without him. It was all a gamble. And it was her gamble, in pursuit of her goals. How could she intentionally put herself in danger and then ask Hunter to keep her safe?

"Go to your island," she said.

Hunter did seem tempted, but then he shook his head. "I'm not sure I can," he said. "I... I don't know if I'm ready to be alone. I only have four friends in the world, and..." He stopped there, defeated.

Despite herself, Phaedra was happy. She might have been lost without a friend to steady her, and he was right – he may easily have been lost without her too.

"You can join me," she said. "I'd love for you to join me. But I don't want you to kill for me, and if that means that I die, I forgive you in advance. I don't need you torturing yourself. I'd rather travel alone than make you hate yourself for what you're doing."

"Thank you," Hunter said, "but you know I'm not going to let you die."

"Well then," Phaedra said, "I'm not going to let you kill."

He smiled wryly, but said no more.

They said goodbye to Bandu and Criton, though they had to wrest the latter away from his new-found kin in order to do it. Criton seemed disappointed, and Bandu outright mournful, but neither seemed terribly surprised. It was possible they had realized this would happen before Phaedra had.

So they embraced their friends and parted, keeping their goodbyes short. "I hope you find what you're looking for," Criton said, because of course, he himself had done just that.

Bandu hugged Phaedra with tears in her eyes. "Learn slower," she whispered, cryptically.

The journey to Atuna lasted three weeks at Phaedra's slow pace – three weeks of tension intermixed with boredom. She and Hunter already knew what each other were thinking much of the time, and neither had the stomach for smaller conversation. Besides, Hunter had always been the brooding type, and not much of a conversationalist at the best of times. As for Phaedra, she was suddenly, awkwardly afraid of talking too much. She was too aware of the difference between a woman traveling with friends and one traveling with a man, and she didn't want to explore the meanings of her choices more than she had to. She had enough to think about, trying to compile everything she knew about magic.

According to Psander, the magic of dragons was completely innate, a part of their nature just like it was part of the Gods' nature. This was not particularly useful to Phaedra, as far as she could tell. The elves were another matter. Their magic certainly *seemed* innate, but if that were the whole story, how would Bandu have learned to replicate it?

Then of course there was Psander. Phaedra tried listing the feats of magic that Psander had performed within sight, and found that they were maddeningly few. The wizard had dismissed her illusory mask in the blink of an eye, far too quickly for Phaedra to observe any action on her part. She had created a light in her palm, much as Criton now could, but that seemed to have taken her little more than some amount of concentration. All the great magical works had been performed either long ago or behind closed doors: the construction of Silent Hall;

the wards that protected it against the watchful eyes of the Gods; the fashioning of the magic-siphoning charms – all these Psander had done outside Phaedra's view. The wizard had claimed she would be generous with her knowledge, but perhaps old habits died hard.

Phaedra wished she still had something to write on. It would have been helpful to record her thoughts someplace where she could review them. Maybe when she and Hunter arrived in Atuna, she'd have an opportunity to buy writing supplies.

Though, come to think of it, how would she pay for them? She and Hunter had no money left, and nothing to barter: Hunter's expensive weapons and armor were gone, and most of Phaedra's belongings had been lost in the mountains. They would have to earn their living once they got there, but how? She could theoretically have done as she'd planned to a year ago and earned her living as a weaver, except that she didn't even have the means to buy a loom anymore.

By the time they finally arrived, both of them had sunk deep into melancholy. Phaedra still desperately wanted to write her thoughts down, so she asked after parchmenters and scribes, hoping to make some arrangement. Thus, to her surprise and delight, she learned of a scribe who was in need of an assistant. He worked near the great Atunaean customs house, writing detailed notes for the traders and financiers, recording debts and exchanges, and at times becoming an arbiter between men with competing claims. It was perhaps the least interesting thing one could do with a pen and ink, but the scribe paid well for Phaedra's assistance, and it gave Phaedra plenty of access to ink, parchment, and the cheap reed paper that was an Atunaean specialty.

The scribe paid Phaedra twice a week, and the

commissions were high enough that she was able to expand her definitions of what counted as a necessity. There was only so long the man could tolerate his assistant looking so disheveled. Phaedra had explained her appearance by saying that she was in mourning for her lost nation, but in truth the anniversary had passed already. The days were growing short. Now she washed and trimmed her hair, and teased it up so that it rose from her head in a frizzy ball of curls. It had been a popular style on Tarphae, easier to keep up than the thousand-braid style that her nursemaid Kelina had so faithfully maintained. How Phaedra missed her.

She bought new clothes too, to replace those she had worn out with rough travel. She was tempted to commission something truly beautiful that might flatter her curves the way her old dresses once had, but she resisted. There would be no dances for her, not now, and she meant to begin traveling again as soon as she had somewhere to go. She had to be sensible.

The scribe had a small room for her to sleep in, but Phaedra was neither able nor willing to extend its use to Hunter. As such, Hunter had had to find his own work at the docks, loading and unloading the shipments that came in nearly every day from the islands and other coastal cities. She saw little of him until the evening after her fifth payment, when he appeared outside her door and told her there was a witch on Mur's Island.

"Come with me," he said. "I'll show you."

Phaedra snatched up a candle and followed him through the darkening streets, wondering where they were going. It was a warm night, probably one of the few pleasant ones left before the rainy season started in earnest, and she did not yet miss the shawl she had left behind, draped over the corner of her bed.

"All sailors carry charms," Hunter said as they walked, "but you have to see this one. The man says his auntie gave it to him. He said she makes them herself."

He brought her to a sailors' inn, a sprawling, stinking building crowded inside and out with men of all sizes and colors. It was only when they arrived outside the door that Hunter suddenly froze, stricken with horror and embarrassment. Phaedra had come along with him unthinkingly, excited at the thought of what he might show her, and now he of all people had put her in danger.

This was not a place for women – only whores came anywhere near there, and that only because they had to. If Phaedra came in with him, people would assume that Hunter had paid for her. If she lingered outside, it would be even worse.

"So he's in there?" Phaedra asked, trying not to seem frightened or angry, trying not to scream *why have you brought me here?* because she knew well enough why. He hadn't been thinking, plain and simple. An innocent mistake, until someone got hurt. At the very best, she would never find another job in Atuna. She worked with a customs scribe – someone here was bound to recognize her.

Hunter nodded wretchedly. "I–" he began, but he sputtered to a stop. There was no excuse, and an apology would do no good.

Phaedra came to a decision. "I'm your sister," she said. "We're going to go in there, we're going to find whatever it is you came to show me, and tomorrow we're going to take the first ship away from here. If we can find one to take us to Mur's Island, all the better. If not, we're still leaving. All right? Don't forget, I'm your sister."

He swallowed. "All right."

Phaedra caught his hand in hers and they approached

the door together. It was propped open by an earthenware jug that stank of liquor, spit and vomit: a distillation of everything Phaedra expected to find inside. She kept her eyes on Hunter's back as he pulled her in with him, imagining the stares as she went limping along behind him. It smelled ghastly in there, and men whistled and jeered at Phaedra as she passed. Someone's hand gave her left buttock a sudden squeeze, and she yelped and turned, but could not locate her aggressor. She looked to Hunter and found him still focused on navigating the room. He hadn't even noticed.

They weaved through the crowd, passed into a narrow hall where they had to physically push by the patrons, and entered a small room with a large bed. The bed already had two men sleeping in it, with room for two or three more. On the side opposite the sleepers sat an islander, conversing with a continental man with an enormous red beard. The two turned when they saw Phaedra, and fell to silence.

"This is my sister," Hunter said awkwardly. "Could you show her your bird charm?"

The islander smiled at Phaedra. She doubted he believed Hunter's story. "Happily," he said.

He reached into his tunic and withdrew a string of shells. On the end was a delicate octagonal pendant made of twine and what might have been cormorant bones – Phaedra remembered the cormorant as sacred to one of the Gods of Mur's Island, though she could not recall the God's name. Tig, maybe? A small piece of driftwood was strung from one side of the pendant to the other, with a tiny beak bone loosely screwed to it. The beak was so small it must have been from a chick, and the screw was made of whittled shark tooth. There was no metalworking tradition on Mur's Island.

"Look at this," Hunter said, as the man placed the pendant on his palm. Slowly, the beak turned to point east.

"It always points home," the islander said, his accent thick and familiar. Phaedra's father had had business partners in Mur's Island, and their Atunaean had always been strongly accented and heavy with the effort of foreign speech. They had talked business with her father in their own language, which he had never taught her. Like Tarphae as a whole, Phaedra's father had always looked west.

"Always? No matter where you go?"

"No matter where. It always points home."

She stared at the little pendant, wondering what it had been that had transformed it from a few pieces of bone and twine into this wondrous thing. She was suddenly glad that Hunter had brought her here. Forget her reputation in Atuna – this was real magic! If charms like this were still possible, then so were her dreams.

Hunter thanked the man and they left again, pushing their way toward the door and freedom. Phaedra breathed deeply as they reached the cooler air outside, glad to have escaped without more unpleasantness. Hunter walked her back to her home before returning to the inn to sleep, promising to ask everyone he met if they knew of any ships leaving for Mur's Island. Phaedra went to bed with a smile on her face. Tomorrow they would abandon this noisy, dirty city, and sail away to meet a witch. The thought delighted her.

9

HUNTER

He did manage to find a merchant ship the following day that would eventually be stopping at Mur's Island, though that destination was not the first on its trade route. Phaedra, unlike Hunter, had managed to save enough money from her work to book their passage. She also had new clothes, and some extra coin left over. It was enough to make Hunter rethink what sort of trade he ought to pursue. While he had neither Phaedra's passion for reading and writing nor her aptitude, his education had still involved practicing these arts until he was competent. It would certainly beat working at the docks.

The ship carried olive oil and guardian wood and steel, which the captain meant to exchange for salt and spices and tukka gum, for medicinal tonics and mineral cures, for pearls and nacre. The smell of the lumber made Hunter miss home again; in its day, Tarphae had been known for its high-quality guardian trees and its tukka gum, which was both edible and a major ingredient in ink. Mur's Island was known for its pearls.

Sailing had a poor effect on Phaedra. It clearly brought

back memories of her drowned nursemaid Kelina, and she spent the first few hours below deck where she would not have to face the ocean that had taken the old woman. Hunter would have joined her, but the rocking motion bothered him less in the open air than it did in the musky darkness below.

So he stood up on deck, watching as the ship crashed through the waves and listening as the sailors called to each other in pidgin Atunaean and sang songs to keep their rhythm steady as they hauled on ropes or bailed out the hold. Every man had his task. At any given time, each knew where he belonged.

Hunter didn't. He admired Phaedra for the way she was always adapting to her circumstances, making new plans and choosing new goals, and never, ever, giving up. He admired her, and he envied her. For better or for worse, his friends had all found their callings. God Most High had plans for them, or else like Phaedra they had plans for themselves. Only Hunter had no plans, and now that he had done his part in fulfilling the Dragon Knight's prophecy, he suspected that no God particularly cared what happened to him.

The following afternoon, as Hunter was trying unsuccessfully to nap and Phaedra was teasing at her hair with a steel comb, a crewman stuck his head through the hatch and called them above deck. They stumbled up the steep ladder-like stairs, wondering if the ship had reached its destination already. When they reached the top, they found that it hadn't.

Even before their eyes adjusted to the sunlight, they could hear crewmen praying. Hunter blinked and stared. Though the sky above the ship was blue, a ring of angry clouds had gathered, some hundred yards out to sea in every direction. The waves underneath these clouds reared up like menacing giants, the waters under the ship remained calm. The ship sailed on, and the unnatural weather moved right along with it.

"What does it mean?" the captain asked, more to himself than to anyone else.

Hunter and Phaedra looked at each other. "God Most High has blessed our journey," Phaedra said. "This is a sign of His power, and His favor."

The cook had abandoned the galley to watch the unnatural weather, and he now turned to Phaedra. "Who is this God Most High?"

Phaedra told him what she knew: that God Most High had slain the Yarek in days of old and built the elves' world out of its carcass, that He had created the mesh between the worlds, and that the dragons had worshipped Him and their descendants still did. Lastly, she told the captain of how she and her friends had brought Salemis back into this world and gained his God's favor.

"I think Hunter and I are responsible for those clouds surrounding your ship," she admitted. "Both Mayar and Karassa have declared Themselves our enemies. But it looks like even here, God Most High protects us from Them. Apparently, Their strength even in Their own domain is impotent compared with His."

The captain gulped. "Change course," he called to the helmsman. "We're going to Mur's Island first, and may God Most High find favor with us."

The crew obeyed without a word of complaint. They were terrified, and who could blame them? Not one but two Sea Gods were trying to tear their ship apart and cast them into the depths of the ocean – what would happen if God Most High stopped protecting them? If they insulted Him by treating Hunter and Phaedra poorly? It didn't even stop there – what if He lost interest in the ship once Phaedra and Hunter disembarked? Would Mayar and Karassa lose interest too?

Phaedra spent the rest of their voyage telling the crew everything she knew about the dragons' God. The sailors listened eagerly and never interrupted, which Hunter supposed must be a welcome change for her. By the time they reached Mur's Island, half the crew had made vows to worship God Most High alone.

Hunter found his new God's activity confusing. Salemis had once claimed that the Gods never slept, least of all God Most High; and yet, if He had not been asleep before, why was He only now asserting His presence in the world? Why had He not protected them from the earthquake when they returned to Tarphae, or from the rough seas on the way back to the continent? Or had He been protecting them then too, but more subtly? If so, why was He being so unsubtle now? What had changed?

It must have had something to do with Salemis' return to the world. Although Hunter couldn't understand why this might be so, it stood to reason. The event that had cast Psander's fortress into the world of the fairies, in exchange for rescuing Salemis and giving the Yarek a foothold here... it must have somehow prompted God Most High to take a more active role. That was a relief, certainly, but Hunter still wished he knew why.

Three abnormally sunny, breezy days later, they reached Mur's Island. Hunter hadn't known quite what to expect of it: on Tarphae, Mur's Island had been known as a backwater. From a distance, it looked beautiful. Ivory beaches stretched all along the shoreline, and the waters were a perfect clear blue. Some cormorants sunned themselves on a rock. Past the dunes, a fishing village was nestled into the edge of a wood. A number of skiffs bobbed cheerfully across the water, their owners waving as the merchant ship approached. It took Hunter a few minutes to realize what was missing: a dock.

The helmsman steered the ship around the island until they came to a small town – or a somewhat larger village, really – with something resembling a pier. Even so, the waters were too shallow for the ship to approach. Instead, they filled a small boat with jugs of oil and lowered it into the water. Hunter and Phaedra climbed down after the captain and two of his crewmen, and they rowed their way to the shallow dock.

They stepped onto the sand, thanking the captain, and walked toward the village while the sailors were still unloading their cargo. Or perhaps walking was the wrong word. After their time at sea, the ground beneath Hunter's feet was too solid, almost brutal, and he fell to his knees in the sand when it refused to move under him. Phaedra managed to keep upright, albeit barely. She tried to stop and steady herself for a moment, then changed her mind and limped along the beach much faster than Hunter could follow. She seemed to have decided that her forward motion could not be controlled and had to be fully embraced instead.

Hunter stayed there on his hands and knees, feeling the sand between his fingers. When he rose, Phaedra was well ahead of him, approaching a young man of about their age. The man smiled, a reaction Hunter hadn't seen since they'd left Tarphae a year ago. It was good to be among islanders again.

"I am looking for an auntie who makes charms," Phaedra said. "Out of cormorant bones?"

"Auntie Gava," the teen said. "She lives by Perrinye. I take you?"

It was a request for coin, and Phaedra obliged. They

followed him across the beach, past the village – perhaps it was the capital? – and into the woods. The boy's name was Tamur, and he was a pearl diver. His Atunaean was weak but passable, and he told them a bit about his work as they walked – how long he had taught himself to hold his breath underwater, and which sand was best for seeding. This last was difficult to understand, both because of Tamur's accent and because Hunter hadn't even realized there *were* different kinds of sand.

He found his mind wandering. What would it be like to live here, on an island so far away from the major cities and ports that made up civilization? If Hunter decided to stay, how long could he bear it?

They forded a shallow stream and turned vaguely leftward, bound to meet the shore sooner or later. Phaedra was doing remarkably well despite her limp; she even seemed to be enjoying their walk. The ground was getting rockier, though, and they were traveling uphill. When they passed the tree line, they found that the hill turned into craggy cliffs up ahead, sloping down to the sea on the left. At the bottom was another fishing village, which must have been Perrinye. Perched on the rocks above was a small hut, built out of what honestly looked like driftwood.

"She lives up there," Tamur said, "but you better take her a gift. Nobody doesn't go without something for her."

Hunter and Phaedra looked at each other. "Like what?"

"Like food."

"Could you buy us some and bring it here?" Phaedra asked. "I can't walk much farther."

She paid him again and he scurried eagerly down the hill toward Perrinye. Then Phaedra sat down on a rock to wait. "Thanks for coming with me," she said to

Hunter. "I don't know what this is going to be like, but I'm glad you're here."

"Of course," Hunter answered, and after that there didn't seem to be anything left to say.

Tamur returned some time later with a bucket of assorted mollusks, covered over with seaweed. Hunter took the bucket while Phaedra thanked the boy and gave him a tip, and they turned back to the driftwood hut.

Hunter's knuckles barely made a sound on the spongy wood of the door, but the old woman who lived there must have had sharp ears. The door opened soon afterwards, and they stood face to face with Auntie Gava.

She was a tall woman, slightly hunched though she was, and her dress was covered in beads, bones, and other small objects that clacked together as it swayed. Her long gray hair was bound only loosely in the back by what might have been dried woven seaweed. She was bulky too, with a formidable heft that told of strength despite her years. Hunter was not sure what exactly he had expected, but this Auntie was far more imposing than anything he had imagined.

She spoke to them first in some of the languages of the eastern archipelago, and switched to Atunaean only when it became clear that they didn't understand a word. She clearly hated that – she spat out the Atunaean words like they were each a bad bite of fruit or a seed half-eaten by insects. At least she spoke it, though.

"I don't know you," she said bluntly. "What do you want with me?"

Hunter looked to Phaedra, who said meekly, "I was hoping you could show me magic."

Auntie Gava began to shut the door again, but Phaedra put her hand in the way. "Please," she said.

"I've got no use for you," the woman said. "Move

your hand or I break it."

"Go ahead," Phaedra answered, finding her voice. "If I
can't study magic, I may as well lose my hand too."

That stopped her. Hunter could see Auntie Gava
reassessing them through her cold dark eyes. She looked
extremely skeptical. She was going to ask what was in it
for her, Hunter was sure, and he doubted that a bucket
of oysters would be enough. But then she surprised him
and said, "Come in then."

She stepped back and they entered her hut, which
was small enough to seem crowded with just the three
of them inside. There was no furniture whatsoever –
the nearest thing to a bed was the single blanket rolled
up in a corner. The floor was littered with junk: bones
and mollusk shells, pebbles and sticks and seaweed.
Gava took the bucket from Hunter and sat down on
the floor, clearing a space for herself with a thoughtless
sweep of her arm. Hunter and Phaedra sat gingerly
across from her, or beside her – it was practically the
same thing in here.

Auntie Gava took up a flint knife and began shucking
oysters, popping them open with an expert twist and
sucking out the contents. She did not offer any to them.

"You want to learn magic," she said after a time.
"Where are you from? You look all right, but you only
speak Atunaean?" She said the last word as if it disgusted
her.

"We were from Tarphae," Phaedra said. "And we've
been on the continent for the last year, ever since the
plague that killed our people."

Gava slurped another oyster. "That would do it.
Atunaean is all you know, I'll bet. Not even a word of
Estric or Lago, and definitely no Tigra. You're rich too.
Fancy words. Tarphaeans always wished they didn't

live on an island. The richer they are, the more they talk like it."

It was an undeniable truth, put forward in the ugliest way possible. For all that they worshipped Karassa and looked like the other islanders, the people of Tarphae had always looked to the continent for their culture and learning. Tarphae was the westernmost island in the archipelago, and aspired to the kind of power that the great cities of the continent were known for.

"Our wealth is gone," Phaedra answered. "What we have now are our skills and our wits."

"And you want to learn magic."

"And we want to learn magic. Or, I do."

"And you?" Gava asked Hunter. "You're along for her, yes?"

"Yes," Hunter admitted, though he didn't like her implication.

"And what makes you think you can learn from me?" she said to Phaedra, and again her implication bothered Hunter. She was questioning Phaedra's aptitude as a student, not her own skill as a teacher. Blunt. Rude.

Phaedra took a breath and recited a speech that she must have prepared beforehand. It was far too formal for their surroundings, but at least she didn't falter once she'd committed to reciting it. She said, "I have seen a continental wizard conjure fire in her hand, and summon books from her shelves with no more than a gesture. But she's gone elsewhere, to the world of the fairies. I have seen more amazing things than could fit in a thousand stories. I want to learn, and I am willing to learn from you or from anyone. Only time will tell if I shall succeed."

Auntie Gava put her knife down and met Phaedra's eyes. "You talk too fancy," she said. "You say the right things, mind, but too fancy. My magic isn't fancy, not like your words. I doubt it'll suit you. But we'll see. You want to try to learn from me, I'll show you what I do here."

10

PHAEDRA

The first thing Auntie Gava did was to finish her oysters, maintaining her unhurried manner. When she was down to the last one, she reached into a fold in her dress and pulled out a thin coin.

"See here," she said.

She slid her knife in beside the hinge and began to pry the oyster open, stopping as soon as there was a gap between the two halves of the shell. Then she slipped the coin inside and pressed the oyster back together with her fingers. It was imperfect, but good enough to keep the coin from falling out again.

She said a word in her language three times. Then she marched out of the hut and climbed partway down the rocks. Phaedra and Hunter followed dutifully. "Now we bury it," Gava explained. "Here, boy, move this rock for me."

Hunter did as she said, and when he had cleared a space, the old woman dropped her oyster in and told him to cover it up again. It wasn't even a proper burial – they hadn't dug into the ground – but when the oyster was no longer visible, Gava began to climb back up to her house.

"What now?" Phaedra asked when they got there.

"Nothing," Auntie Gava said. "That's it."

"What did that word you said mean?"

"Prosperity."

"Is it supposed to bring prosperity to you, or to the whole island?"

Gava shrugged. "Doesn't really make a difference. When things go well, people share."

"Is there some way you can tell when it's working?"

This time, Gava laughed. "Sure. People do well, they come and bring me things."

"And if they don't do well?"

"Then you try again. You just need more oysters and more coins, that's all. If they've got 'em, I've got time to bury 'em."

"Then how do you know when it's magic and not luck?"

Gava looked at her sternly. "This is luck magic, girl. If it works, it works; if it doesn't, it doesn't. The luck and the magic are the same thing."

"Oh."

"I don't know what notions you've got," Gava said, "but you can't separate magic from the world and say, 'this part's magic, this part's normal.' Magic is part of the whole thing. It *is* normal. The Gods are all magic, and They made this place."

Phaedra nodded, but she knew her disappointment was showing. It was all well and good for Auntie Gava to say that magic was normal, but she hadn't seen what Phaedra had seen.

"The Gods put this place together on purpose," Auntie Gava went on. "Some places They made it pretty, some places They made it ugly. They make it how They like it. If you want to do magic, you take a look at what

They made, you try to get some of the pieces so they fit together better than before, and that's it. You've got magic. It's not fancy."

It took all Phaedra's self-control not to argue with the old woman. Whatever one might say about magic, it was definitely fancy. Psander's library, Criton's fire, even Bandu's connection with plants and animals – they were all miraculous, all aesthetic. How could anyone be so prosaic about magic?

But then, maybe she wasn't being fair. Auntie Gava and Psander did seem to share a general attitude toward life. They might have more in common than met the eye.

"Can you show me how you make the sailors' charms? The ones that point back here?"

"What, I'm your private teacher now? Just because I let you watch doesn't mean I'll go out of my way just to show you things. You gave me some oysters, not a fortune in gold. I only make charms for people who need them."

"I'm sorry," Phaedra said. "That's fair. I'll just watch whatever you're doing."

She spent the rest of the day watching and listening without interruption as Gava went about her work. She watched the old woman coax her fire back to life, listened carefully to the songs Gava sang as she prepared her meals – it could all be important. Auntie Gava might not pulse with power the way Bandu, Criton, and Psander all did, but she had been doing this for years, and she sang her songs and performed her rituals with all the confidence that Psander had shown in her own domain.

Her attempt to reconstruct magic theory wasn't off to such a bad start, Phaedra decided. Gava's perspective was useful, especially since Phaedra could compare it to what little the wizard Psander had told her. Psander had spoken of magic as a series of rules that existed above and alongside the "ordinary" rules of reality. She had never revealed what these rules might be, but one did begin to taste their flavor, the longer one watched her. Phaedra thought back to the time a few months ago, when the islanders had tried to open a route to the fairies' world. The Goddess Eramia had given Hunter a flower to help them find their way through to Salemis, and Narky had suggested that Criton bleed on it: "It seems like the kind of weird thing Psander might have you do."

It had worked, too. Once Bandu had added her fairy magic, the gate to Salemis' prison in the elves' world had opened. There had been a kind of poetry to their method, and it had worked.

Phaedra's new theory was that this poetry was essential to magic, that magic itself might *be* a kind of poetry. She doubted that Psander would have put it that way, and Gava would probably have objected too, but it was a theory that resonated for her. So much of the magic she had seen in the last year was, for lack of a better term, *appropriate*. Even Gava's prosperity magic, unrigorous though it was, had that same underlying appropriateness to it. Whatever the details, Phaedra thought that this must be the basis of Psander's "magic theory."

Right or wrong, at least Phaedra had a solid hypothesis now, and a framework with which to test it. If magic was truly a kind of universal poetics, then somehow or other, she ought to be able to manipulate the world through thoughtful composition. For now, she'd observe Auntie Gava in the hopes of witnessing a piece of demonstrably effective magic – something she could practice on. After that, she would have to proceed through trial and error.

Auntie Gava's lack of rigor was excruciating, though. She treated every mundane task as if it were magical and every magical task as if it were mundane. The worst part was that she did it that way on purpose – as she had said, she didn't believe there *was* a dividing line between the two.

In the late afternoon, when Phaedra was already starting to wonder about where they were going to sleep that night, a man with Atunaean coloration came running up from the village to tell the old witch that his wife had gone into labor. Gava made him stay while she cut off a lock of her own tangled hairs and braided a charm for the baby out of it. Phaedra watched, fascinated, as the old woman washed the charm with a few drops of blood taken from her thumb, and presented the man with a necklace just big enough to fit over a baby's head.

"Never let the babe take this off," she warned, "and if it comes apart before six years have passed, you come back to me. My old blood will protect your child from the demons."

The man took the charm gratefully and paid her in gold. Atunaeans were the ruling class here, and Phaedra suspected that this was a massive overpayment compared to what a native islander would have given her, but Auntie Gava did not even thank him. She just took the money and watched him run off, leaving Phaedra to ask what all that had been about.

"Your parents never told you about demons?" Gava asked disgustedly. "It's a wonder you people survive at all."

Phaedra *did* know about demons, at least from the perspective of continental religion, but none of what she knew explained what Auntie Gava had just done with her hair and blood.

"Please," she said, "tell me about them."

"Demons like to steal babes and children and take them off to their demon halls. My old blood keeps our young ones from being found."

"Have demons stolen children here before?"

"Not in generations, girl, but they used to, before we aunties started warding them away."

"What do they look like?"

Auntie Gava sucked on her bloodied thumb and rolled her eyes. "How do I know? I keep them away; I don't invite them in."

Phaedra nodded. She thought she knew exactly what demons looked like. She thought they looked like fairies.

The word "fairy" was a misnomer – the denizens of the first world changed their complexions depending on the lighting. In the dark, their skin was not only pale but luminescent; in daylight, it turned blacker than night. Phaedra and her friends had only barely escaped them a few months ago, rescuing eight human children in the process. The fairies had meant to eat them.

Phaedra was amazed that she had never made the connection between elves and demons until now. Demons were a well-known part of religious lore, a part that Phaedra had always vaguely considered metaphorical. They were supposed to be the cursed children of evil Gods, living to torment humanity through temptation and guile, guiding lovers to ruin or sailors to their deaths. But Auntie Gava said they stole children, and that changed everything. The more she thought about it, the more Phaedra realized how obvious the connection should have been to her. Of *course* elves and demons were one and the same. The people of Mur's Island were right to fear them, and they were lucky to have aunties like Gava to protect them.

There being no place for them to sleep in Gava's shack, at sunset they clambered down the rocks and wandered into the village below, more or less begging to be lodged. A generous widow took them in, and they blessed her in the name of God Most High. Hunter, as usual, had no trouble sleeping, but Phaedra was too excited about her theory to sleep well. If she was right, then magic was an art. She would learn it like a new dance, step by careful step, until she was confident enough to improvise. What glorious days she had ahead of her!

They awoke late, luxuriating in the island's relaxed atmosphere. It was nice to be away from the continent, away from the stares, and from the instant recognition that the five black-skinned youths must be those cursed wanderers from Tarphae. Here on Mur's Island, she and Hunter blended in, at least until they spoke their flawless Atunaean. In any case, the freedom from recognition was priceless.

They ate with their hostess, a breakfast of dried fish and seaweed, and went down to the beach for a stroll. Phaedra had it in her head that they might find some gift for Auntie Gava, but in the end she and Hunter spent more time talking than they did searching for gifts. They had barely spoken for days, but now Phaedra could see that Hunter was worried about something, though he seemed willing to let her chatter on endlessly about her theory of poetic magic. After a time, she gave up on letting him bring his worries up himself and asked him outright what the matter was.

He grimaced. "I don't want to distract you."

He was too stoic for his own good; always had been. "Hunter, the last time you tried to keep everything inside, you forgot to feed yourself and nearly fainted. What's the problem?"

She had embarrassed him. She was a bit sorry about it, but it did get results.

"I don't know how we're going to get off this island," he admitted. "Not that we shouldn't stay as long as you need to, it's just... I don't have anything to do here. They don't need any of the skills I have. And we're going to want to leave eventually, right? How long until another ship comes by? How are we going to pay for our passage on it?"

Phaedra had no answers for him. She was making progress here; was it selfish for her to hope *not* to leave any time soon? After all, Hunter had known from the start that this was what she wanted. That was why he hadn't wanted to admit to his concerns.

They walked on, the silence between them growing. They were both being selfish, both feeling bad about it, and why? It wasn't as if some sea captain had actually offered to sail them elsewhere.

"I keep thinking about Bestillos," Hunter said out of nowhere. "He'd have killed me if Narky hadn't shot him in the back. I keep thinking through our fight, over and over again. He was faster and stronger, but his technique wasn't perfect – I should have been able to beat him."

Phaedra studied him curiously. Bestillos had not been the sort of man to surrender. Had Hunter defeated him in combat, it would have been another death for him to carry.

He seemed to read her mind. "I know," he said. "It's still true, what I said before. I don't ever want to kill a man again. But I still think about it sometimes, just for myself, like I used to when I was learning to spar with my brother. I used to think about fighting all the time, and it felt good."

"I can imagine," Phaedra told him. "I've seen you

fight, Hunter. It was terrible, but it was also like a dance in some ways. Beautiful."

He looked at her with such relief and joy that she wanted to weep. "Exactly. You *understand*. When I tell myself that that part of my life is over, it's like saying I'll never dance again."

Oh Gods above, there were actually tears in her eyes. She could hear Hunter gasping at his own thoughtlessness, then floundering wordlessly as he searched for a way to apologize. But of course, there was nothing he could say.

It took an effort to compose herself, with Hunter standing there awkwardly, remorsefully, watching her. When she could trust her voice not to crack, she said, "I don't think you should stop. You haven't been crippled. Can't you still enjoy it, as long as you don't fight to kill? Maybe you could find someone to spar with."

Hunter nodded hopefully. "My father had a swordsmaster who trained me and my brother. Maybe I can do that – find a nobleman with sons, who needs someone to…" he broke off, looking past her.

A group of five men was running toward them. Three of them were continental. Could it be? Why were those sailors still here – hadn't that merchant ship left almost as soon as Phaedra and Hunter had come ashore?

The sailors reached them, and, to Phaedra's shock, seized them by the arms. "You're coming with us," one of them barked. "You brought this curse upon us – now it's your job to lift it!"

11
DELIKA

Delika knew there was something wrong with Galdon the moment he set foot inside the door. Her adoptive father *looked* all right, and he walked with the same heavy gait as always, but while she couldn't explain precisely what it was, she knew there was *something* wrong.

Or maybe it was her imagination. Rakon didn't seem to have noticed anything – he just kept on picking burrs out of his pile of wool, keeping his head down like he always did. He was better at that than Delika was: she was always sticking her nose out, and getting a beating for it.

She missed her parents. She would probably never see them again, and it was her own fault because she didn't know where they lived. The black islanders had asked, and she hadn't been able to answer. So they had brought the children they could back to their different homes and left Delika, Rakon, and Caldra here.

They had tried to bring Rakon back to Laarna first, but it was gone. His parents were probably dead, which was even worse than for Delika in some ways, but in other ways it was better. Delika knew that her parents were alive somewhere out there, missing her, but the world was too big for her to find them.

It was the same for Caldra, but Delika didn't like her, so she didn't care.

She had thought it would be better here than it was. When the islanders had brought Adla and Temena home to Galdon's brother-in-law, Galdon and his wife had said they would happily raise the last three children as their own, since they couldn't make any themselves. So Delika had thought, foolishly, that it would at least be nice here.

And it had been, for about a week. But then the red priest had come, and whatever he'd said to them, he'd scared them so much that now they spanked the children whenever they talked about the past – especially when they talked about the islanders. Well, Rakon and Caldra were good at pretending that the islanders had never existed, but Delika wasn't. The big one called Criton had saved her from drowning, and she didn't think it was right for her to try to forget him. But whenever she talked about him, well, out came the switch.

Galdon was looking for something by the doorway, and getting frustrated that he couldn't find it, but instead of telling them what it was and demanding that they help him look for it, he was trying to do it subtly, as if he didn't want to keep them from their work.

"What are you looking for?" Delika asked, knowing that it would likely get her in trouble. She couldn't help it.

He looked startled at first, trapped even, but then he frowned. "Did you move my spear?"

She shook her head. Why did he want it? "It's still there," she said, pointing.

He went and got it. "You're a good girl," he said.

"I know you're not him," she answered.

Galdon froze. "What?" he asked.

Rakon's head snapped up so he could glare at her, but Delika ignored him. She'd said it already – if she was going to get in trouble for it, it was too late anyway. "You're not him," she said. "You're someone else. Why do you want his spear?"

At that moment, Galdon's wife Sina came in with Caldra and their baskets of vegetables. "Oh, Galdon," she said in surprise, "I didn't realize you were home! Did something happen?"

She was between him and the door, and Delika could see the terror flash across his face. "The Dragon Touched are back," he said, walking toward her. "We need to drive them off before it's too late."

The Dragon Touched! That meant Criton! Wait, was *this* Criton? Delika squinted at him as if she could force him to turn back into himself, but it was no good. Not-Galdon met Sina at the door, gave her a quick kiss, and fled.

Delika wanted to scream at him to take her with him, but it was too late. He was gone. Sina looked frightened, but she only put her basket on the table and stood with her hands on her hips, staring at Delika. "You've let Rakon do all your work for you, haven't you?"

"That wasn't Galdon," Delika said, trying to deflect. "That was someone else, and he took Galdon's spear! Maybe it was–"

She stopped herself, but it was too late. Sina knew that she had been about to say "Criton." Now Delika was in *so much trouble*.

"What makes you say that?" Sina asked, poison in her voice.

Delika didn't even answer. She backed away around

the table, slowly at first, afraid of Sina's hand and of the switch that it might soon hold. Sina marched toward her, already reaching out to catch her adopted daughter. Delika kept backing away from her, then suddenly changed direction and sped underneath the table and out toward the door as fast as her legs would carry her. She had to dodge stupid Caldra on the way, but she ended up being glad for the other girl's presence, because Sina actually *did* crash into her while giving chase, and had to stop for a moment to pick the girl up and apologize. By that time, Delika was gone.

She tried to find the man who had pretended to be Galdon, but she couldn't spot him anywhere. Had he already transformed into someone else? He wasn't Criton – she didn't want to believe that Criton would visit her new home just to steal a spear and run away. But he was *like* Criton. She was sure of that.

She had to find a place to hide before Sina could catch up to her. She had already turned a corner so that she wouldn't be seen from the door, but that wouldn't be enough. Where could she hide? If she tried running into a neighbor's house, they'd recognize her and bring her back.

Ahead, she saw the Temple of Magor. She hated the place, since it was the fault of Magor's priests that her new parents had started hitting her, but it *did* have lots of little corners to hide in. That, and Sina would never expect her to go there. Delika ran for it.

When she slipped inside, panting and out of breath, the priest was busy pouring sacrificial blood from the altar's four blood-collectors into the big metal vat in the corner. His back was to her, so she had time to hide under one of the benches without him noticing. Then she crawled forward a few rows so that she wouldn't be visible from the door, doing her best to calm down and stop panting.

The priest went about his business, totally oblivious to Delika's presence. She watched him over the top of the bench in front of her as he cleaned the altar, swept the floor around it, and rearranged various items she couldn't see from her vantage point. She tried to breathe more quietly. There was a commotion outside, and she was afraid that Sina and the real Galdon might be looking for her, but then there were some cries and thuds and she realized that it was a fight. Even the half-deaf priest heard it, because he grabbed his spear and turned toward the door.

Before he could leave, another man came rushing in. "What's going on out there?" the priest asked him.

Delika turned to see if she could spot the other man, but he was still too far away. She could only see his feet, which were big and dirty and wearing sandals, just like any man's feet might have been.

"The Dragon Touched are back," the man said. He sounded young, and familiar. Which of her neighbors was it?

"What?" the priest cried. "Impossible!"

"Come and see for yourself," the man answered, coming closer. Now she could see his hair peeking out above the benches. She might have seen more if she moved a little, but she didn't want either of them to notice her.

The priest strode forward, but as he reached the other man he gave a sudden cry. "See?" the second man said. "I told you."

The priest's knees hit the ground in front of where his feet had been, and the second man's feet took a step or two back, transforming before her eyes into scaly claws.

There was a grunt as he yanked something out of the priest, and then the old man was lying prone on the ground, staring straight at her. He wasn't dead yet, and his expression turned to surprise and then to worry as he saw her there, hiding under her bench. But he didn't say anything, and soon the butt end of a spear came down on his head and quieted him for good.

The second man laughed and ran to the altar, breathing flames at it and at the statue of Magor behind it. She got the briefest look at his face as he ran by, and she knew it instantly. It was her teenage neighbor Pilos, who lived with his wife and parents only a couple of houses down from Sina and Galdon. If he was like Criton, how many of her other neighbors were like him too?

Delika tried not to move, tried not to breathe. She didn't want Pilos to notice her. Criton was good, Criton had saved her, but that didn't mean that *all* these people were good. This one had just murdered a priest.

She wanted to run away, but she was afraid that he would catch her and kill her just like he'd done to the man on the floor. So she stayed while he lit the altar on fire, lit the statue on fire, lit the temple on fire. She stayed until he ran laughing from the building, and it grew hot and smoky around her. And by then, it was too late.

The smoke was everywhere by the time she crawled out from under her bench, and the flames too. There were casks of oil by the door, and their tops were aflame – they'd probably burst soon. Delika crawled away from them toward the burning altar, not knowing which way to go. A piece of roof fell down behind her, smashing the bench she had just crawled out from under. When she raised her head even just a little, the smoke choked her. She coughed, and sank lower to the floor.

Where could she go? There were killers outside, and flames inside, and soon she would burn just like that statue of boar-headed Magor. The benches were on fire already. Her skin and lungs felt like they were burning too.

At last, she remembered the vat in the corner. She sucked in a big breath from the good air near the ground, and ran as fast as she could for it. When she reached the vat she fell down again, winded. She felt weak, and her back was so hot – oh mother, it was burning! Her dress was on fire!

Delika coughed, sucked once more for air, and climbed into the vat.

12

BANDU

The men did not stay long. Off they went to get their weapons, with Criton in the lead, leaving Bandu and the baby with the Dragon Touched women. That was no good. The women all avoided her gaze like they were afraid of her. One might have thought she was the one with claws.

Hessina muttered something under her breath, apparently praying. Bandu did not catch the whole prayer, but she kept hearing the word "arise," over and over again. When she thought about it, it made sense that the Dragon Touched should pray like that: others may have believed their God to be dead, but the Dragon Touched only thought He was far away and inattentive. Salemis had even said something like that once. What had it been? That for his God, people's lives passed in the blink of an eye?

It certainly didn't feel like the blink of an eye, waiting like this for her mate to return. Goodweather had woken up and was crying for the breast again. Bandu felt Hessina's eyes on her as she fed her daughter. She met the old woman's gaze and asked, "You have young once?"

The old lady looked surprised, but then her expression softened. "Six. It was a joyous time, before the purge."

"Does your mate help then?"

"Not much. He had duties serving my father, the High Priest."

That explained a few things. "Your father is High Priest for your God? This is how you are important."

Hessina's eyebrows shot up. "Yes. I don't mean to be insulting, but where did Criton find you?"

She didn't mean to be insulting? If she hadn't begun that way, Bandu wouldn't have known that she *ought* to be insulted. Now she was annoyed.

"Criton is lucky he 'finds' me," she said. "You and your God are lucky too. You think Criton wakes up Salemis? I wake him up. You think Criton grows Goodweather's seed so the dragon can come back to this world? I grow the seed. I do these things while you are still hiding. You should be happy and say thank you."

"I apologize," Hessina mumbled. "I did not mean–"

"You think Criton should not love me," Bandu pressed on, not letting the old woman recover. "You think he should love only his kind. You are wrong."

Hessina tried to shrug this off. "When you've lived to be my age and seen some of the things I've seen, you may begin to see things differently. I am grateful for what you have done to help us, and am sorry if I suggested otherwise. But people should stay with their own kind. I make no apologies for thinking so."

"Everyone say your kind is dead," Bandu pointed out.

"Perhaps now that Criton has learned otherwise, he will take a second wife."

Second wife? Bandu felt that like a kick to the stomach. Phaedra hadn't said anything about second wives. She had said that marriage was when people promised not to have others. Or, hadn't she? Maybe Phaedra hadn't said exactly that, but it was what Bandu had understood. How much had Phaedra neglected to tell her?

If marrying was only a promise for her and not for him, then it was no good. Besides which, whatever marriage was *supposed* to be, Criton *had* promised not to have others. If he broke that promise, he could not have her. Not unless she could have others, anyway. But then, that didn't work, because she didn't want anybody else.

She had thought that she and Criton were the same: two wild things without any family except each other. But Criton wanted more. He had always wanted more. And now there were others of his kind who wanted to take him away from her.

Her fury stretched itself in all directions. Below the earth, something answered. Roots connected to roots – the Yarek was listening. It owed her a favor. Did she want it to eat this woman?

It took some strength to resist. Bandu would have liked to see Hessina dragged away beneath the ground to become food for plants, but she knew better. This woman did not deserve that, not for this crime, and besides, Bandu might need that favor someday.

She looked south into the distance, where even now the Yarek was visible. It was taller than the mountains of the Calardian range, so tall and wide that it might have been a pillar holding up the heavens. It amazed Bandu – the great tree seemed so much larger than Castle Goodweather, its parent in the fairies' world. Parent *and* child, maybe – it was hard to tell with these ancient beings. God Most High had torn the Yarek into two pieces in ancient times. Those two halves, Castles Illweather and Goodweather, were the cornerstones of the fairies' world, while their roots made up that world's foundation. The tree before Bandu's eyes had come from Goodweather's seed, but she could see that the new Yarek was stronger, more whole. Less kind.

Maybe the new Yarek's size should not have come as a surprise. This younger world was not built of gnarled old roots; it was made of soil, soil that was rich and yielding and had never known the Yarek. Of course the great tree would take advantage.

Hessina, following her gaze, went back to praying to her God. "You who struck down the Yarek of old, who conquered Your enemies before the first dawn, defeat Your detractors now so that they will not scoff at Your name. Arise, our God, and Your enemies tremble; lift Your hand, and they scatter like chaff in the wind."

Bandu switched baby Goodweather from one breast to the other and smiled a bit to herself. She wondered what Hessina would think if she knew the story behind her daughter's name.

There was a fire growing in the village nearby. Even from here, she could see people running. Whether or not Criton's plan had worked, it had clearly led to some sort of fight.

Bandu considered staying and watching, but she was tired of Hessina's company. Criton might need her help, for all that he wanted her to stay behind to protect Goodweather. Bandu thought she could protect both.

Figures were running out of the smoke, but none of them were Criton. The fire was spreading, too, jumping from house to house. Was Criton trapped in one of those awful wooden houses, with a roof of burning thatch above his head?

She broke into a run. The wind whistled in her ears, warning her to stay away. It was fighting against her now, trying to keep her back. "Stop," she said through gritted teeth. "Stop blowing. You make the fire worse. *Stop*."

The wind calmed at her words, and she ran on. At least the clouds of smoke were rising straight up to the sky now. Without the wind blowing it in all directions, she could see that the source of the smoke was somewhere in the middle of the village. That was bad. Even with a calm wind, the fire would spread unless it could be put out. Bandu clutched Goodweather to her chest and kept on running, past frightened livestock and fleeing villagers, past barns and sheds and houses, until she turned a corner and almost ran headlong into Criton's cousin.

There was a ragged line of Dragon Touched men facing the blaze, with weapons in their hands and rags over their mouths to keep out the smoke. Belkos had clearly only just recovered from a coughing fit – he was still in the process of standing up straight after having been doubled over, and his breath came in gasps.

"They're still there!" he wheezed. "Who the hell set fire to Magor's temple?"

Nobody answered, and Belkos began to stumble forward. There was a shout of, "Where are you going?" and Criton came running to his cousin's side, carrying a shield and spear. He hadn't noticed Bandu yet.

"My family!" Belkos cried. "My Iona! Our house is on that side of town!"

Bandu stepped forward. "Take us there."

Criton saw her, and his expression turned to horror. "Bandu! What are you – you brought Goodweather *here?*"

"So take her!" Bandu yelled at him. "She's yours too. You have your fighting things now – go watch Goodweather while *I* help your cousin and his family."

Criton did not take the child; his hands were full. Instead he made a frustrated sound and said, "Never mind. We can go together."

They followed Belkos as he made an arc around the burning buildings, hurrying toward his house. "They might still be all right," he said. "I'll *kill* whoever set that fire! The rout's no good if our village burns down because of it, and the townspeople are fleeing us instead of helping! At least the wind has calmed down now. Thank God for that!"

Yes, Bandu thought, *thank your God for calming the wind. What do* you *know?*

Goodweather had woken up during the run, and was wriggling with discomfort. She did not like this heat. Bandu raised her to her shoulder, where her grip was better. "Be quiet," she pleaded, and for once her daughter obeyed.

They hurried on, townspeople scattering as they passed, until they came to Belkos' house. A Dragon Touched woman, her scales hiding under a layer of magic, was trying to load her family's possessions onto a wheelbarrow, shouting orders at her daughter while her mother looked on. She saw Belkos and cried out, tears in her eyes.

"Thank God you're here!" she said, then recoiled as she took in his spear and realized he was undisguised. "What's happening, Belkos?"

Bandu did not listen to his answer, because the woman's mother was staring at her. "She-wolf," the old woman spat. "Black Dragon. They have come."

Bandu locked eyes with her. The old woman did not flinch as others did, but stared right back, unblinking and unashamed. In fact, it was Bandu who became disquieted and had to turn away. There was something less than sanity in the old woman's eyes, and Bandu got the impression that whatever was missing had been replaced with magic.

"Come," Bandu said to Criton. "Kill the fire with me."

"You don't kill a fire," Criton muttered, but he came with her.

The lack of any breeze may have helped to slow the flames' progress, but the blaze had nonetheless expanded – there was only one house now between it and Belkos' home.

"So what's the plan?" Criton asked. "I've *made* fires before, but I've never fought them."

Bandu patted Goodweather on the back and thought about it. "Without wind, the fire doesn't jump far. If this house doesn't burn, it is good."

Criton looked at her incredulously. "Yes, but how can we keep it from burning?"

Bandu was about to answer, but just then Goodweather made a sudden attempt to fall out of her mother's arms, flopping backwards with a motion that no spine should have allowed. Bandu did not let her fall, but the baby began to scream anyway, a cry of pure infantile anguish.

"Take her," Bandu snapped. "I can't think."

Criton obeyed, dropping his new shield and spear to take the baby from Bandu's arms. Bandu touched the walls of the house, trying to quiet her mind. Between the heat and Goodweather's near-constant nursing, she was beginning to feel light-headed. She wished she could abandon the fire for a moment and go find a well – there must be one around here somewhere, and she badly needed a drink of water. Her mouth was as dry as the wall she was leaning against.

A strange thought came to her, the beginnings of a plan. This house was made of trees – dead trees, yes, but if they could only be made to remember…

She pressed both her palms against the wall and closed her eyes. She felt her dry mouth, licked her lips, and tried to make the walls feel her thirst. *You must be thirstier than I am,* she told the wall. *Long ago you have roots that reach down to where wells are born, and you drink and drink and grow and grow. Do you remember? Your roots then are not so short like now.*

Remember how you are alive then? You should let your roots grow again, so you can drink. The water is waiting for you!

The boards in this wall did not have roots anymore, but when she told them otherwise, she found them open to persuasion. She commanded them to let their roots grow deep again, and she could feel the wood groaning as it tried to obey. One of the boards beneath her hands splintered with the effort, and dug into Bandu's right hand.

Yes, she told the wall encouragingly, *like that. But don't dig into me to find your water, dig into the ground! There is water there, so much more water than in me. Take it! Let your roots grow down to it!*

They were trying, she could feel it in her hand. The splinter was actually sucking at her as the rest of the boards tried to grow roots. It was small enough that she decided she should let it, if that meant that it would remind the others how it was done. And when at last the roots burst out of the boards and into the ground, she felt their triumph echoed in her pain.

Down and down the roots grew, searching for the water that had been promised them. At last they found it, and Bandu leapt back from the wall with a yelp. How greedily they had begun to drink, both from the ground and from her!

Criton ran to her side, asking if she was all right. Bandu nodded. "I'll take her," she said, reaching for

Goodweather with her left hand. "Pluck that out from me!"

Criton did as she said, passing their daughter over and then inspecting her right palm closely. "That's kind of a thick splinter," he said, pinching the end between clawed fingers. "This is going to hurt."

He was right about that much. It definitely hurt. When he had pulled the splinter out, he muttered an oath and held it up for her to see. The wood had divided into three tiny squiggly roots partway into her hand. Bandu licked her wound and handed Goodweather back to Criton. The baby was miserable in this heat.

Criton threw the root away and looked up, finally noticing what she'd done to the house. "How did you do that?" he marveled.

She looked back and smiled. Water was running down the outside wall as the boards drank and drank from the underground well, lifting more water out of the ground than they could possibly absorb.

"Take Goodweather back to Belkos," she said. "Tell him they are safe."

She touched her good hand to the wet wall and reminded it to share with the roof. Then she picked up Criton's spear and shield and followed him back to his cousin's house.

Belkos and his wife were still loading the wheelbarrow, keeping one eye on the fire's progress, when Bandu and Criton arrived. Their daughter stood motionless, a long dress draped over her arms, staring at the rising smoke.

"Don't worry," Criton said, "the fire won't come here. Bandu's seen to that."

Belkos' wife looked incredulous. "What? How?"

"The She-wolf makes houses weep," the old woman said darkly.

13

DESSA

Grandma didn't like that witch Bandu; that was part of what made Dessa love her. She didn't trust Grandma. Mother always said that she should be grateful because Grandma and Grandpa had protected Mother when she was Dessa's age, and without that, there would have been no Dessa. But at least Grandpa had been nice. Grandma was mean.

Mother said it wasn't her fault. She hadn't always been this way. Mother was probably right – Dessa could almost remember a time when she had loved Grandma more than anyone. But now she never knew what to expect, whether Grandma would smile at her or hit her, and when she did hit, she never said sorry. Dessa always had to say sorry. It wasn't fair.

So when she saw Grandma looking at Bandu with such hatred in her eyes, Dessa decided that Bandu must be wonderful. And she was – look what she had done with that house! Even the nasty name Grandma gave her sounded impressive. The She-wolf. It was like something out of a story.

Bandu was short and skinny compared to the other

women Dessa knew, but that didn't make her any less impressive. She looked like no one Dessa had ever seen before – her skin so dark it was almost black, her clothes dirty, her hair a tangled mass. She didn't look like someone who could be punished for climbing trees. She looked like someone Dessa wanted to be.

Mother made Dessa help with the packing, since Grandma wouldn't leave off staring at Bandu and her husband. That was so unfair, Dessa wanted to scream. Grandma wasn't even talking; she was just standing out there glaring while Father talked. If Dessa had been allowed to stay outside, she could actually meet Bandu!

Dessa wasn't even sure why they were still packing, if their house was safe from the fire. She must have missed something Father had said while she was watching a building cry. Were they going somewhere? What was going on?

She hurried to finish, but by that time Bandu and her husband were gone. "Where's Chalkstone?" Father asked when he came indoors.

"She ran off during the fire," Mother told him. "She was too wild for me to control, and when I turned my back on her for a minute, she was gone."

"I thought I'd tied her up well," Father said. "Partha? Did you see her go?"

"What's that?" Grandma asked. "I don't know who you're talking about."

"The horse," Mother answered.

Grandma just stared at her blankly, for so long that Dessa was almost sure she couldn't remember the question. Then she said, "I didn't know you had a horse, dear Iona."

Mother made a frustrated sound and turned away.

Dessa hoped she'd have the chance to meet Bandu

properly soon, and she couldn't wait to talk to Vella about her. Vella was six years older than Dessa, and she was the person Dessa admired most in the world. She was generous and kind, and even though she was married, she still found the time to talk with Dessa about whatever might be troubling her. These days, it was her impending marriage that bothered Dessa most, and the fact that she would have to leave her home and her family so soon.

Vella helped with that too: Dessa was betrothed to her little brother, Malkon. The fact that the two of them would soon be sisters-in-law was the one nice thing about the whole situation. Even so, Dessa was afraid. Vella and Malkon's parents lived a whole town away. Dessa would be seeing much less of Vella after the wedding, even though they'd be sisters-in-law. She'd be completely alone in a town full of strangers.

Vella tried to make it better for her. She told Dessa stories about her family, reassured her that her grandma Hessina wasn't as scary as she seemed, and did her best to make the move to another town seem normal. After all, if Vella could live through it, so could Dessa.

Now Dessa wondered if she might not have to live through it at all. Everybody she knew seemed to be packing, preparing for some big trip somewhere. From what she heard, it sounded like all the Dragon Touched everywhere would be going together. So she wouldn't be separated from her parents, at least for now. Might her wedding also be postponed, or even better, cancelled?

Dessa's father said that everyone would be gathering that night in front of the weeping house. Where would they be going after that? He didn't know. "Wherever Criton leads us," he said. "God Most High has placed our people in his hands."

It was a strange thing to say, and the way he said it was even stranger. He sounded almost giddy about it.

Mother was *not* giddy. She was worried. Dessa didn't know who to trust about how to feel – Father always said that Mother worried too much, but he was acting too weird right now for her to trust him. Should she be afraid of what was coming?

She and Mother spent the next few hours making bread and wrapping it up for the journey while Father went to find Chalkstone and Grandma watched them bake, muttering angrily to herself. Wherever they were going, Dessa wished they could leave Grandma behind.

They all gathered that evening just as Father had said, bringing their things and their animals with them. Every Dragon Touched person Dessa knew and some she didn't stood before the weeping house while Vella's grandma purified Criton the old way, sprinkling him with bull's blood and counting aloud so that everyone could hear she was doing it right. Dessa had never seen this ritual before, having grown up long after the Dragon Touched went into hiding. She'd only heard of such things, and now watched in fascination. Neither Criton nor Hessina were wearing a disguise – their scales shone in the firelight for all the world to see. Did this mean Dessa's people would be leaving the shadows for good?

And did that mean she wouldn't have to marry yet?

Bandu was standing not too far away, and Mother waved her over. "Would you like me to hold the baby?" she asked.

Bandu nodded and handed her infant over, stretching her back. "Thank you," she said.

Dessa felt paralyzed. Here Bandu was, standing right next to her, and she didn't know what to say. "I want to be your friend" was too blunt, and "Thank you for saving our house" would sound stupid, especially since it sounded like they would be leaving it soon. Besides which, Bandu would just answer "You're welcome," and then they'd be right where they started.

In the end she settled on, "I can hold the baby too if you like." That prompted an appraising glance and a small nod, which was enough to delight Dessa no end. Mother never did hand the baby over, but Dessa was glad to have been considered worthy anyway.

In the meantime, she was starting to gather more about what was going on. Her people were coming out of hiding for good, and would have to find allies to help them retake their homeland. Criton was going to take them northward first, to find allies on the northern plains. They would leave tomorrow.

Dessa was almost certain that that meant she would not have to marry Malkon any time soon. As happy as she was at the thought, there was also a sadness that caught her off guard, because if she didn't marry Malkon, she wouldn't be Vella's sister-in-law after all. She had already started thinking of her as a sister, and had loved the way Vella kept reassuring her that her family would love Dessa. They could still be friends even if the marriage never happened, but it wouldn't be the same.

On the other hand, she was already related to Bandu, sort of. Father said that Criton was his cousin, and that meant that Bandu was family too. Wouldn't Vella be jealous! She was sure Vella would be just as fascinated by Bandu as she was.

She spotted Vella in the crowd, standing beside her husband Pilos. Did she dare to go join them? Pilos had always sort of frightened her: he was so aloof and disdainful. He was the same way with Vella, and possessive too – that was part of what frightened Dessa about getting married. What if Malkon would be the same way with her? Vella said he wouldn't be, that he was a nice boy, but Dessa wasn't convinced that such a thing existed.

Dessa was halfway there before she realized that Pilos' parents were right behind him. She *hated* Pilos' parents. They always acted as if Dessa's engagement was an attack on them – it had been quite a coup for them to marry their son to Hessina Highservant's eldest grandchild, and they jealously guarded the place that gave them in the community. They were always polite to Vella, since her inclusion in their family gave them status, but they also did their best to keep Dessa from her.

Now they would hate Dessa even more, because the Dragon Touched suddenly had two leaders instead of one, and Dessa was related to both. Or, at least, she would be if the wedding still happened – maybe she ought to marry Malkon after all, just to beat them at their stupid game. It was a tempting thought.

In any case, they'd all seen her walking toward them, so it was too late to turn back. She had wanted to tell Vella about everything that had happened to her today, and everything she'd seen, but instead she walked up and said, "Vella, do you want to come meet my new cousins? Criton's related to us, you know, and his wife said I could hold their baby! You should come meet her!"

Vella gave her in-laws the sort of look that said, "This girl's not really my friend, but what can you do? She looks up to me." Then turned back to Dessa and said in an indulgent tone, "Sure, Dessa. I'd be happy to."

She kept up the act until they had put half the crowd between them and her in-laws, and then she said, "Criton's related to you?"

Dessa nodded. "Wait till you meet his wife, the witch. She's *so amazing*."

But by the time they got to where Bandu was standing, the crowd was quieting down to hear what Criton himself had to say about their future. Dessa tried to give a hurried introduction, but her mother shushed her and Bandu just nodded absently and turned to look at Criton while he spoke.

"Today we armed ourselves," he said, "right under our enemies' noses. But if we want to take Ardis, we'll need more than weapons. We'll need an army. So tomorrow, we'll start off northwards. I've heard that the people of the northern plains used to be enemies to the Ardismen, so I'm hoping they'll willingly rise up to help us take Ardis back.

"They might not, though, so I want us all to be prepared. If we're going to build an army big enough to beat the Ardismen, we can't let every other village turn us away. We need a reputation as frightening as the red priest's was, so that people will be *afraid* not to join our cause. That means we'll have to make an example of anyone who refuses to help us. Do you all understand?"

There was a murmur of assent from the crowd, but Dessa wasn't sure she understood. Was Criton saying they'd have to kill everyone who didn't join their army? That *couldn't* be what he meant, could it?

"I hope this war will be short," Criton said, "but there's no way of knowing. We'll just have to trust Salemis that God Most High is with us and will protect us from our enemies."

The adults around Dessa nodded solemnly. That seemed to be the end of Criton's speech, because he thanked everyone and took two steps toward the crowd before suddenly freezing. He was looking at something behind Dessa and to her left, and as she turned to see what it was, she heard frightened cries and gasps of, "Is it an omen?"

A little girl was walking toward Criton, and she was covered head to toe in blood. She had been on the outskirts of the crowd at first, and with all eyes on Criton, few had seen her as she approached. Now there was horror and confusion. Was she real? Or a ghost? A vision of things to come?

The girl couldn't have been older than six, seven at the most. There was no expression on her face as she approached, dripping, dripping. She was leaving a trail of blood behind her – did that mean she was real? Either way, Dessa shuddered at the sight of her.

She looked back at Criton, who had the same look of horror on his face that most of the others did. But as the girl got closer, his expression suddenly changed.

"Delika?"

At the name, the girl broke into a run. Criton bent toward her, and she hurled herself into his arms, sobbing. Nobody in the crowd knew what to make of that. Neither did Dessa, but unlike the others, she was too curious to gossip and wait. Bandu was already walking to join Criton and the girl, and Dessa followed.

"I didn't even realize," Criton was saying. "I should have known, but I never thought – how did this happen?"

Dessa couldn't quite hear the response, muffled as it was by the girl pressing her whole face into him, but she thought Delika said something about the fire in the temple.

"Where are the others?" Criton asked suddenly, kneeling and pulling her away so he could look at her. "Rakon and Caldra, and Adla and Temena?"

The little girl shook her head. "I don't know. I ran away."

Criton sighed. "They'll be gone then, either way. I hope they're all right."

Suddenly, she rushed in and hugged him around the neck again. "Please let me stay with you!"

"Of course," Criton said. "Bandu? Is that all right?"

Bandu nodded, and said nothing. Behind Dessa, a voice spoke.

"You two know this child?"

It was Vella's grandma, Hessina Highservant, and she was just as formidable up close as Dessa had feared she would be. Even from afar, she had seemed terribly judgmental and severe, and proximity only reinforced that impression. The rest of the crowd might react with horror or fascination or wonder or trepidation at the blood-soaked girl who had thrown herself on Criton, but Hessina didn't. Hessina only *disapproved*.

"This is Delika," Criton said. "We rescued her from the elves, and from Mayar…"

"She stays with us," said Bandu. "You don't care."

The "you don't care" was a command, not a statement. Dessa loved the way Bandu talked.

"Well," Hessina said, "as long as you take responsibility for her. But for God's sake clean her up."

Criton looked relieved that Hessina wasn't giving him any more trouble. He turned back to little Delika with a smile.

Dessa was relieved too. More than anything, she was glad that Delika was a real girl and not some terrible omen of things to come. Because if she *had* been an omen – well, Criton's whole neck and chest were covered with blood.

14
NARKY

For three hellish weeks, Narky stayed hidden in the room the Graceful Servant had prepared for him. It was not the accommodations that bothered him – the bed was fine, and the meals they brought him were good. The problem was the crushing boredom. He wished someone had taught him to read, so that he could at least try to amuse himself with the books that were in his room. Not that he thought they'd be especially interesting if he *could* read them, but anything would be better than sitting alone on his bed and waiting for news.

The Graceful Servant or one of her followers always gave him updates on the situation outside whenever they visited to bring him food or take out his chamber pot, whether there had been any real developments or not. He got to know a few of the other followers who came to visit him: Ptera, the young widow who had turned to Ravennis in her grief; Taedron, the big, nervous man who always called the Graceful Servant 'Teacher;' wispy Magara, whose voice was so gentle and soft that it put Narky on edge. They were all clearly intimidated by him, whether because of his history or his general appearance, it was hard to say. Narky found that he preferred the Graceful Servant's company.

On Narky's third day in the room, Ptera passed along rumors of a dragon north of the city, supposedly trying to raise an army of its own with which to conquer Ardis. From this Narky gathered that Salemis must have visited his former home and met the other islanders there – the talk of an army was clearly ridiculous. The next day, the story was that some of the Dragon Touched had survived the purge, and were sure to try to take back their city. Someone had spotted Criton, then.

The Graceful Servant was pleased with all this nonsense. She said, "The people no longer trust Magor to protect them. They see an enemy in every shadow, a dragon in every cloud. Can they cling to their God for long? Just a little longer, and we will show them how weak Magor truly is. When Ravennis reveals His might, the people will flock to Him as their true protector in this world and the next."

"Let's hope so," Narky said. It was hard to feel hopeful after three days lying low in a dark room.

On the fifth day, the news from outside was shocking. The Dragon Touched had raided several villages, stealing weapons from under their servants' noses, and even sacked the town closest to the Dragon Knight's Tomb. Reports on their numbers ranged from hundreds to thousands – it was no longer possible to believe that all this fuss was about Criton alone. There must have been a community of Dragon Touched hidden out there after all, a community that Salemis had rallied during his visit. Criton must be overjoyed.

How had Bestillos missed them all? The red priest had had no difficulty seeing through Criton's disguise, and Bandu had insisted that he could track them by the smell of Criton's magic. A clan of hundreds, of thousands, all lurking near Ardis undetected seemed impossible to reconcile with his knowledge of the red priest's power.

But villages did not sack themselves. A community of Criton's kin must exist, and they were beginning to assert their power, just as the followers of Ravennis meant to. It appeared as if Magor really was doomed. The vultures were circling. Or the ravens, rather.

The days passed slowly, as Narky spent his waking hours waiting for news that didn't come. The Ardisian Council of Generals sent scouts to assess the strength of the Dragon Touched army, but apparently these had yet to return. The generals were raising a massive army of their own, while in the shadows, the Graceful Servant and her followers spread their gospel throughout the city. The time was nearly at hand – they had to prepare the populace for the great confrontation between them and the priests of Magor.

Then at last the day came. The Graceful Servant came to get him, bringing with her a hooded black robe.

"You want me to put this on?" he asked. If the idea was that he could travel through the city unnoticed that way, it wasn't going to work: his dark hands and face would still be visible to anyone who looked. What was the robe for, then?

"The priests of Ravennis wore these garments," she replied. "Do you object?"

Narky sighed and took it from her, and she left the room to wait for him to change. The garment was long, at least, and would hopefully keep him warm in the chillier weather. But Ravennis forgive him, he didn't want to be a priest! Was that what the Graceful Servant wanted from him? If she thought he could do it well, she was very much mistaken.

When they stepped out of the house, Narky was nearly blinded by the light outside. The sky was overcast, but that only meant it was uniformly white and unbearable. Though the alley struck him as deserted at first, soon he and the Graceful Servant were joined by a small crowd of other Ravennis worshippers, and together they set off. People gasped and stared as they marched through the streets as a unit, squeezing through countless alleyways before bursting out into the temple square. It was uncomfortable how right the Graceful Servant had been: though the prophetess of Ravennis stood no more than three feet away from him, all eyes were on Narky. His presence had made the desired impression.

The Ravennis worshippers fanned out, and the Graceful Servant stepped toward the Great Temple of Magor. The temple was a gigantic, hulking edifice of painted stone, with murals of hunting scenes visible past the outer support pillars. There were stylized spearheads seeming to burst out of the roof above each pillar, and the tip of each spearhead was painted a very convincing red. A large permanent altar stood in front of the temple, with gold-coated boar's tusks at its four corners. The sight of it reminded Narky of the Boar of Hagardis, and he suddenly wished he had a spear to hold onto. At least then he'd have something to do with his hands, besides letting them hang impotently at his sides.

"Priests of Magor, I challenge you!" the Graceful Servant cried, and her voice boomed throughout the square and echoed off the temple's walls. It was magic; it had to be. Like Bestillos, the Graceful Servant was not just her God's High Priestess, but His chosen, His representative on earth.

At first, no priest came to answer her challenge. A crowd of citizens, however, was beginning to gather outside the temple, watching to see what would happen. For a good five minutes the Graceful Servant and her pupils stood watching the crowd grow, waiting for the priests of Magor to show their faces. The Graceful Servant even repeated her challenge, mocking the priests with her tone. Why hadn't they come out yet? It made them look weak.

Finally, five priests emerged from the temple, all carrying spears and dressed in red robes. "Who are you to challenge us?" asked their leader, a thin man in his forties. His voice was deep and gravelly, and it did not boom like the Graceful Servant's, but cut through the air as if all distance was illusion.

"I am the Graceful Servant of Lord Ravennis, Keeper of Fates and Lord Among the Fallen. God of the Underworld."

The priest let out a bark that never quite became a laugh. "The God of Laarna, you mean. Laarna, which was destroyed, and its Oracle slain. I am glad to finally meet you face to face, woman. I was beginning to think you no more substantial than your dead God. And yet, here you are. Where did you hide to avoid the fate of your sisters, eh, Graceful Servant? In a stable, with a pile of horse dung to disguise you?"

"Your High Priest Bestillos was no more observant than you are," the Graceful Servant answered. "Perhaps that is why he was so easily killed. Magor's chosen, killed by a boy with a crossbow, a servant of Ravennis. Here he stands today, the slayer of your champion, defying Magor's power in His own city. You mock me to cover for your God's weakness, a weakness that only grows more obvious by the day."

There were whispers and gasps from the crowd as she introduced Narky, but the Graceful Servant barely paused before she moved on. "You have mentioned my priestly sisters," she said. "I was there when our God spoke to us and commanded the Venerable and Youthful Servants of Ravennis to stay behind and die, so that He might conquer the underworld through them. That was their task, and they performed it unquestioningly. If Ravennis had chosen to let them live, they could have evaded Bestillos as easily as I did."

The priest of Magor opened his mouth, but the Graceful Servant went on in her booming voice: "Perhaps Magor lost His eyes when the Boar of Hagardis was slain. Or before, since He tried and failed to eliminate the Dragon Touched. He has certainly lost His strength now, when the Dragon Touched no longer cower in fear but go rampaging across the countryside. I have come here to demonstrate, before all the people of Ardis, that Ravennis is a greater God than

Magor ever was, and that it is His protection the people should be seeking."

At last, the Graceful Servant stopped to let Magor's priest speak. "Those are bold words," he said. "Especially coming from a so-called 'Oracle' of a God whose people were slaughtered and enslaved. I am glad you have come here to us, so that we can teach you a lesson and demonstrate to all your deluded followers that Magor still reigns in Ardis."

At this the other priests raised their spears to the heavens, as if the very existence of their weapons proved their God's power. It was a ridiculous, theatrical gesture, but Narky had to admit that the crowd responded to it.

The Graceful Servant clearly didn't care. "Magor's power is broken," she laughed. "Ravennis, who rules the land of the dead, will soon rule over Magor as well. If you do not believe me, then believe the words of Narky of Tarphae, who slew both the Boar of Hagardis and your God's High Priest."

The square went silent in anticipation of Narky's speech. It was extremely intimidating. Narky had never spoken in front of a crowd before, and he keenly felt the hundreds of gazes that were directed at him. He froze for a moment, a moment that seemed to last for hours. But nobody spoke in his place, and at long last he took a deep breath and addressed the crowd.

"Everything she says is true," he said, speaking at the top of his voice and wishing that he could project it the way the Graceful Servant did. "I killed the boar, and I killed Bestillos. The Oracle of Laarna told us the truth those months ago – the Gods are being judged, and Magor has been judged most harshly. Even His victory at Laarna was an illusion: Ravennis outmaneuvered Him. The people of Laarna sacrificed themselves to make Ravennis the God of the Underworld, and now He can reward them in the world below while Magor's power here in our world crumbles.

"Magor is dying, people. The dragon Salemis burned His army. The boar is dead, and Bestillos is dead, and even the Dragon Touched seem to be coming back to life. I'm only a farmer's son from Tarphae, but Ravennis has marked me and guided my hand, and raised me above the highest of Magor's servants. If I were you, I'd abandon your old God – He can't protect you in this life, and only Ravennis can save you in the next. Join us before it's too late."

There were murmurs among the crowd when he finished, some of them angry. But nobody had thrown anything at him, so Narky considered his speech a success. Even the angrier Ardismen were afraid of being wrong and having to face Ravennis when they died.

The priests of Magor hissed. Their spokesman said, "Nonsense. Ravennis is a dead God, slain by Magor's hand. Two of the three Oracle priestesses were killed in Laarna, and the last has come to us here, pretending that her God still has power? We will accept your challenge, woman, and when we are done, you will be slaughtered like a lamb and bound to the doorway of the temple like your sisters were in Laarna."

With that, the five priests raised their voices as one and cried, "O Great Magor, show these people Your power!"

Nothing happened. That was a relief – Narky had been afraid that he might get struck by lightning or something. He looked to the Graceful Servant. She wasn't mocking the priests just yet. How long would she wait?

The ground suddenly shifted under Narky's feet, and he stumbled back as a hole opened where he had been standing. Rats poured out. Narky hurriedly backed away from them, but they all ran at the Graceful Servant. The woman didn't budge. Before the swarming rodents could reach her, a flock of ravens appeared as if out of nowhere and dove straight at the rats, snatching them off the ground in a cacophony of caws and squeals. People gasped and the ravens flew away over the Temple of Magor and disappeared into the city. In a battle of miracles, Ravennis had won the first skirmish.

Now the Graceful Servant raised her hands in the gesture of her God's priestesses, her thumbs and middle fingers pointed toward each other. "O Ravennis," she prayed, "send a message of Your power to these people."

There was a screech from above and Narky looked up, along with everyone else, to see the frightening visage of a crow-angel hurtling down toward the temple. Like the others Narky had seen, it looked like a pale man with enormous black wings, bald and naked and sharp-toothed. The priests stumbled back as it landed on Magor's altar, talons and pointed teeth bared.

The angel screeched at the priests again, then turned from them to address the crowd.

"Here is the Lord of Fate's message," it cawed, but its words were cut off as Bestillos' successor stabbed it through the back with his spear. The angel made a horrible noise and curled in on itself, shrinking and curling until it was just an ordinary crow skewered on a spear.

"Whatever that monster meant to say," the priest said, "I think we're better off without it."

Narky half expected him to be killed on the spot, but Magor must still have had at least enough power to protect him. Perhaps Narky should have expected that, but he hadn't, and the ramifications of it still amazed him: Ravennis had provided a miracle, and the priest had effectively countered it with a pointed stick.

The Graceful Servant glared at the grinning priest. Then she raised her voice and cried, "Ravennis, if You really are the Lord of Fates and the King of the Underworld, if You are truly undefeated among the Gods, show this man – show these men their deaths. Reveal to them the manner of their demise and let them see what awaits them in the world below!"

There was a hush among the crowd, as a look of real fear came onto the priests' faces. Then the high priest began to laugh. "How weak your God is, to be making threats He can't act upon! I'm to kill myself with a sword three days from now, am I? Well, then. If that comes to pass, let every man of Ardis turn from Magor and worship the Crow God of Laarna. Otherwise, Servant, I will see you bound to the pillar behind me and whipped to death."

The Graceful Servant smiled back, oozing patronizing indulgence, but for someone standing as close as Narky was, it was hard to miss the look of hatred in her eyes. "Liar," she hissed under her breath.

His heart sank. The Graceful Servant had made a terrible mistake, one that Ravennis could not save her from. Perhaps the God of Fate had granted her request, but that couldn't stop the priests from lying about it. Who really knew what that man had seen? There was no point in the Graceful Servant objecting to his words – an argument over what vision the priest had received was one overbalanced in his favor. He had cleverly chosen a 'vision' of his death that he had maximum ability to control, and now there was very little the Graceful Servant or even Ravennis Himself could do about it.

"We shall see what the coming days bring us," the Graceful Servant said, with great poise. "Until then, make peace with your God, but turn to mine before it is too late, for it is Ravennis who will watch over you when you pass on. Farewell, doomed servants of Magor."

They left the square, followed by a large portion of the crowd and the stares of all. Narky was trying not to panic, going over their encounter with Magor's priests again and again. Phaedra had always insisted that men had free will, no matter how the Gods tried to manipulate them. He was starting to see her point, and to see why people were such valuable tools in the Gods' wars. Here was an argument over which God was more powerful, an argument in which the Gods themselves had had a say, and yet it seemed like it would be won not on godly might but on human tactics. There was something darkly amusing about that. It would have been more amusing if he'd been on the winning side.

As they neared the house, the citizens who had

followed them began to peel off, looking vaguely confused. The magic of the place was keeping them from finding it. Impressive. The Graceful Servant had told him about it before, without him really believing her. Now that he saw its effect on the citizenry, he had to admit that it was pretty amazing.

By the time they arrived, there were only five of them: Narky, the Graceful Servant, Taedron, Ptera, and Magara. A pair of lamps flared as they entered, bathing the room in warm light. They closed the door fast behind them.

"That went well," Narky said. "What the hell do we do now?"

"The high priest lied," the Graceful Servant said, explaining to the others what had already been obvious to Narky. "He was never supposed to kill himself, and certainly not this week. Ravennis should never have let him speak like that."

She sat down and sank her head in her hands. "I am to blame for this reversal: I told Ravennis what I wanted instead of offering myself as a vessel for His power, and the priest of Magor took advantage of my poor choice. If I had trusted in Ravennis to provide a miracle of His choosing, this would not have happened."

"Sure," Narky said, "but what's our plan now? That priest out-thought us, and now it's going to look like Ravennis has no power here. I don't suppose we can force him to kill himself?"

The Graceful Servant shook her head. "It is time for you to leave us, Narky. Tonight, before our enemies can move to stop you. Your part here is done for now, and if both of us are martyred at once, the church of Ravennis will have no leadership. I am ordaining you as a priest, to be high priest after my death. Go to Anardis, and convert that city to the worship of our God."

Anardis. The City of Elkinar. A city that had blamed the "cursed islanders" for its bad luck; a city that Narky and his friends had been forced to flee before its people could deliver them into the hands of their enemies. Surely, Narky was the worst-suited messenger for bringing the Lord of Fate's message to Anardis.

Not that he had any intention of switching tasks with the Graceful Servant.

"Why Anardis?" he asked instead. "Why not some other city? Why not Atuna?"

The Graceful Servant looked astounded, as if Narky's question was too foolish to be believed. She asked, "What greater symbol is there of Magor's power than that tributary city, the city that the red priest brought to its knees last year? To lose Anardis is to lose all semblance of worldly power, to be truly isolated and confined to one city. Ardis does not have the strength to put down a second rebellion: though Bestillos burned half the city, the walls of Anardis still stand. Without Magor's chosen as its high priest, Ardis no longer has the power of intimidation on its side. You will be safe there."

"And you? Will you really stay behind here and let the priests of Magor flay you?"

The Graceful Servant nodded, her eyes glowing. "Of course. What have I to fear? The priests of Magor can only hurt my body for a short time. My God will reward me forever."

Her faith and her confidence were astounding. Narky had to wonder whether he would ever show the kind of serenity she did in the face of certain death. Somehow, he highly doubted it.

"How can I even get out of this city?" he asked. "I can't exactly slip out unrecognized."

"One of the night watchmen is a man of the faith," the Graceful Servant replied. "He will let you out without raising an alarm."

"And how will I know which one is him?"

"I will go with you," Ptera said. "He was one of my husband's friends – I know him well. I converted him and his family."

"Take Ptera with you to Anardis," the Graceful Servant said. "Those who stay with me may well perish. Ptera's a clever girl, and her faith is strong. The Keeper of Fates needs her in this world for now."

Narky scratched above his bad eye uncomfortably. "That's... I mean, a man and a woman, traveling together without being married... it's not like I can tell people we're related."

The Graceful Servant smiled patronizingly at him. "I never suggested such an arrangement. Take Ptera as your wife. She has already told me she's willing."

Narky looked back and forth between them, unable to register his shock. When had they had this conversation? Why hadn't he been involved?

He had thought himself oversensitive to flirtation – after all, he had once thought himself in love just because a girl had been nice to him. Back then, he had built up each conversation in his mind and imbued every word and glance with far more meaning and emotion than they deserved. Narky had confronted that girl's lover, and eventually murdered him, all because he had taken her unexpected friendliness far too seriously.

But there had been no flirtation here, not that he had detected. So when, exactly, had Ptera told the Graceful Servant that she was willing to marry him? Narky would like to have known how that topic had even come up between the two of them. And, nerves aside, he wished he knew how he felt about the whole thing. It was too shocking for him to process.

"I..." he said.

"You will do as I say," the Graceful Servant answered, cutting him off. "You will marry Ptera, and together you will go to Anardis to spread Ravennis' teachings. Our God will guide you once you are there; you will know when the time is right to return. Ardis will be His before the year is out."

"And you..."

"I will be with Ravennis. Don't worry, you will see. My martyrdom will change everything in this city – it will open a path for you. By the time you return, Ardis will be begging to hear your holy words."

Narky nodded, though the voice in his head remained stubbornly skeptical. How could the loss of their God's prophet change anything for the better? Why should Ardis clamor for Narky's teachings after they had tortured and humiliated the Graceful Servant, even up to her death?

And what the hell *were* his teachings, anyway?

15

HUNTER

Hunter had no chance to struggle – the sailors were holding his arms too tight. If he had known what they were planning... but then, he still didn't understand what was going on.

"What curse?" he asked them. "What are you talking about?"

"Your God won't let us leave this damned backwater island!" one of them answered. "Every time we weigh anchor, a tempest keeps blowing us to shore. We almost got shipwrecked this last time, so the captain says, 'Find those two kids from Tarphae and bring them back. Their God doesn't want us leaving this place without them.'"

Hunter looked over at Phaedra. Well, that answered that question: God Most High wasn't going to make them wait for another ship or even pay for their passage. It was a shame for Phaedra that the crew had found them so quickly, but then, it would have been too cruel to force these men to stay here a fortnight while the two of them shucked oysters and watched an old woman cook her meals and wash her clothes and take naps. For all that Phaedra might be developing very interesting theories about how magic worked, he was glad it hadn't taken the sailors too long to find them. He was even a bit relieved.

Now if only they'd stop squeezing his arms like that.

"Please let go," Phaedra begged. "You're hurting me."

The sailors who were holding her obeyed, and even Hunter's captors eased up a little. "We're coming with you," Hunter told them. "You don't have to drag us."

They went along meekly, Hunter supporting Phaedra on the uneven ground. If only her ankle hadn't been shattered on Mount Galadron, when they were unknowingly risking their lives to explore a giant ant hole. If only he or the others had known how to set it before it healed wrong. If only he hadn't said that thing about never dancing again.

They eventually reached the dock and were rowed back to the ship. The captain looked relieved to see them, but his relief soon turned to anger as he was finally able to vent his frustration and fear.

"We should have left you in Atuna, you wretches! You may as well be pirates, the way you've hijacked my ship!"

"I'm sorry," Hunter said. "We didn't know."

"You didn't know," the captain repeated, disgusted. "Well, we're never letting you on shore again. Not on this voyage. Not until you can assure me that your God will leave us alone! If we can't have fair weather without you on board, we're just going to have to make you stay. I don't care if I have to chain you to the mast; you're not leaving my ship."

Phaedra said something, to which the captain barked, "What's that? If you have something to say, girl, speak up!"

"I said I wouldn't recommend that."

The captain's face went red. "Are you threatening me?"

"No," Phaedra said. "I'm saying that we don't control our God – He controls us. We had no idea God Most High would keep you here, and we have no idea where He wants us to go next, but I'm pretty certain that wherever we're meant to go, He's going to guide us there. If you try to control our movements instead of taking us wherever our God wants us to be, He's going to find another way. I don't mean to threaten you, but I can't believe that God Most High would take enough of an interest to force you to wait here for us without getting offended if you imprison us. I don't even know why He's taken such an interest in our voyage, but He clearly has. If you would treat your own Gods with caution and respect, you should treat ours with double."

The captain struck her across the face with the back of his hand, and she fell to the deck. Immediately, the hands of the crewmembers seized Hunter's arms to restrain him. It shouldn't have been necessary; Hunter knew full well how precarious his position was. He had wanted to help Phaedra up, not retaliate. But the crew pulled him back, and Phaedra was forced to climb to her feet by herself.

The captain had the look of a man who knew he had crossed a line. He was clearly terrified of what God Most High might do to him, and at the same time giddy with the freedom of transgression. With that blow, his logic had changed dangerously: God Most High might well punish him, but if He meant to do so, there was little the captain could do about it. That meant his fear couldn't control him any longer.

Phaedra, on the other hand, was all control. Though tears were streaming down her cheeks as she struggled back to her feet, her voice was level and strong. "I don't know if my God will punish you for that," she said, "but I will pray that He doesn't. I've seen what happens when Gods punish men."

"Your God won't sink this ship with you on it," the captain answered. "As soon as the other search parties return, we'll be back to our regular trade route. It should be an easier voyage than usual, what with your God keeping the bad weather at bay."

The man's bluster was enough to enrage anyone, but Phaedra remained calm. If anything she grew calmer, and her look was one of pity, not anger.

"I'm sorry we've brought trouble to you and your crew," she said. "I don't want to see anything bad happen because of the way you've treated us. Please believe me that it's not too late to repent. We have a friend who lives today because of the power of his atonement."

The captain looked tempted, hopeful, relieved. Then his expression hardened. "It's thoughtful of you to say so," he said. "I'll make a sacrifice at our next port."

He turned away. "Put them below."

And just like that, they were confined below deck for the rest of the voyage. Days went by as the ship went from port to port, trading goods for coin and other goods. The crew brought them food and took their waste, treating them with embarrassed deference. At the first major port, half of them left the ship. The others told Hunter and Phaedra that they meant to do the same soon – they respected the islanders and their God, and didn't want to wait to see what would happen to the ship and its captain. But for Hunter and Phaedra, this only made the voyage worse. Each crewman who left was replaced with one who didn't know the prisoners' story, and didn't have any cause to fear God Most High. As the captain grew bolder, his crew only grew more obedient, and by the start of the third week, he and the cook were the only original crewmembers who remained.

And why shouldn't the captain be bold? The stormy season should have begun by now, and yet, to judge by the gentle rocking of the ship, the weather remained fine. If the captain's gambit was working just as he'd hoped, maybe the islanders' powerful God didn't mean to punish him after all.

Hunter wondered whether God Most High had indeed forgotten about them, or whether this latest reversal was all part of the plan. He wasn't sure which possibility worried him more. Now that the crew was made up of men who echoed their captain's blasphemy, he found himself simultaneously hating them and fearing for their lives. After the miracles God Most High had already performed on his and Phaedra's behalf, He seemed bound to intervene again soon enough.

Hunter hoped He would be merciful.

It was miserable being confined below decks, even though there were no cells in which to hold him and Phaedra. They stayed in the same old sleeping bunks as before, in a compartment they shared with six crew members. But the crewmembers got to leave, and he and Phaedra didn't, and that made all the difference. Without access to the fresh air above, Hunter developed a constant, low-level nausea that would sometimes quite unexpectedly grow out of control. One moment he would be talking with Phaedra, or perhaps trying to rest, and the next moment he would have to stop whatever he was doing and focus all his energies on keeping his stomach down.

Then one morning it finally happened. Hunter awoke before dawn to the sounds of a fight abovedeck. It was all the stomping that woke him, but soon there was a piercing scream and then Phaedra was awake too, fumbling about in the near-dark with short, fearful breaths. Hunter's brain was still processing the situation – they had dropped anchor two days ago at Belinphae, an island on the western end of the archipelago, not far from Tarphae, and they hadn't moved since. Much of the crew would still be ashore at this hour – he and Phaedra were alone in their compartment. Now there were voices above, barking orders. The anchor was being lifted – they were setting sail.

An unfamiliar head appeared at the hatch. "Anyone down there, you just stay. The fight's all over, and my friends and I are up here waiting to stick anyone who feels like starting another. We'll be away from here by breakfast time, and then we'll let you up."

"All right," Hunter called back. "We'll stay. We don't want trouble."

The man snickered. "Oh, you've got trouble already."

16
CRITON

They washed Delika with buckets from the well, but had no dry clothes to change her into, so they wrapped her in a blanket from Belkos' house while her own clothes dried. The more he gathered about what had happened to her, the more horrified he became. How proud he'd been that he'd found a caring family to adopt those children!

She'd hidden herself in the Temple of Magor, poor thing, and had climbed into a vat of sacrificial pigs' blood when it burned. Apparently, Magor's priests used the blood in some of their rituals, watering it down just enough so that it wouldn't congeal. It still took some scrubbing to get it off Delika's skin, though.

Iona helped them, while Dessa held Goodweather. Criton secretly wished Iona and Belkos would offer to adopt the girl, but he knew they wouldn't. Delika was his problem now, and Bandu's – the fact that they had only become parents a few months ago was irrelevant. Besides which, the girl had sought him out personally, and the last time he'd tried to get her adopted had turned out disastrously. He and Bandu might be only ten or eleven years older, but they would still have to be parents to her.

It might not be *so* bad, though, he thought, as he changed the clothes of a wailing Goodweather. At least Delika could talk.

The next morning, the Dragon Touched began their journey northward. Traveling in a caravan with them reminded Criton of a time nearly a year ago, when the islanders had left another village with all of its inhabitants and made for the shelter of Silent Hall. His people moved just as slowly as those villagers had, traveling as they were with children and livestock, and setting up tents each evening. It was even more or less the same time of year, perhaps a month away from the start of the rainy season.

Of course, that didn't make the two journeys identical. Psander's villagers had been looking for a protector, and they had found one. For the Dragon Touched there would be no shelter, no safe haven at the end of the road.

On the other hand, now he was here with family, venturing into the northern plains with a clan of his own kin. That made him happy in a way he had never felt before.

Bandu was less happy, though he could tell that she appreciated how good it felt to him. And it helped that Iona and Dessa kept offering to hold Goodweather, or to change her clothes, or to help Bandu bind the baby to her back with wide strips of cloth. He had less time to devote to his infant daughter, now that he had to lead his people and watch over Delika too. The girl clung to him like he was still the only thing saving her from drowning. Even when he met with Hessina or with his cousin to talk about strategy or ask about their religion,

Delika wouldn't leave his side without a good deal of cajoling.

That caused its own troubles for him and Bandu. He could tell that his wife resented his inattention to Goodweather, and his supposed favoring of Delika. But what could he do? Goodweather didn't really care who changed her swaddling clothes, and it was barely even his choice anyway. He had duties to his people, and duties to the girl who had braved fire and blood to find him, so at least for now, Goodweather would have to come third. There was nothing he could do about that, and he wished Bandu wouldn't give him so much trouble for it.

Besides, he was doing his best with Goodweather. He held the child plenty, and changed her clothes often enough. He gave her as much attention as he could afford.

But he spent most of his time getting to know the members of his new community, and learning their ways. He had once read a screed against the Dragon Touched that had been written by a friar of Atel, claiming all manner of evils for Criton's people, and he had always wished that he knew which parts were true and which weren't. Now he had the opportunity to find out, and even with his troubles multiplying and Delika clinging to his side, he did not squander it. He asked Hessina all about the worship of God Most High, and she was happy to oblige.

The friar's screed had apparently been right about at least one thing: the respect and worship of other Gods was anathema to God Most High. His worshippers weren't permitted to use other Gods' ritual objects, and they didn't eat other Gods' sacred animals. Magor's pigs, Ravennis' crows, Karassa's jellyfish – they were all forbidden. Criton gasped when he heard this, because he and his friends had all eaten from the Boar of Hagardis, but Hessina assured him that her purifying ritual had wiped his transgressions away.

Even so, he worried. What if he ate other sacred animals without realizing it? He didn't know which animals were sacred to which Gods – what else should he be avoiding? Luckily, Hessina was well versed in these things. Sharks and whales were sacred to Mayar; moths to Elkinar; falcons to Atun; mules to Atel; hares to Eramia; cats both great and small were sacred to Pelthas. There were other animals that she knew were forbidden without knowing which Gods they belonged to: ants and termites, cockroaches, scarabs, snakes, lizards, jackals – the list seemed endless.

"Eat what the rest of us eat," she said at last. "You'll be fine."

Criton wondered what it meant for God Most High to be so firmly in opposition to all the other Gods, but Hessina disagreed with his characterization. It wasn't a matter of opposition, she said. The "Lower Gods" weren't rivals to God Most High, They were more akin to disobedient servants, who would all eventually be punished.

"Are there some He won't punish?" Criton asked. "Are some of Them allies?"

"God Most High does not need allies," Hessina answered. "But He is merciful, and will tolerate those who obey Him."

Criton nodded, but it seemed as if she could no sooner answer a question than he thought of another. "Does God Most High have special holy days? When do you give sacrifices?"

Hessina sighed at that. "In the old days, we used to make offerings during the draconic festivals. After the purge we started making our sacrifices on Magor and Elkinar's holy days, whispering the prayers of dedication so that our neighbors wouldn't suspect us of worshipping any God but their own. But the draconic calendar is not the same as the common one. In the end we lost track of where we were on it, and when that happened, we lost our own holidays."

That was so unspeakably sad that Criton forgot what other question he had meant to ask.

The northern plains through which they traveled were a flat expanse of mostly grasses and farmland, their farmers and herders paying taxes to Ardis without any conceivable benefit to themselves. Criton meant to put an end to that, but in a way he too had chosen for his people to prey on these poorest and weakest of their neighbors, building their army and their reputation on the backs of the desperate. Especially now, at harvest time, his decision to raise an army from these plainsfolk was too cruel. If he took all their able-bodied men just as they were most needed for the harvest, in a few months there would be starvation.

But what could he do about it now? His people had to survive, so they needed an army. He had chosen his path.

It only took them a day to reach their first village, a hamlet of no more than twenty houses whose people immediately surrendered upon hearing the conditions Criton offered them. Criton took a man from each house and some livestock besides, and the Dragon Touched continued on their way. The livestock were mostly sheep and pigs, the latter of which would of course be useless to the Dragon Touched, but perhaps it was a good thing that their allies would have a food supply dedicated to them alone. Hessina wanted to demand that the pigs remain behind, but Criton overruled her. It was bad enough that he was raising his army here. He wanted the northerners to think of the Dragon Touched as allies, not tyrants.

The men from this village did not have weapons of war, but they took sticks, hoes, whips, or whatever else they could use in a fight without harming their families' ability to harvest their crops. Criton doubted these tools would be much use against an Ardisian army, and he hoped it would be a very long time before they all found out. But that day was bound to come sometime. The Ardismen would catch up to the Dragon Touched eventually, and besides, the Dragon Touched would meet resistance among the plainsfolk too, sooner or later.

In fact, the very next village they came to met them with scythes and spears, held by a ragged line of men who yelled at them to keep away. Criton steeled himself and led his kin in the assault.

It was too easy: the Dragon Touched slaughtered their resisters, seized their families and their property, and moved on. Criton put his cousin in charge of dividing the spoils, with instructions to give special privilege to the northerners who had joined them. It was the best way he could think of to encourage more plainsmen to ally with the Dragon Touched.

Even so, Belkos insisted on giving Criton and Bandu a flock of sheep, as well as the widow who had owned them.

"My Ma didn't raise me to own slaves," Criton told him.

"It doesn't matter," Belkos answered. "You're our leader. It's expected."

"They expect me to own a person and call it normal."

"By the old laws," Belkos said, "slaves were kept only

until they had repaid their debts. Would you be happier with that? What debt do these people owe, do you think?"

"How about a year of service?" Criton asked. "Or until we take Ardis, whichever is sooner. For all of them. We're only punishing them for not helping us against Ardis, after all."

"Good," Belkos said. "Then let these people serve us until then."

Criton accepted that, even though it still bothered him. At heart, he knew that these townspeople had done nothing wrong, that it was terrible to punish them at all. But this was war. He was a leader now, a leader of his people, and if the Dragon Touched didn't develop the sort of reputation that would cause villages to surrender and bolster their camp with fighting-age men, they would all perish. The Ardismen would crush them.

Besides, with all his new obligations, he didn't have time to herd all those sheep himself.

So he made an arrangement with their new slave Biva, one modeled on the relationship between Psander and her villagers. Though he and Bandu theoretically owned both the sheep and the woman who herded them, in practice they let Biva keep both her autonomy and her sheep in return for a share of the milk, wool, and meat. They did not speak of her husband, whom his men had killed, and Criton did his best to pretend that she was just a neighbor who owed him money. She ate and slept separately from his family, and their only contact with her was transactional. In a year's time, they would part ways and never speak to each other again.

Criton took to war easily. He did not have the trained, fluid motions that Hunter had displayed time and again, but he was good at the simple, brutal work of beating down an opponent's defenses and sticking him with something sharp. He liked to intimidate his enemies with an early burst of fire, then slip his spear past their guard and finish them off. It was a dumb trick, and unfair to boot, but if he had learned anything from Narky and Bestillos it was that winning didn't have to be fair. And as long as nobody who fought him survived, there was nothing wrong with using the same technique over and over again. It would be new and surprising every time.

Village after village, town after town was given the choice: cooperation or death. And it worked: the ranks of the Dragon Touched were swelling, and over time, fewer and fewer people resisted them. Their growing numbers slowed them down, of course, what with the livestock they were herding and the difficulties of coordinating such a large group, but that was a good problem to have. The important thing was that they really were raising an army, ragged though it was. Their reputation preceded them now, and there were whole villages that welcomed the Dragon Touched with open arms and gladly joined their cause, hoping to free themselves from their southern oppressors. Slowly but surely, Ardis was losing control over its tributaries.

As the weeks went by, Criton began to develop his own reputation among the plainsfolk. They called him the Black Dragon, just like Belkos' mother-in-law had, and his enemies cowered at the sight of him. For the most part, he didn't mind: the name made him sound powerful, even awe-inspiring. Who could stand up to the Black Dragon in battle? It was a catchy name, too. Soon a number of his kinsmen were using it, and even Hessina occasionally asked him semi-sarcastically, "What does the Black Dragon think?"

On the other hand, being the Black Dragon also made

him less of a person. If his enemies were frightened by the idea of him, all the better, but he should have been more than an idea to his own kin. It was alienating, and he didn't deserve to be alienated from the family he had wanted his whole life. He could feel that added distance turning him into a harder person. He didn't think his mother would have liked that.

It helped in the evenings to retreat to his own tent with Bandu and Delika and the baby. They all loved him in one way or another, and not because he symbolized anything to them. It was frustrating to have Delika there sometimes, since her presence made it harder for him and Bandu to be intimate, but he appreciated her presence anyway. She was a talkative girl, which could be nice when Bandu was in one of her quiet moods, and despite all she'd been through she smiled and laughed much more easily than the two of them did. If Bandu's presence was full of love and of wisdom, Delika's was full of joy.

And there was need for joy. This war of conquest did not sit well with Bandu. It struck her as savage and pointless – what did the Dragon Touched need all these sheep and slaves for, anyway? Criton tried to explain how it was really about gathering force, a necessary step toward defeating Ardis, but she didn't seem to care for that goal either.

"Why your people need Ardis?" she asked. "Why not go far away where they don't try to kill you?"

"They want us dead everywhere," Criton reminded her. "Ardis is where we belong."

"So you kill other people and take their things? Why? Ardis is *that* way!"

"I know, but they're too strong for us right now. We're building an army, Bandu, just like Bestillos did when he moved against Psander."

Bandu gawked at him. "Like Bestillos? Let me remember you something."

"Remind."

She waved a hand dismissively. "Let me remember you something: Bestillos is a wicked man. Very, very wicked. You hate him. So why you want to do things his way?"

"Because that's how it works! The world hates us just for existing. Just for being. We need an army, and this is the only way to build one right now."

Bandu rolled her eyes. "Does Bestillos' army help him?"

"That's not fair," Criton answered. "We had Salemis then, and the element of surprise. But Salemis said he wouldn't be coming back. We *have* to build an army."

"If your God is so strong, he can send Salemis back. Or he can do something Himself instead. You want to make army the red priest's way, the wicked way. Why your God helps you if you are wicked like Bestillos?"

"I'm not wicked like–" Criton began, but it was no good. Whether she was being purposefully obstinate or not, he knew very well that she couldn't see the distinction between borrowing an enemy's tactics and borrowing their wickedness. And when it came right down to it, *was* there such a distinction? It was hard for the Dragon Touched to remain morally superior when they were emulating their enemies.

Her words nagged at him all that day and the next. His strategy was a good one – wasn't it? The Dragon Touched and their allies were over a thousand strong now, with some four hundred warriors among them. The plainsmen who had joined of their own volition now owned slaves and livestock, and fought with as much zeal as any of the Dragon Touched warriors. It was the right way to fight a war, he had come to believe. The only way. They would still be far outnumbered if they faced Ardis now, but with a few more weeks to grow...

The next day, word came from the south. The first towns to ally with the Dragon Touched had been sacked. Ardis was coming for them.

The news threw the camp into disarray. The men who had allied with the Dragon Touched now spoke of leaving to protect their homes. A council of their elders, one from every town and village, came together and demanded that the Dragon Touched do something to protect their families from the Ardismen. There was no question what that 'something' might be. Criton hadn't thought his people ready for a confrontation, but it seemed they had little choice: they had to face Ardis now, before any of their allies could desert.

Hessina said he was being too hasty. Ardis was goading them into an open fight long before the Dragon Touched could be ready for one. Criton agreed with her logic completely, but it didn't change his calculus. This was as clear a sign as they were going to get. The time had come to prove their faith in God Most High. The Ardisian army was rumored to be two thousand strong – in battle, they would outnumber the Dragon Touched five to one. But if this was what God Most High wanted, so be it.

They turned back southward. All talk turned to battle tactics, and Criton rediscovered his kin's weakness in harnessing their magic. He had thought his own magical skill limited, after seeing all that Psander could do, but the truth was that he had taught himself a lot. He could summon a light. He could change his appearance, clothes and all. He could fly. The Dragon Touched universally knew how to hide their draconic heritage, and breathing fire came naturally enough, but that seemed to be all. Was it the three decades of repression, or an actual lack of talent that kept them from using their magic as he did?

He hadn't flown since the battle at Silent Hall, when the high priest of Magor had ended his flight with a single word of command. It had taken him over a month to fully recover from his fall, and he was not eager to take to the air again, but flying would have made for an amazing advantage over the Ardismen now that Bestillos was gone. Ah, well. He could still do it himself, if he found the courage to, but it seemed that there was no hope of his commanding a flying army.

Hessina insisted that his greater magical ability was a gift from God Most High. Perhaps she was right, but he would have rather his God granted these abilities to *all* the Dragon Touched, so that their enemies' greater numbers wouldn't be so devastating an advantage. It was bad enough that nowadays only an eighth of his force even *was* Dragon Touched.

Their tactical options were limited. Outnumbered as they were, there was no sense in keeping some part of their force in reserve. He would have liked to throw up his hands and say that God Most High would take care of everything, but his allies had no reason to trust in God Most High as of yet, and he needed their support. If he couldn't find a way to embolden them while demoralizing his enemies, it would be a rout. Or, worse still, the majority of his army that wasn't Dragon Touched might panic and turn on his people. No, he couldn't leave the tactics to his God.

It was Bandu who gave him the idea, by pointing out that the food supplies were soon going to run low if they didn't start eating pigs. There had been a feast after every victory, and after every northern village joined their cause. It was a way of keeping their allies happy; of convincing them they were on the right side of this war. But Hessina had not allowed these feasts to include pork, so the supply of sheep had dwindled while the number of pigs grew. Criton wondered if this was a metaphor for the foolishness of recruiting an army the way they had, and that was when the idea came to him. A metaphor. Yes.

Pigs were Magor's animal, and the Dragon Touched had access to an enormous number of them. The plainsfolk kept stores of rendered grease that they used to cook their meals. And the Dragon Touched could breathe fire.

Criton sent scouts ahead as the Dragon Touched and their allies marched south. It would take some time to coordinate the display he had in mind, and he didn't want to be surprised by the Ardisian force before he was ready for it. He hoped the plainsfolk wouldn't give him any trouble about the use of their pigs.

They did, of course. Criton called their leaders together that night, once they had made camp. The elders listened to him as he explained that he meant to light their pigs on fire and drive them toward the enemy, and they scoffed at him.

"How are you going to make sure they don't run back at us?" an elder named Paedros asked. "Once you light a pig on fire, there's no telling which way it'll run. If you think they'll all charge toward the enemy, you're a fool."

"I'm no fool," Criton insisted, feeling ever more foolish as he said it. But these were desperate times, and he was prepared to try any tactic, no matter how unorthodox. Their survival depended upon it. "They ought to at least run away from the direction of the fire, right?"

The elders looked at each other. "Probably," one said.

"But not necessarily," Paedros added.

"I think they will," Criton said, "and keep in mind that we don't need them to charge the enemy in unison. The point isn't to use the pigs as part of our army, it's to send a message to the Magor-worshipping Ardismen. They'll watch their God's sacred animals burning and squealing and running away from us, and they'll understand that we mean to do the same to them."

"And if half the pigs turn on us instead?" another elder asked. "What message will that send?"

"You've managed to herd them up to now. Make sure that doesn't happen."

"They haven't all been on fire up to now!"

Criton sighed. "If you like, I can ask Bandu to help you. My wife has a way with animals."

That quieted them down. Even among the Dragon Touched, Bandu had a reputation as an unpredictable foreign witch. The plainsfolk feared her even more, knowing that this was how their fire-breathing allies spoke of her powers.

"Again," Criton said, "the goal is to shock the Ardismen into forgetting that they outnumber us. If we don't face them like we're afraid we might lose, they'll start to wonder whether we know more than they do. Let a few pigs run the wrong way – as long as they're mostly running at the Ardismen, we'll have gotten the point across. By the time our armies meet, *they'll* be ready to run."

There was silence at first. Criton was not sure whether he'd convinced them – they kept looking wordlessly at each other, as if they were elves and could hear each other's thoughts.

"That may be true," Paedros conceded at last. "We can

try it, if you'll compensate us for our lost animals."

Criton promised that they'd be well compensated in spoils once they defeated the Ardismen, offering them a greater share than they had taken from their conquests so far. It was a fair offer, since they were bound to win such spoils if they defeated the Ardisian army. Once he'd left, he let out a great sigh of relief. He had thought it foolish of God Most High to put him in charge of this army, but maybe he was better at the tasks of leadership than he had realized. That was somewhat reassuring.

In any case, he felt confident in his battle plan. The Dragon Touched and their allies would not fight like a force outclassed, would not stake out a position on some hill and wait for their foes to try to overwhelm them. They would set Magor's pigs aflame and then charge their enemies, giving no time for tactics and no room for maneuver. They would fight like people who knew that with God Most High at their backs, defeat was impossible. And when they did that, Ardis would believe them.

He couldn't wait.

17
GENERAL MAGERION

As far as Magerion was concerned, the council spent far too much time discussing the Dragon Touched threat, and not nearly enough talking about the threat from within. The generals argued over how long it was taking to raise their army – which was quite a long time, delayed as they were by the harvest. They argued about the ideal field of battle too, as if they would have a choice, and lastly about who should command the force that faced down the Dragonspawn. Some of the talk was worthwhile, but to Magerion's mind, a lot of it was meaningless.

The Dragon Touched had moved north, gathering their strength for the inevitable battle with Ardis, so it was probably true that the sooner Ardis marched out to meet them, the better. Still. Most of the council's disagreements were about ego, not strategy.

Had he still been alive, Bestillos would have resolved these questions easily. He would have dominated the discussion, and doubtless led the army himself. Now that he was gone, everyone wanted the chance to supplant him as the champion of Ardis.

Magerion was the exception. He had never minded

the priest's dominance, nor his greater visibility. Bestillos deserved it, after all, for having led the Great Uprising that put them all in power in the first place. Championing Ardis was a job for someone theatrical, and Magerion was not one for theatricality. He thought the others were overly concerned with the dramatic reappearance of the Dragon Touched, when the death cult of Ravennis threatened to tear Ardis apart far sooner, from the inside.

The cult had grown so rapidly that the other members of the Council of Generals had yet to register its importance. Or perhaps they believed on principle that the Ravennis worshippers shouldn't be taken seriously, after the way Magor had trounced Ravennis at Laarna. Whatever the reason, they were being foolish. Magerion had been listening to the death cult's followers, and he had seen yesterday's confrontation with the priests of Magor. These people were dangerous. Their theology would appeal to the masses now that Bestillos was gone – it already *was* appealing to them. The army of Ardis had been routed by a *dragon*, for Magor's sake. If the dragons' God was still alive after centuries of abuse, and still so vital that He had summoned up a dragon and a whole clan of Dragon Touched out of nowhere... well, who was to say that Ravennis was really gone?

And if the cult of Ravennis won over the people of Ardis, what would happen to its current rulers?

Magerion had been a young revolutionary during the Great Uprising, when Bestillos had led the people in toppling their king and his Dragon Touched lackeys. The dirty secret of those days was that thousands of Ardismen had been true believers in God Most High right up until the forces of Magor had won – the Magor-worshippers had been in the minority. Perhaps the others had forgotten, but Magerion still remembered how the people had turned on their God and His representatives. Men who had prayed next to their Dragon Touched neighbors in wholehearted devotion had quickly, so quickly joined in the slaughter once the tide had turned against the Dragonspawn. Why shouldn't something similar happen again, if the followers of this death cult were to prevail?

Yet none of the other generals saw the danger. They were still arguing over who ought to lead the forces that took on the Dragon Touched – it looked like General Xytos might well win that argument, but Choerus and young Scrofa still weren't letting it go. Magerion decided at long last to interrupt them.

"Why don't you all go?" he suggested. "All three of you. There is glory enough for everyone, presuming you win. What I ask is this: leave me a hundred picked men with which to defend the city. We have deadly enemies right here in Ardis that we ignore at our peril."

"Enemies?" Xytos asked. "This isn't about those Ravennis-worshippers again, is it?"

Magerion nodded, and the other men sighed and rolled their eyes.

"A hundred men," he insisted. "Then you won't have to listen to me repeating myself. Besides which, if Magor is with you, you won't need another hundred. And if He's not, another hundred men won't do you any good."

"And if we are evenly matched?" Scrofa said. "What then? What if Magor and the dragons' God both watch silently, or if They both intervene equally?"

"Then when you have fought the Dragon Touched into the night, and both sides pull back to regroup, you will be glad not to come home to a city overrun with Laarnan death cultists."

Xytos smiled. "At first I was concerned about our

convening a meeting without replacing Bestillos first, but I see the priests of Magor are well represented."

"Bestillos was a true general," General Stellys said, frowning. "He wasn't on our council to represent the priesthood."

"True," Xytos agreed, "but he represented them anyway. And now Magerion appears to have taken up the cause. Have your hundred men, Magerion. We'll make do without you."

They moved onto other topics, , and the next day Magerion went to meet with Bestillos' successor as high priest. He found High Priest Melikon surprisingly optimistic about the prospect of exterminating the Ravennis death cult, especially considering what they both agreed they were up against.

"The people are losing faith, it is true," Melikon admitted, "and there is some truth too in the death cult's philosophy. Ravennis was clearly not defeated as we had thought – the miracle of the crows proves that much. But with the failure of our death-prophecies to materialize, and with your men rounding up Crow God worshippers for public executions, this revolution will be over before it begins. Then Ravennis will truly be dead, and the faith of Magor's followers will be restored."

The men Magerion picked for his anti-Ravennis cleansing were all either personal loyalists or members of his clan: his sons Mageris and Atlon, his nephews, close friends and distant cousins, all people who owed him their positions in society. Their mission would involve slaughtering their neighbors – he could not afford doubters.

They started with that leftover Oracle, the so-called Graceful Servant. Magerion had expected her followers to keep her hidden until he could torture her location out of them, but he had thought wrong. The Graceful Servant delivered herself to them the very next day, striding up to the Great Temple of Magor as if she believed herself untouchable. She cooperated fully as they tied her to one of the temple's pillars, and though her mouth was full of prayers to her God, she did not pray for Ravennis to save her. Rather, she locked eyes with General Magerion and prayed for Ravennis to bring His truth to the world, and to grant His followers peace and joy in the world below. It was unsettling. Though an enormous crowd had gathered to view her execution, Magerion felt that she was saying something directly to him. It wasn't a plea, either – if anything, she seemed triumphant.

He had her flayed. After that, he had her lieutenants found and flayed as well – all those who were known to have associated with the Graceful Servant were put to death in as public and painful a way as possible. The priests of Magor delighted in this, but Magerion grew more and more uneasy as time went by. The Oracle's followers all did their best to follow her example, praying to their God to reward them in the underworld rather than to save them, and their unnatural bravery was having an impact. Many found the cultists' attitudes inspirational. It was Laarna all over again: no matter how many of His worshippers they killed, Ravennis only seemed to grow stronger.

The trouble was that Ravennis' worshippers weren't universally reviled by the city's leaders. The priests of Elkinar declared neutrality in the conflict, having received no directive from their high priestess in Anardis to take one side or the other. Without the Elkinaran priests' help in chasing Ravennis from the city, the Crow God's worshippers found enough of a safe haven to persist.

To make matters worse, the biggest prize had already escaped him. Narky the Black, the one-eyed slayer of Bestillos, had vanished as if he had never existed. Rumor had it that he had escaped the city even before the Graceful Servant's death, fleeing under the cover of night. High Priest Melikon might laugh that Ravennis' champion had fled in terror, but as far as Magerion was concerned, the point was that he was *alive*. He didn't have to be brave to be dangerous. From what Magerion had heard, Bestillos had been shot in the back.

He began questioning Ravennis worshippers about Narky before killing them, but it seemed that anyone who knew anything was long dead. The general had to own up to his poor planning on that front.

Not all the Ravennis worshippers were suicidal, of course. A good many of them practiced their religion secretly, when none of Magerion's men were around. He would take that. The fact that his men were driving the death cult into the shadows and not the other way around was in itself something to be thankful for. The question was, how long could this situation last?

The army of Ardis had marched off two weeks ago with all the fanfare that that entailed, parading out of the city with three generals at its head. As Magerion saw it, there were only two possibilities now: either Generals Xytos, Choerus, and Scrofa would crush the Dragonspawn and return triumphant, in which case the Ravennis worshippers would likely remain underground for another generation… or else they would lose. If they lost, he was sure the citizens of his city would abandon Magor and embrace the Raven God of Laarna, and if that happened, Magerion's head was bound to be discovered atop a spear before long.

The Graceful Servant began haunting his dreams.

Night after night, he dreamt that he rose from his bed and went to stand below her corpse at the Temple of Magor. Even skinless, even tied to a pillar of her enemy's temple, there was an awful majesty to her.

"You cannot resist us forever," she would taunt him. "Ravennis knows your destiny. Ravennis *is* your destiny."

When he tried to reply, his voice came out a caw and he discovered that he had been transformed into a raven.

He slept less.

He ordered ten of his men to try to track down Narky the Black, wherever he had disappeared to, though at this point he was not sure what to do with the man once he had him. The Graceful Servant had endured public humiliation, torture, and death, and still had the power to keep Magerion awake at night. He was no longer sure this monstrous cult *could* be beheaded.

He was beginning to understand that no matter what he did, it would not be enough on its own. For any of this to be worthwhile, Magor would eventually have to demonstrate His supremacy. So long as the situation with the Dragon Touched lay unresolved, all of Magerion's efforts against the cult of Ravennis could only postpone a revolution, not prevent it.

So he joined the priests when they prayed for victory against the Dragon Touched, repeating their words so many times that he could have led the prayers himself. He prayed when he awoke in the morning, and went to bed with still more prayers on his lips. He prayed as if the power of his worship alone could give Magor the strength to keep fighting against His enemies. And maybe it would – who knew how these things really worked?

Let Magor give His generals, Xytos, Scrofa, and Choerus, the strength and cunning to win their war against the Dragon Touched, and win it soon. Magerion could try to keep the death cult at bay until their return, but victory was not his to aspire to.

And he couldn't hold out forever.

18
CRITON

"You are wicked! Your thoughts are wicked!"

Bandu hated his plan. She hated it with a passion so strong he could barely comprehend it.

"Why you do this to pigs? Why you kill them and not to eat, and not to give to your God, and not to do anything, just to kill? It is wicked, wicked, wicked!"

Goodweather was wailing too, while Delika cowered in a corner of the tent. Criton took the baby from his shouting wife and rocked her from side to side, for all the good it did. He was sure the whole Dragon Touched camp could hear them.

"Your God is wicked like you?" Bandu demanded. Criton winced to think of who might be listening. Who might hear her say such things. Probably everybody.

"Answer me! He is wicked like you?"

"God Most High isn't wicked and you know it," Criton hissed. "This is blasphemy, Bandu – how well do you think I can protect you?"

"If your God isn't wicked," Bandu retorted, "then He hates what you do to pigs. He punishes you for being so wicked to them. You take fat from dead ones and use it

152

to kill more, to *murder* them."

"It's not murder," Criton said. "You had it right the first time."

"No, murder is wickeder than kill. I know your words."

Criton sighed. "They're just pigs, Bandu. Murder is for people."

"If your God likes this," Bandu spat back, "He is wicked. If your God is good, He hates this."

Criton was glad he was holding Goodweather, or he might have struck her. His anger was starting to take over again, in that dangerous way that had only ever led to pain for them both, but which he somehow remained powerless to stop. He had struck Bandu once, and she had shunned him for more than a month afterward – he couldn't let that happen again. Yet how dare she claim that God Most High could not support him and be good at the same time?

"This," he said, his voice rising, "will demoralize our enemies and bring us victory. We're planning to slaughter our enemies on the battlefield, Bandu. God Most High won't mind if we slaughter some pigs too, on the way."

Bandu glared at him, but she spoke no more blasphemies. She only took Goodweather from him and left him to calm down without them. Eventually, he did.

The Dragon Touched met the army of Ardis two weeks later, in a field flatter than an altar top. There were very few hills in this country anyway, though the Calardian range still stood imposingly in the distance. A light rain fell on the armies as they faced each other across the field, the Dragon Touched wary and the Ardismen gleeful.

The entire multitude of the Dragon Touched and their allies stood together in a mass, Criton having declined to keep the women and children separate. Even so, his people were easily outnumbered by the army across the field. The Ardismen banged their spears against their shields as they marched forward, still too far away to begin their charge. The Dragon Touched slathered lard on pigs.

When they were no more than a hundred yards away, the Ardismen sent forth their champion. He strode forward, spear held high, his shield emblazoned with a gold-leaf depiction of the boar of Magor standing before a city gate. Criton wondered if that was a family crest or a symbol belonging to the Ardisian Council of Generals. Either way, it was impressive.

"I am Scrofa," the man cried, "general of the Ardisian council and slayer of dragons! Send me your champion, Dragonspawn, to be a sacrifice upon this sacred battlefield. Magor stands with me!"

For a moment, Criton was sorely tempted to take the bait and enter into single combat with this man. Did he think Criton would be intimidated by this dragon slayer nonsense? Whatever position General Scrofa held, he clearly wasn't old enough to have been active during the purge of the Dragon Touched. Criton would have loved to drive a spear through him personally.

But no. The Ardismen were known for their warriors, and this was one of their generals. All of Criton's war experience amounted to one dumb trick that he used over and over again. A fight against Ardis' champion would be no more equal than the size of their respective armies.

General Scrofa turned back to his troops as if to say, *see what cowards these Dragon Touched are?* "Send me a champion," he cried again.

Criton lit a pig.

It didn't even run in Scrofa's direction so much as diagonally away from Criton, squealing pitiably as it first approached the Ardismen, then turned away from them again. Finally it collapsed.

On Criton's signal, the plainsfolk stepped back and the Dragon Touched breathed fire on the rest of the pigs, keeping up a steady flame to dissuade the animals from turning back toward them. It was mostly effective, as the vast majority of the pigs surged toward the enemy and not at the rest of the Dragon Touched army. It wasn't perfect, though: Criton was nearly run down himself, and had to leap into the air to keep from being trampled. He stayed there, hovering, and called the attack.

The Dragon Touched charged.

The Ardismen charged too, but their ranks were already broken. Though many of the pigs were collapsing before they ever reached the enemy, they had done their job admirably: the most disciplined force in the world was fighting on the same level as the Dragon Touched and plainsmen. Warriors from both sides dodged around flaming sows, slipping in the mud and the wet grass, and most of the Ardismen were too afraid of offending their God to put the pigs down and get them out of the way. Their ranks broke around Magor's dying animals, and when the two armies met, the disorganization turned to chaos.

Above it all, Criton searched the crowd for Scrofa. He found the Ardisian general a little nearer than he had expected, already showing his deadly efficacy with spear and shield. Two men lay dying at the general's feet as he ducked and thrust at a third, never slowing his onslaught. Criton was glad he hadn't chosen to face General Scrofa one-on-one: the man was fast, fearless, and a cunning fighter.

But he wasn't looking up.

Criton dropped toward him feet first, readying his spear. The spear was seven feet long and sturdy, but not terribly useful at this angle, what with the general's helmet and armored shoulders as the only real targets. That was all right, though. Criton meant to surprise him with a hard landing and a burst of flame before skewering him through the chest.

The first half of the plan worked marvelously. Scrofa didn't even notice his approach until the last moment, when the man he had been fighting saw Criton coming and backed off. He looked up just in time for Criton to land on his shoulders, sending him sprawling. He dropped his weapon and his shield in the process, but was fast – God, he was fast! He wriggled back away from Criton's first spear thrust and sprang to his feet, unarmed but back in a fighting stance. He had a short sword in his belt, but didn't draw it yet.

Criton didn't give him the chance. He advanced, jabbing at the general with his spear. Amazingly, Scrofa managed to evade him even while moving closer, catching the spear by the haft and nearly yanking it from Criton's grasp. Criton panicked and shot back into the air, but Scrofa held tight, forcing him to remain suspended directly above, unable to escape. The general pulled at the spear with a frightful determination, trying to drag Criton nearer the ground.

Criton was straining too hard to effectively breathe fire, but though his muscles were being taxed to their limit, his magical strength suddenly grew to accommodate his needs. Instead of pulling Criton down to earth, Scrofa found himself pulled off the ground, and together they began to rise.

If this turn of events surprised the general, he didn't

let on. Hand over hand he climbed up the wet spear toward Criton, even as the wind and rain blew at his face and the two of them rose farther and farther into the air. They were actually speeding up – where was this extra power coming from? Was this what an intervention from God Most High felt like? Scrofa should have let go when it was still safe to; now, even if he killed Criton, he might well be injured by the subsequent fall.

But Criton had no intention of dying. He meant to live, and he meant to live victorious. Just as Scrofa got to the top of the spear and reached for his arm, he caught his breath enough to blow fire in the general's face. There was nowhere to dodge to, so Scrofa simply grunted through the pain and tucked his chin down to avoid the flames, his hand falling back to the spear's haft.

This would likely be Criton's only chance. Once the general caught his arm, he didn't doubt that Scrofa would be able to snatch that sword from his belt and deal a death blow. He didn't mean to wait for that to happen.

"Goodbye," Criton said, and let go of the spear.

They had not risen high enough for the fall to kill Scrofa outright, but that hardly mattered. The whole battlefield had seen them rise, and the whole battlefield saw Scrofa fall. He cried out as he hit the ground, probably breaking a leg or two in the process, and the Ardismen, whose front lines had backed up to give him enough room to land, were in no position to prevent an opportunistic plainsman from leaping forward and driving a spear through his chest. The army of the Dragon Touched hollered out its triumph and surged forward, and the Ardismen broke and ran. Just like that, the battle became a rout.

The Dragon Touched and plainsmen chased their enemies across the fields, slaying every Ardisman they could catch. Criton flew above them, leading them onward, until the pursuers began to thin out for lack of endurance. Then he called off the pursuit and came back down to earth.

He landed to cheers. Belkos lifted him up and his men carried him back to the camp on their shoulders, reveling in the victory despite their well-earned exhaustion. Criton laughed, giddy with his army's triumph. Who could deny God Most High now? And who could deny that He had chosen the right man to lead His people in battle?

Bandu's warnings had all been nonsense – the dragons' God had clearly blessed their army, whatever she said. She might still scowl at him for a few more days, but what did that matter? He had images of the Dragon Touched marching their army through the gates of Ardis and taking back their city. If they could win this battle, no army could stop them.

Hessina's son Kilion disagreed. "I have made a count of the bodies," he told Criton later that evening, during the victory feast. The rain had thankfully ceased, though its chill remained. "We lost thirty-eight men, seven of them our own kin, and killed an even hundred and eighty. At that rate, we'll run out of men before they do."

Criton frowned. He was an odd one, Kilion, a man who exuded quiet diligence even as Hessina, his mother, was all force of will. Criton had thought at first that he was simply too terrified of his mother to speak up, but it seemed that his voice barely rose above a whisper even when she was absent. It was as if Hessina had kept all the force of personality to herself and left none for him. What kind of a man spent the first moments after a great victory counting bodies?

"We routed our enemies and killed their general,"

Criton pointed out. "You're saying we have to do *better?*"

"If we mean to outlast Ardis, yes."

Belkos, who had overheard, came to Criton's defense. "We humiliated the Ardismen today. How many more times do you think they can be humiliated before they refuse to meet us in battle? And what other fool would take up arms against us now?"

Kilion shrugged. "The army of Ardis is still five times our size."

"You are wrong," Bandu interjected from her seat beside Criton. "We are here too."

"We're only counting combatants," Criton said. "Only people who can fight. I know *you* could fight if you wanted to, but the other women? The children? And what would people say if we had to rely on women as a part of our army?"

"They say our army is bigger."

Criton smiled, though he knew he shouldn't. "I don't think that's what they'd say."

"So what do we do now?" Belkos asked. "Do we chase them down, even though they still outnumber us?"

"Of course," Criton said. "We can't give them time to regroup. If we can catch them tomorrow, they'll have to fight with less than their full army. God willing, after another defeat, half of them will desert."

Belkos frowned. "We can't catch them at our children's pace. Are we leaving them and our wives behind?"

Criton didn't answer. He sat silently, saying nothing, knowing that every moment made him look more foolish. It was absurd that he hadn't even considered how much faster the Ardismen would be, having left their wives and children safe at home. Now, he realized, he was faced with a terrible choice: if the Dragon Touched held to their current strategy and moved together as a unit, the Ardismen would have time to recover from their surprise defeat. If they separated the warriors from the rest of the camp and advanced more quickly, there was the chance that they might drive the Ardismen all the way back to their city walls – but there was also the chance that they would be outmaneuvered, and see their families massacred. How likely was that worst of possibilities? How unlikely would it have to be to make the risk worth it?

Delika was looking at him fearfully, already anticipating his abandonment. Bandu just looked frustrated. It would be a lot of work for her to watch both children at once.

"No," Criton said at last. "No, let them stay with us. If that gives the Ardismen time to recover from their losses, we'll just have to live with that. I'm not going to risk our families' lives on the assumption that the Ardismen will fight us honorably. Their army is so much bigger than ours, what's to stop them from sending a quarter of their force to attack anyone we leave behind?"

Relief passed across Belkos' face, and then shame. Despite himself, he had clearly been hoping Criton would say something like that. They were giving up on the biggest opportunity they had to finish off the Ardismen once and for all, and they both knew it, but their families were more important than a swift victory.

Besides, who cared if the Ardismen regrouped? Bandu had been wrong – God Most High had favored Criton's tactics, and would favor His people forever. They couldn't lose.

19
NARKY

Getting out of Ardis was as easy as Ptera had said it would be. Her connection nodded when he saw them and turned the other way as they slipped past the walls. Then it was a long trudge down the open road, with only the moon's light to guide them.

Narky didn't say anything – he was far too self-conscious. Ptera expected him to marry her, and he wasn't sure how he felt about it. He had never imagined himself with a continental girl, and certainly not with a woman so many years his senior. How many years, actually? Eight? Ten? He wanted to ask her, bluntly, just as he did with all awkward questions, but he couldn't bring himself to risk the trouble it would cause. She'd likely find it insulting, after all, and what if it turned out he wanted this? He didn't want to ruin their marriage before it had even begun.

He wished he still had Phaedra to talk to. She would have been able to clarify his position, to show him where his duty lay. Why did he have to be cut off from his friends, the only Tarphaean who had to figure things out for himself?

He'd finally, finally gotten used to being part of a group rather than outside one, and it had felt so good. The others didn't all like him – certainly not all the time – but they had still been friends to him, every one of them. They had supported him, and fought for him, and taught him how to live. They had valued his opinions and tolerated his poor manners, and whatever he said, he had secretly loved being with them all. Now he'd been given this ridiculous responsibility of leading the church of Ravennis, and he wouldn't even have his friends' support to get him through it.

Ptera wanted him to rely on her instead. The Graceful Servant had *commanded* him to rely on Ptera. But could he?

This marriage was so far from what he'd imagined for himself. He had known all along that he had no chance with Phaedra, and he had never meant to return to the archipelago, but still, a continental wife? He had thought it more likely that he'd stay lonely and unloved forever.

So shouldn't he be jumping at this opportunity? Sure, it was sudden, but so had been his exposure to Bandu's dimly lit nakedness, and that hadn't stopped him from wanting to see more.

It was the motivation that bothered him. What reason did Ptera have to want to marry him? Was it a matter of ambition? Attraction? Sacrifice to the cause? And had it been Ptera's idea, really, or the Graceful Servant's? He didn't like *that* idea at all.

"Why?" he said aloud.

Ptera turned to him. "Why what?"

"Why did the Graceful Servant say I should marry you? She said she'd talked to you about it already – why?"

She blinked at him, her features so bright in the light

of the full moon that it reminded him of the fairies. It was outrageous of him to connect the two, but he couldn't help it. He felt as though he was Ptera's prey, just as the islanders had been prey to the elves. What a ridiculous exaggeration on his part.

But was it, though?

Yes, yes it was.

"What did the Graceful Servant say to you about me?" He was trying to be gentler, but it wasn't coming out that way. "Was this her idea, Ptera, or was it yours?"

Another long pause. "Hers," Ptera admitted at last. "She said that you would be vulnerable to other people's influence so long as you were unmarried, and that this way, your head would be clear to make better decisions. She thought you should marry within the faith as soon as possible."

Oh.

"So you're just doing your duty, then? That's disgusting."

She shook her head, smiled tentatively. "Sometimes Ravennis gives us the opportunity to choose which duties we prefer."

That made Narky laugh. "I see. So I'm better than being tortured to death. Can't argue with that."

"You're too hard on yourself."

Ptera's face was serious, and Narky suddenly realized what it was that made that face distinctive: her left eye was ever so slightly higher than her right. It was striking, now that he noticed it. He couldn't decide whether it bothered him or not.

"You're a handsome boy," she continued, "and no one's done more than you in the service of Ravennis. Why shouldn't I choose you if I get the chance?"

He had no answer for her. It was the most flattering

thing anyone had ever said to him, and he didn't know what to do with it. Was that really how she saw him? A handsome boy, despite his lack of muscles or height or chest hair, despite his prominent scar and missing eye? His instinct was to be skeptical, to wonder what she was concealing from him, but nothing made sense. If she didn't really find him desirable, why had she connived to marry him? Even if it had been the Graceful Servant's idea in the first place, it sure didn't sound like she'd resisted.

Still, he hated not having a say in the matter. They had ambushed him, the two of them, and they expected him to simply fall in line and bind himself to Ptera for the rest of his life. No amount of flattery could cover over that fundamental truth. He was traveling to Anardis with a woman whose help had likely saved his life already and whose support he would certainly need in the days ahead – he could hardly afford *not* to marry her and keep up his end of the bargain. But it was a bargain she had made without him.

It was best to have out with it. "I don't like what you're doing to me," he said. "You haven't really given me a choice, the two of you. I'm not such a bastard that I'd send you away, and you're taking advantage of it."

Ptera winced. "I'm sorry you feel that way."

"I do."

They walked on in silence. Oh Ravennis, what was he going to do about this? He was wide awake, but his legs were growing tired. Where would they sleep tonight? *How* would they sleep tonight?

Ptera seemed to have read his mind. "We don't have to sleep together if you don't want to. I think you'd like me if you gave me a chance, but I don't want you to think you have no choice. We can sleep separately, and I'll still be your ally in all things. Ravennis is more important than me or you."

He nodded unhappily. That was the other thing. She was supposed to help him spread the word of Ravennis – how was he supposed to tell her that he didn't know what that was?

The biggest trouble with spreading the word of Ravennis was that Narky wasn't sure how he should relate to God Most High. Ravennis was Narky's God, Ravennis owned him, but Criton's God was the true power in the world, the builder of the mesh, the slayer of the Yarek and so on, and it was His prophet who had rescued the islanders from Bestillos and his army. Was Narky supposed to pretend that God Most High had had no role in his salvation?

And that was only the beginning. Whatever relationship Narky had with Criton's God, the real question was what relationship *Ravennis* had with God Most High. The Graceful Servant had viewed God Most High with something bordering on contempt, as if He was some doting old fool who would eventually tire of the world and wander off somewhere. That didn't strike Narky as right, but where did the truth lie? Was Ravennis an ally to God Most High? A rival? A high-level servant? Or was He perhaps a sort of divine parasite, feeding off God Most High's plans to further His own agenda? Narky worshipped Him and belonged to Him, but he was allowed to wonder. It was his *duty* to wonder, if he was to be Ravennis' high priest.

He wished his God would give him a sign, perhaps appear to him in a dream and explain what was expected of him. If Eramia could appear to Hunter in a river, why shouldn't Ravennis appear to Narky in a dream? Would the Keeper of Fates really leave him to his own devices on this most important of missions?

He hadn't been left *just* to his own devices though, and so his thoughts wandered back to Ptera. What was he to make of her? She certainly knew how to say the right thing. She was trying her best to win his heart, despite their bad start. He had to admire her effort, at least.

Did he find her attractive? It seemed almost like a silly question – he had never *not* found a woman near his age attractive, at least attractive enough to distract him a little. She was no Eramia – the girl, not the Goddess – and no Phaedra either, but those were awfully high standards. Yes, her hips were narrow, and her hair was limp and brown, but her face was fascinating to look at now that he had discovered its secret. It pulled him in. And she had something that neither Eramia nor Phaedra had ever had: she wanted him.

They stopped at a house that had Ravennis' mark painted on its door. After a little while, the bleary-eyed owner answered their knocks and gave a little yelp when he saw them. Narky barely had time to explain who they were before the man said, "My wife and I will sleep in the barn. Please, take our house and may Ravennis bless us all."

Ptera thanked them, and a few minutes later they were alone inside, staring in the darkness at the single bed.

"Shall I take the floor?" Ptera asked innocently, and Narky shook his head. Hunter would have offered to take the floor himself, and he would have thought to do it before Ptera said a word. Narky, unfortunately, was not Hunter.

"I think there's room enough for both of us," he said. "We can lie head-to-toe."

"All right," Ptera said, but they both just stood there.

The dry season was coming to an end, but it was a warm night for the time of year. In weather like this, Bandu would have stripped her clothes off without a thought. No! He shouldn't have thought about that. Now he didn't feel like sleeping anymore.

Ptera was staring at him. "I heard that Ravennis gave you a sort of mark," she said at last. "May I – may I see it?"

"I don't think you'll be able to in this dim light," Narky said, but Ptera just stood there waiting until he gingerly took his shirt off. She stepped closer and ran a hand along his chest, feeling the ridges where Ravennis' mark had cut into his skin.

"I didn't realize it was so ornate!" she said.

"He nearly killed me," Narky told her. "When I repented for what I'd done, He let me live and gave me this."

Ptera nodded. She didn't ask him what he'd done. She also didn't take her hand off his chest until he gently pushed it away. She was testing him, he thought.

"Thank you," she said, and went to lie down in the bed.

Narky lay himself down by her feet and did not sleep. He kept thinking of her hand touching his skin, and of the fact that she wanted him, she wanted *him*, and she was right here beside him. He had resented Bandu once, for keeping him up at night without even realizing it, but how could he resent Ptera when she had made it clear that he could have her if he would only ask? If he could not sleep for thinking about her, he had only himself to blame.

He sat up in bed.

"You win," he said. "I want you."

20

PHAEDRA

Pirates. Kidnappers. Where was their ship headed now?
She and Hunter sat on their bunks, unable to do anything
but worry. Perhaps they were in their new God's hands,
but who was to say whether He had really planned this?
It didn't feel particularly like they were in His hands – it
felt like they were in the hands of men.

Piracy had always been a danger in the archipelago,
but there had been a treaty struck when Phaedra was
young, making every island responsible for patrolling
its shores and harbors for pirated ships and goods in
an effort to eradicate the problem. Its effectiveness had
made her father rich, since investing in merchantmen
had swiftly become a much less risky proposition. But
the problem had never gone away completely, and now
it had become *their* problem.

Did they want a ransom? There would be no one to
ransom her and Hunter. Was it the ship and its cargo
they were after? If so, the two of them were completely
expendable. And if this was God Most High's punishment
for the captain, Phaedra failed to see how it could
improve the lives of His servants. Before, they had been

trapped. Now they were likely doomed.

Their new voyage lasted a few hours before their captors called them above deck. Up the ladder they went, limbs stiff and aching, blinking in the morning sun. There were men around them, and a good number of them too, but Phaedra could not focus on them, because she saw now where their ship was headed.

It was headed for Tarphae.

Someone had repaired one of the docks in Karsanye's harbor, and to this they were headed at full speed. Phaedra's heart pounded thunderously in her chest and she had to force herself to breathe. The cursed island. Home. Apparently it was now a pirate haven.

The ship's captain was still alive, but he was tied to the mast. A half dozen other sailors knelt beside him, staring terrified at the pirates who had taken their ship. The cook wasn't among them, though he had been on the ship last night. Had he been killed and thrown overboard? That wasn't necessarily surprising, but it was undeniably horrifying.

The pirates were predominantly young islanders around Phaedra's age, but their leader was far older. His beard was flecked with hints of gray, while his eyes sported the beginnings of crows'-feet. He smiled as his crew forced Phaedra and Hunter to kneel beside the others.

"Hello there," he said. "My name is Mura. You haven't heard of me; nobody has, except my friends and a sizable number of dead men. Now, let me tell you what is going to happen. There are nine of you now. Three will not survive the afternoon. The rest may live a good deal longer if you obey my every command and make no attempt to free yourselves. Do you understand?"

They all nodded dumbly. Mura's men tied their hands

behind their backs, and soon they were being helped
onto the new dock. Phaedra winced as her foot touched
the planks, terrified that Karassa would notice her
presence and take offense. But nothing happened. Was
God Most High shielding them from the Goddess' vision?

How long had these pirates been using Tarphae
as their refuge? The island had been deserted when
Phaedra and the others had come back for their king,
and that was only a few months ago. Karassa had tried
to swallow them with an earthquake, and now even Her
great capital of Karsanye was mostly rubble.

But out of this rubble, the pirates had built an altar. It
was made of uneven stones, probably from the remnants
of the nearest building, and it stood just past the end of
the docks, waiting for them. *Three of you will not survive
the afternoon.*

Which of them would Mura choose for his sacrifice?
Surely, God Most High would not have protected
her and Hunter all this time just to allow them to be
sacrificed to Karassa. Even so, Phaedra knew better than
to complacently assume His continued protection. It was
too easy to accidentally offend a God, and if they ever
lost that protection, their first and only warning might
well be their deaths.

Hopefully He was still protecting them, and Mura
would choose others instead. The captain would be
a tempting target, Phaedra was sure. He was also
responsible for the crew's defiance toward God Most
High, so if Mura *didn't* choose him, it would mean that
the dragons' God had had no part in this latest turn of
events. That was too frightening to contemplate, so as
horrible as it was to hope for anyone's death, Phaedra
dearly hoped the captain would be chosen.

But after him, it was anyone's guess who would

most appeal to Mura's bloodlust. The tallest ones? The brawniest? The weakest? It all depended, she supposed, on what he meant to do with those who survived.

In the end Mura did choose the captain, and two continental sailors besides. The three sailors who were islanders heaved a collective sigh of relief, while the last remaining continental shifted his gaze from person to person, looking hunted. Mura smiled at this and turned back to the captain, unsheathing a long knife from his belt.

Phaedra closed her eyes while the horrible deed was done, squeezing them together so hard that tears formed in the corners and blurred her vision even after she opened them again. She wished her hands had been unbound so that she could cover her ears as well. What she heard made her want to bury her head in a pillow and never take it out again. The screaming, the pleading, the gurgling... she felt sick.

A sudden burst of heat made her open her eyes. All three dead men on the altar were wreathed in flames.

"The Goddess has accepted our sacrifice!" Mura cried. "Praised be Karassa, who protects us and grants us the use of Her islands."

"Praised be Karassa," his men echoed. This wasn't their first time, Phaedra thought. That only made it more horrifying.

"God of Dragons protect us," she muttered under her breath.

The heat of the altar was intense, despite the lack of any visible fuel. The flames ate greedily at the bodies, turning them to ash before her eyes. Karassa was taking to these pirates' sacrifice far better than anything Phaedra had ever seen on the holy days of her childhood. How easy it had been for Her to discard the Tarphaeans and start anew!

Phaedra felt a true hatred for Karassa growing within her. To think that they had spent months worrying that some other God had overpowered Her to slay Her people! Phaedra hoped the Oracle that had warned of a Judgment of the Gods had been right – Karassa deserved to be judged, and judged harshly. May God Most High cast Her out of the heavens!

When the bodies were little more than charred husks, Mura collected some of the ashes in a bag that had been hanging around his neck, tucked into his shirt. That struck Phaedra as odd. Did the ashes have a ritual purpose? The Tarphaean priests of Karassa had never collected the ashes of a sacrifice to Phaedra's knowledge, and Phaedra's knowledge was extensive. These ashes were different, of course, and not just because they were made from the corpses of men: they were a direct sign of the Goddess' favor. They were the kind of thing Psander might have used to bolster her home's defenses.

Was Mura a wizard? Phaedra had been wondering what God Most High meant to do with her and Hunter, but now it suddenly seemed clear. In one blow He had punished the captain and crew for imprisoning her and Hunter, and brought her to a place where she could learn more of magic! If she could survive the place, anyway.

The pirates dragged the prisoners to their feet and led them roughly onward, through the rubble of Karsanye. Her captors had no sympathy for Phaedra's handicap, shoving her nastily when she fell behind, and slapping Hunter when he asked to help her.

"What good is she to us?" one of them asked Mura. "You should have sacrificed her, too."

Mura ignored the man. He strode ahead, leading the way through the ruined city, and then past its borders and out into the countryside. After another hour's walk, Phaedra spotted their destination: a farmhouse and mill on the edge of the Sennaroot river, active with people and animals. These pirates were also farmers, then?

Not exactly, it turned out. The farm and mill ran on slave labor, its seven workers overseen by four more of Mura's followers sporting weapons and whips. This was where the pirates came for supplies and safe harbor in between raids. It was also where Phaedra and the others would be staying.

When they got closer, Phaedra spotted the six graves outside the farmhouse. The pirates had been courteous, then, when they arrived here, and had buried the former inhabitants. They must have thought it necessary for securing Karassa's favor. Phaedra wondered if they were right, or if the Goddess had watched them with amusement as they reverently buried the very same people that She had so carelessly slaughtered.

Mura caught her gaze, and seemed to read her mind. "Do you worship Karassa?" he asked.

The four remaining sailors all nodded vigorously. Phaedra felt Hunter's eyes on her, waiting to take his cue. He was like that, Hunter. Never comfortable being the first to speak.

"No," Phaedra said, assessing the situation and deciding that Mura was unlikely to be deceived. "But I respect Her power."

That seemed to be the right thing to say. Mura laughed a big, genuine laugh and said, "Who wouldn't, after what She did here?"

He knew, then. How?

"Oh yes," he said. "It was Karassa who drowned the people of Tarphae; She told me Herself. She came to me in a dream and invited me to claim Her island, if I would devote all my worship to Her. She has provided for us ever since, and in return we have given Her sacrifices and kept Her holy days, as will you."

Phaedra nodded along with the others, and said nothing more. If Mura ever found out that she and Hunter were Tarphaean, that would be the end of them. He'd be delighted, *honored* to sacrifice them to the Goddess of their childhood.

One of the overseers, who introduced himself as Bennan, surveyed the new captives about their skills. Luckily, Hunter had the sense to lie and say that he had grown up as a merchant's son. It was at least a plausible background for such an obviously well-bred person, and it didn't encourage anyone to pick fights with him the way that the truth might have. If he had told them of his nobility, it would only have made them want to further demean and humiliate him. If he'd told them of his combat training, they'd surely have taken it as a challenge.

Phaedra was able to be more truthful. She told them of her grandfather, the master weaver, and of her mother who had taught her the craft. Her father really had been a merchant and financier, so she claimed that her mother had been his second wife, and that Hunter was her half-brother. Bennan nodded and told her she would be mending clothes. Hunter, like the other men, would have to work in the fields.

The separation was nerve-wracking. Setting foot in the farmhouse, Phaedra felt the same pervasive danger she had felt in the Atunaean sailors' hostel. She was inside – trapped! How could she protect herself in a place like this, surrounded by these young men with their hungry stares, without even Hunter's protection?

One of Bennan's companions led her to a room with

a pile of clothes and a sewing kit, and told her to get to work. "My name is Terrin," he said, standing at the door. "I'm the cook here. If you want to eat, you'll be good to me."

Phaedra nodded, and he left. She stared at the door, momentarily paralyzed by fear and dread. She didn't have any plan, and she badly needed one. She knew she could find the strength to tolerate any ordeal – the ants of Hession's cavern had proved as much – but not without a plan. Without some way forward, all she could do was despair.

She picked up needle and thread, and began patching a tunic. It was simple work, work that didn't require any real skill and left an unpleasant amount of room for thought. It didn't take a weaver to sew on a few patches here and there – all it took was basic competence.

If only she had the same level of competence when it came to magic. She didn't need Psander's ability to ward a castle against the Gods, she just wanted to protect herself and Hunter. God Most High may have had plans for them, but He wasn't likely to do much more than keep them alive – would He even notice if they were harmed more subtly? Gods were not well known for Their subtlety.

What if there were some way to alert Him? If God Most High could be coaxed into taking a more personal interest in them, she wouldn't even need her own magic. Normally, this kind of coaxing was accomplished through sacrifice and prayer, but there was nothing here for her to sacrifice. Would He listen to prayer alone?

"O God Most High," she mumbled, so as not to be heard by anyone nearby, "God of Dragons, Builder of the Mesh, Constructor of Heavens: help me. Protect me among my enemies – among *Your* enemies. Turn their evil intentions from me and Hunter. Save us from their gazes."

Her hands began to tremble, and she put down the needle. Could God Most High hear her, or was His attention elsewhere? Was there something she could do to amplify her message?

She thought of Auntie Gava, burying her oysters under the rocks; of Psander, who had called magic theory a framework for reusing the Gods' magic for one's own purposes; of Narky, who had justified his suggestions by saying that they seemed like "the kind of weird thing Psander would do." She thought of Mura, whose magic seemed to rely on Karassa's favor. She had all the tools she needed, she was sure of it. She just needed to figure out how they went together.

"The Gods are all magic," Gava had said, "and They made this place. You take a look at what They made, you try to get some of the pieces so they fit together better than before, and that's it. You've got magic."

You've got magic.

What she really had was her prayers, a needle, and a pile of clothes that needed mending. It would have to do.

Phaedra took up her needle again, and began sewing her prayers into her seams. Nobody who had even the most basic domestic skills would have let the pile get this big, and that meant that nobody would be checking her work before they wore it. She made an extended prayer out of multiple garments, picking up the thread wherever she had left off on the previous one. She whispered the prayer as she sewed it, giving it the power of her voice as well.

God Most High, protect me from the men who wear these clothes. Turn their thoughts away from me and my friend, Hunter of House Tavener, and shelter us from their gazes.

Let them feed us and forget us, never knowing that they have forgotten. Make them memory boxes like Bandu's, and put all thought of harming us inside, locked tight with a thousand locks and a thousand missing keys. God of Dragons, Slayer of the Yarek, who made the seas calm for Your servants, nothing is impossible for You. Say the word, and it will be so.

It took hours to complete the prayer, and when she was done only a third or so of the garments had been mended. Her fingertips were bleeding from having been poked with the needle, and her eyes throbbed from staring so intently at such short distances. But she was on the right track, she was sure of it. Whether or not her prayers would be answered, she did not doubt that God Most High would hear them.

A noise made her look up. Terrin stood in the doorway, grinning at her. He pulled off his tunic.

Phaedra threw him a mended one. He caught it, surprised, and looked down at the garment. Phaedra held her breath. Terrin seemed confused for a moment, like he wasn't sure what the mended tunic was for. Then he put it on.

"You've made progress," he said, looking around and noticing the shrunken pile of torn clothes. "Keep it up."

And just like that, he left.

Magic, Phaedra thought. *It works!*

21
BANDU

At first, Criton's war went well for him. After a few days the Ardisian army regrouped and tried to fight them again in the open field, but they were too afraid of Criton and his God. Their ranks broke before the Dragon Touched even reached them, and they lost more men in the stampede than in the fighting.

But the victories didn't last. When they regrouped a second time, the Ardismen stopped trying to confront the Dragon Touched and split their army, sending one half to burn the plainspeople's villages while the other stayed behind to keep Criton's army from catching up. They killed any stragglers who fell behind the camp, so the Dragon Touched couldn't hurry to save the northern villages without leaving their slowest and weakest to die. Criton refused to let that happen, so they moved at a crawl instead.

In the meantime, a sickness spread through the Dragon Touched camp, slowing them down further and making everyone miserable. Criton had the worst of it, coughing and wheezing and blowing sparks everywhere. The sparks were all he produced, though – his fire was gone. He wasn't the only one, either. Most of the Dragon Touched had lost their fire. They were lucky the Ardismen hadn't found that out yet.

Bandu feared for Goodweather's life when she saw all the breathing troubles Criton and his kind were having, but luckily she and the children were spared the sickness. "Your God is angry about the pigs," she told Criton. "You are sorry you don't listen to me."

"But we won the battle!" he objected, right before another coughing fit left him gasping for breath. "God Most High favored us!" he croaked.

"He doesn't now," Bandu pointed out. "You should say sorry, like Narky does. If Ardismen know your God is angry, they kill us all soon."

"Our God isn't angry," Criton insisted. "It's just a cold with a bad cough."

"You burn pigs," Bandu said. "Where your fire is now?"

Criton sighed, which turned into more coughing. "Maybe you're right. I'll make a sacrifice and ask for forgiveness."

"Good," Bandu said. "Ask me too. You don't listen to me when I tell you before."

He made an aggravated sound, but then he said, "You're right. I'm sorry. I promise I'll listen to your advice from now on."

Bandu decided that that would do.

She was glad he was listening to her now, at least. She was also glad about the sickness, as long as Goodweather had been spared. If Criton's God was punishing him for what he'd done, then maybe He wasn't so bad after all.

Criton made his sacrifice the following day, giving his God three of Biva's ewes. Hessina gave another, as did several elders among the plainsmen. It bothered Bandu that they should repent of needlessly killing animals by killing more animals, but it must have been what God Most High wanted, because Criton and his people all recovered from their illness within a day or two.

What did Gods do with all those animals people gave Them? Did the fires that burned the animals' bodies act like a frog's tongue, catching an animal's essence and sucking it into the heavens for Them to eat? Bandu might be able to forgive the Gods for all that death if They were only eating.

Anyway, she was still angry at Criton, whether God Most High forgave him or not. It wasn't just about the pigs. Criton was more concerned with killing Ardismen than he was with making her happy, and he spent more time with Delika than with his own daughter. Some of that wasn't his fault: Delika clung to him whenever she could, and Goodweather preferred Bandu because Criton couldn't nurse her. But it was also more than that. Criton actually avoided the baby. Bandu thought he was afraid of Goodweather, not because of the girl herself but because of his own instincts. He didn't trust himself with her.

Sometimes Bandu didn't trust him either. When Goodweather's clothes were wet and she awoke with a long, continuous wail, Criton would jerk up angrily and change her with hatred in his eyes. He always calmed down a little while after the baby did, and then came the shame and fear. What if he had hurt her this time? He hadn't, yet, but he had been close. He was always close.

Bandu, on the other hand, was growing to love their daughter more and more. Goodweather smiled now, sweet thing, real smiles that expressed such joy it pained her. The girl was happier to see her mother's face than Bandu had ever been about anything, as far back as she could remember.

But Criton hardly noticed his daughter when she wasn't screaming, because he was too busy parenting Delika. He was more comfortable with the older girl, and why shouldn't he be? He didn't have to guess what she wanted, because she could tell him. She also didn't wet herself, didn't wake him up at night, and didn't respond to inattention by screaming. But for all that Bandu understood this preference for the older girl, she still hated it. A man shouldn't love someone else's little girl more than his own.

At least Bandu did have help with the baby, even if it wasn't usually from Criton. His cousin's wife Iona was full of helpful advice for how best to calm Goodweather or bind her safely to Bandu's chest while traveling, and her daughter Dessa was always asking if she could hold her baby cousin. Dessa also came now and then with her friend Vella, whose younger brother was supposed to have married Dessa later this year. Vella was about Bandu's age, and was herself married to some man Bandu never saw, a soldier in Criton's army. She wasn't as helpful as Iona or as friendly as Dessa – she mostly seemed afraid of Bandu. But she came, and she was usually willing to carry Goodweather, and Bandu would take all the help she could get.

Certainly if the rest of the pack had been more welcoming, Bandu would not always dream of taking Goodweather away and leaving Criton with his not-daughter and his war. She wouldn't wish that she still had Four-foot instead of him. But the pack was *not* welcoming. Almost everyone looked at her with suspicion, and even Belkos' family wasn't always nice – Iona's mother was worse than anyone else in the pack. She hated Bandu, and never bothered to hide it.

"I know why you're here," she would hiss. "My daughter will not be widowed."

That was a new word, but nobody would explain it to her. Iona would only apologize for her mother and tell Bandu to ignore her, which was her one piece of advice that was not at all helpful.

Criton didn't want to tell her either. She asked him, after Delika and Goodweather had both fallen asleep, and all he said was, "It's not important."

"Yes, it is."

"No, it's not," he insisted. "Whoever told you you'd be widowed is a liar and a fool. You shouldn't listen to people like that."

"She doesn't say that."

Criton snorted. "Of course she doesn't *say* that she's a liar, Bandu."

"No, not she is a liar. Not that I am."

Even in the dark, she could tell he was frowning. "You're not making any sense. You're not going to be widowed, Bandu! Don't worry about it."

She wanted to hit him, but she didn't. "She doesn't say that! She doesn't say I am widowed."

"Then what are you worried about? I'm going to be fine, Bandu. We're all going to be fine."

"You don't answer me."

"Don't be angry."

"I *am* angry."

He sighed. "To be widowed is to lose your husband."

"Lose where?"

"Nowhere. It's to have him die, Bandu. If I die, you'll be a widow."

Bandu groaned. "Stupid," she said. "Stupid words. All your words for me are stupid. First Phaedra says I am virgin, then we mate and I'm a wife, and if you die I am widow? Why do all your words for me care so much about you?"

"I don't know," Criton said. "I'm not sure why it annoys you so much. Anyhow, you wanted to know what it means to be a widow, and I told you. But you don't need to worry about it."

"You don't tell me when to worry."

She turned away from him. Criton only thought about himself sometimes. Too many times. Maybe she should have mated with someone like Hunter, who only thought about other people. But then, Hunter hadn't interested her.

Anyway, now she had her answer. But why did Iona's mother think that Bandu and Criton were going to kill Belkos? As far as Bandu could tell, Criton's cousin was his closest friend now. They talked about their war all the time together, and there was more to it than that. For Belkos, Criton was a leader to be proud of: his cousin was head of the pack. For Criton, Belkos was his closest connection to the family he had always wanted: his *cousin* was a part of the pack.

Belkos was also the cause of Bandu's connection to Iona and Dessa, her only real friends among the Dragon Touched. No matter how she looked at it, she couldn't find a reason for the old woman to think that she and Criton meant to kill him. It made no sense.

But she couldn't just ignore it the way Iona and Criton wanted her to. Iona's mother may have lost much of her sense, but that didn't make her harmless, and it might not even make her wrong. Her magic was so strong Bandu could smell it. Maybe the old woman saw something in them that was really there, something they didn't even know about. Bandu couldn't ignore that possibility. It worried her.

Criton was under a lot of strain these days. His plan to catch up with the northern army of Ardis wasn't working, but nobody could agree on what they wanted him to do instead. The plainsmen wanted him to hurry to protect their villages, even if it meant losing a few stragglers to the Ardismen's southern army. Belkos wanted him to deal with the southern army first and then move straight on to Ardis while the northern force was still distracted. And of course, Bandu wanted help with Goodweather, and Delika wanted Criton to take her along no matter where he went.

The short days and rainy weather weren't helping anyone's mood either. Everyone in the camp was miserable; many took it out on Criton.

"What am I supposed to do?" he asked her one evening as they were making camp. He was holding Goodweather while Delika played with rocks and Bandu tightened the canvas on their tent. Criton was no good with tents.

"This isn't sustainable," he went on. "We can't do anything with that army on our tails. We're going to have to attack them, try to drive them off. Then we can deal with the other half."

"Yes," Bandu agreed. "You can't help other people if we go so slow."

"The trouble," Criton said, "is that there are still more of them than there are of us, and they'll be ready for us if we try to attack them. Their scouts will tell them when we get close. Hessina thinks they'll avoid our full army if they can – their old general Xytos is known for his patience. He'll wait for the plainsmen to desert us if he can, and only face us in an open battle if he has to. So we should try to catch him, I guess, but if we do fight a battle and lose, we're all doomed.

"Maybe if we could surprise them somehow, we could drive them off for good. But even if we attacked at night, they'd be ready for us – their scouts are everywhere. We're lucky their General Xytos is so cautious, or they'd have ambushed *us* by now."

Bandu nodded thoughtfully. "Night is good, I think."

"We don't have any scouts at all," Criton confessed. "I figured we couldn't afford to lose any. I've just been flying straight upwards in the evenings to see where they've lit their fires, and that's how we know where they are."

"That is good enough!" Bandu said. "If you know where they are, that is good. You can fight them."

"They'll know we're coming though!" He was repeating himself, and his voice was becoming a whine. She loved him, but this was very annoying.

"Maybe they know you are coming," she said, "but they don't see good at night. You can go with only Dragon Touched, and send plains people after."

Criton looked at her as if that was the dumbest thing he had ever heard. "We can't lead a raid with *just* the Dragon Touched, there aren't even sixty of us who can fight anymore! It's not a number that can attack a force of twelve hundred!"

"It is," Bandu insisted. "Their eyes are no good at night. We do just like when Narky kills Bestillos: you are Hunter, and plains people are Narky. You say that Ardis people know you are coming, and everyone is ready? Good! So everyone goes together first, and Ardis people see you and they are ready. But then, after, you go a different way with Dragon Touched only. You breathe fire and make noise and they all go that way. Then plains people go from other side and surprise them, and they run away."

Criton considered that. "So you want to use the Dragon Touched as a decoy?" he said. "That... well, it *could* work. And it's better than waiting for our allies to abandon us. I'll bring it up with the others."

"Good," Bandu said. "I talk to Iona about watching Delika and Goodweather then."

Criton had begun to nod, but suddenly stopped when he realized what she meant. "Hold on, what? You're not coming with me, are you?"

"No," Bandu explained. "I go with the plains people. They need someone to show them the way and help them be quiet, and you're no good for that. You need to go with your kind so the Ardismen think you have everyone. So I go. I can talk to Iona now."

She saw his face turn sour. "I do this," she said. "You don't stop me."

"I don't want to stay with Iona!" Delika said suddenly.

So she had been listening to the two of them after all. Of course she had. Bandu took Goodweather back from Criton and left him to argue with Delika while she went to ask Iona about watching the children.

She wondered if Criton would give her any more trouble about joining the plains people when they made their attack. He was probably worried that they wouldn't let her go with them, but she didn't think that would be such a problem. She knew she wasn't a member of their pack, but she also knew they were afraid of her. They called her "witch," which Iona had said was a bad name for a woman who used magic. That meant they were afraid, she thought. Anyway, Bandu *did* use magic, and she was used to being called wicked. She suspected that the plains people would be too afraid to say no to her, and that was enough. She didn't need them to like her – just so long as they did what she said, they could call her whatever they liked.

They weren't really one mass, of course. There were many clans from many villages, and she and Criton would have to convince each and every one of them to let her lead them in the raid. When she had sorted out her arrangement with Iona, she made Criton take her with him to talk to those elders. It was long and frustrating and took two full days – the plainsmen preferred to be led by one of their own, and they preferred to be led by a man – but in the end, they agreed just as she had thought they would.

What convinced them was the story of the weeping house, which many of them had heard from the other Dragon Touched and which Criton told them again anyway, just in case. For all their objections, the story was powerful. It was one thing to be led by a foreign woman, but no one could say they didn't want to be led by a miracle worker.

And so, two nights later, Bandu led an army through wet grasses toward the enemy camp. The whole of the army had gone together to a spot maybe half a mile from where the Ardismen had set up tents, so that the scouts would tell their leaders that all the Dragon Touched were coming. Then the Dragon Touched themselves split off, and it fell to her to lead the plainsmen the rest of the way.

First, she asked the wind for its help in keeping their steps silent. A breeze picked up and began whistling in their ears, blocking out the sound of their shuffling feet. Good. As long as they could still hear the battle when it started, this breeze was their friend.

They approached as quietly as a three hundred man army could. There was only a sliver of moon, and they stole forward in the darkness, straining their eyes to

catch the first light from the Ardisian camp. When they
had come as far as Bandu dared, and the lights of the
camp were readily visible, she gave the order to stop. She
whispered it through the wind, which made many of the
plainsmen stare shocked in her direction. But they did
all stop, and they did it without anyone having to yell
out a command or make a hard-to-see hand signal in the
dim light. They would be glad they'd let her lead them.

The camp looked asleep from here, to Bandu's
surprise. Criton had thought they would be ready for an
attack, but apparently he had been wrong. This might be
easier than they had expected.

The Dragon Touched made their attack a few minutes
later, and Bandu quickly saw her mistake. The Touched
came in unexpectedly from the west, but the Ardismen
were far more ready than they looked. A guard sounded
the alarm long before the Dragon Touched reached him,
and masses of soldiers streamed from their tents fully
armed and ready for battle. It wouldn't take long at all
for Criton's group to be overwhelmed.

Bandu whispered her command and the plainsmen
broke into a run, making no sound except for the
pounding of their feet and the laboring of their breaths.
The closer they got, the more Bandu wished she had
given the order sooner: the Dragon Touched were so,
so outnumbered. For all their blazing breath-fires, it
wouldn't be long before the Ardismen killed them all.

But the tactic worked. The Ardismen didn't call a
second alarm until Bandu and the plainsmen were
practically on top of them, and by then it was too late.
They weren't ready for the real army to appear out of
the night, running them through from behind. Bandu
wasn't in the front by the time they arrived – the others
ran too fast – but she was still there in time to join the

battle. She drove her way through the crowd and toward the clump of Dragon Touched, swinging the farming tool she had been given to fight with – a hoe, did they call it? Whatever it was called, she used it to smash people in the head.

The Ardismen broke quickly, even quicker than she had expected. They made their retreat in total confusion, trampling each other in their hurry to escape. The Dragon Touched and plainsmen cut them down as they fled into the night, slaughtering them by the hundreds. Another battle, another rout.

We can win this war, Bandu thought. *Nobody can stop us.*

22

NARKY

They had glorious sex that night, and then again the next morning. Now that he had given himself permission, he couldn't get enough. Ptera had been married before and knew exactly what she liked, which was wonderful since it meant he didn't have to guess. The morning was also a better time for it, because he liked seeing everything. He sorely missed his left eye – he'd have grown ten more if he could have.

When they finally stumbled out of the house that morning, they asked the older couple whose bed they had borrowed to witness their wedding. It was a slapdash affair – Narky might have been high priest of Ravennis, but he had no knowledge of the old Laarnan wedding rites, so he had to invent new ones himself. To his secret shame, he modeled them after Bandu and Criton's ridiculous wedding, with an exchange of vows and a few words connecting the whole thing to their God. He told Ptera and their witnesses that the Lord of Fate had decreed that they should be married long before any of them had even been born, a claim that he was not sure he even believed. It was plausible enough,

190

sure, but did Ravennis really care that much about His servants' affairs?

They set out again. Now that Ptera was officially his wife and he was no longer preoccupied with the question of whether or not to marry her, Narky found that he was desperate to know more about her history. He barely knew *anything* about her! How long had she been married before? What had her first husband been like? Why hadn't she had any children, if she had all this experience with lovemaking?

He was going to ask her about all of it – he just hadn't figured out how to yet. He was still trying not to be too blunt, at least not until she knew him better. Besides which, if he had the chance to improve himself a little bit, and before she could really get to know him – well, he was going to take it.

To think that the Graceful Servant had thought that marrying Ptera would make him *less* distracted! Now his thoughts were consumed with the tactics of tact and the dangers of upsetting his bride. What if, over the next few days or weeks, she discovered that she didn't actually like him? That would mean a miserable life for the both of them, and it also wasn't terribly unlikely. What did she really know about him? Nothing. No more than he knew of her, anyway.

But she seemed happy enough so far, and Ravennis below, she was beautiful with her clothes off. Whatever anger he had felt toward her and the Graceful Servant for arranging this marriage, it was gone for now. If it could last, this was the life for him.

He tried again to imagine what Phaedra might say if he told her which questions he meant to ask Ptera. The question about the children was definitely the wrong one to start with, he was sure she would have said that much. How about her first husband? No. Questions on that subject might bring up painful memories, besides which, what if her first husband had been better than Narky in every way? It wouldn't have taken much.

He had probably been tall. Tall and muscular and manly, and better in bed. He'd probably swept Ptera off her feet, and now she was trying to make do with a mere shadow. She called Narky a boy; her first husband had been a man. Maybe he'd died doing something suicidally brave, like wrestling a lion away from a small child. Or maybe he'd died by drinking too much and falling in a river. That would be better.

Narky wished she would volunteer something about the man. He didn't want to have to ask, to open the old wound all by himself. Why couldn't she make this easy for him?

What if he made his questions as generic as possible? He didn't think Phaedra would have objected if he asked a really basic question in a soft tone of voice. How about, 'Can you tell me about your first husband?' That was a nice, simple request, not judgmental or prying in any way. He rehearsed it in his head.

He was about to ask it when Ptera said, "You don't regret it, do you?"

"Huh?"

She sighed. He shouldn't have made her have to explain herself – that was already a mistake.

"Marrying me," she said. "You're right, I didn't even talk to you about it before we sprung it on you. And I'm much older than you, and I've been married before... is it all right?"

The question brought back all his resentment, so plainly laying out the reasons that it had been justified. He almost said "No," and left it at that. Instead, he took his time before answering. Yes, she had done the wrong thing, but hadn't he been thinking just a few minutes ago about how happy he was with the result? If he drove her away, that would be his own doing, not hers. If he wanted more mornings like this one, he had to find a way to salvage the situation.

"I don't know yet," he said. "I wasn't angry today until you asked me."

"This morning was good, right?"

He nodded. "Yeah, it was good this morning. So far, it's not so bad."

She sighed again, and seemed to accept that. He didn't want her to look so unhappy, but then, he also didn't want her to think that he was no longer mad at all – or that it was all right to cut him out of decisions she made for the two of them.

"It's got nothing to do with your age," he told her. "I've got no complaints with your looks or anything like that."

She smiled wryly at him. "Thanks, Narky, that's quite a compliment."

He felt his face get hot. "Sorry, I… This is how I talk."

"I'd noticed."

"You had?"

She laughed at that, and Narky couldn't think of anything else to say. She had already noticed how blunt he was – did that mean he should give up on trying to be tactful with her? That would certainly make things easier. Still, he was surprised at how much disappointment was mixed in with his relief. Perhaps he ought to keep trying anyway.

On the other hand, if she was already aware of his manner of speaking, that sort of gave him permission to ask his awkward questions, didn't it? He hoped so. As a test, he asked, "What was your first husband like? I know I'm young, but I don't want to live in his shadow."

She raised an eyebrow at him. "You're not in his shadow, Narky. He barely cast one."

"Yeah? I bet he was taller than me, and stronger and everything."

"Well, yes."

"So?"

She sighed. "It was no good, Narky. How can I explain it?"

"Try. Did he hit you or something?"

She shook her head. "He wasn't a brute, he just wasn't right. At all. He married me after Magor's fertility festival because he said he liked how I looked under him, and I was young enough that I thought it was a compliment. We had a few decent months, but it went sour fast. We just didn't get along that well, and he was annoyed at how long it was taking me to conceive. He was actively looking for a second wife when he died.

"He wasn't cruel," she added hastily. "He'd have kept supporting me either way. But I wasn't exactly looking forward to the rest of my life."

Narky swallowed. "So... when you say it took you a long time to conceive..."

"I didn't conceive at all," she said tersely.

"And you were married for...?"

"Three years."

"How did he die?"

"A man killed him," she said disgustedly, "in a fight over a woman. His brothers avenged him, and killed both his killer *and* the girl. Then the girl's father stabbed one of *them*, and the priests of Magor had to step in and threaten to eradicate all three of our families before the feud resolved itself. The whole thing was stupid from top to bottom."

"Oh."

He felt foolish now that he knew the story. "I thought you'd turned to Ravennis out of grief," he said.

"Over *him*? No."

"Then…"

"Even before he died," Ptera said, "I was starting to question my allegiance to Magor. The God of Strength seemed to want me to be powerless, now and forever. And then suddenly my husband was dead and the Graceful Servant appeared at my door, offering me a place in the church of Ravennis and the eternal protection of a God who cared about me."

She smiled with the recollection. "She gave me this name, Ptera, and it suits me better than my old one did. Did you know that I was the first Ardiswoman she converted? She said that our God had special plans for me, and that I would help her build a church that would last for the ages. And now here I am."

"Yeah," Narky said. "Here you are."

They fell into silence again. He was going to have to get better at talking to her. They kept starting and stopping, leaving more unsaid than he could really process.

"Anyway," he said, "I'm glad you don't have any children I didn't know about."

"I may not have any with you either, Narky."

He shrugged. "We can worry about that later, or never. I'm not ready to be a father yet anyway. I've seen a bit of what it's like."

Her expression was priceless, a mixture of shock, confusion, tentative relief. "Really? You don't care?"

"What do I want with a baby?" he asked her. "I can barely handle myself right now."

She clearly couldn't tell if he was joking or not. He

wasn't. It was a relief to know that they wouldn't be following Criton and Bandu's path any time soon. Gods, how he had hated spending time with that yowler of theirs.

It might be different with one of his own, of course. Gods knew, Criton and Bandu didn't seem to have noticed how hideous their child was. Parenthood seemed to cause a sort of blindness in that respect. Even they had noticed how loud it was, though.

In any case, maybe by the time it came up for him and Ptera – if it ever did – he'd feel differently about it. For now, he wouldn't have minded a guarantee that she *wouldn't* conceive for a little while.

"So," he said, "what is Magor's fertility holiday like?"

He shouldn't have asked. Ptera was clearly trying to find a way to avoid the question, or at least avoid telling him all the details.

"It's much kinder to men like my first husband," she said, helpfully leaving off the obvious follow-up, *kinder to them than to men like you*. "The Graceful Servant called it barbaric, and she wasn't really wrong. It could be good, though, and it definitely taught me a lot about lovemaking. I'm sure that makes you uncomfortable."

It did, but he wasn't about to admit it. If they had had an orgiastic holiday on Tarphae, he was sure he'd have grown up even more miserable than he had been already.

"You're really good at what you learned," he said diplomatically.

"Thank you."

There was nothing to say to that, so they stopped talking yet again. These frequent silences were killing him.

"We should get off the road," he said after some time,

just so he could hear *something* beside crickets. "We don't want to meet anyone who will tell Magor's priests where we are."

They did as he suggested. They stopped only at doors marked with the symbol of Ravennis, which grew more common as they traveled farther south. The cult of Ravennis seemed to have grown fastest in the lands between Ardis and its southern neighbor, Anardis. Magor had been widely worshipped in Anardis before His defeat at Silent Hall, and yet the people there lived far enough from their northern neighbor not to feel immediately threatened by Magor's priesthood. Some doors they found marked with both Elkinar's moth and the crow of Ravennis. It seemed that, at the very least, Ravennis was rapidly displacing Magor as the secondary God of this area.

What would Narky's reception in Anardis be like? Did they still blame the Tarphaean islanders for the destruction of their city at the red priest's hands? Would Narky be seen as a representative of his God, or as a symbol of their weakness and subjugation?

He had stalled long enough: he ought to tell Ptera about the last time he'd been to Anardis. The islanders had come there last year after Phaedra broke her ankle, hoping that the priests of Elkinar would be able to heal her. Which they had, sort of. When they had arrived, Phaedra had been completely unable to walk. The high priestess Mother Dinendra had rebroken the bone and set it properly, and now she could walk with a limp.

The islanders, Narky explained, had had a reputation back then for bringing bad luck wherever they went, but Mother Dinendra had shielded them from those who wished to see them gone. They had spent weeks in the inn across from Elkinar's temple, visiting every day to help in the rooftop garden or, in Phaedra's case, to read. But then the army of Ardis had come through the gates, preempting any plans the Anardisians' king may have had for breaking free of their dominion. The islanders had fled without saying goodbye, leaving the city burning behind them. He didn't know if Mother Dinendra had survived, or if so, how she felt about the islanders and their "bad luck" now.

But the two of them were about to find out.

The first thing Narky noticed as they approached the city was the wall. The city wall had never come down, it seemed. Criton had thought once that Bestillos might be chasing him, trying to slay the last of the Dragon Touched, rather than taking the time to fully subjugate Anardis. Did the wall's presence mean he was right? Had the red priest really tried to chase them so soon after taking the city?

He and Ptera approached with caution. The gate was wide open, and Narky could already see the devastation that had been wrought by the fire the Ardismen had set. Many of the old houses were still there, burnt-out husks that would serve as a reminder of that day's events for years to come. Others were new, or had blackened sides where the fire had passed by without destroying them.

He took a deep breath and walked up to the guards who stood by the open gate. "I am Narky of Tarphae, High Priest of Ravennis. I'm here to speak to Mother Dinendra, or whoever is high priest of Elkinar in these times."

The men's hostility was unconcealed, but they didn't turn him and Ptera away. "Mother Dinendra still lives," one said, "not that you wanderers of Tarphae would have cared should the Ardismen have slaughtered her as they did so many others. Ravennis is respected here, but you are not. Enter, but know that you are not welcome."

He supposed that was as pleasant an interaction as he could have hoped for. They entered the city and went straight to Elkinar's temple, trying to ignore the many stares they received along the way.

The temple's sides had been blackened by the fire, and none of the hanging greenery that he remembered was visible on its roof. Had the priests' rooftop garden perished in the fire?

One of the younger priests, Father Taemon, met them at the door. "I am here to speak with Mother Dinendra," Narky told him.

The priest said nothing and was about to turn away when Narky added, "You're the one whose wife was having a baby when Ardis came. How is your family?"

Taemon looked surprised. "They're well. I thank you for asking." He bowed slightly. "I'll tell Mother Dinendra you're here."

They stood outside the triangular building, waiting. What could Narky say to the High Priestess of Elkinar to make up for the misfortune they had brought to Anardis? He had to keep reminding himself that Dinendra hadn't believed any of that stuff about the islanders being cursed. She had thought her nephew, the king of Anardis, was to blame, because of the way his actions had goaded their northern neighbor into attacking them. Did she still feel that way? He hoped so.

Mother Dinendra arrived a moment later, opening the door and looking beyond and all around Narky before accepting that he and Ptera were the only ones there. The elderly high priestess was a welcome sight in this place. "You've lost your friends," she said. "And gained a new one. What's this about your being High Priest of Ravennis now?"

"The Graceful Servant named him high priest," Ptera answered. "And Narky has gained more than a friend: I'm his wife."

Dinendra smiled indulgently. "Welcome, Narky's wife, and welcome to you too, Narky. But what did you do with the other islanders?"

"They're among the Dragon Touched in the north," he answered. "At least, I assume they are. I left them before they got there."

"And now you have returned to Anardis. Well, come in."

They entered the dimly lit hall of worship, where pillar-chimneys stood waiting for worshippers' prayer notes, each pillar containing an oil lamp. There were three women inside praying, one of them noticeably pregnant. They stared at Narky, their gazes unfriendly at best.

"We can speak in the library," Mother Dinendra offered, "and you can tell me what brings you back here."

She led the way, slowly and carefully, to the chamber beyond, which was perhaps even dustier and more disorganized than Narky had remembered. Scrolls and codices were stuffed onto their shelves in a jumble, joined by earthenware jars, empty bowls, half-spent candles, and various other kinds of debris. In a corner sat a familiar sack of plaster and a pile of rags. It was here that Mother Dinendra had bound Phaedra's ankle, allowing her to walk again, though with a limp. At the time, they hadn't realized how permanent that limp would be: Phaedra had hoped that Psander might heal her ankle with magic someday. Those hopes had been dashed upon their return to Silent Hall.

"What happened to your garden?" Narky asked the priestess.

"The temple walls are made of stone," Mother Dinendra said, "but the garden was flammable. We were able to bring some of the clay pots down to the library, but we had to cast the heavier ones off the roof to keep the fire from spreading to us. So the garden remains, but the hanging plants that you'd have seen from the street outside are no longer. We will replace them eventually, I'm sure. There would be no better symbol of Elkinar's resilience than the display of new plants to replace the old. Elkinar's cycle continues, as it always has."

Narky nodded. "I've noticed that my God has taken up residence in Anardis as well. Have the worshippers of Magor all converted on their own?"

"Almost. If Bestillos' humbling of our city made Magor less popular here, his death dealt a mortal blow to the cult of Magor in Anardis. The temple was defaced within days, and its priests fled. Ardis might have punished us for that, but we sent our tribute early to placate them. Without Bestillos, and with our city walls still standing, the Council of Generals chose to accept our payment with grace."

Ptera made a subtle noise that caught Narky's attention and made him put off what he was about to say. "Does Magor's defaced temple still stand?" she asked.

"It does."

He saw the meaning in her eyes. "We can claim it for Ravennis," Narky said. "Good thinking."

She smiled. "Thank you."

"You'll be staying in Anardis, then?" Mother Dinendra asked.

"Yes, at least until Ardis is ready to welcome us back."

The old woman eyed him skeptically. "And when will that happen?"

"When Criton slaughters their army."

23
HUNTER

The first couple of days were the hardest. Phaedra disappeared into the house and didn't come out again, while the field slaves and their overseers worked and ate and slept outside. He worried about her constantly – what were they doing to her in there? But there was nothing he could do besides pray for God Most High to protect her, and hope that his prayers would be enough.

The overseers were cruel, violent men, and quick to use the whip. It stung more, knowing that this land may well have belonged to his father: House Tavener owned much farmland on the outskirts of Karsanye. His father had taken him and Kataras out to the fields when they were children, but Hunter hadn't shown enough of an interest to be brought back. Neither had Kataras, really, but as the eldest son, Lord Tavener had forced him to learn about managing their lands anyway.

Hunter wondered whether the slaves his father owned had been treated like this. He hoped not, and he honestly doubted it. Under the Tarphaean system of slavery, slaves could bring suit against their masters for unreasonable treatment and win back their freedom.

Hunter hadn't always retained what his father had taught him of Tarphaean law, but this much he remembered: the contracts by which men sold their families into slavery were taken seriously. Any breach of contract could be prosecuted.

He didn't remember what qualified as mistreatment under the old Tarphaean law, but he was pretty sure his captors would have been in breach of contract. They allowed no rest during daylight, and beat their workers on a whim. When one of the continental sailors collapsed, they threw him in the river and watched as he nearly drowned trying to get out again. By the end of the day, every prisoner was aching and weary, and the continental men had sunburns.

On that first day, they built a barn for the captives to sleep in alongside the six sheep and one cow that the pirates had somehow found and brought back here to supply them with labor and, hopefully, milk. Hunter was surprised, frankly, that any domesticated animals had survived the last year without turning wild or being eaten by predators. Farming had always seemed like such hard, tedious work to him that he had imagined a whole year's neglect would surely ruin everything. And yet, even if only a hundredth of Tarphae's crops and animals could be recovered, that would be more than enough to feed such a small group of people.

He was glad of the barn, in any case. The rainy season might have held off for him and Phaedra while they were on the ocean, but the unnaturally fair weather didn't last for long. No sooner had they erected the barn than the downpours began. But if he had thought that would spare him from laboring outside, he was wrong: the overseers gladly sent their slaves out in the deluge to catch river fish.

By the second and third day, though, Hunter began to notice a mysterious change in the pirates' attitude toward him. In short, they stopped paying attention to him. He still did as they directed, not wanting to test the limits of their leniency, but the difference was noticeable. The whip never touched his body again, and he was able to be occasionally inefficient without fear of violence. The other captives looked on him with envy and loathing, but they also began praying to God Most High. They might not know *how* Hunter was being protected, but they had some very concrete suspicions about *why*.

Mura returned a few days later, collecting men to help repair the new ship. The hull had apparently sprung a mysterious leak – he suspected foul play, but could find no motive for sabotaging what was, as far as anyone knew, the only way off the island. Almost as soon as he had arrived, Mura sniffed the air and announced that something was wrong.

"Somebody's been casting spells here," he told Bennan. "There's magic so strong I can smell it."

"Really?" Bennan said. "I haven't noticed anything unusual."

Mura gave him a long stare, frowning. "Gather everyone," he said at last. "The slaves too. We're going to get to the bottom of this."

While Bennan was gathering the others, Mura commanded Hunter to build a fire. The ground was muddy, but he seemed to want a bonfire outside, so Hunter chose the driest spot he could find and made a few trips to the woodpile in the barn. Mura did not light the fire with magic this time – perhaps that required Karassa's intervention – so Hunter had to do it by hand. By the time he had set the tinder alight, everyone had gathered around.

Everyone but Phaedra.

Hunter felt that familiar fear gnawing at him, the same fear he had felt when Phaedra had fallen into the ants' nest in Hession's cavern. What had happened to her? He prayed that she had somehow escaped, but he didn't really believe that was possible – not with her limp, and not without a word to Hunter first. Had they hurt her? Had they killed her and forgotten even to taunt him about it?

No. No, he couldn't believe that. Why would God Most High protect him from these men, while allowing her to die? That just could not be. It was all wrong.

Mura noticed Phaedra's absence as well. "Where is she?" he demanded.

"Where is who?" asked Bennan, playing dumb. There was only one 'she' on the island, besides Karassa.

"The girl. This one's half-sister."

Bennan looked sheepish. "Oh, her. I'm sorry, Mura. I forgot all about her. She must still be up in that attic."

"Get her."

Hunter allowed himself to breathe a little. They had simply forgotten her. It was hard to believe, but it was true. Somehow, Bennan and the others had managed to *forget* that there was a woman living among them. Hunter was no wizard, but he was starting to understand what Mura meant by "magic so strong I can smell it."

Had Phaedra had some sort of breakthrough, and laid an enchantment on their captors? He couldn't imagine who else would have done such a thing, and it would explain the overseers' lenient treatment of him. So what had changed? What had Phaedra discovered?

Mura paced in front of the fire while everyone waited for Bennan and Phaedra to return. They arrived a short time later, Bennan mumbling an apology. Mura gave the

two of them a contemptuous glare and commanded the
whole crowd to look into the fire.

"Karassa," he intoned, "let the nature of this
enchantment reveal itself to me." He added three foreign
words, pulling the pouch from under his tunic and
sprinkling some of its ashes in the fire.

The flames leapt skyward for a moment, drawing
Hunter's eyes upward. A vulture was circling overhead.
An omen? If so, then for whom?

His heart was pounding. What if Phaedra really was
behind this enchantment and Mura found out? God
Most High may have protected the two of them from
Karassa and Mayar, but hadn't Phaedra always said
that humans had free will? That was the whole point of
the mesh, wasn't it – to protect people from too much
interference by the Gods? Could anything really stop
Mura from killing them if he set his mind to it?

"Look into the fire!" Mura spat.

Hunter glanced about, startled and frightened, but
luckily Mura was not just talking to him: several other
people were as distracted as he was. One or two of
them were overseers, which was also lucky. If none had
been, Mura would likely have punished all the captives
without even waiting for his fire ritual to bear fruit.

Hunter turned his eyes back to the fire, wondering
what he was supposed to be seeing. He hoped that
whatever Mura had planned, it wouldn't work. But
now that he was really looking, he saw that the embers
were glowing green as if they'd been burning copper.
Mura threw in another handful of ashes, and the flames
turned a startling purple. At the third handful the fire
flashed such an intense white that Hunter shut his eyes
involuntarily, an after-image of the fire still glowing
beneath his eyelids.

"An enchantment of the mind," Mura said, probably to himself and yet loud enough to be heard. "No surprises there – far too inattentive to be natural. Well, I can fix that."

He turned away from the fire and began circling behind the crowd, sprinkling holy ashes on each of their heads. He was mumbling the whole time, and when he got close enough for Hunter to hear him, it became clear that these words were in no language Hunter had even heard before. Were they real words in *any* language?

Hunter began to feel something, a tugging at his mind. He thought the ashes must be acting as a wick, trying to tease the enchantment out through their heads. The sensation went away fairly quickly, but then Hunter was pretty sure he hadn't been a target of the original enchantment. Perhaps this was having more of an effect on the others.

It sure didn't seem like it, though. Mura was growing increasingly frustrated. "Karassa," he pleaded, "aid Your servant. Break the shackles that have imprisoned these men's minds and give them the freedom to think as before. I cannot do this alone!"

He threw another handful of ashes in the fire, but this time, nothing happened at all. He tore the pouch from his neck and flung the whole thing in, but the flames only burned on, unchanging. Mura stood there with a look of disbelief, watching his pouch of sacrificial ashes, his sacrifice of sacrifices, blacken and disintegrate to no effect.

"Listen, the lot of you," he shouted. "I'm going to get to the bottom of this, and when I do, whoever cast this spell on my men will suffer like no one has ever suffered before. I will offer him to Karassa piece by bloody piece, all while he lives and watches. If magic will not break the enchantment, death will."

With that he stalked away indoors, leaving his men and their captives looking wonderingly at each other. "Mage Mura is angry at us," the cook said dumbly.

"As well he should be," Bennan answered. "We let ourselves get enchanted, and now he has to fix it. You just pray he figures it out before he starts cutting *us* into pieces. I've never seen his magic fail before."

"Best to keep away from the house," said an overseer called Tarphon. "I don't want to get in his way."

The others agreed, so they all spent the next few hours outside, fishing and tending to the livestock. "We need to leave tonight," Phaedra whispered when she and Hunter were briefly next to each other. "It's not safe to stay, and I think an escape might be possible."

"On what ship?"

Phaedra shook her head almost imperceptibly. Nobody had noticed them talking yet, and there was no reason to change that. "Even if we have to live in the forest, it's better than staying here with Mura."

"You think we can make it far enough away with your limp?"

They separated for a minute, seeing Bennan glance in their direction. When the danger of their conversation being witnessed had passed, Phaedra said, "I think we'd better find out."

They had to wait until late that night to make their attempt. Shortly after their conversation, Mura returned from the house and took a lock of hair from every person on the estate, presumably so that he could use them to identify whoever had cast the spell on his men. However he meant to use the hair, he was apparently waiting for morning to do it, because they heard nothing more about it that night. That was a great relief: the two of them had no intention of waiting to find out whether his second ritual would identify Phaedra as the culprit.

They made their attempt shortly after midnight. Hunter slipped out of the barn while its watchman was relieving himself against a tree, and set off to get Phaedra from the farmhouse. It was midmonth, and the moon was bright overhead. He slunk over to the house, keeping low so that he would be harder to spot. Nobody stopped him. The cook, Terrin, was on watch at the house tonight, but he seemed to be half asleep in his chair by the door. What had Phaedra done to these men?

Whatever it was, Hunter had no complaints. He had been on the cusp of thinking this might be *too* easy, but that was nonsense. Being caught would mean their deaths, whereas escaping would save their lives – there was no such thing as "too easy."

Something touched his shoulder and he spun around, his heart pounding. It was Phaedra. "I was starting to worry you wouldn't make it," she whispered. "Let's get out of here."

They picked their way around the house until they were sure they could not be seen from either the house or the barn, then picked up their pace. The moon was bright enough that they were able to find their way with little trouble, breaking from the road once the farmlands and tukka orchards gave way to true forest. Hunter kept looking back in case they were being pursued, though of course they weren't – if nobody had noticed them leave, they weren't likely to be missed till morning.

But for all that they had a tremendous head start, he worried about Phaedra's slow pace. She had grown used to traveling with a limp, but that mostly meant that she stopped to rest and stretch her muscles far more often than he'd have liked. He took the time during one of these breaks to find her a good walking stick, but though she seemed to appreciate it, it didn't much improve their speed. They walked on.

The hardest part came when the initial excitement and anxiety of their escape finally wore off, and they were left sleepily plodding along, trying to keep their eyes open and focused and to get just one more mile farther away, and then another, just past these trees and after that, those ones. The night winds were chilly at this time of year, and all Hunter wanted to do was to curl up in some reasonably dry place and fall asleep.

At long last, when Phaedra had decided that they should go no farther that night, they curled up back to back on the most level patch of ground they could find and passed swiftly into unconsciousness.

When they awoke, a familiar face was staring down at them.

24
PHAEDRA

Phaedra blinked, trying to place that face. It was a skinny continental face with close-set eyes and long brown hair, and it belonged to a girl who must have been at least a year or two younger than Phaedra. Where did she know her from?

"I know you," Hunter said to the girl. "You're from that village that Psander took in! How did you get here?"

"She sent me through," the girl said. "She wanted me to get some things to help her fight off the elves."

"Like what?" Phaedra asked.

The girl looked uncertain, as if she thought Psander might not have wanted her to say. "Like what?" Phaedra repeated.

"Like relics from your lives. You islanders. She said you'd been to the elves' world before and survived, and if I brought her some of your things she could use them against the elves."

For a moment, Phaedra just gawked at her. Psander meant to use relics from the Tarphaeans' lives – from her life – to fight the fairies? How was Phaedra supposed to feel about that? Except, obviously, she wasn't supposed to feel anything about it. She wasn't meant to know.

She vaguely remembered having fed this girl, back when Psander's villagers had all been sick and weak from the wizard's overreliance on their latent magic. Psander had made them pendants that siphoned off unused magical potential and used it to buttress her wards, and upon the islanders' last visit they had found the villagers too weak to stand.

"Have you all recovered from the pendant-sickness, then?"

The girl nodded. "Mostly. Psander had us take the charms off after we got to the world of elves, so she could look them over and make some changes. They don't make us as weak anymore, and we also don't wear them all the time – we go one week on, two weeks off, in cycles. It's not so bad now, and if it keeps the elves away, that's worth more than anything we could give."

"How have you held them off?" Hunter asked. "They even knew you were coming!"

"They didn't know where, though," the girl said. "We had a few days before they found us, for Psander to turn her wards around."

"Turn her wards around? What does that mean?"

"I don't know. It's what she said."

They went silent for a time, until Hunter pointed out that they had to keep moving if they were to stay ahead of Mura's men. The village girl was confused. "Psander said the island would be empty when I came."

Phaedra explained the situation, and that ended the questions. They fled deeper into the forest. The girl followed them, occasionally consulting with a map she had brought with her. It was a strange sort of map that seemed to be marked differently every time Phaedra glimpsed it. It was made out of a patchwork of five or six pieces of cloth sewed together. Just over half of it was covered with signs and squiggles that shifted as they walked, but the other almost-half seemed to be permanently blank.

"Those are your pieces," the girl explained when she saw Phaedra looking. "They're all supposed to go empty like that when I'm close enough to something of yours. These two parts must be from the two of you."

"I see." The material this map was made from looked familiar somehow… Ah, that was it. They were patches of bed sheet. Psander must have made this map out of the linens the islanders had slept under when they came to Silent Hall. It was poetic magic, just as Phaedra had suspected: Psander was looking for relics from the islanders' homes, so she had used the material she had that was closest to being their home at Silent Hall. Phaedra would never have thought to have done that, but it made fine sense now that she recognized it.

"What's your name?" she asked the girl.

"Atella."

"Did Psander choose you for your name?"

The girl looked confused, though she shouldn't have. Atel was the God of travelers and messengers, and it was too fitting for a girl named after Him to be sent back to this unfamiliar place to seek and find relics of its native children. There might have been some magical benefit to sending a girl with a name like that. But then, perhaps you had to be a student of magic to recognize such things.

"How are you going to get back to Silent Hall when you're done here?" Hunter asked.

"I'm supposed to find my way back to where I came through, and if I'm in time it'll open for me. I've only got eleven days to find everything and get back, or Psander said I could be lost for years."

Elevens again. Phaedra wished she could make them all add up. Everything that had to do with the world of the elves seemed to come in elevens, but there was no rhyme or reason to it as far as she could tell. Perhaps Psander could explain it all, if she had mastered the theory of elevens so quickly.

"We'll go back with you," Phaedra said. "It'll save you time finding things to represent me and Hunter."

That, and it would get them away from Mura.

"Thanks," Atella said. "I hope we can get back in time."

Phaedra smiled reassuringly at her. "We will."

It was an incredible, overwhelming relief to think that Psander might once again save her and Hunter from their enemies and pursuers. Phaedra had thought that she and Hunter were trapped on the island for good this time, but now there was the possibility of leaving this world behind and seeing Psander again! In eleven days, she might sit in Psander's library and learn how the wizard worked her magic without the support of a patron God.

So far, the magic Phaedra had done was more similar to Mura's terrible rituals than anything else: just as Mura seemed to rely on Karassa's blessing for his power, so Phaedra had relied on God Most High. Their magic was at best an amplification of their prayers, a way to get more attention from their respective Gods than they might have warranted otherwise. Yet this was obviously *not* the way Psander worked – she didn't have to rely on some God's favor to disguise herself, or to summon a flame, or to make her fortress invisible. Phaedra wanted to know how she did it.

On the other hand, what if it was this non-reliance on Them that had turned the Gods against the academic wizards, after a centuries-long tradition of tolerance? Perhaps magic was *supposed* to rely on the blessings of Gods, and it was the decoupling of magic from worship that had both empowered and doomed Psander's colleagues.

They followed Atella's shifting map until another of its patches went blank, in a part of the forest that looked like any other. There were guardian trees here, and a healthy undergrowth of plants that Phaedra could not identify – she had never been that interested in plants. She scanned the trees and forest floor for any reason for them to have stopped. What could be here, among the guardian trees, that could be called a relic of the islanders? It must be something of Bandu's, but what? What significance did this place have? Was it the place where she had met Four-foot? The place her father had left her when he first brought her to the forest to live or die without him? Was it the place where the fairies had first abducted her, some eleven years ago?

Atella didn't seem to know any more than Phaedra did. She turned round and round, looking lost. "What's here?" she asked despairingly.

"I don't know," Phaedra said.

Hunter beat about in the underbrush, looking for anything that might be hidden among the vines and bushes, but it was no good. There was nothing there to be found.

"What do we do?" Atella asked.

"Take some of everything," Phaedra suggested. "Some dirt, some bark, some leaves and twigs. If we leave without what you're looking for, Bandu's part of the map will start working again, won't it?"

The girl looked relieved. "I think so. Oh, thank you!"

She pulled her satchel around and began harvesting

little pieces of their surroundings. "We'd better get moving soon," Hunter pointed out. "Mura can't be that far behind us."

"Do you think we could try to find a road again?" Phaedra asked. "If they're tracking us, they won't still be on the roads anymore."

"It's worth trying," Hunter said. "Besides which, I'm not Criton – I can't catch us a dinner with claws and fire. We can try throwing rocks at birds, but I think we'll have better luck foraging around the old towns."

He was right. The three of them proved completely incapable of hunting for themselves, and the little streams they found along their way were not deep enough for fish, though their water was sweet. They walked in the direction they thought most likely to lead to a road without taking them back toward Mura's outpost, but they found none that day, and broke for the night still surrounded by trees. Atella luckily had brought dried meat, hard bread, and cheese with her on her journey, but it was meant to last her a week and a half, and they had to share it in tiny portions to make it last. They settled down to sleep still desperately hungry, shivering in the cool winter night and listening to the howling wolves.

The wolves made Phaedra think of Bandu and her wolf Four-foot, who had died of an infection so short a time after saving the islanders from Magor-worshipping highwaymen. Phaedra had always found the wolf terrifying, but she knew how Bandu loved him, and she loved Bandu. She missed the other girl, her generous soul, her insight, and even her infuriating lack of understanding about the norms of civilization. Bandu would surely have felt at home here, and Phaedra would have felt at home with Bandu.

It was too hard, having all split up like this. Phaedra had lost her first family, found a new one, and now lost that one too. Would she ever see Bandu or Criton or Narky again? She wished she knew what they were all up to, or at least that she could have gotten some assurance that they were all still alive. Who knew what had transpired in her absence?

She thought the wolves might be getting closer – their howls seemed to be becoming louder and louder. She prayed to God Most High to protect her, Atella, and Hunter while they slept. But her prayer felt hollow, so she got up and scratched it into the ground all around them with a sharp rock, reading it through three times, both for the power of the repetition and to make sure she was satisfied with her wording. That would have to do, she decided. She was a novice at magic, but Criton's God had shown them such favor so far that hopefully He would forgive her amateurish work.

They awoke the next morning and moved on, coming at last to a path that led them to a village. The village square was full of bones, where villagers had died during the divine plague and then been preyed upon by birds and wild animals. Some skeletons were mostly intact, others scattered by the rougher scavengers who had fed upon their flesh. The blackened bones of a ram still lay upon the altar in the center of the square, grinning at them.

They went into the houses, looking for the stores of grain that had never seen another sowing season. It was an eerie feeling, walking into other people's houses unannounced, knowing that the owners were inevitably among the bones outside. They found what they needed, though, and spent most of the day grinding flour and baking hard bread for their journey. She thought that would still give them enough time to collect everything Atella needed – from what Phaedra knew of Narky's past, his village couldn't have been more than a day or two away. With Psander's map to guide them, they ought to reach it with still five or six days left before their eleven-day window closed. That ought to give them just enough time to get back to Karsanye for something of Criton's before returning to the forest and, hopefully, Silent Hall. The only trouble was that Mura and his people still existed, and, unless he gave up and turned back, might catch the three of them at any point along the way.

They left the village that evening and soldiered on despite their lack of rest, stumbling down the road weary and half asleep. They were glad they did: after dark, they spotted a light no more than a day's journey behind them. Mura might not have reached the village tonight, but he surely would tomorrow morning.

How many men could he possibly have with him? Presumably he had left his captives behind with overseers to guard them, and taken a small group to track down the escapees. He would kill them when he found them, that much was certain. Hunter wouldn't give up without a fight, so he would die first, but Phaedra would be sacrificed and her ashes harvested for more spells. She had no idea what they'd do with Atella. Probably the same.

They didn't sleep at all that night. When Atella tried to sit down and rest, Phaedra snatched the map from her and kept limping on, forcing her to rise and follow. Mura and his men would be much faster than them – the only way to outpace them was to never ever stop.

By midday the next day, Phaedra was seeing things she was pretty sure weren't there. The fairies on their horses, pursuing them through the woods – that was a memory, right? But she kept thinking she saw or heard them, riding toward her and the others with their sky-nets and elvish sickles ready for slaughter.

By early evening, when they arrived at the village that Atella's map indicated as Narky's, Phaedra could have sworn the skeletons in the yard were moving. She shied away from them as she passed through, afraid that they might snatch at her. The map led them just out of the village before Narky's corner went blank.

"I don't understand," Atella said, tears streaming down her face. "There's nothing here but a clump of trees."

Phaedra's vision was blurring too, and her eyes kept closing. She slapped herself in the face. "There has to be something. Narky isn't like Bandu – places aren't important to him. Whatever's here, it's concrete."

Hunter nodded. "I'll look in the trees, you look on the ground. Atella, check that stream over there."

"Where?"

Hunter blinked a few times. "Sorry. Just help Phaedra look on the ground, then."

This would have been much easier had they slept before their search. Phaedra kept finding things that struck her as full of significance, only to realize a moment later that they were simply rocks or sticks or blades of grass with interesting coloration. She crawled about on the ground, examining every pebble and trying not to be fooled by her own imagination. Even when she found what she was looking for, she almost ignored it on the assumption that it wasn't really there.

But it *was* there. No matter how many times she blinked or felt it with her fingers, she had found the front half of a crossbow bolt. Someone had snapped the thing somewhere near the middle and flung it away –

the other half must be around here somewhere. Phaedra knew what it was, and she knew why it was important: it had been pulled from someone's body after Narky had put it there.

"I have something!" Phaedra cried. "Come here. We need to find the other half."

"It's an arrow?" Atella asked, looking confused.

"A crossbow bolt," Phaedra corrected her. "Find the other half."

She did, lifting it out of the grasses a few minutes later. "So this is it? This is what we're here for?"

"This is what we're here for."

Phaedra didn't tell her any more than that. Hunter seemed to have figured out the bolt's significance on his own, but it was not the sort of thing one said aloud. They knew that Narky had murdered someone, probably not long before they had met him. They had learned it not from his mouth but from a prophecy, one that had referred to Narky as *he who was murderer*. Narky had been the one to point out the other verses' resemblance to the five islanders, but though Hunter had claimed to believe that he himself was the murderer for the things he had done in self-defense, Phaedra thought he must have realized the truth by now. Narky had fled his home after killing someone; that was why he had been so desperate to get on the boat that took them to the continent. Here then was the crossbow bolt that had turned Narky into a murderer, and saved his life.

"So," Hunter said, rubbing his eyes. "So. What... how are we supposed to get to Karsanye now? Our enemies are between us and where we need to be, we haven't slept – there's no way I can fight them off. What do we do?"

Phaedra sighed and looked around. A dark cloud was

coming across the island from the east, promising rain and maybe lightning too.

"We go back the way we came," she said. "And we pray."

25
NARKY

It took them almost two months to convert the former Temple of Magor into an acceptable temple of Ravennis. At first they worked alone, but as word spread of their presence, new followers of Ravennis began volunteering their support. Narky and Ptera set them to work destroying all the statues and figurines that had been so prominent in Magor's temple and painting over the devotional murals with pitch. It didn't look beautiful by any means, but it would do.

During their breaks, Narky preached. Phaedra had once read him a scroll by a priest of Ravennis, and he did his best to recall what he had learned from it. He was lucky that the people of Anardis knew even less about Ravennis than he did, because they never complained about his spotty knowledge, and when he didn't know the answer to one of their questions, he could always invent one. He wasn't much of a public speaker, but he was quick on his feet, so he would give only the barest of speeches and then spend the rest of the time answering questions.

The personal quarters of Magor's temple had had

room for four priests to live there at one time, but Narky and Ptera kept it to themselves for now, luxuriating in its space and making prodigious use of the beds. They pushed two of these together to give themselves more room to sleep once their lovemaking was done, and slept more comfortably than Narky had in his life.

They made love constantly. The excitement of being newly married was mutual and overwhelming, and Ptera's reactions convinced him that he was getting better at it. He had never felt so confident, so alive.

He was starting to really like Ptera. She was a schemer like him, even if she wouldn't admit it, and they shared a similar sense of humor. It was a wonder he hadn't discovered this back in Ardis, or perhaps it was no wonder at all. He had barely spoken to her at the time, except when she was delivering news. Their similarities hadn't come up.

Twice a week, Narky would go to visit the Great Temple of Elkinar and speak with Mother Dinendra. For all that she had forsworn politics, she was a very practical, political sort of leader, and Narky was convinced that her support was the key to converting Ardis. Elkinar had a real and widely-accepted presence there, and as Magor's power waned, Dinendra's influence in Ardis was not to be overlooked. What her priests taught, the people would accept.

The trouble was Dinendra's second-in-command and likely successor, Father Sephas. Sephas was a true theologian – Phaedra had loved him – and he would not accept the notion of an alliance between their two priesthoods without an airtight theological reason for thinking that Elkinar and Ravennis were really allies. Dinendra liked Narky and enjoyed their meetings, but she agreed with Sephas on this matter, so unless Narky could somehow convince him on a theological level, her support would remain tacit.

He thought he could manage it, if he just framed it the right way. Elkinar and Eramia were supposed to be siblings, and the islanders had guessed that Eramia and Ravennis must have been working together to fulfill the Dragon Knight's prophecy and bring about a Judgment of the Gods. It was the Oracle of Ravennis that had told Hunter's father to send him to the continent, Ravennis who had kept an eye on Narky and marked him with His power. Eramia, in the meantime, had goaded the island's patron Goddess just as Narky and Hunter, Phaedra, Bandu and Criton were about to leave. As a result, the five of them had escaped the island at the last possible moment, sealing their fates as wanderers of the continent. Without this, the dragon Salemis might never have been rescued, and Magor's army never destroyed.

Narky even wondered sometimes whether Eramia had had a direct hand in turning him into the prophesied murderer. The girl he had loved back in his village had been called Eramia too, and it was her lover Narky had killed. How much of a coincidence could that possibly have been?

The trouble was that Elkinar did not seem to have had a part in any of this, for all that His sister was so deeply involved. But then, perhaps that shouldn't have surprised anyone. Phaedra had once told Narky and the other islanders about a theory that all the familial relations between Gods were invented by people, just as the Gods' genders supposedly were. According to this theory, the Gods were all equally related or unrelated, but had been grouped together thematically into 'families' because people understood the world better that way. If this was true, there was no real reason to expect Elkinar to be on Eramia's side.

It was interesting that Elkinar and Ravennis were not said to be brothers, considering that Narky would have thought Their domains must overlap quite a lot: the God of the Life Cycle and the Lord of the Underworld should have had a lot in common. But then, Narky was no theologian – he was just some poor sap who'd been named high priest by an Oracle who should, of all people, have known better.

At least he had Ptera to talk to about it, if he ever had the courage to tell her how little he knew. He thought that if he could only speak freely, as he had with his friends, he might talk his way through to something really meaningful. But he didn't dare reveal the depth of his ignorance – not yet, anyway. For all that she might enjoy him physically, he knew that it was his supposed connection to Ravennis that had attracted her to him in the first place.

So he stayed silent, and learned nothing, and felt once again like a coward. And all the while people came to him with their gifts and their labor, and looked up to him as if he knew something. What would they do if they ever realized how little he deserved his position?

Of course, he also felt ridiculous for failing to appreciate their respect, now that he finally had some. He'd left home less than a year and a half ago, and look how far he'd come! In Tarphae he'd been miserable, alone, disrespected, and full of self-doubt. Now here he was: High Priest of Ravennis, happily married, sought out by followers for his wisdom... and still full of self-doubt.

Was this something immutable about his personality? He should have been confident, considering how well things were going. The new Temple of Ravennis was looking less and less like a painted-over Temple of Magor, and worshippers were beginning to come by not to help convert the building, but to make sacrifices. They made sacrifices when a loved one died, begging the Lord Among the Fallen to watch over their departed family members in kindness, and they made sacrifices when things went well for them, thanking Ravennis as the Keeper of Fates. Narky did his best for them. They weren't exactly wrong to come to him: no living person knew more about what Ravennis had been up to than Narky did. The trouble was that only he seemed to realize what a tragedy that was.

For there had been news from Ardis: the Graceful Servant had been publicly executed, as had every other follower of Ravennis that could be found. General Magerion had been given free rein at home while his companions on the council were at war, and he had made his focus the persecution of the Ravennis worshippers. The remarkable thing was that the cult had survived, even in Ardis. He knew this because a trickle of Ardismen kept making the pilgrimage to Anardis and Narky, to give sacrifices and receive guidance on how to proceed. It had happened just as the Graceful Servant had predicted: she had been martyred to their God, and it had only made Him stronger.

Narky wished he had a good answer for the Ardismen who came to him. His instinct was to tell them to stay away from Ardis, to save themselves and, if possible, their families, and make new lives in this safer city. Ardis was fighting a two-front war against him and Criton's army, and things were bound to get worse before they got better.

But he couldn't say that. It didn't matter that the cult of Ravennis was growing in Anardis, and that the people here were safe for now: Ardis was the prize his God wanted. The Graceful Servant had ordered him to come back someday soon, to wrest Magor's city from its doomed God and make His punishment complete. The Ravennis-worshippers left in Ardis were there to pave the way – they could not flee.

So Narky told them to go back, and to keep converting their friends and neighbors in secret. Yes, many of them would be captured and killed, but Ravennis would watch over them in the underworld, and He would favor all those who had died in His name. He told them to show no fear, no matter what happened. Life was short; Ravennis was eternal.

His followers loved that. He wished he did too.

It was wrong of the Graceful Servant, wrong of Ravennis to make Narky His High Priest. Narky was a coward and a coward's son, a man who would never give his life voluntarily for *any* cause. Ravennis was forever, yes, but life was *now*. How could such a man be asked to send people to their deaths, to encourage them to *love* their deaths? It was too cruel, to them and to Narky too.

But this was what his God demanded of him, and he could not shirk his duty. He'd had Ravennis angry at him before, and didn't ever want to put himself in that position again.

If only the priests of Elkinar had been able to grant their support and not just their neutrality, Narky might have felt that he could send his followers back to Ardis as the vanguard of an army instead of as martyrs. He must try to convince them. It might be hard, but the options didn't get any easier from there. It was certainly better than the Graceful Servant's path.

This time when he and Ptera visited the Temple of Elkinar, Narky did not shy away from theological debate.

They were all sitting crowded around the library table, sipping a strong wine that had been donated to the temple, when Narky asked, "Have you wondered why there haven't been any real fights between the followers of Ravennis and the followers of Elkinar? A new God has come to power here in Anardis, but Elkinar doesn't seem to mind."

"Well," said Mother Dinendra, "I don't mind taking a little bit of credit now and then. I've practically encouraged Magor's followers to turn to Ravennis as a secondary God, once it became clear that they would not turn over their whole being to Elkinar. Magor always satisfied people's needs for a God of power and domination, and Elkinar was never one to fill that role. Our priests are healers and midwives, and our God a sustainer of balance. Let Magor's place be filled by your God – as long as there is life-sustaining balance, Elkinar can never be threatened. That was my theory, anyway."

"Are you saying you think your God has stepped aside to let Ravennis in, just because Elkinar hasn't historically been the only God of Anardis? Why shouldn't He try to take more?"

"Because 'taking more' is not Elkinar's way!" Father Sephas scolded. "He is not some crafty nobleman, always maneuvering for more power. All of life is His domain."

Narky snorted. "In one breath you say that He has no interest in power, and then you turn around and say He's in charge of all of life. If claiming all of life as your domain isn't maneuvering for power, what is?"

Mother Dinendra's countenance hardened. "Have you come today to insult Elkinar in His own temple?"

That stopped Narky short. Why was he so bad at this? He was trying to build a theological argument for a pre-existing alliance between Ravennis and Elkinar, one that he thought was really good, and his base rudeness was getting in his way. Even Ptera was staring at him, aghast. She hadn't understood what he was trying to do either – he'd done a truly terrible job of explaining himself.

His mistake was that in his attempt to point out how welcoming Elkinar had been to them, he hadn't expected Sephas to push back against the very notion of godly ambition. That had thrown him off, and he'd fallen back on his usual argumentative style. Idiot. If he was going to make this work, he had to control himself.

"I'm sorry," he said. "I haven't come to insult Elkinar, but to exalt Him for the warm welcome He's shown to me and my God. I only meant to say that Elkinar didn't *have* to be so welcoming, He *could* have tried to fill Magor's role by Himself and become the only God of Anardis. Instead, He and His servants have welcomed us into His city and even into His house, this temple. I meant to express my gratitude."

"You are young," Mother Dinendra said indulgently. "Tact is not one of the strengths youth has over age."

Narky nodded, relieved. "Thank you. You're absolutely right."

Father Sephas waved a hand. "Go on, then. Let's start from the point you were trying to make."

Narky looked to Ptera for strength and tried to regain his composure. "Well," he said, "in any case, Elkinar *could* have made a play for sole patron of Anardis, but He didn't. You might say that's because ambition isn't in His nature, but I think He's been uniquely welcoming to Ravennis. I can't imagine that He'd have supported, say, Atun, if the Sun God had tried to capitalize on Magor's weakness here."

"Perhaps not," Dinendra conceded.

"I think it's not a matter of Elkinar lacking for

ambition. I think He *wants* Ravennis here."

"You think They are allies," Father Sephas concluded. "Yes, Narky, we've heard this from you before. You even make a very good case for it—"

"That's not what I'm saying," Narky said, to his own surprise. "I'm saying They're the same God."

The room went silent. Narky closed his eye and waited. Would Ravennis slay him for saying what he'd just said? Would Elkinar? What had possessed him to say such a thing? He was practically *begging* the Gods to smite him.

Nothing happened. Narky opened his eye. They were all staring at him. Of course they were.

"What?" Ptera asked.

"I think," Narky said, and stopped. His hands were shaking. "I think that may have been a prophecy."

"What do you mean?" asked Father Taemon.

No God had smitten him yet. How could he make sense of this?

"I don't think those were my words," he said. "I mean, I said them, but they just came to me as I was saying them, and, well, and They haven't killed me yet. Is it – is it possible that Ravennis and Elkinar are one and the same?"

"We've had no reason to think so," said Father Sephas. "Up until now."

"But it's possible."

"Anything is possible, if the Gods say it."

"No," Narky said, "I mean, yes, but I think it's plausible too. When I was with the other islanders, two Gods were clearly guiding us: Ravennis and Eramia. We had no idea why those two should be allies, but Eramia and Elkinar are brother and sister, right? If Ravennis *is* Elkinar, the alliance makes perfect sense.

"When my friends and I came here, to Anardis, it was the priests of Elkinar who took us in and sheltered us before Bestillos invaded. And it was Elkinar's sister Eramia who gave us what we needed to find the Dragons' Prisoner and rescue him, and to destroy the armies of Magor and Mayar. I think this really is a prophecy. I think Elkinar is the sole God of Anardis; we've just been worshipping His two halves.

"Their domains are perfectly complementary. Keeper of Fates; God of Birth, Life, Death, and Rebirth; God of the Life Cycle; God of the Underworld. They're the same God."

"If what you say is true," Sephas asked, "how could Magor not have known it? Why should He and Elkinar live in peace even as Magor sent Bestillos to destroy Laarna?"

"I –" Narky began, but he had no answer, nothing beyond the fact that he had said the two Gods were one, and neither had killed him for it. "I don't know," he finished.

"Thank you, Narky," Mother Dinendra said, indicating the end of his visit. "You have given us a lot to discuss – it will take much more than an evening, I think, to tease out the various implications of what you have said tonight. It may be too early to assume that neither God has taken offense, but if in a week's time you still have not been punished, we may have to accept that both Elkinar and Ravennis endorse your statement. Hopefully by then we will have arrived at a good theological explanation."

They bowed to their hosts and left, still trying to process what had been said.

"She's being too cautious," Ptera said during their walk home. "Ravennis spoke through you. Anyone could see that."

"Not everyone, I guess. And she's right that I don't have all the answers. I don't think it'll hurt for them to spend a week figuring out what all this means."

Ptera's mouth twisted. "And making sure that Elkinar remains the dominant half here in Anardis."

"You think so?" That gave him a lot to think about. Ptera didn't stumble into her words the way he did – she always thought before she spoke. If she thought that power-hunger played a role in Mother Dinendra's thinking, she wasn't just saying so reflexively.

Ptera gave him a look that expressed just how naïve his question sounded. "She has a priesthood to protect."

"You're probably right," he said, when they got indoors. "And she'd be wise to make sure of it, really. Who knows if what I said tonight was even true?"

Ptera stopped dead, one hand already reaching for the door of their bedroom. "Are you telling me you were lying?"

He shook his head. "Of course not. Ravennis put those words in my mouth – I'm sure of that much. But what if *He* was lying? For all I know, the two of Them have been separate Gods all along and now He's trying to swallow Elkinar while He's got the chance. The Gods can shield us from each other – if this is a surprise attack, Elkinar won't be able to smite me unless He wins the struggle with Ravennis first."

"Narky!" she cried. "Do you even know what you're saying?"

He smiled. "You're only just getting to know me, Ptera. This is how I talk."

"But you're accusing your own God of treachery! You're His high priest, Narky, you can't go saying–"

"Do you think I know how this all works?" Narky snapped. "I'm seventeen, Ptera, for the Gods' sake! I'm not a theologian, and I was nobody's holy man until the Graceful Servant told me I was going to be high priest. I'm just trying to figure out the truth for myself, and to follow Ravennis' path wherever He leads me. If He's been Elkinar all along, great! If He's trying to usurp and co-opt Him, that's fine by me too. Ravennis is my God no matter what. But until He gives me clear guidance, I have to make guesses and talk these ideas through so I can figure out what I'm going to do about it. If He has a problem with that, He can send me a clear message for once and tell me what to do!"

Ptera was staring at him silently, her expression inscrutable. He wished he knew what she was thinking.

"I don't know what's going on right now," he admitted, "and if you want to know what I *think*, it's that we'll never really know. If Ravennis swallows Elkinar, there'll be no way to know for sure that They weren't the same God all along. I think Mother Dinendra is right to be wary of my prophecy. Our Gods might be united, but They also might be fighting in a life-or-death struggle as we speak, in which case Elkinar can't afford for His own high priestess to give up on Him. She can't trust me; she's doing the right thing for her God."

He could tell that Ptera didn't agree with him about something, but about what? Why wasn't she saying anything?

"I don't know," he sputtered on, unable to stop talking. "Maybe it's over already. Maybe They weren't the same God before, but They are now. The thing is, if it *is* a fight, and the fight isn't over, this could get really ugly. Even if Ravennis can shield me from other divine powers, an independent Elkinar might be able to tell Mother Dinendra the truth – assuming for now that the truth is different from what I said it was."

At this, Ptera finally spoke. "Stop doubting yourself, and stop doubting our God. Ravennis doesn't lie, Narky."

He shrugged. "Ravennis made the world think He was dead, then wormed His way into Magor's territory and started undermining Him from within. He made me shoot a man in the back, or at least rewarded me for doing it myself. You can say that Ravennis doesn't lie, but what do we know? No straightforward, honorable God would have chosen me for His high priest."

To Narky's surprise, Ptera caught his face between her hands and kissed him hard. With her hands still firmly on his cheeks, she said, "I love you, Narky, but you don't understand yourself at all. I'm sure you have all sorts of flaws, but dishonesty isn't one of them! Whatever His reasons, Ravennis didn't choose you because you're a good liar. What man in your position would admit to his wife that he doesn't know what's going on? What high priest would speculate that his God chose him for nefarious reasons? You can't even hold your thoughts inside you for long, let alone mask them in deception. The truth shines through you."

"Thanks," Narky said. "Are you going to let go of me now?"

"No," she answered, and kissed him again. There was no more talk of Gods that night.

In the morning, however, the work began. Ptera was right, after all: it wouldn't do for Narky to doubt his own God. Even if the prophecy wasn't strictly true yet, Ravennis would want him to act as though it was.

So Narky called a festival in honor of the prophecy he had been given, and sent Ptera to spread the word throughout the city. The priests of Elkinar were caught flat-footed – they had apparently not settled on a response yet, nor had their God given them any visions to contradict Narky's prophetic words. As such, Narky was able to spread his message of the Gods' unity for two full days without any story competing with his. That was perfect: without disagreement from the priests of Elkinar, people assumed that Narky's version of events must be true. When they asked him what would become of the two separate priesthoods, Narky demurred magnanimously, saying that the One God had yet to guide him on such political questions. The priesthoods need not merge overnight.

As for the people's everyday practice, Narky told his followers to dedicate all future prayers and sacrifices to "Ravennis, who is Elkinar". He defied the priests across the way to find a reason for complaint – after all, wasn't he doubling the number of prayers and sacrifices directed at their God? Of course, it was quite possible that Ravennis and Elkinar had always been one. That was what Ptera thought. But if there *was* a struggle in the heavens, he meant to win it for Ravennis.

The next time he and Ptera visited, Father Sephas was furious. "What is this you've been spreading while our backs were turned? We were to coordinate our teachings!"

"I'm sorry," Narky said, "I thought you were just waiting to see if Elkinar struck me down. He still has time to, you know. I'm sure if He smites me tomorrow, the people will reject my teachings without any argument."

Ptera was right – he was terrible at concealing his thoughts. That had come out far more biting than he'd wanted it to, and exactly as biting as he'd meant it.

"Be careful," Father Taemon said. "The Gods can work through men as well, and this is still Elkinar's city."

Narky's stomach clenched. Oh Ravennis below, why hadn't he thought of that? If Narky was beaten to death

here in the Great Temple of Elkinar, who would deny
that his teachings had proven false? Could he make a
break for it if he needed to?

Mother Dinendra smiled innocently at him. "I'm sure
Narky didn't mean to offend us. He is young, and has yet
to learn tactful speech. He was not raised to be High Priest
of Ravennis, but had the position thrust upon him."

"Yes," Narky said, sizing up the room. "I apologize."

Without Mother Dinendra, who was old and frail,
there were still five priests of Elkinar and only Narky
and Ptera to face them. What's more, the door behind
him was closed – he doubted he could get it open and
slip out before they were upon him, and of course, there
was Ptera to consider too. And even if they did escape,
where would they flee to? The very act of running would
be seen as a defeat for Ravennis, a proof that Narky's
teachings had all been lies. There was no way around it:
he was at the priests of Elkinar's mercy.

"We have a theological quandary here," Mother
Dinendra said. "I have discussed it with Father Sephas
and we see two distinct possibilities: either Narky's words
the other night were truth, and Elkinar and Ravennis are
one, or else Ravennis is attempting to usurp Elkinar's
place in the heavens even as He festers in the world
below. If I had to guess, Narky, I would say that you were
operating under the latter assumption."

Narky gulped. "I considered the possibility."

"And yet," Mother Dinendra said, "you are as ignorant
of the truth as we are. Without Elkinar's word on the
matter, we can't know whether the right course of action
is for us to join our priesthoods together or, if you'll
pardon me Narky, to kill the two of you immediately."

"Ravennis doesn't lie," Ptera said, but her voice shook
with fear.

"Well," said Mother Dinendra, "therein lies the quandary. If our Gods are truly one, then to kill the two of you would be unspeakable blasphemy. Elkinar may well do to us what Karassa did to Tarphae. I would rather not risk it, which is why I had *suggested* that we take a week to sort out the truth. By spreading word of the prophecy, however, Narky has forced our hand."

"If you guess wrong," Narky warned, "it'll mean the death of your people."

"If I guess wrong on the other side, it'll mean the death of my God."

Narky fell silent. His talking wasn't helping. He hadn't thought that Mother Dinendra was especially attached to her God – she had told him once that she had only joined Elkinar's priesthood as a way to keep herself and her children out of politics. Only now did he realize how little contradiction there was between that fact and the possibility that she might take her role as high priestess of Elkinar seriously.

"What are you going to do?" Ptera asked.

"Barring an answer from the heavens," Dinendra said, "I'm going to have to devise a test. Luckily, just such a test has presented itself."

"It has?"

The old priestess smiled. "Oh, yes. I received word today that General Magerion of Ardis is on his way here with a hundred men. Apparently, he wishes to take Narky back to Ardis with him. Ravennis has proven quite well that He can take advantage of His followers' deaths, but if He is truly one with Elkinar, He will also be able to sustain their lives. So I propose that you go with Magerion peacefully, and see what happens.

"I do not enjoy being rushed, Narky, so let me be clear and precise this time: today is the seventh day of the eighth month. If in a year or more you come back to Anardis and give a sacrifice on Elkinar's altar, then it will be proof that our Gods are one."

26

BANDU

The Ardismen never recovered from Bandu's ambush. Though their general had escaped, their army did not reform, and after two days in pursuit, Criton turned the people northward again. By now, a steady trickle of refugees was joining them, bringing news of the second army's movements. Criton did not think it would take long to catch them.

He was wrong. The second army managed to slip by them and hurry homeward, and Criton was left trying to chase them down with no real hope of catching up. Belkos said they should march straight down to Ardis and besiege the city. Bandu begged Criton not to try.

"They are so many more than us," she said, "and they have walls. You can't win there, but you already win here! They are too afraid to fight you. The plain people are happy without Ardis. We can make a new home for the Dragon Touched here!"

But Criton would not listen. He was angry because the second army had gotten away from him, and it was no good talking to Criton when he was angry. He stopped listening. Even Delika avoided him for a day or two, and

239

Bandu wouldn't let him handle Goodweather until she was sure he'd be able to control himself. That made him even angrier, which made her trust him less, and on and on it went.

She relied even more on Dessa and Vella to help her, since Iona's time was often spent now taking care of her mother. Partha was getting worse, it seemed. Her balance was bad, and she couldn't walk so fast, so she rode on a friend's mule when the camp was moving, and made demands of Iona whenever they stopped to rest. It was enough to make Bandu glad that she had no mother of her own.

Dessa split her time between visiting Bandu and helping take care of her grandmother, but Vella was available almost every evening. She still seemed scared of Bandu, but at least she was useful. She doted on Goodweather, really, and she also had much more patience for Delika than Bandu did. Bandu was too unkind to her.

Vella and her husband were not close the way Bandu and Criton were, for all their fighting. They were not friends, and from what Bandu could tell, they spent very little time together. That was the problem with choosing mates the way the Dragon Touched had – parents chose mates for their children not to make them happy, but to keep them safe. This might have worked to keep their neighbors from finding them, but it was too easy to make mistakes and pair children who didn't like each other.

It would not always be this way, at least. Dessa had been supposed to marry Vella's younger brother, but that had been put off when the Dragon Touched went to war. There was no time for weddings and no need to hide now, so Dessa might even get to wait until she was Bandu's age and could choose for herself. Dessa was very happy about that.

But then, Bandu sometimes wondered if even that was old enough – sometimes she thought she might have chosen Criton too soon. She loved him, and the two of them knew each other better than they knew anybody, but he was not a good mate – he was easily distracted, he let his worries spill onto Bandu and their daughter, and of course, he had never been good at controlling his anger. His father had broken that in him.

He *wanted* to be better, of course – that was why she hadn't left him yet. He always tried, or almost always, and if he failed… well, it was still his fault, and she didn't forgive him for it. But at least it was understandable.

It scared her how little she wanted him sometimes. She had once needed him so desperately that any separation had been painful, but now… well, she had changed. Baby Goodweather needed her more than Criton did, and she took up so much of her mother's time and energy that Bandu had less interest in trying to fix Criton. Now if he said or did something bad, or ignored her when he should have been paying attention, Bandu just rolled her eyes and went to someone else for help.

Sometimes she dreamt she had Four-foot back, and could live just with him and Goodweather in the shadow of the Yarek. The wolf and the tree would protect her from harm better than any army could, and they would never make her feel like the pack was more important than she was. That was how life should be. Why couldn't Criton have given her a life like that?

She knew why, of course: because he would have been miserable all alone with her. As much as he loved her, being alone with a mate and a child was not his dream. He too had grown up in isolation, but his isolation had been very different from hers, and he had hated it in a way that she knew she would never completely understand. He had always wanted to be part of a big pack that loved and accepted him – he needed the Dragon Touched even more than they needed him. Bandu couldn't ask him to abandon the people he had been looking for all his life.

But then, when had Criton ever asked Bandu if she wanted to be part of a Dragon Touched army? If the pressures of being part of this pack were too much for him, serve him right! Maybe if things got bad enough, he'd be willing to try it her way for once.

She had never felt so powerless as she did now, among these people, with a baby to take care of. It was one thing to choose a mate and then rely on him for support, and it was another thing entirely to have to rely on help from his cousin's family so that she wouldn't be overwhelmed. It was one thing to travel with a pack that didn't always understand her, and it was another to be surrounded by people who called her a foreign witch.

When she needed reassurance, Bandu looked to the Yarek. It was always visible, at least from here, stretching from the ground to the sky like a living pillar holding up the world. It was her connection to who she was, and it was ready to help her if she called.

But though she drew strength from its presence, she never reached into the earth again to speak to it. She was afraid of what it might offer her. It may have come from Goodweather's seed, but it wasn't like a child. The Yarek was dangerous, much more dangerous than people realized. It wasn't just a tree, and it didn't really hold up the world. It split it.

But it was tempting to look toward it anyway whenever she felt misunderstood. Unlike the Dragon Touched, the Yarek was grateful for what she'd done on its behalf. Unlike the Dragon Touched, it did not fear her. And unlike any person she had ever met, it did not fear the Gods.

Bandu didn't fear the Gods either, not the way other people did. All her kind worshipped the Gods out of fear, because that was what They wanted. There was good reason to be afraid, of course – Bandu had seen the Gods do great and terrible things – but that only made her angrier about Their meddling. It made her want to stand like the Yarek and cry, *You cannot destroy me. You can cut me down and tear me to pieces, but I will always grow back.*

She did not say these things to Criton.

She wondered if Hessina knew; if that was why the high priestess was so unwelcoming to her. Could she sense that Bandu did not respect her God? Was that why they all shunned her, why they seemed so afraid of her? Maybe it wasn't her foreignness that bothered them. Maybe it was her fearlessness.

One evening, when they had all made their camp again and Criton was out with Delika, learning prayers or rituals or something from Hessina, Bandu decided to make Vella tell her what made her so scary. The other girl was playing with baby Goodweather while Bandu arranged the bedding for the night, and Bandu turned on her and asked, "Why you're so afraid of me?"

Vella's eyes widened in horror. She looked trapped.

"You are always afraid of me," Bandu said. "I don't do anything to you, but you are afraid anyway. Why?"

"You're a bit intimidating," Vella answered quietly. Her face was starting to turn red.

"Then why you come here, if you are so afraid?"

"I like coming here."

Bandu didn't believe her. "You don't look like that. You don't look happy – always you're scared of me just like everybody else. Why do you come here?"

"Do you want to see less of me?" Vella asked meekly.

Bandu made a frustrated sound. "No, I want you to answer."

"Because you're so beautiful," the girl nearly whispered.

"What?"

"I said, because–"

"I hear you; I don't understand. What do you mean, I am beautiful? Why that makes you afraid?"

Vella stood shakily and handed Goodweather back to her. "Do you want to hold her again? I have to go."

And like that, she fled.

Bandu stood holding Goodweather for a long time. What had just happened between them? Did Vella want to be Bandu's mate? She hadn't said so, but that was what it seemed like. But Bandu already had a mate, besides which, she hardly knew Vella – the girl had always been too afraid to talk to her. It almost made her laugh, though, to think that she had thought Vella could explain why everyone was afraid of her. She had assumed that Vella had the same reasons as everyone else, but that obviously wasn't true – she was fairly sure the other Dragon Touched weren't afraid of her because she was beautiful.

It was a nice thing to hear, that someone besides Criton thought she was beautiful. The thought made her smile. She liked Vella much more now that she knew why the other girl had been shy with her. Bandu thought they might talk a lot more after this, since Vella had apparently said the thing she'd been so afraid to say before. She looked forward to it. It had been so lonely thinking that everyone hated her.

But she did not see much of Vella for the next few

days. Maybe the girl was too embarrassed to see her.

In the meantime, the Dragon Touched camp moved closer to Ardis by the day. As time went on, Criton was beginning to admit that his plan for attacking made no sense. He had won his battles against the Ardismen by making them run away, but as he said now, no army would run when its city was at its back.

Not everyone agreed. Sitting in the tent where they held their meetings, Criton's cousin said that the Dragon Touched ought to march straight to the gates of Ardis and demand that they open, just as the gates of Anardis had opened to the red priest.

"And what if they don't open their gates?" Criton asked. "If they shoot arrows at us, and throw rocks, and never open the gates? What'll we do then? We've won our battles so far, with the help of God Most High, but we've won them by making our enemies flee us. For those in Ardis, there is nowhere to flee. I'd love to think that they'd surrender to us, but we can't afford to assume they will."

"What do you mean to do, then?" Belkos said. "Give up on Ardis? Settle in these lands and worry about them attacking for the rest of our lives and our children's lives? Let them laugh at our God, and say that He was unable to overcome a stone wall? We can't do that."

"You can," Bandu pointed out, burping Goodweather.

Belkos pointed at her angrily. "Why is she here? She's not one of us; she doesn't represent any clan of Dragon Touched or plainsmen. Who does she speak for?"

"I value her judgment."

His cousin snorted. "I don't."

"It was her idea that won us the fight against Xytos' army!" Criton cried. "How can you say she doesn't belong here?"

"We didn't win on your wife's tactics," Belkos said. "We won because God Most High willed it. She doesn't even worship Him! Consult with her in the bedding of your tent if you feel the need, but she doesn't belong in this council. Think for yourself and speak for yourself, cousin – God Most High named *you* our leader, not this girl wife of yours."

Criton looked into Belkos' eyes for a long time, while Hessina, her son, and the elders of the plainsfolk all stared at Bandu. Their gazes made her angry. Why shouldn't she be here? She was no less a leader than Hessina's timid son, and she had done as much as anyone to help these people win their stupid war. What's more, she had had to beg Iona to watch Delika for her – or really for Criton, but he was always ready to foist the girl on Bandu for these sorts of occasions – so that she could come to this meeting and be heard.

She secretly hoped Criton would lose control and yell at his cousin, maybe even threaten him. She knew from experience how frightening it could be when Criton lost his temper, and Belkos had insulted both of them, on purpose. He deserved to be scared.

Instead, Criton just sighed. "You'd better go, Bandu."

"No." He had promised to listen to her, after the pigs. He had promised!

Criton's eyes flashed. "Go, Bandu."

Bandu stood up, barely able to contain her shock and her fury. "You are sorry later," she said.

"The longer it takes you to leave, the sorrier I'll be."

27

CRITON

Hessina was the first to speak after Bandu left. "You need a new wife, Criton. A Dragon Touched wife. Bandu presumes too much."

Criton resisted telling her to mind her own business and tried to turn the conversation back to Ardis, but the others would not let him. "Your high priestess is right," said Endra, an elder from one of the larger clans of plainsmen. "My first wife was like yours: she thought she could control me. Take another wife, and she'll realize she has nothing you couldn't find elsewhere."

Another elder, Kana, added, "She'll hate your other wife for it, though. Two is not enough. Two wives will become enemies, and their rivalry will consume all your happiness. Take at least a third, and maybe a fourth. They'll learn to live together and be kind to you when they realize that a fight between two of them will only benefit a third. Take several more wives, Criton. The Dragon Touched have married all their older girls away already – take a few from among our daughters while you wait for your own to mature."

Criton shook his head. Their advice was all self-

serving, besides which, it was horrible. Criton had
promised. These men just wanted to weaken Bandu's
influence, and to raise their own. They wanted to bind
their families to the leader of the Dragon Touched, to
strengthen their positions and claim a larger say over the
decisions of the group.

But then, what was wrong with that? A handful of
plainsmen had already made marriage pacts with the
Dragon Touched for after the war, and a good number
had pledged themselves to God Most High and begun
abiding by Hessina's rules for them. Perhaps the time had
come to cement these alliances, to call the plainsmen
Dragon Touched as well and stop treating them as if they
were lesser allies for their lack of claws. Even if it meant
sacrificing his promise to Bandu not to take another
wife, might it not be worth it? He was the political leader
of his people. Could he afford to be so selfish?

He could see the disapproval in Hessina's expression
– she didn't want him to marry outside his kin. But
she was letting her prejudices get the better of her: the
political benefits of accepting the plainsmen's offers were
unmistakable. Right now, this alliance was held together
only by the common enemy of Ardis, and by the fear
that otherwise the Dragon Touched would maraud across
the plains themselves. If Criton cemented his alliances
with a few marriages, he could then call the northern
plainsmen a *part* of the Dragon Touched. Then his people
would not even be so many fewer than the Ardismen.

Besides, what if the elders were right? What if the
addition of wives could actually improve his relationship
with Bandu? There had been tension between them,
always. The other women could help with Delika and
Goodweather, and make the times when Bandu was
angry with him more bearable. And if that made him

more patient, might it not be worth it for her too?

"I'll think about it," he promised the clan leaders. "Now can we please get back to the question of Ardis?"

"So long as God Most High takes our side," Belkos said, "we can't lose. Everyone knows how Bestillos took Anardis without the loss of a single soldier. It was the fear of him that opened the city's gates, not the strength of his army. What has given us our victories over the Ardismen time and again? Their fear of us."

"Their fear of God Most High," Hessina corrected him. "It is the God Above All who granted us these victories, and set His terror upon the soldiers of Ardis. Do not take our God for granted, as our ancestors the dragons did."

"We shouldn't doubt Him either," Belkos countered. "You think you know better than He does whether we're worthy of taking Ardis? Let our God judge our readiness. If He favors us, we can't lose."

"But if He doesn't favor our attack," Criton pointed out, "we're unlikely to get a second chance. If we assume that God Most High wants us to conquer the city and we're wrong, the Ardismen might easily take advantage and annihilate us entirely. Our God hasn't actually told us we ought to take Ardis, and we've been wrong about His wishes before. All Salemis said was that if we followed God Most High, we would be safe. But for that, we need to know where He's leading us."

"Where to, then?" Belkos said. "If not Ardis, then where?"

"To the Dragon Knight's Tomb," said Hessina. "We will pray for guidance in the holiest place we know, and camp at the base of the mountain. It is near enough to Ardis to show them our lack of fear, and defensible in battle should they choose to risk another confrontation. We can stay there until God Most High lends us His guidance."

Kana turned to Criton. "What say you?"

"I say she's right," Criton answered, standing up. "Now I need to go and speak with my wife."

"Will you follow our advice?" asked Endra. "Will you marry a daughter of the plains?"

"Or several?" Kana put in.

Criton sighed. "You can put together a list, if you like. Women whose marriage to me would satisfy everyone here. I don't promise I'll take any of them."

He went back to his own tent, where he found Goodweather asleep and Bandu pretending. She hadn't bothered to go get Delika back – the girl must have been asleep in Belkos' tent by now.

"Bandu," he said, putting a clawed hand on her shoulder.

"Don't talk to me," she snapped.

"I'm sorry," he said. "But that meeting was necessary, and you weren't helping."

"Don't talk," Bandu repeated. "I don't care."

"Don't stop talking to me over this," Criton said. "That's not going to help either of us."

Bandu said nothing.

"Bandu, you can't keep doing this to me."

Silence.

"They want me to take more wives," Criton said, "and I have half a mind to listen to them."

He'd expected that to make her turn around and look at him at least, but she only stiffened and kept her face turned away from him.

"It makes sense," he said. "If I do it, it'll signal to the rest of the Dragon Touched that the plainsmen aren't just allies, they're brothers. Our people will intermarry and we won't be a big conglomeration of allied clans with the Dragon Touched at the top. We'll be one people.

Bandu, are you listening? It makes sense, and the only thing stopping me from doing it is you. If you don't want me to take other wives, you have to say so. You have to talk to me."

Bandu did not turn. Why did she have to be so stubborn? They both knew that she hated the idea – if she had changed her mind, she'd have said so. Had she resigned herself to his doing whatever seemed right to him? Her body language didn't strike him as resigned.

Well then, it was her job to dissuade him! He wasn't going to spend the night arguing with himself.

"Fine," he said, "we'll talk about it in the morning, when you're ready to act like a civilized person."

He hated going to bed angry, but there was nothing for it. He lay down beside her, facing the opposite way, and went to sleep.

When he awoke, Bandu was gone.

28

HUNTER

They stumbled back the way they had come, toward Karsanye and toward their enemies. Phaedra led them in a prayer to God Most High which she seemed to have composed herself. Hunter and Atella repeated the words after her as they shuffled down the road, trying not to collapse in their exhaustion. After a couple of times through, Phaedra realized that they could set her prayer to a tune that had once been popular at Tarphaean dances, so they sang it instead. Hunter was not very tuneful, and Atella was altogether unfamiliar with Tarphaean music, but Phaedra was very musical herself and her voice was clear and precise, so they soon caught on nonetheless.

Hunter kept his eyes down, watching his feet move, because whenever he looked up at the way ahead, his eyes blurred and he became dizzy. Even with his head down, he kept seeing things moving at the corners of his eyes, things that clearly weren't there. Stars shooting past. Giant insects. The disembodied heads of men he had killed.

He focused on the road.

If they were bound to be caught anyway, he wondered, why couldn't they just go to sleep? They'd had a sunny day or two now, and the dusty road looked like a perfectly good place for it. He imagined lying down with his head on that rock over there, and he nearly cried for wanting to. But no: if they slept, they could not pray, and they needed the prayers more.

Besides, the rock was shuddering. Gods, he needed to sleep.

If people had free will, as Phaedra was always insisting, then what good would all their prayers do them? God Most High could not force Mura to let them go, nor could He make them merciful. Could He? Maybe he could. Phaedra was very knowledgeable about these things, but she wasn't infallible.

Hunter chose to believe that the God of Dragons could do anything. It was easier to pray that way, and easier to stay awake too. To stay awake, and pray.

He thought he might be losing his mind.

Phaedra led them through repetition after repetition of her prayer-song, and Hunter began to grow impatient for Mura's men to meet them here already. What was taking them so long? They ought to get on with it, so he could see if God Most High would really answer their prayers. Did he dare to look up and try to spot them?

He chanced it, lifting his eyes from the road and willing them to focus, focus on *something*. He blinked. He stopped walking. He slapped himself in the face.

"Phaedra," he said.

Karsanye was standing before him, not half a mile away. He knew those ruined buildings. He slapped himself again, blinked again, again, again, again. His foolish eyes wouldn't stop seeing the city.

"Phaedra," he repeated, and the girl stopped and looked up.

"Karsanye?" she said. "How is that possible?"

Hunter fainted.

It was night-time when he awoke, still lying in the road. Phaedra was asleep beside him, with Atella softly snoring on her other side. They had apparently decided to sleep instead of rousing him, a decision for which he was extremely grateful. In fact, he thought he might sleep some more if he could – he had a bit of a headache still. He'd had the headache since sometime yesterday, he thought, but it had been so low on his list of problems that he'd barely noticed it before. Now he looked at the road ahead, saw that Karsanye was still there, and went back to sleep.

He woke to rain falling on his head. He groaned and sat up, wiping the mud off his cheeks and looking around. It looked to be dawn, though he couldn't be sure. The clouds were dark.

"How long have we slept?" Phaedra asked in a panicked voice. "We should go!"

"We should," Hunter agreed, rising to his feet and shielding his eyes as he gazed toward their ruined city. "How did we get here?"

"God Most High brought us here. He shortened our path somehow."

"I know, but how? Or why?"

Phaedra frowned. "I wish I knew. He's sent miracle after miracle, and I can't believe that it's because He wants me to learn magic. We must have something big we're supposed to do, He just hasn't revealed what it is yet. Let's find some shelter. Maybe Psander will know."

Psander. Would they truly be seeing her again, just a

few short months after her departure from this world? He had hoped never to see the world of fairies again, and with that hope had come the assumption that he would never see Psander either. Wrong and wrong.

They took shelter under a tree until the rain lessened from a downpour to a steady patter. If God Most High was protecting them here, would He be able to do so in the world of the elves? Bandu had said – and everyone who knew anything about it had agreed – that instead of a mesh between the heavens and the fairy world, God Most High had built a wall. The Gods no longer had influence in the world of the fairies. If Hunter and Phaedra found themselves endangered there, there would be no miracles to rescue them.

At least it sounded like Psander was still alive, for now. That had hardly been guaranteed when they had helped her transport Silent Hall to the other world.

"Well," Atella said, "whatever reason your God has saved us, I'm very grateful to Him. I'd make a sacrifice, if I had an animal."

"Pray to Him," Phaedra suggested. "It's not much, but it'll have to do."

The girl nodded. "What do I say?"

So Phaedra led them in a thanksgiving prayer and they resumed walking toward the city. Atella tried to follow her map, but she needn't have: Hunter and Phaedra both knew where they were going. The only remaining patch on Atella's map belonged to Criton.

Up until he had joined them on the last boat out of Tarphae, Criton had lived with his mother in the prison of his father's house. Criton's father had hidden him from the world by claiming that his wife was deathly ill, and that only he could tend to her. Knowing Criton's side of the story, it hadn't taken them long to guess who his father had been. And that meant they knew where he lived.

It had been a two-storey house, but the earthquake had reduced it to two walls and a pile of rubble. Phaedra steered them to the door that still stood in one of the two walls – Criton's mother Galanea was bound to be somewhere in that pile of rubble, undevoured by scavengers who could not shift stone. There would be more of her than bones, and they had no desire to find out how much more.

But the door was locked, a sad irony that did not escape Hunter. So they went around after all, picking their way over the wet stones and hoping to find something that would represent Criton's essence, besides the corpse of his mother. There were plenty of objects in the rubble, so they collected as many as they could – the leg of a chair, the remains of what might have been a tapestry, feathers from some pillow that must still be trapped beneath the stone. But once they were a few feet from the house, the last corner of Atella's map always came back to life. They hadn't yet found what they were looking for.

"I sure hope..." Phaedra said, and didn't finish. Hunter knew what she was thinking, even if Atella didn't.

"It'll be some object," Hunter insisted, in an attempt to reassure the both of them. "It has to be."

Atella raised a hand to stop them. "Do you hear that?"

Someone was whistling.

They scrambled to get behind one of the walls, praying that no one would find them. "Mura's ship is still at the docks," Phaedra whispered. "There must be some sailors around here."

They waited until they couldn't hear anything but their beating hearts, and then waited some more. When they felt the danger had passed, they left Atella as a lookout while they continued their search. That cut their manpower by a third, but at least Atella was still able to make runs back and forth away from the building to test each item they found. But every time she left them, the map came back to life.

The clouds passed, and the sun came out. Eventually Phaedra gave up her part in the search and sat down on the ragged edge of one of the walls, resting her uneven and aching legs. Hunter was left to pick through the rubble on his own.

"Try over there," Phaedra would say now and then, and Hunter didn't know if she had any special reason for indicating the spots she did, but he obeyed anyway.

He had just painstakingly freed a mangled pair of hearthside tongs when Atella called out to him.

"This is it!" she said. "You found it!"

Hunter dropped the tongs with an annoyed grunt – how many heavy stones had he had to lift to get the useless things out? – and stumbled his way over the wreckage to see what Atella was talking about. He couldn't even remember what the last item he'd given her had been.

Phaedra got there first. "Really?" she said.

It was a broken wooden bucket, with a metal handle bent and dangling from one side. A little rainwater had managed to collect at the bottom.

"The map stayed blank," Atella insisted. "See for yourself."

They walked twice as far from the house as usual, just to make sure. "If there's a story behind this," Phaedra said, "I don't know it."

"Well," said Hunter, "let's get out of here."

They left Karsanye for the forest, making sure to avoid the route that led to Bennan's farm.

"I wonder what the map would have chosen for us," Hunter said, "if we hadn't been here ourselves."

Phaedra pondered that silently, chewing on one of their soggy breads. It was late afternoon by now, and Hunter had lost track of how many days they had left before their window closed. For one thing, he didn't know how long they had slept on the road. It could have been sixteen hours or forty. Considering their state in the days before, he didn't want to assume that it was the lower number.

"Do you think we'll be able to find the place where I met you?" Atella asked. "Because I'm completely lost."

Hunter looked to Phaedra, who shook her head. "I've been hoping that God Most High will lead us there. The mill has to be somewhere northeast of here, but I don't know how far west we'd gone before we met you. I wish Bandu were with us – she'd know."

Yes, Hunter thought ruefully, she would. Even on the continent, Bandu never failed to find whatever was needed at the time, be it food, water, or a safe path through the mountains. She probably knew the forests of Tarphae better than the wolves did.

Hunter had known that he would miss the others, but he hadn't realized how much. There were holes in his life where they belonged, just as there were holes for his parents and brother, and a hole for the man he had thought he would become. He had imagined once, vaguely, that the king's army would become a second, realer family the next time Tarphae went to war. That war had never come, but his need for its comradeship remained. He had grown to appreciate being one of five, but now even those five were dispersed. Phaedra alone was not enough.

"This way," Hunter said. "We should go north first

and see what we reach."

He was no tracker, but he had studied a map of Tarphae some years ago, back when the thought of being invaded had been exciting rather than horrifying. When he thought back to those times, studying the maps, he realized that he could still visualize all the little blue squiggles that represented rivers and streams. If they went north early enough, they were bound to meet the Sennaroot river that ran past Mura's mill. From there, he might be able to retrace their steps.

They followed his instincts and his lead, and within an hour or two they found a little stream that ran northwest. They drank there, pondering their next move. Hunter was sure that this stream was too narrow to be the Sennaroot, especially after the morning's rains. It must be a tributary, in which case it should meet the river at some point. He thought if they came to the place where the rivers met, he'd know how to proceed from there.

So they crossed the stream and followed it westward as the clouds and rain returned, turning the whole world gray. The stream did meet a larger river not long thereafter, much to Hunter's relief. If memory served – and if this was indeed the Sennaroot – there would be a ford not too far upriver. They changed directions again.

As they walked, Phaedra asked Atella what interactions the people of Silent Hall had had with the elves.

"They're horrible," Atella said with a shudder. "Their queen came to talk to Psander, and promised to leave us alone for ten years if we'd give her four 'breeding pairs.' Psander said they want to eat us. She said no to the queen, but every week or two she comes back with her guards and asks again. We didn't want to go outside after the first time she came, but we had to cut down the trees and try to farm or we'd have had nothing to eat.

Psander made a ward that tells us when the elves are close, so we run back in when they're coming."

"They have a queen?" Hunter asked. "We met a prince, but I didn't know they had a queen."

"I don't know anything about a prince. The queen is so frightening I can't even say, and her guards are just as bad. They have no tongues, and they clack at you."

"Did Psander let them in?" Phaedra asked, horrified.

"No, I saw them from the walls. Everyone told me not to climb up there and look, but I thought I wasn't afraid."

Hunter shook his head. "The elves are worth fearing."

"I know that well enough now. You don't have to tell me."

They spent that night in the forest, which was somehow infinitely less comfortable than the road had been the night before. Hunter suspected that this had very little to do with the wet ground and much more to do with their better-rested state before they went to sleep this time. Whatever the reason, Hunter awoke cold, wet, and sore. His neck was stiff, his right arm numb from having been used as a pillow, and when he tried to rise, he found that one of his feet was still asleep. It tingled for nearly a minute after he got up, and hurt whenever he stepped on it.

The others followed his lead for the rest of the day, and for the entire afternoon he felt that they were maddeningly close to the spot they were looking for. He had brought them as far as his memory for maps could take him, but that still wasn't enough to take them the rest of the way. At best, he had narrowed down their location to somewhere within two or three square miles of where they wanted to be. He missed Bandu even more.

Phaedra went back to praying, and Hunter began to wonder whether she might wear Criton's God out with all these requests for successively smaller things. God Most High had shortened their path to Karsanye and thus allowed them to evade their pursuers – could He be bothered to help with this last insignificant task, which any competent woodsman would have been able to figure out on his own?

On the other hand, why shouldn't He? If God Most High had taken them this far, how strange would it be for Him to abandon them right before they could reach their goal?

Hunter didn't ask Atella any more about Psander's dealings with the fairies, but that did not stop him from thinking about them. He had felt guilty knowing that the islanders' salvation from the armies of Magor and Mayar had come at the cost of exposing Psander and the villagers to a world full of child-eating demons – Auntie Gava's term for the elves had been a good one. But he had had the comfort, at least, of not being forced to think about it terribly often while he and Phaedra were busy following her quest for magic. Now he had to face the reality of what they had done to Psander and her villagers, and it was horrifying.

He wished he could believe that Psander knew what she was doing; that she could stand up to the elves and win; that she could protect herself and those she had come with. From what he'd heard so far, it seemed highly unlikely. The very fact that Psander was relying on Hunter and his friends as magical ingredients for her wards was damning. After all, it wasn't as if the islanders had actually *defeated* the elves – their greatest success had been in running away. If Psander was building her wards on the strength of such questionable victories, she must

be desperate. An arrow from Narky's life; a bucket from
Criton's; a handful of dirt to represent Bandu – these
were not the stuff of powerful magic. For the Gods' sake,
Psander would be getting Hunter and Phaedra in the
flesh, and it *still* wasn't worth much of anything.

"When did Psander tell you she was a woman?"
Phaedra asked suddenly.

"The day after we arrived," Atella said. "That was a
shock to everyone. It sounds stupid, but we all felt safer
when we thought she was a man."

"Well," Phaedra said, and then cut herself short. She
had been shaking her head, but now she stopped. "Yes,"
she said. "That *is* stupid."

There was silence for a time, a silence Hunter did not
understand. He had the sense of a second conversation
occurring outside of his hearing, a conversation in which
somehow Phaedra's insulting words were not rude
but complimentary, encouraging. Such was Phaedra's
expression, anyway.

They kept walking, turning whenever Hunter thought
they had gone too far in one direction. At this point they
were not so much on their way somewhere as they were
attempting to find a place that looked familiar.

They still hadn't found such a place by nightfall, when
the cooler air brought forth a stagnant mist that rose
up from the ground and made any further navigation
impossible. So they huddled together, trying and failing
to find a comfortable position to sleep in. Just as Hunter
finally began to drift off, his back against a tree, the wind
picked up and roused him halfway with its cool touch on
his cheek. He opened his eyes and yawned.

The wind was doing something very strange up ahead,
swirling the mist round and round in an ever-growing
spiral. Hunter scrambled to his feet. He knew what an

entrance to the elves' world looked like.

"Get up!" he cried to the other two. "We're here – we found it after all."

The girls got up hurriedly, Atella grabbing her satchel as she rose to her feet. Together, the three of them walked into the swirling mists. Psander awaited.

29

GENERAL MAGERION

The word of Xytos' defeat shook Ardis to its foundations. How could a city famous for its warriors be losing to an enemy that had appeared so completely out of nowhere? First a dragon and now the Dragon Touched were proving that the greatest warriors in the world could not stand against them, that all talk of their extinction had been very premature. It was shocking. How short a time ago had Magor's city been paramount in the world, its people respected and its army feared? One moment, High Priest Bestillos had been like a demigod, conquering every city that resisted or denied Ardisian might. Now he was gone, and it seemed as if Magor had gone with him.

What good was a leader like Magerion against a reality like that? What chance did his city have, with the Dragon Touched defeating their armies and the worshippers of Ravennis trying to devour them from within? Perhaps it was time to prioritize his enemies differently. He had worked for nearly two months to prevent Ravennis from expanding on His foothold in the city, but he did not fear Ravennis the way he feared God Most High. He had spent his youth in an Ardis ruled by the latter, and he did not mean to go back.

Magerion had succeeded so far in keeping Ravennis and His death cult at bay – that much, at least, he had accomplished. But even if the worshippers of Ravennis did not respond to Xytos' defeat with jubilation – after all, it was their brothers too who were dying in these battles – the Dragon Touched were nonetheless strengthening their hand. How long until revolution swept Ardis? How long until the Great Temple of Magor fell?

Magerion had no intention of dying in a second purge. His family, his clan, had risen to a place of prominence in the city on the strength of his leadership, and he would not let them down. It was time to switch sides.

The cult of Ravennis could not afford to turn down the support of a man like Magerion. He could bring them an aura of legitimacy and the allegiance of a powerful clan – he would be indispensable. So what if he had spent weeks now slaughtering their worshippers in the most public and gruesome ways he could devise? Their God was a sneaky one – He would see Magerion's sudden change of heart as a major coup, regardless of its motives. The only question was how to engineer this change of heart in such a way as to deliver the city to him in one clean stroke.

The priests of Magor had to be gotten rid of, that much was a certainty. But would Elkinar then rise from His slumber and make a play for God of Ardis? It was possible. What Magerion needed to avoid was a power vacuum, a moment when the fate of Ardis was unclear. He needed to make sure that none of the other generals survived the new order to take sides in a conflict between Elkinar and Ravennis.

He wanted to get them together somehow, to gather Magor's priests and the Council of Generals in the same place, where a surprise attack by his loyalists could wipe them all out at once. But how best to arrange such a thing?

It was his scouts who brought him the solution. Narky the Black had escaped to Anardis and was now spreading the message of his cult to the people of that city, where once again Elkinar's priests seemed to have taken a stance of neutrality. Perhaps they had learned from Magerion's example that killing the Ravennis worshippers did not always have the desired effect. Or maybe their God was secretly dead, and no one had told them.

In any case, Narky was the key. The capture of the young high priest of Ravennis could draw both the generals and the priests of Magor to a meeting, and the black priest could bless Magerion once he'd disposed of them. It would be perfect.

But first he needed to capture Narky, and that might not be so simple. With Bestillos gone, the people of Anardis could not be counted upon to capitulate to an Ardisian general who had no army to back up his demands. A hundred men would not do for that purpose – but perhaps the priests of Elkinar could help him. They might be officially neutral, but they stood to gain a lot from Magor's collapse, unless the cult of Ravennis could co-opt the Wilderness God's following. They had every incentive to get rid of Black Narky.

But how to get a message to them without tipping him off? If Narky discovered that Magerion and the priests of Elkinar were in communication with each other, he was liable to run off and disappear again. Conversely, if Magerion revealed that he was seeking Narky's aid and not his elimination, word was bound to get back to Ardis long before he was ready for it. It was far too risky a thing to be so open about. This had to be very delicately done.

In the end he settled on his niece, who was a great devotee of Elkinar and very friendly with His Ardisian priests. She would travel to Anardis as a pilgrim and deliver the high priestess of Elkinar a message: Magerion would be coming to town in another week with a hundred men, so that he could take the pesky Narky away from their city and bring him to justice. He would be much obliged if the priests of Elkinar would send the boy out to him when he arrived.

In the meantime, he informed General Stellys of his plan to capture the high priest of Ravennis. "Why do you bother?" Stellys asked. "You executed their first leader, and dozens after her, and what good has that done you? What good has it even done Magor? The cult hasn't died – if anything, it's grown stronger. Why not just leave them alone?"

"And pretend that that would make them go away?" Magerion retorted. "Black Narky is more than just their latest leader, Stellys; he's the man who killed Bestillos. He's their proof that their God survived Magor's victory at Laarna and came out the stronger for it. A public execution of Narky would do more than humiliate the cult of Ravennis – it would unravel them."

"So you say. I say they'll just find another leader. These people lost their army, their city, and their famous Oracle. They saw their God's sacred birds fall dead from the sky, and they still insist their God is greater than the one that killed Him. *Nothing* can convince people like that, Magerion. No matter what you do to them, they'll find a way to call it a victory."

Magerion twisted his mouth to conceal the smile that was trying to creep onto it. "We'll see."

When he left the city, his hundred men with him, he

had still told no one of his true intentions. He informed his men on their third night outside Ardis. They were shocked at first, but eventually they fell in line. Who cared if they had been slaughtering cultists yesterday, so long as Ravennis accepted their conversions and rejoiced at their support? Human life was cheap to the Gods, and to Magerion's loyalists, it didn't honestly matter which God ruled the city so long as He ruled through Magerion. For with the other generals gone, Magerion would be the sole ruler – the new king of Ardis. His clansmen would be royalty, his loyalists favored in all things. Who among them could object to that?

When Magerion was king and Ravennis ascendant, Ardis would again be strong enough to turn its attention outward, to the defeat of the Dragon Touched. Ravennis could unify the city as a weakened Magor had failed to, and then Ardis could face its enemies with the backing of a rising God rather than a declining one. With Magerion's leadership, his city could make this transition without wasting its manpower or resources on a prolonged civil war. His Ardis would be stronger than the one that had purged itself of the Dragon Touched so many years ago.

When they arrived at Anardis, Black Narky was waiting for them. He was standing outside the gate with his wife and a crowd of followers, and as Magerion's army approached, he parted with the crowd and came forward to meet them.

Magerion did a quick reassessment of the situation. He had more or less expected the priests of Elkinar to deliver the man to him in chains, yet here he was, walking toward the men of Ardis of his own volition. Had his God already told him of Magerion's plans? The general had thought that he was using Ravennis and His cult to his own ends, but perhaps he had it backwards.

Perhaps he was a tool of the Gods after all.

But no, Ravennis had not told Narky what to expect. When the two met face to face, the young man struck him as barely holding in his terror. "You came here for me," he said. "Well, here I am."

"Yes," Magerion agreed. "Here you are."

Black Narky was much younger than Magerion had expected, and shorter than he had remembered. But then, he had only seen him the once, from a distance. In person, the High Priest of Ravennis was an average-sized teenager, neither particularly impressive physically nor wise beyond his years in any obvious way. Magerion had to remind himself that it was this boy who had killed Bestillos and this boy too who had slain the Boar of Hagardis. There was clearly more to him than met the eye.

Speaking of eyes, from what Magerion had heard, nobody knew how Narky had lost his left one. The rumor he'd heard most often was that Narky had given it to his God in exchange for wisdom. Up close, Magerion could see what nonsense that was. He could tell a scar from a blade when he saw one: that eye had been slashed by some enemy, not sacrificed to a God. It had been burned too – it looked a mess. But it was not so recent a scar that Narky could have lost it in the fight against Bestillos. It had been healing for a few months longer than that, Magerion thought.

Narky was clearly uncomfortable with the way Magerion was looking at him, sizing him up. Magerion let it stay that way for a little while, savoring the feeling of power that came from intimidating a high priest. He and Narky would be partners, but he now knew that they would not be equal partners. That was a pleasant surprise.

"Well?" Narky said at last. "Are we going to Ardis, or…?"

"We are," Magerion assured him. "And I thank you for coming out of Anardis on your own, and not wasting my time. Is this your wife?"

The girl nodded. "Yes, general. My name is Ptera."

"You moved quickly," Magerion noted. "Did you smuggle him out of Ardis as a wedding gift?"

Ptera's lips tightened, but Narky said, "More or less."

Some of Magerion's men grinned at this, and his son Atlon actually laughed. Mageris, the younger of Magerion's sons, did not. He had admired the late high priest of Magor greatly, and had once been given the honor of tracking the Tarphaean islanders alongside his idol. Mageris would obey his father, but Magerion knew it would be a long time before he would forgive him for betraying Bestillos' legacy. Among his men, his own son was the least happy about his new alliance.

Well, Mageris would have to get over it. Bestillos was dead, and the Tarphaeans were clearly favored by the Gods. Of the forces threatening Ardis, both were led by islanders – the cult of Ravennis by Narky, and the Dragon Touched by his erstwhile companion, whom the people called the Black Dragon. Perhaps Narky would have some insight on how to defeat his former friend.

Magerion waited until evening to tell Narky of his intentions. Let the boy think he was a prisoner. Let him think he would be martyred as the Oracle had been. The memory of this moment might keep him from overstepping himself later.

When the camp was set and a fire burning, Magerion called Narky over in front of his men and told him he was needed. "I have a task for you, before we arrive in Ardis."

Narky gulped visibly. "Yeah?"

"Yes. My men and I haven't known your God except through slaughtering His followers, but that will not do now. We will soon be bringing you before the priests of Magor and the full Council of Generals, and we must be better prepared for the task ahead of us. You can help us with that."

"I can?"

"You can. I have had a vision, a vision that I need you to help me fulfill. These hundred men are my closest kin and most faithful friends. All are loyal to me and will do as I tell them. I want you to teach us about Ravennis, and convert us to the worship of your God."

The boy's jaw dropped. For the first time in what felt like ages, Magerion laughed.

30
VELLA

Vella spent much of that night crying. It was the terror, the terror and the relief. She had opened up her heart in a way that she had never done before – opened up her heart, and endangered her life.

What would her husband do to her if he learned of her desires? He would probably kill her. Even with Vella's lineage, nobody would stop him.

She hoped Bandu knew not to tell a soul. She was unpredictable – it was part of what made her so enchanting. It always felt as if she could see through Vella, as if she could look into her and *see*. But of course, she hadn't known. She hadn't known, or she wouldn't have asked.

Would she? Vella never knew what was going on in Bandu's head. Maybe she had known, but wanted Vella to admit it out loud.

Oh, Vella didn't know. All she knew was that she had finally told someone, and she had told the only person who mattered. Her sobs were sobs of happiness. Happiness. And fear.

She was saved, for now, by her husband's indifference.

Pilos didn't even ask why she was crying, he just lay down and snapped at her to shut up and go to sleep. She tried and failed,

but he didn't press the issue, just grunted his annoyance and took his own advice. An hour later, Vella was still crying.

What did Bandu think of her? She desperately wanted to know, and to ask Bandu if she felt the same way, but she was too afraid. What if Bandu rejected her? What if she didn't even understand? One could never be sure from the way she talked. Sometimes it seemed like she was simply letting people's words wash over her unexamined, while at other times she seemed to understand a good deal more than had even been said.

Vella was too afraid to go back and talk to her. She felt like a coward and a fool, and she tried telling herself that she was just going to go walk beside Bandu while they traveled southward, maybe offer to hold Goodweather for a bit – but her courage always failed her.

It would have been all right had her life been otherwise bearable, but it wasn't. She and Pilos had consummated their marriage last year, but hadn't made love since – had never really made love. There was no love between them, and never had been. She resented his treatment, and he seemed to resent her very existence. If he had fallen in love with someone else – and perhaps he had – then she would hardly have felt betrayed, since he had never loved her to begin with. But not everyone felt that way, and Pilos in particular did not do well with humiliation. She hoped, for her own sake, that he never found out.

So she didn't go to see Bandu, didn't play with Goodweather or change her, didn't walk beside them as they moved south toward Ardis. And she lived a week of utter misery.

Then one night she awoke with Bandu kneeling beside her. Vella had slept in her clothes, it being a chilly night, and she stumbled out of the tent after Bandu as hurriedly and quietly as she could. Pilos turned over, but did not wake.

"What are you doing?" she whispered, suddenly realizing that Bandu had Goodweather strapped to her back, atop a traveling pack. Oh God. "Are you leaving? Are you here to say goodbye?"

"No," Bandu whispered back. "I don't say goodbye. I want you to go too."

Vella gasped. Her heart was beating so fast it was starting to feel irregular. It was actually hurting her chest. "You want me to come with you? Where? Who else is going?"

"Only Goodweather."

"But where are you going? Bandu, we can't just—"

Bandu caught Vella's head with both hands and kissed her, longer than it took to make her point. "Just come."

Vella followed Bandu out of the camp, her head in a blur. There was a watch, but the guards didn't seem to notice them as they left the tents behind. The moon was high – it couldn't have been much past midnight. They walked and walked until Vella lost her sense of direction entirely, but Bandu seemed to know where she was going. They came to a stream, which Bandu began to ford before abruptly changing direction and following the current northward – it had to be northward, because Vella thought it must be the same stream that their camp had crossed yesterday evening. Why were they going north? She splashed after Bandu, but they soon turned again – was it eastward?

"Bandu, where are we going?"

"Away."

"Away to where?"

Bandu didn't answer, and on they went. How long had they been walking? The moon was a good deal lower than it had been when they started out.

Vella repeated her question. "Away to where?"

"Away from Criton. He doesn't follow us here. He can't smell magic like I can, and this is the wrong way for him."

"But why? Why are you leaving him? Why take me with you?"

Bandu stared into her eyes in the moonlight. "I need your help. And I like you."

The second part sounded like an afterthought, but Vella pushed that down. It was too late to turn back. She was lost now, the camp was nowhere in sight, and she had no story to tell her people if and when she did find them again. She was at Bandu's mercy, a thought that thrilled and terrified her in equal measure.

She had to believe that Bandu didn't just want her help with the baby. "You like me," she repeated.

Bandu nodded. "I can mate with you," she said. "I don't want Criton now."

The more Vella allowed herself to think, the more complicated this was getting. It wasn't just the baby, it was Criton too! Did Bandu really love her, or did she just want to punish Criton? Now the thrill was wearing off, and Vella was just terrified. What had she gotten herself into? Why had she followed Bandu?

Bandu kissed her again, but Vella pulled away. "You don't love me," she said, and her heart sank as she said it. She knew it was true.

Bandu shook her head. "I don't know you yet," she admitted. "You are so quiet."

"Then why did you bring me here?" Vella almost shouted at her. "Why are you doing this to me?"

"Maybe I don't know you now," Bandu answered, "but I like you. You like me. You want to be my mate, and I don't want Criton now, so this is good."

"No," Vella groaned, "no, this isn't good. You're angry at Criton, but you can always go back if you change your mind, because he loves you. My husband hates me, Bandu. If I go back now, he'll kill me."

"Criton wants other wives," Bandu said quietly. Goodweather stirred with a soft moan.

Vella bowed her head. "I'm sorry," she said. "But you didn't have to take me with you."

Bandu pulled a strap over her shoulder and began to take Goodweather off her back. "I don't have to," she agreed. "I *want* to. If your husband hates you, why you want to stay? You don't. You are not happy there. That's why you come with me."

She sat down with Goodweather and began to nurse her. Vella sat across from them, grateful to the earth for its stability. Dawn was breaking, and her world was falling apart. And what would replace it? Nothing real, it seemed. Nothing true.

"This isn't going to last," she said. "You're just going to go back to him when you're done with me."

Bandu shook her head. "Never. Criton is not a good mate."

"It doesn't matter. You'll go back."

Bandu made a frustrated sound. "Why nobody listens to me? I don't go back, Vella. You want me to say again? I don't go back!"

She laid Goodweather's wrappings on the ground and gently lowered the baby onto them. Goodweather had gone back to sleep.

"You don't even know me," Vella said. "You brought me out here to be your lover, and you don't even know me."

"So tell me about you," Bandu said. She motioned the ground next to her.

Against her better judgment, Vella joined her. She felt suddenly afraid.

"Tell me about you," Bandu repeated, but what could Vella say? Where could she start? The whole of her life seemed insignificant now, and when she tried to think of something to tell Bandu, she couldn't think of anything worth mentioning. She had been with her parents, and then she had been with Pilos. Her childhood had been pleasant, and she loved her parents, but she also resented them for having chosen Pilos, and besides, she didn't want to talk about her parents or her husband, she wanted to talk about herself! But what was there to say?

Bandu kissed her again, so tenderly it made Vella weak. "Don't be afraid," she said, but Vella had no choice in the matter.

The sun rose and they lay down together, exhausted from their walk but nowhere near sleep. Vella tried to let go of her fears and live in the beautiful moment, the moment that she had not even dared to imagine. They kissed and kissed, and then Bandu's hand found her and Vella gasped, but didn't stop her. Bandu looked into her eyes the whole time, unashamed of what they were doing and confident, always confident in her power over Vella.

It was too much, too strong. Vella's head snapped back and she shouted, the fire escaping from her lungs and out into the world. Each cry sent another burst of flames up toward the trees, but Bandu didn't stop until

one of those cries awoke Goodweather. Then she rose
and changed the baby's clothes, lifted Goodweather
with one arm, and went back to the stream to do the
washing. Vella lay on the ground waiting for them to
return, drifting in and out of sleep, feeling more relaxed
than she could ever remember. Then Bandu came back
with Goodweather strapped to her chest and the washed
clothes hanging from a stick, and told her they had to go.

Vella sat up slowly, languidly, savoring her last
moments of delicious relaxation. "When are *you* going to
sleep?" she asked.

"Later."

They walked on, Vella following meekly, not knowing
what destination Bandu had in mind. What sort of town
would be welcoming to the three of them? Did such a
place exist?

Bandu seemed confident that she knew where she
was going, so Vella chose to trust her. Besides, the farther
they walked, the greater the distance between them and
Criton.

After most of a day, they reached a town whose men
had pledged themselves to the Dragon Touched. Vella
told them that she and Bandu had been sent there to rest,
since the army's pace was too much for them, and she
was relieved when their hosts acccpted this explanation
without too much suspicion. All the men of fighting
agc were gone, so there was more than enough room
for Vella and Bandu. They thanked their hosts for their
generosity and lay down in comfort, if not in privacy.

Bandu fell asleep before Vella did, Goodweather
cradled in her arms. Vella watched them sleep, her
heart aching. Could this last? She wanted to believe
that Bandu would never go back to him. She wanted to
believe that the two of them could make a life together,

that they could care for each other and for Bandu's child without the angry world tearing them apart. Oh, how she wanted to believe!

31
NARKY

Narky could hardly believe his good fortune. Magerion was not here to kill him, to torture him to death, even to humiliate him! Ravennis was executing yet another of His maneuvers, and it was glorious.

Most of Magerion's men were very amenable to being taught about Ravennis. They learned His ways the same way they might have learned to use a new weapon – with a sort of professional, utilitarian engagement. They asked about the underworld – everyone always did – but they were more focused on the here-and-now. How would their everyday practices have to change in order to accommodate Ravennis instead of Magor? What animals did Ravennis favor in sacrifice?

Narky told them that they could continue sacrificing the same animals as before, so long as they left the eyes for Ravennis. He had grown more comfortable with inventing new practices during his time in Anardis. Nobody would be judging him, he had learned, for the ways in which his teachings might differ from the old Laarnan practices. He was the high priest of Ravennis, and it was assumed that Ravennis spoke through him. If

the men of Laarna had worshipped their God differently,
perhaps they were the ones who had been wrong. They
were all gone now, after all.

Magerion was just as engaged as his men were,
listening attentively and asking the occasional question
himself. This mass conversion may have been a power-
play on his part, but he was still taking it seriously. He had
apparently decided that Magor's defeat was inevitable,
and he meant to be on the winning side. While Magerion
the man frightened him, Narky was quite sympathetic to
this line of thinking.

Narky was relieved that his martyrdom no longer
seemed to be a major part of Ravennis' plans, but he
was still nervous about the days to come. The plan was
for him to remain a prisoner right up until the moment
when Magerion and his men turned on their former
leaders. What if their coup failed? What if it succeeded,
but Narky was killed in the struggle? Would Ptera take
up the mantle of high priestess?

It wasn't such a bad thought. Ptera might not have
the reputation that Narky had, but she knew as much
about Ravennis as anyone, and in some ways her faith
was much stronger than Narky's. She certainly never
questioned that Ravennis was a good and moral God,
whereas Narky had his doubts on that front. She would
make a fine high priestess, if it came to that.

He hoped it wouldn't. Ravennis might protect him
in the land of the dead, but Narky preferred to take his
sweet time getting there.

As they neared Ardis, word got out that Narky had
been captured, and people began meeting them on
the road to cheer Magerion or jeer at Narky, or else
just to stare. Narky hated those last ones the most – he
wished he knew what they were thinking. Were they

worshippers of Ravennis, watching despairingly as their high priest returned to Ardis in captivity? Were they Magor worshippers, come to watch their God's triumph but suddenly struck with suspicion? Or maybe they were all witless fools, gathering to gawk at the soldiers and captives just for the spectacle of the thing. Either way, he hated their presence.

When they arrived in Ardis a few days later, an enormous crowd was waiting for them. Magerion had sent messengers ahead to tell of Narky's capture, and people of all ages lined the streets to watch the procession go by. Narky and Ptera had been put in chains for the occasion, and walked with at least three spears pointed at each of them. This was all for show according to Magerion, but Narky was still keenly aware of his vulnerability. The general's son, Mageris, was one of those with a spear, and it was terrifying to realize that he had the power to kill Narky quite suddenly should he choose to. By the look of him, he was strongly considering it.

Narky had recognized Mageris by his voice as one of the men who had been waiting for the islanders when they got back from their first conversation with Salemis. His father might be a shrewd and ambitious man, a worshipper of whichever God was likeliest to increase his power, but Mageris was a Bestillos loyalist. Narky didn't trust him.

They reached the Great Temple of Magor, where the priests and the other members of the Council of Generals were waiting for them. The crowd cheered them on as Narky and Ptera were marched inside. The bulk of Magerion's men stayed outside to control the crowd while the general, his sons, and the others who shared the duty of guarding the prisoners entered the temple.

The Great Temple of Magor was a magnificent

building, its walls covered in murals and painted friezes depicting victories for the God and His city over various enemies. Here, a band of soldiers led a jackal-headed Goddess in chains toward the throne of the Boar God. There, a young High Priest Bestillos rammed his spear through the chest of a mounted Dragon Touched warrior. Narky even spotted a corner where someone had recently added a scene of Laarna's destruction, with Bestillos standing before the twin pillars at the entrance to the Temple of Ravennis, a flayed Oracle lashed to each. Above this scene, the boar of Magor trampled on a desperate-looking crow, its wings spread as if in an attempt to escape.

If everything went the way it was supposed to, Narky would have the privilege of watching these works of art destroyed. He would have that boar repainted as a corpse, with its eyes pecked out and the raven perched triumphantly on its back. He would tear down Magor's statue at the temple's center, behind the altar, and... and first he had to survive the afternoon.

The soldiers forced Narky and Ptera to their knees as a group of men came forward to meet them. These were the same five priests of Magor that Narky remembered from the Graceful Servant's confrontation, and three other men who must have been members of the city's Council of Generals. These were dressed formally, their armor polished and their swords hanging from their belts in ornate decorative scabbards. A boy stood behind them, near the altar, holding the priests' barbed spears.

"Welcome back, General Magerion," said Magor's high priest, "and congratulations on your capture of Narky the Black. His sacrifice will be holiest to Magor, and send a message to his brother the Black Dragon that there is no escaping Ardisian might."

"Perhaps," said one of the generals, turning a critical eye on the two who stood beside him. "But if we wanted to send that message to the Dragon Touched, defeating them in battle would have worked better."

"Quiet, Stellys," said the older of the two. "You have not fought the Dragon Touched yourself, nor have you worked to suppress the cult of Ravennis as Magerion has done."

"You let the Black Dragon rout you, Xytos. I'd call that worse than doing nothing. And Choerus didn't even engage with our enemy before fleeing homeward."

"Which is why Ardis still stands," the one called Choerus retorted. "With Xytos' army routed and the Dragon Touched between me and our home, our enemies could have easily stormed the city and burned you alive if I hadn't outmaneuvered them and made it here first. Only fools criticize without thinking."

High Priest Melikon ended their quarrel with a clap of his hands. "Save your arguments for later," he scolded. "Ardis faces enemies both within and without. Today marks our victory against the former – defeat of the latter is bound to follow. The day is Magerion's."

"Thank you," Magerion said. "I believe this day is getting better and better."

Melikon nodded. "Today marks the end of the death cult of Ravennis. With them no longer weakening our people from within, Magor will once again bless His city with victory. The strength of Ardis will be restored."

"No," Magerion said, "not restored. Renewed. Ardis can never be what it once was. It must become something new and stronger."

Every muscle in Narky's body tensed. It was coming. Soon.

"I don't follow you."

"Then let me show you," Magerion answered, and with a sudden leap forward he thrust his spear straight through Melikon's stomach. The other generals cried out and drew their swords, but Magerion's retainers skewered all three of them before they could do much more than that. The remaining priests of Magor scrambled to retrieve their spears from the boy by the altar, but Atlon hurled his spear into one of their backs while Magerion drew his own short sword and whistled for his men outside to join them. The priests of Magor and their young assistant were quickly surrounded and dispatched.

Narky looked over to find that Ptera had squeezed her eyes tightly shut. Narky would have loved to do the same, but his sense of self-preservation wouldn't let him. What if one of Magerion's men turned on him? What if he had to dodge a stray spear thrust or worse, an intentional one? So he watched the horror that unfolded before him and sighed in relief when all of Magerion's former colleagues were dead.

When it was over, Atlon helped Narky to his feet and untied his hands while another of Magerion's men did the same for Ptera. Magerion turned toward them. "Are you ready?"

Narky shook his head. High Priest Melikon was staring at him, clutching at the spear that had gone through his belly and was poking out the other side. He was trying to say something.

Narky approached him warily – he wouldn't have put it past the man to have hidden a knife in his palm on the off chance Narky got close enough for a kill.

"It's happened," Melikon gasped, barely audible over the sounds of the agitated crowd outside the temple.

"It has," Narky agreed.

"Just like she showed me," Melikon continued, his voice getting weaker with each word. "Only she never showed me who. I only saw the spear, and felt... betrayed... surprised..."

"You should have expected it, then," Narky said. "The Graceful Servant showed you the death Ravennis meant for you, and you didn't even guard against it? You're an idiot. I'd have spent the rest of my life suspecting *everyone*."

Melikon blinked and looked up into his eyes. "I thought if I killed her... a prophecy is only..."

Narky nodded. "A prophecy is just a God's boast, sure. But you didn't kill Ravennis, you killed His servant. That's not the same thing. Not even close."

Melikon closed his eyes and said no more, waiting for death to take him. Narky turned away.

They stepped out into the sunlight, where the crowd stared at them all in shock. They had heard the screams, but the soldiers outside the temple had held them at bay until it was all over. Now they just stood, waiting for someone to explain away the sudden horror.

Magerion raised a bloodstained hand. "Magor has fallen," he announced, "defeated by Ravennis, Keeper of Fates and God of the Underworld. The senior priests of Magor are all dead, beside our failed leaders Xytos, Choerus, and Stellys. A new age is upon us: the age of Ravennis. All will worship Him or be put to the sword."

There were gasps, and muttered exclamations, but nobody was brave enough to object aloud. Magerion turned to his men. "Round up the families of the slain generals and tell them that they can pledge their loyalty to me and be named nobles, or refuse and be slaughtered. Narky, as high priest, I leave the conversion of the city in your hands. Wherever a worshipper of Magor refuses to give up the old religion, don't hesitate to have him slain. Tell me or my men, or do it yourself – I don't care, so long as the city unites under Ravennis and under me."

Narky nodded, and the old general looked at the crowd and smiled.

"So begins my reign," he said, aloud but clearly to himself. "Ardis has a king once more."

32

DESSA

Dessa couldn't believe Bandu and Vella had left her behind. Why, why would they have gone off together and not taken her too? They hadn't even told her that they were going – they'd just disappeared one night without warning, leaving Dessa to cope all by herself. How could they?

She'd thought Bandu was so wonderful. She'd ignored Grandma's warnings, and why shouldn't she? Grandma had said Bandu and Criton would take Dessa's father away, not her best friend!

Nobody knew where they'd gone – not Criton, not Vella's parents, not Pilos or his awful parents. Dessa kept trying to think back to what had happened over the last few weeks, what warning signs she might have missed, but there was nothing. Vella hadn't even visited Bandu in days and days! Could they have planned this so far in advance?

No, she was sure they hadn't. Vella knew that Dessa could keep a secret – if she and Bandu had been planning to leave together, she'd have said something. It was comforting to think so, anyway. Maybe it had been a sudden emergency, and they'd had to hurry off without any time to tell Dessa about it. That would have been almost excusable. Almost.

So what could she do now? Who was left for her to care about, now that the two people she admired most were both gone? That little girl Delika didn't even care. Mother suggested that Dessa talk to Malkon about it, since he was sure to be missing his sister too, but that was such a grown-up way of looking at things. Having 'things in common' didn't help anything, it was just an excuse to try to shove the two of them together. Dessa had just lost her two favorite girls – she didn't want to talk to some boy about it.

Instead, she avoided talking to anyone. Mother found that distressing, but she didn't push Dessa too hard because she also had Grandma to worry about. Grandma was getting worse and worse – she sometimes thought that rocks were mushrooms and tried to eat them, or else she would try to leave their tent without being properly dressed. Now when Mother said Grandma "wasn't herself," Dessa believed her.

She was still herself *sometimes*, though. Sometimes she would look at Dessa with such clarity and speak with such sense and purpose that it was hard to believe her mind was really going, that she wasn't just pretending the rest of the time.

"I know I'm going mad," she said once, when Mother and Father were busy and Dessa was alone with her. "I can feel it slipping away, Dessa. It's horrible, just horrible. I'm sorry I can't be like I was. Once…"

She broke off, sobbing. "I'm sorry."

Dessa gingerly patted her on the back. That only made Grandma cry harder, but Dessa didn't know what else to do, so she kept going. "You'll be all right, Grandma," she said.

"No, I won't," Grandma insisted, wiping her eyes. "Don't lie to me, child. This never gets better, it only gets worse. I'll lose more and more until there's nothing left."

Dessa didn't know what to say to that. She had never considered what it would be like to go mad, and she hadn't realized that you could *know* you were going mad, hate that it was happening to you, and be unable to stop it. She suddenly felt bad for having hated Grandma before. Mother was right: it wasn't her fault.

"We'll take care of you, though," she said. "We won't let you eat rocks or anything."

"What?" said Grandma, looking up. "What rocks?"

"You try to eat rocks sometimes."

"I do not."

Dessa should have known better than to take the conversation in this direction. "Oh," she said. "You're right. I'm sorry, Grandma, that was a mistake."

Grandma smiled. "It's all right, child. We all make mistakes."

We sure do, Dessa thought.

She told Mother about their conversation, and Mother nodded sadly. "It's very hard for her," she said. "It's hard for all of us. I hope you'll be kind to her, Dessa, and don't take what she says sometimes to heart."

"I'll try," Dessa told her. "But Mother?"

"Yes?"

"Why does she hate Bandu and Criton so much?"

"I don't know, maybe they remind her of someone."

Dessa didn't think that was very likely. There weren't any other Dragon Touched who were dark like Criton, and she didn't believe there could be anyone in the world who was quite like Bandu. But then, there was no telling what was going on in Grandma's mind. She called Dessa 'Iona' sometimes, and at other times she thought that Mother was *her* mother. For all Dessa knew, maybe the Tarphaeans *did* remind her of someone – someone who was nothing like them.

But it was Grandma who had called Criton the Black Dragon, so she had to have recognized that his skin was darker than any of the other Dragon Touched. And the fact that she kept saying Criton would kill Father didn't have anything to do with her confused memories. That scared Dessa. What if Grandma was right? It was hard to believe – Father was so warm and solid, and he and Criton seemed to be the best of friends. But grown-ups could change quickly. There was a whole level to them, underneath the surface, that Dessa couldn't understand. So she worried.

She would have liked to pretend that Grandma was just confused again, that she was mixing Father up with Grandma, who really was dead. But then, she couldn't have been mixing up their deaths, because Grandpa had died peacefully in his sleep.

Still, Grandma *was* going mad. Maybe she had just dreamt something, and thought it was real. That seemed likely enough. Just so long as it was a nightmare and not a prophecy, it would be all right. And it *had* to be just a nightmare. Why would God Most High give a prophecy to a madwoman?

33

PARTHA

That feeling of slipping, slipping. For Partha, losing her mind wasn't a sudden snapping, it was a grueling ongoing process: an assault on her *Partha-ness* that raged on and on as she faltered and retreated, falling back from each position as it became impossible to hold. Her husband had been a soldier, a captain, so she thought of it in his terms. Her husband, her husband – oh God, what was his name? Belkos? Belkos! No, that wasn't right, that was someone else's husband. Shit!

At first she had thought it was simply her memories slipping away, but it was far worse than that. They were failing to form in the first place now, dying stillborn before she could catch hold of them and drag them into the light. This whole thing was like sleeping on a hill. Every day you woke up lower down than you remembered.

And it was infuriating, losing her mind. People thought she would do something crazy just because she couldn't catch it, whatever it was. Her mother watched her day and night, told her what to eat and what not to – she was a nuisance, really. Partha could take care of herself, she was a full grown woman, except... had she just called

Iona her mother? That was a mistake, a terrible mistake. She hoped she hadn't made it out loud. She didn't want Iona to catch on to the fact that something was wrong with her – there was no telling what would happen to her then.

Her eyesight was going too, along with her mind. Or not exactly her eyesight, since her eyes could still see, but her mindsight. The things she saw with her eyes made less sense to her now. She would say, "Careful, Iona! Don't step in the hole!" and Iona would turn to her and say, "It's not a hole, Grandma, it's my black wool coat. I took it off while we were putting the tent up." But Partha couldn't trust her, of course, because Iona was always lying. Here she was, lying again, because she had called Partha "Grandma" when Partha knew damn well that Iona was her daughter, the insolent girl.

But while her ability to see and understand faltered, she was receiving visions in its stead. That should have been a holy thing, except she thought she might be stealing them. Or maybe not stealing, that wasn't right – it was more as if she was standing on the wrong path, on *their* path, and intercepting them by mistake. Was that holy, or unholy?

She saw that devil, that Black Dragon, giving her little girl a mealy-mouthed apology for killing her Belkos. It was a fake apology, she knew. He didn't even mean it, the liar! And that witch, the She-wolf, she had scurried off into hiding somewhere, but she was the one responsible for it all. Partha could feel her presence *inside* the Black Dragon, influencing him, sustaining him.

That was the only true thing she knew, at least until it slipped away too. She was afraid it might if she didn't keep thinking about it. Sometimes the vision was blurry, the words indistinct, and all she could remember was that those two had betrayed her. They had killed her father, Belkos.

No! Damn her, that wasn't right either! But it was close, close enough. The point was that they had done it to her, either long ago, or later on. It was the betrayal that mattered. She had to sustain her fury, because someday it might be all that sustained *her*.

But more often than Partha was angry, she was frightened. There were times when the fear of losing herself pushed all other thoughts to the side and she wept out of sheer terror, unable to hold onto the parts of her that mattered – unable to even explain which parts they were. She clung to the notion of the Black Dragon's betrayal like a reed on the edge of a cliff, not because it was strong or even important, but because it was all she could reach. The fear of falling governed everything.

Sometimes she prayed for her God to take her before she could lose any more. She didn't know how old she was – seven, maybe? – but she knew she was old enough to die. They probably wouldn't even weep over her grave, just say, "Too bad about that girl Partha," and move on. They were all liars and false friends anyway.

This one here, this one who was pretending to be Partha's daughter – Partha knew better than to trust her. She might pretend that she was a dutiful daughter, just looking after her poor aging mother, but it was all a game. She was after something – was it her money? She had hidden Partha's real daughter away somewhere, and was trying to ingratiate herself.

"I know what you're really after," Partha told her. "You can't fool me."

Not-Iona sighed. "And what am I after, Mother?"

Partha didn't know for sure – it *might* have been the money, but it might also have been something else, so instead of answering, she repeated herself. "You know what you did. You can't fool me. You're not really her, you're one of *them*."

"One of who?"

"You know who."

It was morning, time for them to help her onto that horse of theirs; the horse they had stolen from the *real* Iona. Partha considered resisting, but then she decided it might be best to go along, to pretend that everything was fine. She didn't want to tip her hand too early.

She was tired of riding that damned horse day in and day out. Her arse was sore. They were trying to tire her out so that she'd give up and they could steal her money. She had gathered it up off the ground, but they had somehow changed it so that it all looked and felt like little rocks and pebbles. They wanted her to give up and abandon it so they could make off with it and turn it back into money afterwards. She was onto their tricks.

Now the little one was angry at her for some reason, giving her nasty looks as if Partha had done something to her. "Stop looking at me like that, you horrible little girl," Partha said to her. "What did I ever do to you?"

"You chased Bandu away," the girl said sullenly. "You were mean to her. Maybe that's why she left. I bet you're happy."

"Dessa!" her mother scolded. "How could you say such things to your grandmother? Apologize. Now."

"I'm sorry," Dessa mumbled, obviously not meaning it.

Was the She-wolf gone, then? Partha hadn't known. She hadn't known, and she actually *didn't* feel happy about it. She was sure it was a trick – the witch would stay away until Partha couldn't recognize her anymore, and then she would strike when Partha was defenseless against her. She knew that Partha's memory was failing, and she was taking advantage of it. Partha tried to resist, but she was already having trouble visualizing the girl. It was fiendish and underhanded, and it played on her weaknesses. If she forgot the She-wolf, forgot to hate her, what would remain?

Not much, she feared.

34
CRITON

It took him far too long to realize that Bandu had really left him, and by that time he had little hope of tracking her down. He spent over an hour wandering through the camp, insisting that she must simply be elsewhere – lingering with Iona while picking Delika up, or visiting Biva and her flock of sheep, or perhaps washing Goodweather's clothes somewhere nearby. But nobody could remember seeing her, and though he felt her presence when he came to the stream's edge, he could not tell in which direction she had gone.

What began as bewilderment quickly turned to panic. She was gone! She had left him! Would she ever come back?

The others could not understand his desperation. None of the Dragon Touched had liked Bandu except for Belkos' wife and daughter, and Kilion's daughter Vella. Speaking of which, Vella had disappeared too. It was Kilion, rather than his son-in-law, who discovered her absence and brought it to Criton's attention. Kilion looked absolutely sick about it; he was the only person who seemed to care almost as much as Criton did.

Where had they gone? Had they left together, or was there some other explanation for their simultaneous disappearance? Had one gone in chase of the other?

He questioned Belkos' daughter Dessa, who was friends with Vella, but she didn't know anything. Neither did little Delika, and worse, she seemed viciously glad to have Criton to herself. But he shouldn't get mad at Delika for that – she was so young, too young to understand or care that his heart was breaking. His panic meant nothing to her.

Criton wished Bandu hadn't taken a friend with her. He was increasingly sure that that was what she had done, and it worried him. If she had been alone with Goodweather, she might grow tired and lonely without Criton and come back to him. But like Phaedra, a woman friend would probably encourage her to stay away longer.

And he deserved it; that was the worst part. He had made a promise to Bandu that he would never take another wife, and then talked openly about breaking that promise for the sake of a political message – and, he had to admit, because he had secretly hoped that Bandu wouldn't mind the idea of his taking multiple wives. After all, he had thought to himself, the notion of exclusive marriage hadn't come naturally to her: it had taken Phaedra to explain the concept.

That secret hope had been quickly dashed, but he had still thought that she would argue, that she would force him to choose her above all others. He hadn't expected her to forfeit.

What was the matter with him? He didn't even *want* other wives, not really. It may be a good idea politically speaking, but there were other ways to encourage camaraderie between the Dragon Touched and the plainsfolk. And though the idea had intrigued him, he hadn't taken it all that seriously – and clearly not as seriously as Bandu had. Now he was miserable. He only really wanted Bandu, couldn't she see that? When would she return to him?

There was nothing he could do now to bring her back. He wanted to send out a search party, but he knew that if Bandu didn't want to be found, no search party would find her. Besides, Hessina and the elders wouldn't approve of his sending such a party. They didn't want her back. It was all he could do not to scream at them.

Bandu's absence only made them press harder for him to take new wives, but he put them off. The very thought made him sick now. It was the threat of his betrayal that had chased her away – if he followed through, he feared that she would never come back.

At least she knew how to find him. The Dragon Touched were hard to miss, and she knew where he was headed. That was all he had now, the hope that she would seek him out in a month or two and let him apologize to her for what he'd done. Until then, all he could do was to pretend everything was fine, to raise triumphant Delika as if she was his only daughter and to lead his people as if half his soul hadn't disappeared overnight.

He led his people back to the Dragon Knight's Tomb, just as Hessina had suggested, encountering little resistance on the way. The people fled before him, leaving their houses and farms for the protection of Ardis' walls. The army of Ardis seemed content for now to hide behind those walls as well, and the Dragon Touched reached Dragon Knight's Tomb without incident. There Hessina asked – or, rather, demanded – that Criton accompany her into the tomb alone. He had less energy for disagreement without Bandu at his side, so he left Delika with his cousin again despite all her protests and ascended the mountain at the old woman's side.

At first, Hessina didn't even talk to him. She knelt by the Dragon Knight's sarcophagus, praying silently to herself. Criton tried to do the same, closing his eyes and trying to find the words for a prayer. But the only prayer he could think of was *please send Bandu back to me.*

At last Hessina shifted, causing Criton to open his eyes. "You wanted to speak to me?" he asked warily. The last thing he needed right now was a lecture, but he was sure he was about to get one.

"I am sorry for what has happened between you and Bandu," she said, grimacing as she sat on the hard floor of the cave. "I understand your pain. But you do not have the luxury of grief. You must marry again, and soon. Speak to Kana and the other elders, and marry the women they suggest to you."

"I thought you were against intermarriage."

She sighed. "Hession was my ancestor," she said, indicating the tomb. "I'm sure you didn't know that. Though not Dragon Touched himself, he was married to a Dragon Touched woman, and my lineage traces back to them. Our people have never been pure in that sense – there have always been intermarriages. Despite my reservations, I have come to the conclusion that such intermarriages are necessary for the survival of our people.

"That means I owe you and Bandu an apology. Though she was not well suited to living among us, you were not wrong to marry a girl from your own island."

"You didn't make her feel very welcome," Criton said bitterly.

"I know."

N S DOLKART   301

"She left me because I was considering listening to you. I promised her when we married that I'd never want another woman, and you made me question that promise. You practically chased her off yourself!"

She eyed him sternly. "My suggestion was not wrong, Criton. It still isn't. I think that with time, you'll come to understand the wisdom and the necessity of marrying again. You are no longer simply a man, but a symbol. You owe it to your people to marry the women the plainsmen suggest to you, to give us the strength of the plainsmen's numbers and turn them to our ways. I believe it is for this purpose that God Most High chose you to lead us – I am too old to make political marriages."

"Or maybe He chose me because I make better decisions than you do."

He had meant to insult her, to make her hurt for the way she was scratching at his wounds, but to his shame and fury, she only regarded him with that disapproving gaze that made him feel like a child, one who could be indulged now and punished later.

"Your tactical decisions have helped our cause more than they've harmed it," she said. "But this one choice is more important than any of those you've made so far. If you do not marry the women the elders suggest to you, our people will suffer."

"We'll see."

She spoke on, unfazed. "I do understand your grief, Criton, whatever you may think. A first marriage is special. My husband had no other wives, but from watching others, I can tell you that more wives are unlikely to make you happier. They may dislike each other, or dislike you, and you may well curse us, your elders, for suggesting this course of action. But these marriages are a political necessity. You must realize that."

She sighed. "You should know that while I did not especially like Bandu, I did not bear her any ill will. She was an impediment to you politically, but I know her abandonment has hurt you, and I am sorry for that."

He hoped she could see the hatred in his eyes. "You knew she'd leave me."

"Of course not. But we should look to the future. Our victory is close."

"Really? You think we can take Ardis?"

"God Most High will not abandon us. Now that I am here, I am sure of it. Soon Ardis will fall, and we can make its citizens pay for what they did to us. Which brings us to the second thing I wanted to say. As with your marriages, I want to be sure that you understand what we must do, and why."

That sounded ominous. "Has the plan changed? When we take Ardis, we'll reward our allies and settle in to live as we used to."

"No," the old woman said, her face grim. "It will not be the way it used to. We used to live in relative peace, protecting the king and protected by him as well. Now there can be no peace, not so long as the worshippers of Magor live within those walls. They slaughtered us, Criton. You were never here to weep with us at our losses, but there is no punishment too severe for those who killed our people."

Criton recoiled from her. "What are you saying? You want us to slaughter the whole city? We're not monsters. The goal is to live in Ardis righteously, not to destroy it ourselves!"

Hessina shook her head. "We cannot live with the Ardismen after what they did to us. I had five sons, Criton. Five. Eight grandchildren. Kilion was my youngest, the only one I was able to save. All the others were killed –

my sons, my daughter, and all their children and babies. We *cannot coexist* with the Ardismen. As long as we live, they will be our enemies. As long as *they* live, they will be a danger to us. They will dream of murdering us in our beds."

Criton said nothing. The story of Hessina's family – even the short version – was devastating. He had once witnessed the red priest executing an entire family. He had watched children die then, and the horror had been unfathomable. But now, as a father, these things affected him so much more deeply. The reality of Hessina losing her children and grandchildren was so overwhelming it robbed him of his power of speech. He nearly burst into tears thinking of those children, and of his own daughter now absent. Goodweather had been a frustrating chore right up until the moment that she became a hole in his heart.

It was that pain that brought him back. He shook his head, choking on his grief and on hers. Hessina was justified in her hate, but she was also wrong. She could not ask him to inflict her experiences on other parents, other grandparents. Whatever she said, he would not accept that as the only way.

Hessina was studying him. "You've given me a lot to think about," he told her. "I'll ask God Most High for guidance, but you should know that I disagree with you. I'm not going to become the kind of killer Bestillos was. Not willingly, anyway. If I can find a new arrangement with the Ardismen, a peaceful one, I'll take that peace over the kind of victory you're hoping for."

"This is the victory we have *all* been hoping for," Hessina said vehemently. "Our people will not settle for less."

Criton frowned. "Then I'll have to convince them.

Maybe *this* is why God Most High chose me to lead the Dragon Touched – because I'm willing to make peace with our enemies when others won't."

The old woman's eyes flashed. "Nobody who grew up before the purge will accept your position on this, Criton. You are young and idealistic, and foolish. Don't imagine for a moment that your stance will be popular."

"Thank you for your guidance," Criton said acidly. Then he closed his eyes and pretended to pray so as to cut off any more communication.

Bandu would be happy with his position when she found out. She had never believed this war was necessary, and would never have endorsed the slaughter of an entire city. If by some miracle he succeeded and the Dragon Touched made peace with their enemies, she was bound to hear about it and come back to him.

Wasn't she?

35

PHAEDRA

They came through the mists right into the courtyard of Silent Hall, where they were greeted with cheers by Atella's people. Psander was there too, looking both pleased and astonished at Phaedra and Hunter's presence. "Oh, well done, Atella," she said, and to Phaedra added, "I did not expect you two to be on Tarphae – what were you doing there?"

"We'd been taken there," Phaedra answered. "Karassa has turned our home into a haven for pirates. Without God Most High's protection, we'd have been sacrificed to Her as soon as we touched shore."

"And yet here you are."

"Here we are."

Psander took Atella's bag and thanked her. "You surpassed my expectations, and even my hopes."

Phaedra found herself a bit overwhelmed. This was so much more a homecoming than she had expected, certainly more a homecoming than their return to Tarphae had been. Even the villagers, once suspicious of the Tarphaeans for their association with the Gallant Ones, now looked on her and Hunter with admiration and hope. The whole group of them had gathered to witness Atella's return through the mists, and they looked just as happy with Phaedra and Hunter's surprise appearance as Psander did.

It was early morning here, unlike on Tarphae, which confused Phaedra somewhat. The hours of the two worlds had been more or less aligned before, from what she could remember. Had she been wrong about that, or had the release of Salemis somehow thrown this alignment off?

A young boy spoke up. "Are you here to save us?"

It was a heartbreaking question, and one that Phaedra did not know how to answer. If the situation was as dire as Phaedra feared it was, nothing could save these people.

Hunter stared at her. He'd been waiting for her to answer, she realized, and her hesitation had already caused a ripple of fear to spread through the crowd. He turned to the boy. "Yes," he said. "We're here to save you."

The tension remained among the adults, but the boy smiled. "Good. We need you."

You *need us most of all*, Phaedra thought. The boy was right around the age that elves preferred for their food.

It was good to see the villagers looking so lively. The last time Phaedra had seen them, they'd all been too weak to stand. So far, the move into the fairies' world seemed to have done them more good than harm. The trouble was that they couldn't expect it to last.

How reckless of Hunter, to say that they were here to save these people! They were neither of them some devastating weapon that could hold the elves at bay. Psander's interest in them as such was a mark of her desperation. And yet, looking at Hunter's face, Phaedra

was surprised to see confidence there. It might make no
sense, but he clearly believed himself. He thought he
could save them.

Perhaps this was what Hunter needed, what he'd
been looking for all along. He had wanted to lead the
army of Tarphae once, and when that dream had died,
he had fought to protect the remaining islanders from
whatever dangers they encountered. Now Psander's
villagers needed rescuing from the elves, who meant
to capture them and breed them and eat their children.
What better fight could Hunter join?

They broke their fast all together in the courtyard,
joined even by Psander. She had apparently been
much less aloof from the villagers since revealing her
true nature to them, and a sort of camaraderie had
developed in the months since then. Hunter asked the
villagers about their interactions with the elves so far,
and Phaedra was relieved to hear that nobody had yet
been taken. As Atella had told them, Psander had set
up wards that alerted the villagers whenever elves were
near, and they would flee for the protection of Silent
Hall any time the alarm sounded. What protection the
walls offered them was unclear, but Psander's reworking
of her God-evading wards had apparently been effective
so far. Phaedra hoped she would explain how she'd done
it.

When they had finished with their meal, Psander
asked Phaedra and Hunter if they would like to speak
privately with her. To Phaedra's shock, Hunter declined.
He was polite about it, but firm: he preferred to stay with
the villagers. Phaedra was left to talk to Psander alone.

As they walked to the wizard's library together,
Psander asked her to explain how she and Hunter had
come to be once more on Tarphae. So Phaedra told her

of the events of the last few months, and of her ambition
to recreate academic wizardry for herself.

"I am glad you came here," Psander said, "and it is a
great relief to know that God Most High sent you. My
old mentor was right, then: the dragons' God is alive and
well, and growing more active in the world. If that is so,
and He sent you to me with His blessing, then there is
hope after all. I had grown desperate."

"I know," Phaedra told her. "I figured if you had
sent Atella to find ingredients that would represent us
islanders, the situation must be dire. All we ever did to
the fairies was escape from them."

Psander eyed her skeptically. "You give yourselves
too little credit. My understanding was that Bandu
had bested the elves in one of their games, Criton had
defeated one of their living castles in a battle of wits,
and Hunter had slain more than one elf in hand-to-hand
combat. I'm sure if all this is true, your support and
Narky's were not immaterial."

"Thank you," Phaedra said. She felt herself blushing.
Psander clearly respected her; respected all five of them.
Phaedra knew that Narky would have scorned her for
feeling so flattered, but she couldn't help it. Psander did
not express respect for people often, and she respected
them.

"But I will admit," Psander added, "your overall
assessment was correct. I reached for these shadows of
you because I am running out of tools. Any day now, the
fairies may recognize our weakness and slaughter us all."

"How have you kept them away so far?" Phaedra
asked. "Atella said you turned your wards around, but
your wards were for keeping the Gods from seeing you.
I don't understand how those could be useful against
the elves, even reworked. My conception of magic is

as a sort of universal poetics, where ingredients are all representational. Am I missing something?"

The wizard shook her head. "You are not. My wards *are* useless against the fairies. But they don't know that, and their lack of knowledge is what has kept us safe so far. Atella is repeating what I told her, which is more or less the truth. I have reversed my wards entirely: where once they were keeping my hall invisible to the Gods, they now project a *feeling* of the Gods' might. That is all. When the elves come to my walls, they feel that projection and, so far, they have chosen caution. I have not told the villagers this truth because their minds are so easy for the elves to read – they have not learned to guard them as I have."

"But you're telling me?"

"I am telling you. And that means that I cannot let you leave my hall until you have learned to protect your mind."

Phaedra gaped at her. "You'll teach me?"

Psander smiled at her shock. "You have proven yourself fully capable of learning, and I am in need of an assistant. I will be glad to teach you everything I know."

36

HUNTER

Hunter stayed with the villagers when Phaedra went to talk to Psander. He asked them about their food stores, their foraging habits, their ability to avoid starvation, and found that they had adapted themselves quite quickly to their surroundings. Psander had deemed it too dangerous to go out hunting, and they had responded by becoming quite good trappers. They set their traps well within Psander's wards of alarm, where the elves could not ambush them, and they caught enough meat to supplement their remaining stores of grain while they waited for more to grow. They had cleared most of the tents out of Silent Hall's courtyard so as to leave room for a small field of wheat and oats, and the displaced families had moved into Psander's tower. They had also cleared away space for a modest vegetable patch just outside Psander's walls.

The trouble with trapping was that nearly every animal in this world seemed to be omnivorous, if not altogether carnivorous. If the villagers were too late in checking their traps, they were liable to find their prey already feasted upon by a great blue cat, or an unfamiliar pig-thing, or a flock of pigeons.

When he asked them to show him what defenses they had in case the elves did eventually attack, they pointed to the walls.

"That's all?"

"That's all."

"Then you need weapons."

They had axes, at least, for chopping wood, but they were not balanced the way a weapon ought to be, and Hunter knew how fast the elves could be with their war sickles. So he set off with Atella's father and two younger men to gather boughs for halfspears and quarterstaffs. He had learned stick fighting as a boy, before Father had given him his sword, and he thought he could teach it passably. Besides, he knew nothing of forging swords.

They would want weapons with some reach on the elves anyway – the elves were fast, brutal fighters, and the villagers would need every little advantage they could find. When the boughs were gathered and cut, Hunter set himself to teaching anyone who had time to learn. He started with the simplest drills, repeating them over and over until his students dropped their staves out of exhaustion. Then he had them gather more, smaller branches so that the children could practice with them too.

It would take months for the villagers to be even passable with their weapons, divided as their time was between training, trapping, and farming. He knew that. He also knew that in an actual fight, the elves would have every advantage. So when they broke for the evening meal, he set about devising a way to turn the elves' advantages against them.

Phaedra tried to talk to him while they were eating, but he had to apologize multiple times for inattention.

His mind was fully engaged with the problem of fighting the elves, and he could not be distracted. He gathered only that Psander had offered to train Phaedra in magic, and that she was very excited about it – of course she was. He congratulated her and went straight to bed.

He awoke before dawn and went outside to repeat the drills he had taught the villagers, adding some other ones and refamiliarizing himself with the weapon. At his peak, Hunter's swordsmaster had always said, a warrior would become one with his weapon. He would stop thinking and engage fully with each moment, seeing and responding to the slightest motions of his opponent with a perfectly blank mind. Now Hunter tried to build a further step on top of that: he tried to train himself to think while he acted, but in ways that contradicted his motions. If he could teach himself to cut high even as he *thought* about attacking low, then he could turn the fairies' mind-reading against them.

It was surprisingly difficult. With his swordsmaster, he had reached the point in his training when one no sooner thought of an attack than one had done it. He frequently found himself accidentally letting his actions match his thoughts, or vice versa. The village children, watching from the walls, must have wondered why he kept making frustrated sounds after each perfectly executed cut.

But he needed this to work. If he could master his new contradictory-thought fighting style, then one day his students would too. The elves would find them far more capable of defending themselves than they expected.

His life became a never-ending cycle of military preparations, both internal and external. He began introducing his theories into his training of the villagers, hoping to skip straight over the empty-minded fighting that had taken him years to learn. Most of the villagers were frustratingly slow to learn even the basics of stick fighting, but he thought that could have been expected. His swordsmaster had always called him an exceptional talent – he could not expect others to catch up to him so quickly.

"Cut low!" he would bark at his students while they were practicing a high parry. The trainees looked at him with annoyance and confusion, but he had already explained his reasoning, and could only tell them to keep not-quite-ignoring his instructions.

"Memorize my words," he would say, "visualize what I am asking you to do. But do the opposite."

The villagers hadn't realized that fairies could read minds – it had shocked and horrified them when Hunter had explained the truth. Their reactions to that information convinced him to wait before explaining how nearly impossible elves were to kill. He had seen elves survive beheadings, which made him wonder if they were altogether immortal. He didn't *think* so, but he couldn't know for sure.

He hoped it wouldn't matter. Mortal or not, elves were still made of flesh and bones – bones that could be broken. If an elf was crippled and incapable of fighting, that was sufficient. A live elf might even be useful to Psander, if they could capture one.

Psander watched with apparent amusement while he tried to train the villagers. She clearly didn't believe they would ever be able to resist the elves in arms. He meant to prove her wrong. What did Psander know of armed combat, anyway? Many of the villagers were coming along quite well, by Hunter's standards: Atella's father took naturally to the training, as did a pair of brothers who were grandsons of old Garan, and there was one nine year-old girl, Tritika, who imitated Hunter with such adroitness that he was sure she would be quite formidable given five or six years. He hoped they would live that long.

Of course, there was no knowing how well everyone was doing on the mental side of the training, visualizing movements other than those they were making. Gods knew, Hunter was having enough difficulty himself. At best, he could manage a mental-physical split about half the time, and that was never mind the fact that he had no proof the technique would work at all. He was relying on the assumption that these mental acrobatics would confuse the elves more than a closed mind would have – if he was wrong, then all was for naught. The elves had probably spent hundreds of years mastering the use of their long-handled sickles. Weapons training alone would never overcome them.

There were other benefits to his interactions with the villagers, though. Hunter and his friends had first met them a year and a half ago, when they had generously helped nurse Narky back to health, and sheltered and fed the islanders while they waited for the boy's recovery. They were good, kind people, and yet they had grown suspicious of the Tarphaeans after they had joined with a group of bandits on Psander's orders. Later, the wizard had used ingredients the islanders had brought her to make charms that sickened the villagers while bolstering Silent Hall's defenses. And then, to cap off their betrayal, Hunter and his friends had helped transport them all to the horrifying world of the fairies.

During all this time, the islanders had taken advantage of these people just as Psander had, and barely given them more thought. Now Hunter was finally getting to know them, making friends, sharing meals, and working with them in the courtyard and the vegetable garden when he wasn't too busy teaching them to fight. He inspected traps with his new friends, chopped wood with them, lived his life with them.

He even considered moving to live with them instead of in his room in Psander's tower, but that would have taken him farther from Phaedra. True, she spent most of her time now holed up with Psander learning the mysteries of the universe, but she still stopped by sometimes to talk, and to give him an update on her progress. He didn't want to lose that.

He thought he loved Phaedra. No, that was a lie – he *knew* he loved her. Seeing her so happy only reinforced how important she was to him, how much he liked to see her so excited about her life. She was radiant, her troubles forgotten as she limped hurriedly toward the library, day after day. He wanted her to look that excited about him.

He had never expected for them to come back to the elves' world, let alone for them to be happy there, but strange as it was, they really were both happy. Phaedra wasn't the only one benefitting from their time here – training the villagers to fight the elves filled Hunter with such purpose that he sometimes forgot that he had not always meant to be a combat trainer. Here was the aspect of his life that had gone missing when Tarphae was drowned. Here was the nation he would fight for, the army he would lead in battle. His answer to that little boy, Emmer, felt true: he was here to save them.

Even the older villagers believed that now, and the admiration and respect they showed him made him feel stronger, wiser, more attractive. He wondered if Phaedra could tell.

He was out one day checking on traps with Atella

and her father when the alarm sounded. Or perhaps 'sounded' was the wrong word – it was more like a very loud *feeling*, telling him that one or more elves had passed within the range of Psander's wards. Hunter and his companions immediately broke into a run, cursing. They had been right on the edge of the wards' range for that particular trap – if they were unlucky, they might not make it back to Silent Hall before the enemy did.

They were lucky this time. They made it to the fortress just as the door was closing, and after some small amount of shouting, Psander opened the door to let them in. "You were cutting it awfully fine," she scolded them.

"We ran back as quick as we could," Atella's father said, panting.

"You were almost too late," Psander answered. "They're just testing the boundaries now, but they still would have loved to catch you outside these walls."

"They're testing the boundaries?" Phaedra asked, horrified. She had come hurrying along behind Psander to open the gate to Hunter and the other two. "Can we afford for them to do that?"

"Not at all," the wizard answered grimly. "These tests are building up to an attack. But I don't see that there's much we can do about it. Today's scout will try to sniff out the nature of our defenses, as will each future one, and they will report back to their queen. If I could capture them before they returned home, I would."

That stopped Hunter in his tracks. "I can," he said.

Psander looked at him appraisingly. "Are you sure?"

"Is there just one of them?"

She nodded. "So my wards tell me. If they have found a way to make my wards lie to me…"

"Hunter," Phaedra said, but when he looked at her, she said no more. She was smarter than he was – she knew full well that letting him try to capture the scout was worth the risk to Hunter's life. If he couldn't defeat an elf in single combat, he was of no use to the people of Silent Hall. And anyway, if *he* couldn't defeat an elf, they were probably all doomed.

But her eyes expressed more than resignation, and more than pain at his risking of himself. They expressed trust. Belief. Love.

Atella brought him a staff, and Psander opened the door for him. Hunter took a deep breath and stepped back outside.

He walked as far as the edge of the trees before he stopped. He had seen elves disguise themselves as thorny bushes once, and had no intention of being caught off guard. "Come out and fight me," he called into the woods. "You want to test our defenses? Test me."

A gentle breeze blew out of the forest, but no one answered his call. Hunter stood waiting. Had the elf scout failed to hear him? Was he being ignored on purpose? Or was this long wait only a ploy to make him nervous?

"Maybe you've heard of me," Hunter shouted. "I am Hunter, who beheaded Raider Two of the Illweather elves, who rescued human children from that castle and left this world in triumph. If you're too afraid to face me, I don't blame you."

A buck trotted into sight, standing among the trees and staring at him. Hunter eyed it skeptically. He hadn't seen any deer here before, and he expected this animal to turn into his elf scout any moment. "What are you waiting for?" he asked it.

The creature bared its teeth at him – sharp, pointed teeth that never belonged to any deer. Then it lowered its antlers and galloped.

Hunter didn't have long to realize that this creature was

not going to transform into the expected human shape before it was practically upon him. He tried to imagine smashing its head in while he crouched and swung at its legs instead. His blow connected with a sharp crack and the animal ploughed into the ground beside him. He rose quickly and went for the head this time, jabbing his staff into the base of its skull. The creature began to crumple forward, but it was already transforming as it tucked in its head, did a front-somersault, and rose as a man.

In the daylight the elf's hair and skin were blacker than night. His hair flowed past his shoulders, and he wore clothes that looked like they were made of silver. In his hands he held one of the cruel elvish sickles that Hunter had grown all too familiar with. He looked, dismayingly, no worse for the wear despite Hunter's blows. Then he grinned, baring those same pointed teeth, and leapt to the attack.

For a time, Hunter forgot all about his new strategy and let his mind go blank, acting and reacting on instinct alone. He blocked and thrust, dodged and swung, never planning his next move until he was already doing it. He was glad then for every obsessive moment he had put into his training over the last few years: even against the ancient warriors of this godforsaken world, he could hold his own. The staff might not be his weapon of choice, but he still fought like a natural.

The trouble was, so did the elf. Hunter's opponent dodged or parried each attack Hunter sent his way, grinning all the while. No droplet of sweat shined off his unnatural skin as the elf leapt and spun, pressing the attack. Soon, Hunter began to realize his disadvantage in this fight – he might be just as fast, but his weapon was inferior. It cracked as he was blocking one of his opponent's swings, and then broke in two.

Hunter retreated, still blocking his opponent's blows with what now amounted to two jagged clubs. He considered throwing one of the clubs at the elf warrior, and saw the elf react to the possibility with a slight adjustment of his weight. The technique could really work, then! Hunter feinted with his mind again, and swung both clubs together at one of the elf's hands.

It was a ludicrously small target, but he hit it nonetheless. His opponent cried out in pain as Hunter broke his fingers and then, with another hard swing, knocked the sickle out of his hands altogether. Hunter dropped the club in his left and swung again, this time for the head. His swing should have ended the fight, but the elf raised his good hand and caught the club in an iron grip, twisting until the splinters forced Hunter to let go. So he changed tack and leapt after the sickle.

He got the sickle off the ground just as the elf landed his first blow on Hunter's skull. There was a cracking sound – from the wood, thank goodness – and his vision went fuzzy for a moment, but Hunter was not one to let this throw him. He jabbed upward and retreated, getting his bearings. The elf advanced again. As he did so, Hunter swung for his legs with his mind, and with his body, aimed instead for a killing blow.

The blade was sharp, and his aim was true. The elf, caught off guard, missed his parry, and the sickle cut through muscle and bone until his head tumbled from his shoulders.

The elf's head screamed as his body collapsed, then glared at the man who stood above it. "How?" the head screamed.

Hunter pulled a splinter out of his hand and picked the elf up by the hair. "You're too confident that your mindreading is an advantage. You shouldn't trust everything you see."

The elf gnashed his teeth at him even as blood dripped out of his remaining sliver of neck. "You will pay for this. Your ploy can only work once, and then–"

"It'll work as many times as it needs to," Hunter interrupted. "I'm taking you to Psander, elf. You'll be lucky if you can still *think* by the time she's done with you."

He walked back to the fortress walls, where a crowd was watching from the battlements – not just the villagers, but Psander and Phaedra too. He held up the head and sickle, and his audience erupted in cheers and applause.

It was the moment of glory that he had spent years imagining, and it came with all the pride, all the emotional power he had dreamt it would. This was how he would have felt if Karassa had never turned on his people, if Hunter could have gone on to live as the king's champion just as he had meant to. It felt incredible.

But hadn't he left all this behind? He had thought his days of killing were over – was it different now, just because he was killing elves instead of people? The fact that the elf could talk even after being beheaded did nothing to lessen the savagery of Hunter's victory. He was still waving a head around, indulging in the primal glory of having slain an enemy with his hands. And what if the Kindly Folk only lasted an hour without their heads? What if their seeming immortality was itself an illusion? Would he feel remorse then? He didn't think the elves' deranged foreignness should give him an excuse to feel good about killing.

"My young will grow up fatherless," the elf said, and Hunter looked down at him in shock. He had never considered the possibility that elves might have children. Did they? Could it be true? Or was the elf simply trying to make him feel worse, reading his thoughts and striking where he found a weakness?

"Of course we have children," the elf admonished him. "We are older, wiser, and more worthy than you, but we are still your cousins. We were made by the same cursed Gods who made you."

"Then why aren't there more of you? If you have children, and you live even after your heads have been cut off, why isn't this world completely full of you?"

The elf didn't answer. Was it a sign that Hunter had caught him lying about having children? Or did it mean that elves *could* die, and this one was too afraid to reveal the fact of their mortality? Hunter reached the gate of Silent Hall, which now stood open to him. Luckily, he would not have to guess these answers on his own. That was what Psander was for.

"You put too much faith in your Psander's abilities," the elf scoffed. "She cannot protect you for long."

Hunter swung the head into a wall, just hard enough for the elf to get the point. "Keep underestimating us," he suggested. "That's how you end up like this."

37

BANDU

Bandu had no intention of staying in town for long, whatever Vella might think. It was a good place to stop for now, but she did not like living with so many people around to look at her, to stare, to wonder, to judge. She would be happier, she thought, in a forest or maybe the mountains, where she could live away from all these people. It had been one thing to travel with her pack, with just the four other islanders, but the last few months had been too much for her. She did not like living with these crowds, with what her kind called "civilization." If it hadn't been for Criton, she would have fled all these crowds long ago.

She had let his needs outweigh hers for too long, and though she'd done it out of love, it had been the wrong choice. Criton probably thought she had left because of his promise to her, because he had told her he would never want others and then he'd changed his mind. That was a part of it, but their problems had been building since long before, in some ways since the first time they had kissed. He had never cared more about her than he did about his dragons, his heritage, his imaginary family.

She had worried it might be that way, but because he was also brave and strong and did his best to protect her, she had overruled her good sense and stayed with him. Until now.

Now she knew how much of a mistake it had been, and she vowed to trust her instincts better. So if her instincts told her it was time to go back to the forest, that was what she meant to do.

Maybe she could take Vella and Goodweather back to the Yarek, to live in its shadow and under its protection. Nobody was likely to bother them there, and she was confident of her ability to find food. But that was a long way to go, and she was not sure Vella would want to be quite *that* far away from her home. She didn't want to do the same thing to Vella that Criton had done to her, valuing her own desires so high above her mate's.

The trouble was that Vella was so out of her depth that it was hard for Bandu to be sure what the girl even wanted for herself. She wanted Bandu, of course, but what else? Bandu was not sure Vella even knew.

They were probably the same age, really, but Vella was still so much younger than her. She still compared everything to her life with her parents, which sounded as if it had been nicer than anything Bandu could relate to. What was it like to have parents who loved you like that, who fed and clothed you and even tried to make you happy? Bandu could only guess. It had made Vella younger and sweeter than Bandu or Criton, and more fragile. Bandu smiled when she thought of it. In some ways, Vella reminded her of Hunter.

She hoped Goodweather would grow to be as sweet and playful as Vella was. Perhaps if they loved and cared for Goodweather as Vella's parents had done for her, she would have that same sweetness to her that Bandu so appreciated in her new mate.

It was amazing to even have these thoughts. Before, she had worried about what influence Criton and his people might have on their daughter; now she felt free to dream of how she and Vella would raise the girl on their own. What would she be like, their Goodweather? Would she have her father's bravery? His obsessiveness? Would the wind whisper to her as it did to Bandu?

Bandu liked to watch Vella play with the baby. She would cover Goodweather's eyes with her claw and then pull it away, and the two of them would laugh and laugh. Play came so naturally to her, in a way that Bandu could recognize and admire but never understand. She tried to play the same game with Goodweather a few times, but the baby just looked confusedly at her and Bandu never really knew what was supposed to be so funny to begin with.

Vella was a good mate too, gentle and loving without any of Criton's impatience. She looked at Bandu almost worshipfully when they were alone together, and Bandu liked the way they mated. It was different, and very nice. She took a special delight in making Vella breathe her fire – Vella had learned as a child to suppress that fire, and it only came out when she lost all ability to think. The downside was that this meant they could only mate when they were out 'taking a walk' together with a sleeping baby, because they didn't want to accidentally burn down the house they'd been allowed to sleep in.

She was glad when the townspeople started looking at them suspiciously, because it gave her an excuse to drag Vella away from there. Vella was too used to the comforts of beds and pillows, and did not like to travel. But she was no fool, and didn't argue when Bandu said it was time to go.

So they left, taking some provisions with them, and continued on their journey. To Vella's delight, they found a place to stay before nightfall that had a roof and a bed. It was a woodcutter's house, sitting on the edge of a small wood. Vella was worried at first that the owner would come home and find them there, but Bandu pointed out the thin layer of dust on the table and the empty hooks above the doorway. The owner had been among those who marched against Psander behind High Priest Bestillos. He would not be coming back.

It was a good place to stay, dry and safe from animals but not too close to other people. There was even an overgrown vegetable garden outside, which Vella knew more about tending to than Bandu did, and it did not take Bandu long to find the well that the unknown woodcutter had dug out in the woods. He had abandoned his food store along with the house, so between that and Bandu's foraging, they ate quite well. The food store was all dried grains and lentils and chickpeas, and Bandu was glad for Vella's experience cooking these things. She even knew how to grow them, she said, if they stayed here long enough.

Bandu was not sure what she thought of that. She knew Vella wanted to stay, but she did not like the idea of staying quite this close to Criton and his people. If and when his war ended, he would eventually hear that they had passed through that town, and this house was less than a day's walk from there. But for now, she supposed it would do. Vella was so happy.

At least, she seemed happy. Sometimes Bandu would catch her looking pained and miserable, and every time she asked what was wrong, Vella would say, "You're not going to go back to him, are you?"

And Bandu would say no, and Vella would nod a few

times and try to smile, saying something like, "Forget about it." And then a few days later it would happen again.

That was one bad thing about Vella: when something bothered her, she would keep talking about it over and over again, even when there was nothing left to say. It was fair for her to be afraid that Bandu might change her mind and go back to Criton – Bandu was afraid of the same thing, sometimes – but what good did it do for her to keep coming back to it? Bandu was growing to love her more and more as time went by, but having to keep reassuring her about this was frustrating.

"I don't go back," she would say. "Criton is never a good mate."

"But do you love him?"

"Yes, but he is a bad mate, so I don't go back."

That answer always upset her, but what did she want, for Bandu to lie? Of *course* she loved Criton – he was a part of her pack, and always would be. He had comforted her after Four-foot died, had protected her from their enemies more times than she could count, and for all his problems, he had made beautiful little Goodweather with her. If only for that, she would never stop loving him. That didn't mean she wanted him as a mate again.

But that was more than Vella could understand, not knowing their history together. Bandu had neither the words nor the patience to explain how she felt, and she worried that trying would only hurt Vella more. She might feel bad for not being part of Bandu's pack.

Bandu wondered sometimes whether the rest of her pack would like Vella, if they ever got to meet her. She thought Phaedra and Hunter would. Vella was kind and gentle, and Bandu thought they would have a lot in common. In any case, they were unlikely to object to her even if they didn't like her at all. They were both dishonest in that way, with the funny sort of dishonesty that most parents apparently taught their young, where you didn't say what you thought if it wasn't friendly enough.

Narky was much more honest in that way. He also didn't seem to like anyone, at least at first. You had to force Narky to like you – it didn't happen on its own. He still didn't like Bandu, as far as she could tell – though there was no doubt that he respected her, and from Narky, respect was almost as good.

Would he respect Vella, if he ever got to meet her? Bandu wasn't sure. She didn't think he would appreciate her gentleness the way Bandu did. A lot of things were different when you had a baby to think about, and wanting to be with someone gentle was one of those things. It had been easier to stay with Criton before she had had Goodweather's safety to worry about.

She felt bad now, because Criton loved Goodweather too, and Bandu had taken her away. If it had been the other way around – if Criton had been the one running off in the night, taking Goodweather with him – Bandu wouldn't have slept until she had her daughter back. Criton probably felt the same way, and it was wicked of her to have done that to him. But then, it had been wicked of Criton to take such bad care of them. She was sure she had done the right thing. She just wished she could have done it without hurting him.

This was one of those things she couldn't talk to Vella about, because Vella didn't like knowing that Bandu cared so much about Criton. She wouldn't understand Bandu's complicated thoughts, not with Bandu's halting speech, and that meant there were some conversations that shouldn't even be started.

That caused its own problems, though. Criton might

have been bad for her, but Bandu had always been able to tell him how she felt. It was lonely keeping her thoughts to herself, and she didn't think it was right for a mate to make her feel lonely.

So that night she told Vella everything, as best she could. It was just as hard as she had expected, but at least Vella didn't interrupt. When she was done, the other girl looked her in the eye and said, "I don't know why you're doing this to me."

"Doing what?"

"Torturing me. You took me away from my family and my people, and now you're telling me you feel bad because of *Criton?* That's not right."

"That *is* right!" Bandu insisted. Vella had clearly understood her words perfectly, so why did she think otherwise?

"I mean that it's not fair," Vella snapped, noting her confusion. "It's not fair to me. You don't feel guilty for wrecking my life, so why should I care how guilty you feel about leaving your husband? It was all your idea!"

"You think I break your life? So why you come with me?"

"Because I love you. That doesn't give you an excuse to be selfish."

Vella was right, but if Bandu couldn't tell her how she felt, even about Criton, then that meant she couldn't tell anyone. The thought made her feel lonelier already.

"You don't want me to tell you what I feel."

Vella sighed. "No, no, I didn't mean it like that. Of course I want you to tell me how you feel, it's just... you hurt me this time. I wish you cared as much about me as you do about Criton."

"I do," Bandu said, but she knew Vella didn't believe her.

Bandu hated fighting. She *hated it. It had felt* like all she and Criton did sometimes was fight with each other – was this what it would be like with Vella too? Would they stop speaking for weeks sometimes, and only start again when Bandu weakened? Maybe Bandu should not have a mate, if it would always be like this. Maybe she should have left Criton by herself.

"*You* are not fair," she said. "You don't want me to care about Criton, but he *makes Goodweather with me*. If he is important to me too, that is not bad. I don't want him anymore, I want you. I can still *think* about him."

She thought Vella was going to say something, but she just sat there, eyes shining. "You're right," she said at last. "I'm sorry. I get jealous sometimes."

And just like that, their fight was over. Bandu leaned over and kissed her, and they lay back down. Nestled between Vella and her sleeping baby, Bandu marveled at how much better she felt now. This was not like with Criton after all. This was nothing like with Criton. Somehow, instead of causing hours and days of pain, this argument had brought them closer together.

"You don't need to be jealous," she told Vella. "You are good for me, better than Criton. And I love you."

38
NARKY

The next few days were bloody and decisive, as Magerion moved with blinding speed to consolidate power and eradicate his enemies before anyone could organize an opposition. Narky was given a squad of six men as guards and servants, and he led them in defacing the Great Temple of Magor and rounding up workers to recreate it and rededicate it to the glory of Ravennis. The artist who had painted the temple's murals converted as soon as he was called for, and hurriedly volunteered to rework or paint over every image in the building. The statues of boar-headed Magor were attacked with hammers until they were little more than rubble-covered pedestals. Within a week, Magor's one great city belonged entirely to Ravennis.

It was everything a dishonorable God could want.

Narky became high priest to the whole city, and the people flocked to him with fear in their eyes. They wanted him to tell them that Ravennis would be magnanimous in His conquest and kind to His former enemies. Narky was happy to oblige. So long as people gave themselves freely to Ravennis before their deaths, he told them, He would watch over them kindly and lovingly in their final rest. But those who opposed Him would be subjected to eternal torment, at least until their Ravennis-worshipping descendants prayed to Him for leniency on their behalf. Narky felt he had to add this last bit, because otherwise all those who had died before Ravennis came to Ardis would be doomed through no fault of their own. He had no idea if it was true.

He was growing more comfortable inventing doctrine though, as he spent more time in the role of high priest. Given his God's clear ability to put words in his mouth if need be, every sentence that Narky uttered on his own now carried the Keeper of Fates' implicit approval. The lack of further divine intervention suggested that Narky was guessing right about the true teachings of his God – or else that Ravennis didn't particularly care. Either way, he no longer worried that his teachings would conflict with his God's position.

What did worry him was that Ardis was now undergoing its *second* mass conversion in thirty years. What if Magerion somehow lost control, and Narky got swept away in the backlash? The old artist who was repainting the temple told him a bit of the city's history, and it turned out that the Great Temple of Magor – now of Ravennis – had been built on the same site where God Most High's great temple had once stood. The architect for the new building had been murdered once it was finished so that he could never design any building greater than Magor's temple. That sounded horrifying to Narky, but the artist said it with a certain pride. That was easy enough for him – his painting services didn't come with an end date.

The temple wasn't the only building that had been transformed during the "Great Uprising." The armory across the square had once been the Ardisian Hall of Records, where the Dragon Touched and the royal family had kept all the documents of state, from histories and rare, precious texts of academic wizardry, to tax records and bills of sale. When Bestillos and his followers had come to power, pillaging the Hall of Records had been their second act after tearing down the temple of God Most High. They had burned every document in the building, torn out half the shelves, and turned it into an armory. Narky could only imagine how much that would have horrified Phaedra.

Though his position seemed secure enough for now, he'd have felt better about it if he'd had better relations with the priests of Elkinar. He was too afraid to even meet with them, after the way Mother Dinendra had humbled him. They were staying neutral for now, and if he made it through the year, they would have to accept the merger of the Gods and become his underlings. But a year was a long time. In the meantime, he ought to make sure they didn't hate him.

Here Ptera was indispensable. She acted as his liaison to the Elkinaran priesthood, representing his gospel without insulting their faith or intelligence, which was likely more than Narky could have done. Narky envied her tact, and wished sometimes that he could secretly go with her just to see how she did it. He hoped he'd learn from her over the years.

A second bloody week came and went, and Magerion sent Narky a messenger saying that he would be needed for the coronation. Probably owing to Narky's youth, Magerion was handling all the details himself, and the messenger intimated that Narky would need to do little more than show up on time to crown and bless the new king. That sounded easy enough, so Narky asked no further questions and sent the messenger back with his acceptance.

After all, the coronation was probably the least of their worries. Magerion's takeover came at a particularly perilous time: the Dragon Touched were on the move. The latest reports were that Criton's army was already marching for Ardis, bent on destroying the city. With any other people, the notion of such a small army threatening Ardis would have been laughable. With the Dragon Touched, it was credible. Criton's people had yet to lose a battle, despite their modest numbers, and though the bulk of their army was northern plainsfolk, it did not take many flying soldiers to imperil a city's defenses.

Narky worried about his inevitable confrontation with Criton. Such a confrontation would come, he knew – he would have to somehow convince his friend to leave the city alone, despite the very real claim the Dragon Touched had over it. It wouldn't be easy – he and Criton hadn't always gotten along so well. He still had memories of Criton's clawed fingers closing around his throat from when the two had argued over a scroll, and in the case of Ardis, all of Criton's strengths and weaknesses as a person were aligned: his insane bravery, his short temper, and that childlike confidence that he was the hero in his own story. They all pointed toward a confrontation.

Narky hoped he would be able to appeal to Criton's overall decency and generosity. If Ptera had taught him anything, it was that flattery really did work. Maybe he could appeal to Criton's sense of himself as a hero, by telling him that only he could bring peace to the region. Narky hoped that would work, especially since it might well be true.

He supposed he ought to be thankful that Criton was in charge at all. It was hardly a given that the one foreigner among the Dragon Touched would be the one to lead them, but just as the islanders' reputation had once led to doors being slammed in their faces, now their reputations were opening new doors. People didn't even call them by their names anymore: they were the Black Dragon and the Black Priest. In theory, this latter title could have been a reference to Narky's robes – Bestillos had been known as the red priest, after all – but everyone knew that was nonsense. Narky would have been the Black Priest even if he'd been wearing mauve.

Magerion wore him like a talisman. Narky was doubly strange, the foreign priest of a foreign God, and he got the impression that he was expected to bring some kind of foreign magic to the service of Ardis. He was their answer to Criton.

But Narky knew better. He had no magic, and his powers of persuasion were limited at best. He was friends with Criton, sort of, and that was all.

What's more, Magerion seemed to be under the false impression that Ravennis could protect the city against God Most High. Narky, who had spoken to elves, to a wizard, and to the dragon Salemis all face to face – well, he knew better. God Most High had not gotten His title by accident.

If they were all lucky, Ravennis might be a high-level servant to the dragons' God. He was allied to the Goddess Eramia, after all, and she was married to Salemis. If they were unlucky then that alliance might have been merely temporary, but either way, Narky did not think his God could ever stand up to Criton's in battle. He would be crushed like a bug.

He could see how, from Magerion's perspective, it

might seem as if Criton and his God had prevailed in war only because Magor had been terminally weakened, caught between two stronger Gods. Magerion thought that by aligning with the other of the two, he would be on even ground against the marauding Dragon Touched. He was so, so wrong.

Was Ravennis powerful? Definitely. He had lost Laarna and its Oracles, and still lived – if you counted being Lord of the Underworld as "living". But God Most High had power on a different order of magnitude. He had abandoned the *dragons*, on purpose, without fear of being consumed by His rivals. The dragons, who had themselves killed Gods in battle! If there was a comparison to be made between the two, it was not to Ravennis' benefit.

The trouble was that Narky was terrified of explaining this to Magerion. If he thought he had chosen the wrong side, the new king of Ardis might well execute Narky and start all over again. He might ally with the Dragon Touched and welcome them into Ardis, just as another king had done generations ago, and lift them up as his prized advisors and lieutenants. It would cause much whiplash for his other subjects, but they were all afraid of him now, and they would not stop him. Then Narky would have failed his God completely, and he would reach the underworld as the most hated of creatures. He would probably be tortured and tormented until the day Ravennis was destroyed by some other rival, and then the new God of the Underworld might well torture him too.

Narky had no intention of failing his God. One way or another, he would have to dissuade Magerion from battling the Dragon Touched, without revealing the true supremacy of God Most High.

But first, the coronation. Magerion held it in front of the armory, an unsubtle message if ever there was one. Though it was drizzling, citizens flooded the square to watch Narky place the old crown of Ardesian kingship on Magerion's head. The crown was an interesting story in itself: it had been sitting atop the statue of Magor in the temple, and Narky had assumed that it was gold leaf over stone until someone told him that it was in fact the real crown. Magerion's men had removed it before the statue was destroyed, and the old artist had explained that it had been placed there after the tyrant king's death, as a symbol of the end of the kingship and the beginning of Magor's reign. Of course, it had taken many months to carve the statue, so the red priest had held onto the crown until then. That didn't surprise Narky in the least. Council of Generals or not, it seemed that Bestillos had been in charge all along.

Now Narky placed the crown on Magerion's head, and blessed him in the name of Ravennis below. Magerion rose to deafening cheers, whether genuine or forced it was not clear to Narky. To some degree, it didn't matter. Magerion didn't seem to care about his city's love, only its obedience.

The city would be safe under his rulership, the new king told the crowd. The weakness of Ardis had been vanquished with the last of the red priests, and the city would soon know glory again. The crowd loved that, and they roared their approval. Narky had to hand it to Magerion: the man knew how his city wanted to be ruled.

The tyrant king of Ardis had once had a great palace within the richer quarters of the city, but this had long been torn down and disassembled for its stone. Mage...

a mansion two stories tall with beautiful decorative weapons and shields adorning the walls. There they dined on choicest veal and discussed their next moves in the war.

Criton's army had come all the way to the Dragon Knight's Tomb, and Magerion wanted to strike at him there despite the unfavorable terrain. He was afraid that given time, the Dragon Touched would summon the great dragon that had once lived there, and which had incinerated so many Ardismen. The Dragon Touched had won all of their battles so far, despite their army's unimpressive size. With a dragon, they would be unstoppable.

They were unstoppable anyway, but Narky didn't say that. Instead, he suggested that Magerion offer a truce. What if it was too late, and Salemis was already on his way? Better to make peace now, when the terms would be more favorable and the Dragon Touched might be convinced to settle for the territory they had already conquered.

"Peace?" Magerion scoffed. "There can be no peace with the Dragonspawn. They will not have forgotten that Ardis was once theirs. They will not have forgotten what we did to them."

"No," Narky admitted, "but they can't hope to rule the city through armed occupation. Even if we surrendered, a few targeted murders a year would chase them out again."

Magerion shook his head. "You are naïve. They have found allies in the north, allies who would be happy conquering our territory and tilling our fields. They could burn our houses, slaughter every last man, woman, and child and start from the beginning. Ardis isn't the buildings, boy, it's the land."

That was sobering. If such widespread slaughter was an option, how could the Dragon Touched ever be persuaded to give up? Criton might hesitate to sentence another Tarphaean to death, but that didn't mean he would turn his people away from their only goal just because a friend's life was at stake. Besides which, Narky had always been a mediocre sort of friend.

Yet surrender was impossible with Magerion as king. "Let me pray for guidance," Narky said. "The God that outmaneuvered Magor will have an answer for us."

Magerion shook his head. "Pray while our soldiers march. With the Keeper of Fates' blessing, they will destroy our enemies before any dragon comes to their rescue."

"No," Narky begged, "please. Ravennis hasn't given us His blessing yet. At least wait until He sends us an omen."

"He sent us an omen," Magerion said. "He made me king."

39

PHAEDRA

The apprenticeship was everything Phaedra had imagined it to be. Having discovered the essence of magic theory for herself, Phaedra was able to skip directly to the practice of individual techniques and the elucidation of the theory behind each. Psander was not a patient teacher, but neither was Phaedra a patient student, and their progress was rapid. If magic was poetry, Phaedra was finally being taught composition.

That was certainly how she thought of it, though Psander took a different view. She talked of magical "resonance" as if it was a natural force, when to Phaedra even that choice of words suggested poetry. The more a composition resonated with the natural ugliness or beauty of its context, the more powerful it became. The trick – and the thing that set academic wizardry apart from any less rigorous form – was controlling one's composition with such precision as to yield the desired effect and no more.

This had been the major work of the academics: testing and retesting individual techniques in specific contexts until the effects of their magic could be reliably predicted. Many of the scrolls Psander gave Phaedra to read dripped with the tedium of their authors' work, and yet there were few things more exciting than to read about a discovery in a book and to be able to prove its worth within minutes.

Under Psander's tutelage, Phaedra quickly learned how to replicate the ghostly light that had once impressed her so; she constructed her own flawed illusions and practiced her wizard sight; she even learned how to call books down from the impossibly tall library shelves. This last task turned out to be deceptively easy: all the effort had gone into threading the ghostly tethers that connected each book to its spot on the shelf and to the library floor. Pulling on those tethers was as simple as widening one's weak magical field and calling out the right name.

Phaedra's training was not all rote, of course: the principles of magic theory allowed for plenty of improvisation. This improvisation was most effective in areas where the wizard had a deep knowledge of the related symbology, and for Phaedra, that field was travel magic. She had spent a year of her life deeply obsessed with Atel the Messenger God, and she knew the imagery of His domain better than she knew anything. Whenever she read about a travel-related spell, her mind would fill with dozens of modifications that could make the spell more effective under varying circumstances.

The hardest training, and the most necessary, was in the realm of mental defense. There were two components to such a defense: detection, and willpower. Pushing a known intruder out of one's mind was actually fairly easy, Phaedra discovered – one fought that fight on one's home turf, after all. It was detecting the intrusion in first place that caused all the difficulty. It was like training oneself to recognize a dream before anything implausible happened. It did not come naturally or easily, no matter how often Psander attacked. She had the humiliating habit of slipping past Phaedra's defenses undetected while Phaedra was studying a book, and then reading aloud from its pages using Phaedra's own eyes. Psander might be across the room and facing the other way, but all of a sudden she would speak the very words Phaedra was reading, and Phaedra would know that she had failed her test yet again.

The elves, Psander insisted, were stronger in their mental attacks and at least as stealthy, but Phaedra had reason to believe that she was exaggerating their subtlety. For one thing, it was much easier to catch an intruding Psander when Phaedra knew she was being tested. The elves could be expected to make an attempt on Phaedra's thoughts any time they were present, so she would already be on the lookout whenever she was near one.

"True," Psander said suddenly. "But that's no excuse to leave yourself unprotected in the meantime."

Phaedra groaned and pushed her out again.

She was glad, though, to be learning from Psander. Phaedra's spellcasting on Tarphae had had the desired effects, but it had relied entirely on God Most High's willing intervention. This state of things, it turned out, was to be avoided.

"You used the most inherently dangerous form of magic there is," Psander said when Phaedra told her of her exploits. "Gaining the attention of a God is extremely perilous, Phaedra. You're lucky God Most High didn't smite you on the spot."

Phaedra looked at her incredulously. "Might He have?"

"Of course. The Gods are made of such powerful magic that They are liable to burn any creature that gets too close to Them. They *are* made of magic, you know, as far as we can tell. Corporeal bodies may or may not be sustainable on Their side of the mesh. In any case, we must keep our distance whenever possible, even those of us who don't already have a target on our backs. The attention of a God can be disastrous at any time, *especially* if you are attempting to perform a feat of magic. The fact that you may be practicing devotional magic is no defense. One false move, one mislaid cue, and They will destroy you."

That was alarming, if true, but it didn't seem to match up with Phaedra's experience. "I don't know," she said. "God Most High kept the sea at bay on our behalf even before I learned to enhance my prayers with magic. He went to the trouble of keeping the merchantman from leaving Mur's Island until we were aboard. Do you really think He'd have turned on me a few weeks later over a poorly executed spell?"

"Yes," Psander said. "And it wouldn't have been the first time, either. God Most High in particular is said to have once struck down His own high priest over a misworded sacrifice. You are intensely lucky that you didn't get burned."

While Phaedra spent her days learning from Psander, she was happy to see that Hunter was putting his time to good use too, training the villagers how to fight with staves and spears. She doubted the training would do the villagers much good, but no one could deny its positive effect on Hunter. Gone was the brooding, melancholy man she knew – Hunter had a project now, and he was as focused on it as Phaedra was on her own. She thought this must have been what he was like when he had first learned to use his sword – intense, tenacious, obsessive – except that he was also making friends among Psander's villagers, set as he was on training them. In her few breaks from studying, she would watch him from one of the tower windows as he drilled his students or practiced by himself, or even helped out in the garden. She could tell he was growing into his own, and she was glad.

Psander used much of Phaedra's reading time setting up new wards in an attempt to dissuade the elves from attacking. It was a miracle that they had waited this long, but Phaedra supposed they could afford to be patient. From what Psander told her, it sounded as if Silent Hall had arrived in this world much nearer to Castle Goodweather than to Illweather, and the Goodweather elves might well have been concealing Psander's arrival from their enemies. Either that, or the two elven camps were still negotiating what to do with Psander and her people once the fortress was breached. Phaedra hoped not.

Phaedra told Psander about Auntie Gava, and how the old woman had warded the "demons" away with her own blood. Psander was impressed.

"That is a very clever ward," she said. "Now that I've seen something of the elves, I have to admit that we academics spent far too much time trying to learn *about* them and far too little time trying to protect ourselves and the world *from* them. We never liked to give hedge witches credit, but if Mur's Island hasn't seen an elven raid in so many generations, their 'aunties' have done far more for them than the academics did for our own people."

"Can we use Gava's ward to keep them away now?"

"No, not here. It is far too late to keep them from detecting us, and for once they don't seem to be looking for children. My impression is that the queen of the elves means to set up a breeding program."

Phaedra tried not to think about that.

For now, the greatest danger came from the possibility that the elves might soon realize how illusory Psander's defenses were. If a fairy scout discovered the extent of the deception, they were all doomed.

So when a scout did breach the outer wards and Hunter volunteered to capture it, Phaedra didn't have the luxury to object. Instead she waited on the battlements with Psander and the entire village, hoping. Hunter was just visible, standing right before the tree line with his staff.

"He'll do it," Atella said, a little further down the row. "He'll win."

They were able to see the whole fight from their vantage point. They gasped when Hunter's weapon snapped, and broke into cheers when he disarmed his opponent. But when Hunter cut off the elf's head, Psander snorted disgustedly.

"I'd have preferred it if he'd captured one alive," she said.

"He did," Phaedra told her. "We're not even sure elves *can* be killed."

Sure enough, it soon became obvious that Hunter and the elf's head were carrying on a conversation. "Amazing!" Psander exclaimed, sounding more genuinely surprised than Phaedra had ever heard her. "I wonder."

Psander was not a talkative woman, but she couldn't help speculating, while Hunter brought the head back to the fortress, about how and why elves might survive their beheadings.

"Do you suppose their souls remain in their heads

because this world has no underworld?" she asked. "If that were the case, one would expect us also to survive beheadings here. That seems unlikely, but we have yet to fully disprove the possibility. Alternatively, could it be that the elves' souls are sturdy enough that they don't even need a functioning body to cling to? What does it mean that the body has stopped moving, while the head still speaks?"

Phaedra asked, "Will you be able to learn the answers from this one? Is there some way to make sure the head won't lie to you?"

"Maybe," Psander said. "If so, it will take some experimentation. There are known potions for truth telling, but I possess the ingredients for none of them, and what's more, I am uncertain of whether such a potion would have any efficacy without a stomach to digest it. I will have to learn my answers through interrogation and experimentation."

They greeted Hunter at the base of the tower, where the elf's head met them with rageful obscenities, sharp teeth gnashing. Psander shoved a rag in its mouth. "You will be less useful to me if I have to cut your tongue out," she told the elf, "but I will do it if I must. I'm sure the tongue of an elf would make for a fine ingredient if it turns out I have one lying around."

The elf looked hatefully at her, but he stopped trying to speak. "Should we bring the body in too?" Hunter asked.

"Absolutely. I have a long table in my study – Phaedra, show him the way. I'll bring the gentleman's head myself."

With the help of a few village men, they retrieved the elf's body before some scavenging beast could devour it and brought it up the stairs to Psander's study. The

wizard's study was a large room near the top of the
tower, past the heavy door that had once stymied the
Tarphaean islanders in their attempt to interrupt one of
Psander's experiments. Psander had cleared the raised
stone slab that stood in the middle of the room, so they
laid the body down there beneath its head. They wanted
to stay to watch Psander work and perhaps to ask about
the various bottles, vials, and tools that lined the walls,
but as soon as the body was positioned on the table,
Psander said, "Everybody out."

Phaedra was about to reluctantly file out with the
others when Psander said, "Not you, Phaedra. You can
stay. I'm too accustomed to working alone – I forgot
about you."

"Oh," Phaedra said, sighing with relief. "Thank you."

"You're welcome. Now hand me that bottle over
there. Yes, the grain liquor. And that dish, too. Let's see
if we can't set some ground rules for our friend."

Phaedra did as she was told, and Psander was soon
pouring a clear liquid into the dish. The elf's eyes
followed her movements, showing only contempt.

"I hope to learn a lot from you over the coming days,"
Psander told the elf, "but I want to be very clear about
what I expect from our conversation, and that is first
and foremost civility. You may lie to me all you please
without consequence – I expect plenty of lies. But if you
open your mouth to curse me or my people, if you say
a word of denigration or abuse, here is what I will do. I
will lift you up by the hair, and I will place you in this
dish. Do you want to know what that feels like?"

She did not wait for a response – the elf's mouth was
still stuffed with that rag, after all. His eyes betrayed no
fear, no doubt, no curiosity as she followed through on
her threat, placing the head chin-deep in the alcohol.

It must have been agony, because Phaedra suddenly felt his presence in her head as he lost control and let out a long psychic wail. She covered her ears instinctively, though it had no effect – the scream went ringing on and on in her skull until she finally gathered her wits and banished him from her mind.

She dropped her hands again and looked back to the table. The elf was making a muffled sound through the rag in his mouth, and tears were dripping from his eyes as he squeezed them shut against the pain. Psander had turned from the elf and was looking on Phaedra with disappointment. After all their training with mental defense, she still hadn't been prepared. She would do better in future, she promised herself. Now Phaedra knew what an elf's presence felt like, she would notice it even when it was subtler.

With a grimace, Psander lifted the elf's head once more and placed it back on the table. She waited calmly while the elf slowly recovered, then pulled the rag out of his mouth and said, "Do I make myself clear?"

"Ohhhhhhhh," the elf moaned, still weeping. "Clear, yes."

"Good. I'm going to start with some very simple questions. What is your name?"

"Olimande."

"And your orders here were?"

The elf stared up at her defiantly.

"I'll answer that one, then," Psander said. "Your orders were to test my defenses, to learn how they worked and how they can be avoided or dispelled. Have you satisfied yourself on that account?"

Olimande's head wobbled on its remaining portion of neck, and Phaedra was fairly sure he was trying to shake it. "Hunter got to you first," she said. "And after that, you weren't paying attention."

"The raids will not end," the elf said. "We will find a weakness, and then our queen will destroy you. She will eat your heart herself, wizard."

"That is always a danger," Psander admitted magnanimously, "but I am beginning to doubt it, frankly. After all, I am about to learn a good deal more about her than she knows about me."

"I will tell you nothing."

"You've already told me that your queen means to eat my heart. So now I must ask, why? Is there something special about my heart, of all organs, that is more precious to her? I have eaten heart, though not a human heart, obviously, and it was neither tender nor especially enjoyable. If she hopes to eat my heart, therefore, I imagine that it must be for symbolic reasons and thereby magical ones as well."

"You understand nothing," Olimande sneered.

"Nonsense," Psander replied. "You have every incentive to turn me away from the truth. When you call me a fool, that is when I can be most confident of your lies."

The elf had nothing to say to that. Psander really was on the right track, then. If the fairy queen wanted to eat Psander's heart, that meant there was a special power in the act.

"Perhaps I ought to try eating *your* heart," the wizard mused. "Would it give me an advantage of some kind?"

"There is no advantage you can gain over us," Olimande said. "Sooner or later, we will devour you."

Psander raised an eyebrow. "Why this fixation on eating us? I recognize the symbolic power of doing so, but you have yet to connect it to a specific purpose, which suggests that it is not part of a given spell but a ritual of some inherent value to you. Is eating a human's heart a method for permanently absorbing their magic, or perhaps their soul? If it's a matter of absorbing people's souls, then your own souls must not be kept in the heart at all, but in the head somewhere. Otherwise, it would be your body that was moving without your head, rather than the other way around. Could your own souls be stored in your brains, rather than your hearts?"

The elf closed his eyes. "I have said already, I will tell you nothing. You will learn no more from speaking with me."

"Mmm," Psander said. "Then I shall have to begin experimenting. Phaedra, there is a saw on the far wall, second shelf. Hand it to me, will you?"

40

CRITON

Criton had sent scouts to watch the city of Ardis, so they were ready when the assault came. They had moved their livestock to the other side of the mountain, supervised by a few hand-picked youths, and had themselves hiked up to secure their dominance of the high ground. They waited for the Ardismen to come creeping up the mountain in the hope of surprising their quarry, whom they believed were still asleep. Then Criton's men came down on their assailants with a roar, routing them before the two sides could even come to blows.

More Ardismen fell to them that night than at any other battle. They had to wait until morning to properly assess the devastation, but when they did, the results were astounding. Only six of Criton's men had lost their lives. On the Ardismen's side, it was nearly four hundred.

"Enough hesitating," Belkos said to him when the count had been made. "It's time to march on Ardis. If they know what's good for them, they'll surrender."

"Let's bury our dead," Criton said. "We can discuss our next move after that."

If that was the best he had, he must be getting truly

desperate. His people were growing suspicious. He had told himself for long enough that he was being prudent, cautious, when in fact he was simply reluctant to commit to the destruction of Ardis. And why shouldn't he be reluctant? He knew what the rest of the Dragon Touched didn't: that Narky was in there.

They had left Narky on the road to Ardis, where his God had separated him from his friends and sent him into the city of their enemies. There had always been the question before of whether he had survived – the Dragon Touched had kept no prisoners, and Criton knew nothing of what had been happening inside the city. But he hadn't failed to notice that many of the dead Ardismen from this last raid wore raven charms.

How cruel would it be if Narky had survived his inevitable struggle with the worshippers of Magor, only to be caught in the slaughter of a Dragon Touched victory? It was one thing to kill Ardismen – they had shown the Dragon Touched no mercy a generation ago, and Hessina and Belkos insisted that they deserved no mercy in return. But it was another thing to condemn his friend.

Criton had so few friends now. Narky had left; Phaedra and Hunter had left; even Bandu had left, and taken Criton's daughter and another man's wife with her. Belkos was his friend, of course, as well as his cousin, but somehow it was not the same. Delika didn't count either – she saw him as a sort of father, not a friend. Only the other islanders knew him for who he was. Only they knew *Criton*, and only Criton had friends – no one could be friends with the Black Dragon.

But there was no way he could say all this to Hessina or Kilion or Belkos or anyone. So what if Narky was in Ardis? Why should Criton's people care? He wasn't the only person in the city who didn't deserve to die. To condemn a city was to condemn its peaceful dissidents too, and its innocent children. Criton still had memories of Bestillos spearing the little princes of Anardis. The Dragon Touched would do the same in Ardis, when they breached its walls – to pretend otherwise was naïve. Hessina had told him as much. That was what victory looked like.

Had Criton become a hard enough man that he could welcome such horror? Why should Narky's presence have been the only obstacle left, the only signpost to remind him of the nature of the path he was on?

It was too late now anyway. After this victory, the Dragon Touched and their allies expected to take Ardis. They had fought this war for that purpose alone, and Criton did not think he could dissuade them. So when the Dragon Touched had buried their dead, Criton told his people that it was time to march on the city. At this point he thought they might have done so even if he'd told them to march the other way, but at least this way his cousin smiled at him instead of frowning.

Narky met them on the road late that afternoon, flanked by a few guards under a banner of peace. He was dressed in black robes, and looked very official. Official, and nervous.

Criton was relieved to see him. He wondered if he could keep him as a "prisoner" so as to save him from the pillage of Ardis. It was worth considering. In the meantime, he had the meeting tent erected and called for the council of elders to gather there and hear what Narky had to say.

When everyone was in attendance, Narky began his speech. "I'm here on behalf of Magerion, King of Ardis, who wants to broker a peace between our peoples."

Hessina interrupted him. "Ardis has no king. Magerion is only one general among many."

"Oh," Narky said. "So I guess I'm the one who's been away for months, pillaging the countryside? Because if I were, I wouldn't have any idea what was going on in Ardis."

Criton winced. With Narky's diplomatic skills, they'd be lucky if Hessina didn't insist upon a public execution before they even reached the city.

"The other generals are all dead," Narky went on, "and so are the priests of Magor. Under Magerion, the entire city has converted to my church. Ardis worships Ravennis now."

"Are we supposed to care?" Belkos snarled. "Ardis is still Ardis. Its people are still our enemies. No new God can change that."

"Let me respectfully disagree," Narky said, sounding in no way respectful. "It's Magor who stood up against your God when Bestillos and the generals came to power, and Magor who tried to exterminate your people. Magor was your enemy, but Ravennis has only helped you. Criton can back me up on this – we left Tarphae together. Ravennis helped us get off the island, and Ravennis kept us together afterwards. Our Gods are allies. Magor tried to destroy you, and Magor tried to destroy Ravennis. Or were you too busy hiding to hear about what happened to Laarna?"

If Hessina or Belkos had been in any way open to Narky's arguments, he lost them with that last gibe. Criton was glad the elders of the plains were there to keep the two of them from tearing Narky apart.

"We know what happened at Laarna," Kana said. "We had heard your God was dead."

"My God *is* dead," Narky said, "just not in the way

other Gods have died. He rules the underworld, while your God rules the heavens. There's no conflict between the two, unless you insist on starting one."

Belkos waved him off. "We haven't fought and bled all this time to make peace on the eve of our victory. Ravennis may not be Magor, but He's still taken the side of the Ardismen."

"Isn't that the whole point of war, though?" Criton nearly begged. "To make peace on our terms?"

"The point of *this* war," Belkos answered, "is to take Ardis."

Hessina turned back to Narky. "You say our Gods are allies? You are a fool. God Most High needs no allies. If you and your God stand in the way of ours, you will both be crushed."

"Maybe," Narky said. "Or maybe God Most High will abandon you if you condemn His friend, just as He turned on the dragons for condemning Salemis. A God as powerful as yours doesn't rely on His people to survive. He can always start again."

Those words struck a blow. The council fell silent, pondering Narky and his threat. Then Belkos said, "Kill this man. He may be your friend, Criton, but he's here to spread poison and doubt. He and his God are liars and cowards – they know that their armies are useless, so they're trying to defeat us from within. Kill him and take Ardis – God Most High will bless us."

"The alliance could be real," Criton said. "Magor and Ravennis have been enemies all along."

"That doesn't make his God and ours friends," Endra pointed out.

"Kill this man," Belkos said again. "Put his ugly head on a spear and drive it into the heart of Ardis."

"Listen to me," Narky said, beginning to sound

desperate. "I'm the man who killed Bestillos while Criton was lying helpless on the ground. Ravennis gave me strength, and guided my aim. I'm one of His fingers. Ravennis did as much to rescue Salemis from his prison as God Most High did – without Him, the Dragon Touched would still be in hiding and the plainsmen would still be paying Ardis tribute. You can call Ravennis your ally, you can call Him your God's servant, you can call Him God Most High's son, I honestly don't care. Whatever you want to call Him, He's been on your side."

"That's a very convenient position for you to take," said Hessina, "now that we are at your gates. Where was this alliance two nights ago, when your army tried to surprise us as we slept?"

Narky bowed his head. "I tried to stop that. Magerion thought that Magor's weakness was responsible for your victories, not God Most High's strength, so he figured by aligning himself with a stronger Ravennis, he could beat you. I told him he was wrong, and that Ravennis wouldn't bless the attack, but… it didn't work. I'll take responsibility for not convincing him. I'm here because he's learned his lesson, and is willing to make peace with you."

"Willing!" Belkos laughed. "You hear that? The new king of Ardis is *willing* to make peace with us. Magerion, who was the red priest's lieutenant during the purge, who slaughtered our parents and brothers – he's willing to make peace with us, now that we're about to give him and his people what they deserve."

He spat on Narky's face. "Here's your peace."

Narky wiped his face with his robe, and Criton could see the rage building within his friend. "Criton," Narky asked, "who is this idiot? Can you send him away?"

"Belkos is my cousin," Criton said. "My mother was his aunt."

"Wow. I guess your side got the decency *and* the brains."

Criton folded his arms. "If you want us to make peace with Ardis, you're doing yourself more harm than good. Apologize to my cousin, or this meeting is over."

Narky looked back at him with something like distaste. He'd expected more indulgence from Criton, as if they were back with the others all together, where everyone would forgive him for being blunt. He was reassessing now, and it clearly pained him.

"I apologize," he said, keeping his good eye locked on Criton. "Please forgive me, all of you. I wouldn't want the Dragon Touched to react to my personal rudeness by murdering thousands. So many people are relying on the Dragon Touched to be merciful, the way your God is supposed to be."

"Our God is merciful," Hessina cut in, "but only to the repentant. A city that abandons the worship of a cruel God only to turn to an underhanded one has shown no signs of repentance. Frankly, Ardis does not deserve our mercy."

"Your king sent an army first," Kana agreed, "and when that failed, he sent us his city's rudest messenger to *argue* for peace when he should have been pleading for it. Your lack of respect is staggering."

Criton loudly cleared his throat, hoping to cut off any further escalation. "We'll talk it over and give you our terms," he said.

Once Narky had been led away, the others turned on Criton. "Our terms?" Belkos asked, his voice shaking. "Our terms are that they die! We're not going to let Ardis and its leaders mock us just because you're friends with their high priest!"

"Narky made good points!" Criton objected. "He's not the most polite person I know, but he's one of the smartest, and he's no liar. He believes what he says."

Hessina snorted. "What he says is nonsense."

"How do you know? How do you know Ravennis isn't a servant of God Most High, just as we are? Has our God told you otherwise?"

Hessina shook her head, but she didn't look any less skeptical.

"You don't know, then," Criton said. "I was there when Narky killed Bestillos, and I was there when he killed the giant Boar of Hagardis. I think his argument about Ravennis being a servant of God Most High is a good one. What if he's right? What if God Most High has judged Ravennis worthy of serving Him in this world and the underworld? Our God reigns supreme in the heavens – He doesn't need Ardis. What harm will come to us from offering peace terms?"

"You're young," Belkos said, "and you're foreign. It's easy for you to say that Magor was responsible for the purge, but we remember those days. It wasn't Magor who killed our families, it was the Ardismen. After what they did to us, they think that running to another God will protect them now that we're here to take our city back? Our God is merciful, but Ardis doesn't deserve His mercy. It definitely doesn't deserve ours."

"The purge happened almost thirty years ago," Criton countered. "When you take the city, will you spare those too young to have participated in it? No, you'll kill everyone you can get your hands on, and thirty years from now, the remnants of the Ardismen will try to take *their* city back and punish the people who killed *their* parents."

"Let them try," Belkos sneered. "You think the children of Ardis deserve our mercy because only their parents and grandparents sought to wipe us out? What do you think these children will try to do when they're of age?"

Hessina nodded. "A guardian tree doesn't produce carob seeds, Criton. A poisoned tree bears poisoned fruit."

"That's an argument for perpetual war."

"No," Belkos said, "it's an argument for winning *this* war once and for all. If God Most High is on our side, our enemies will never rise again."

Criton turned to the plainsmen. "Do you agree with this? The Ardismen have been your enemies and your overlords for generations. Do you think we should ignore their pleas for mercy?"

Endra spoke first. "I think with favorable enough terms, a peace might be granted. If Ardis were to pay *us* tribute, and if their walls were to come down as those of Anardis once did, I think that might be suitable. With tributes of gold, bronze, and stone, a city of the Dragon Touched could rise in the north."

"It is a possibility," Kana agreed.

Criton turned back to Hessina. "Our God has named you our leader in matters of religion. What religious tribute would you require the Ardismen to make, if we were going to make peace with them?"

He could tell that Hessina didn't like the question, but she found it unable to dismiss as the others turned to her expectantly. He had asked it well, he knew, reminding her that she was a religious leader and not a political one, and that their God had entrusted him with the authority to make peace as well as war.

At last she said, "Abandoning Magor is not enough, if

they have simply adopted another false God in His stead. The people of Ardis would have to accept God Most High as the Lord Above All, and the master of their new patron God. If your friend Narky is serious about saving Ardis, he can stand before his people as the high priest of Ravennis and proclaim that his God is subservient to ours, a heavenly lieutenant tasked with the mission of bringing God Most High's order to the world below. If the people embrace this teaching and repent of their actions in the purge, Ardis will be worthy of God Most High's mercy."

Endra raised his eyebrows. "That's a lot to ask."

"It's perfect," Criton said. "Narky has the authority to make God Most High's supremacy official dogma for the worshippers of Ravennis. If he wants to save Ardis, he'll do it. He suggested the idea himself; let him own it."

They spent the next hour discussing the specifics of the proposed tribute Ardis would have to pay, and then sent for Narky. He grimaced when he heard their conditions, but promised to deliver their message to Magerion and return with his answer. Then he left with his guards, and it fell to Criton to calm his cousin.

Hessina might have given Criton her blessing to negotiate terms despite her skepticism, but Belkos was inconsolable. "You're selling our victory away for smoke and vapor," he said. "This decision will doom us. Our grandchildren will be slaves."

"That's ridiculous," Criton said. He didn't understand his cousin's anger – why should Belkos be so attached to this war when even Hessina was willing to see where Criton's negotiations would lead?

"Magerion may not accept the terms," Kilion pointed out. He had been nearly silent throughout the meeting, but apparently he too was bothered by Belkos' irrationality.

"That won't forgive what you've tried to do here," Belkos said. "You would give Ardis away for nothing."

"How can you say that?" Criton asked. "If Magerion accepts our terms for peace, it'll mean the end of Ardisian rule over the north, a yearly tribute in gold and stone, and the elevation of God Most High even among the worshippers of Ravennis! How could you dismiss all that?"

Belkos looked at him with contempt. "All those things would be ours if we conquered Ardis as we always meant to. There's nothing they can give us that we couldn't take ourselves, but with the surrender of Ardis to Magerion and his people, you leave open the possibility that some day they'll stop paying the tribute, that their religious doctrines could change or their new God be abandoned, and that they will seek to destroy us again. You are selling us for nothing."

"We're selling them their own lives for peace," Criton said. "It seems like a fair enough trade to me."

But Belkos only stormed out of the tent.

"Give him time," Hessina counseled. "He too will be glad when this war is over."

Criton nodded absently. He wondered.

41
PHAEDRA

Phaedra did not stay to watch Psander take a saw to the elf's head. It was the most she could do just to ask Psander how her interrogations were going the next day, when the wizard poked her head into the library.

"Most profitably," Psander answered. "The elven anatomy appears to be built much the same as ours, and yet now that the head has been removed, it is operating on magical rather than anatomical principles. I believe – though I do not yet know – that the head gathers all the magic into itself upon severance and uses it as a backup system until, presumably, it is either reattached or destroyed. From what I've gathered so far, the magic is stored in the heart prior to severance, which is why the elves believe that devouring a heart will increase one's power. Presumably, now that the magic has transferred from heart to brain, the elven way would be to devour the latter."

"Oh," Phaedra said, trying to keep her disgust from showing. "Do you plan on... doing that?"

"I'll admit I've considered it," Psander said, "but I think there is more to be learned before I take such final measures. Olimande can still talk, you know, even with the top of his skull removed. And with greater access to his brain, I think I may be able to disinhibit him and improve the quality of his answers. I shall have to be very careful, but I think it can be done."

Psander finally seemed to take note of Phaedra's discomfort as she said this, and twisted her mouth thoughtfully. "Perhaps while I am conducting my experiments, you should take the opportunity to conduct some research of your own. Independent research used to be a staple of magical schooling, back when such a thing existed. I believe we will both be glad to see you put to good use here in the library rather than getting in my way upstairs."

Phaedra nodded. "That sounds perfect."

"What have you been reading this morning?"

"Nothing in particular," Phaedra lied. In actuality, she had been scanning the first few lines of scroll after scroll and codex after codex, searching for any sign of healing magic. Psander had once told her that healing magic was a lost art, that there was no way to fix her ankle, and yet Phaedra knew that *some* texts still existed from the days of academic healing magic – after all, she had brought Psander just such a scroll from Anardis. *Developments in Magical Surgery* it had been called, and she doubted it was the only one of its kind.

So far, her search had been unsuccessful. Besides *Developments*, which covered magical techniques for wound cleaning and ultra-localized cautery, the only other scroll of healing magic that Phaedra had found so far described a rather horrifying surgery for the male anatomy. She was very glad that she had put that one away before Psander came in.

"I meant to ask you," she said, pointing to a side table

piled high with scrolls. "What are all those doing there? Were you researching the underworld?"

"I wasn't," Psander answered, "though I had meant to at one time. In return for her help with the Boar of Hagardis, I had promised Bandu that I would tell her how to retrieve her wolf from the world below. It's a ridiculous notion, of course – you don't risk your soul for an animal that was barely going to last the decade anyway. But for a brief while, I thought I might have time to research the question."

"But you won't now," Phaedra said with disappointment, noting the finality in Psander's voice. The wizard might have opened her tower to the villagers, might have finally revealed herself to them, but that didn't mean she had changed. Promises meant nothing to her, except as tools for getting what she wanted.

"No," Psander agreed, "I won't. There has always been a more pressing concern, and I imagine there always will be."

Phaedra looked over at the pile of books. "Then I will."

"You will do no such thing. I've given you all the tools you need to be truly useful – I won't have you squander your skills on such frivolity when there is much more urgent work to be done. It won't be long before I'll be sending you back, after all."

"What?" Phaedra cried. "You need me to go back? Why are you only telling me this now?"

She could have answered her own question. Psander never volunteered information until it was convenient for her to do so, and she never acted out of the goodness of her heart. Bandu called her a wicked woman, Narky called her a blackmailer and a manipulator, and neither of them were wrong. It was the thing Phaedra disliked most about her mentor, even as it was nearly inseparable from the quality she admired most: Psander's unapologetic use of power.

After a meaningless, defensive answer to Phaedra's second question, Psander went back to answering the first. "When we first arrived here," she said, "the ground shook, and so did the sky. Was there no such effect in the other world?"

"The sky shaking?"

Psander nodded. "It only happened here, then. Had it happened on your side, you would have known. A skyquake is not a subtle effect. If you stay here for long enough, you're bound to witness one – which, I assure you, you don't want to do."

"I trust you," Phaedra said. It was hard to imagine quite what a skyquake would be like, but that only made the concept more frightening.

Psander went on: "I assumed at first that the skyquake was a temporary aftereffect of our arrival. But there was another soon afterward, and another three months after that. The first came during an assault by the Goodweather elves, and I'm sure it was that more than anything that convinced them my wards were too strong to be overpowered through sheer numbers. The coincidence is responsible for our survival.

"Even so, the phenomenon itself is extremely ominous. I have had some time since then to determine what causes these skyquakes, and I believe that this world is being dragged closer to yours, to a dangerous extent. Our arrival here and the introduction of the Yarek on the other side have bound the worlds closer together, and they are moving closer still. As far as I can tell, if the connection isn't loosened then the two will eventually crash, most likely killing everyone on both."

Phaedra couldn't help but gasp – it was too terrible to

believe. Would God Most High really have allowed the islanders to plant the Yarek's seed in their soil even if it meant the eventual destruction of both worlds?

"Then why haven't we seen any skyquakes on our side?" she asked. Surely, Psander had made some mistake.

Or maybe she hadn't. It was true that God Most High had been kind to Phaedra and her friends so far, but that didn't mean she could know His motives. Maybe the islanders had been *meant* to bring about the worlds' end?

"I had assumed," Psander told her, "that there had been skyquakes on your side as well. I cannot pretend that I understand the situation fully, but my first guess is that this world's much smaller size makes it more vulnerable to such disturbances. Presumably as the two worlds move closer together, your side too will begin to see these effects."

"But you think we can fix this?" Phaedra asked, sounding desperate even to her own ears. "You think we can stop the collision from happening?"

Psander shrugged. "Maybe. In any case, it seems wise to try."

"So what will I be doing?"

"Sealing gateways," Psander said. "I have come to believe that the gateways between the worlds are not only areas of thinner mesh but in fact points of connection, tethers that keep the worlds from drifting apart. The new one between my hall and Tarphae seems to have thrown off the balance, but presumably sealing some of the other gates will have an effect similar to cutting loose a mooring line – the distance between the worlds should grow with each severance until eventually the system becomes stable again.

"This newest connection will be the strongest, of

course, built as it is on the Yarek's power. It may take
the severing of many gates to make up for the one new
one. But to cut the connection at my hall would be to
cede all power over interworld travel to the elves, and
I am unwilling to do that – besides which, a severance
may be a good deal more difficult to accomplish here
than elsewhere. In any case, my preference is to sever
the connections at the other gateways instead, releasing
some of the tension while leaving me in possession of
the only active gate.

"The flaw in this plan, of course, is that I'm still afraid
to leave my house. I may be safer here than in my
previous location, but I cannot afford to meet any elves
without the protection of my walls and wards. Your
presence solves this problem. If you could go back and
seal the gateways from the other side, it would put both
of us at lower risk without lessening our effectiveness.
That is my hope, anyway."

Her words were heartening. As long as they had a
plan, Phaedra felt she could move mountains. "How do I
seal a gate?" she asked.

"That's the bad news," Psander said, gesturing to the
walls of books that surrounded them. "Your guess is as
good as mine. Nobody's ever attempted to close a fairy
gateway before – I'm proud enough for having learned
how to open one. It is up to you to answer your own
question if you can, and in the meantime I will study
Olimande to determine if and how an elf can die."

"Wait!" Phaedra cried, realizing that her mentor was
about to leave. "Can you at least point me to the right
shelf?"

Psander thought for a moment, but then she shook
her head. "The answer itself is in none of my books –
as I said, to my knowledge nobody has done anything

like this before. The hope is that you will find something tangentially useful in this library, and use it to develop a spell of your own. I cannot tell you where this inspiration lies – if I could, I'd have done it myself. If it were me, I might start with accounts of the War of the Heavens, since that was the last time the mesh underwent significant changes. But that is only a thought."

With that she exited, leaving Phaedra to a roomful of books. Phaedra stared up at the shelves that rose so impossibly high and felt nothing but despair. Even if the answer *was* here somewhere, what were the chances she would find it?

She laughed sadly to herself, a puny "huhuh" that dissipated into the many folds and crevices of the stacks that surrounded her. Who would have thought that she could ever feel so intimidated by a pile of books?

She started where Psander had recommended, with accounts of the War of the Heavens. But her mind kept wandering, and whenever she thought a scroll was about to tell her something useful, it would veer off into some other topic entirely. How had the mesh been torn at the war's onset, and how had it been repaired at its end? The dragons had torn it, the latest scroll attested. The Gods had repaired it. And without another word on the subject, the author would turn to a discussion of casualties or of human reactions or of the Gods-damned weather.

It was horrendously frustrating, and all the while that little side table kept calling out to her. Psander had promised Bandu that she would research the underworld, and then she hadn't. But Phaedra was Bandu's friend – didn't she owe it to her to read those books? Psander might have abandoned Bandu and her hopes and dreams, but how could Phaedra? She might even have the opportunity to visit Bandu and Criton someday soon, after she returned to her world. And it would have been one thing if her reading so far had turned up some hint of progress, but it hadn't. More and more, the fact that Phaedra had to save their world felt like an excuse.

Besides, even Psander didn't know where to look for their answers. What if the clue to the sealing of gates was hidden somewhere in those books about the underworld?

Phaedra went to bed that night dreaming about that pile of books, the only part of the library that Psander had deemed "frivolous." When she awoke the next morning, she promised herself that she would devote this day, just this one day, to reading through them. If there wasn't anything useful there, she'd have only lost a day.

To her slight shame, she found the books in Bandu's pile endlessly fascinating. Her mind didn't wander once as she read account after contradictory account of journeys to the underworld, or of what steps people took to avoid getting there in the first place. The first scroll she read was the story of a man who had gone down in search of his dead wife, only to return empty-handed. In the second scroll, the same man came back victorious. The contradictions were maddening, and yet each reversal only made her want to read more.

Over the course of the day, a picture of the world below began to emerge. It was a depressing picture, to be sure. The general consensus was that the dead spent the eternity of the afterlife sleeping, dreamless and inert. Most of the clerical sources Phaedra read were preoccupied with the question of how to avoid this miserable place. The followers of the Sun God cremated their dead, hoping that Atun would take their souls up into Himself instead of letting them sink into the earth; Mayar's followers had a similar reason for their burials-at-sea. There was a southern vulture God whose worshippers performed sky-burials. There were others who didn't seek to avoid the underworld, though: Atel's priests buried their dead much as the Tarphaeans had, and called death the Final Journey.

The second most common theme after avoidance was in the many stories about journeys to the underworld and back. And yet, while these stories were common, there was only one man whose success was entirely verifiable: Maira, the wizard-king of Parakas, had retrieved his wife from the underworld some hundred and thirty years ago, a success that had been much celebrated at the time. When she came across the fact, Phaedra's heart leapt. Here finally was the information Bandu had sought! Even if she never used it to bring back Four-foot, she would know that Phaedra had kept Psander's promise for her.

So yes, dinnertime had come and gone and Phaedra was starving and weary, but surely this merited a second day of study.

That second day began with another fascinating reversal: though the contemporary accounts of Maira's feat all agreed that he had succeeded, there was no agreement on how. The wizard-king had told his story to scores of people, and each version was notably different from the others. The monsters and demons Maira had bested on his journey seemed to change with the telling, as did the manner of his victories. Phaedra tried to determine which version of the story he had told first, but even that wasn't exactly clear. Unfortunately, the rescued wife didn't seem to have contributed to any of the accounts. She had apparently gone silent within days of her return and refused to speak to anyone besides her elderly mother, who had taken their conversations with her to the grave.

The most awful scroll Phaedra read that day was a list of wizards and heroes who, inspired by Maira's success, had attempted similar journeys over the last century-and-a-half and never come back. Most of them had been trying to bring back children, those they had lost to disease or accidents or, in one case, a grisly murder. It broke Phaedra's heart to read summary after summary of the tragedies that had prompted grown men – and they were almost exclusively men – to willfully hurl themselves into the abyss in the hopes of seeing their beloved sons and daughters once more. When she was finished reading the scroll, Phaedra found that she had no strength to keep researching the matter. She skimmed a few more scrolls to see if she could find the method by which Maira had journeyed to the underworld, but gave up before she found it. After reading that horrifying list, the idea of helping Bandu reach the underworld was no longer appealing to her.

So she turned back to the question of the gateways, unsure, as always, of how to proceed. How many gates were there? How many would she have to seal to make up for the new one? And were they like simple threads connecting the worlds, or could each gateway on the fairy side connect to multiple human-side gates? If they formed a sort of web, then would closing a gate on just one side even work?

She had spent too long with books – she couldn't think straight anymore. Psander was still shut in her lab, conducting Gods-knew-what horrible experiments on Olimande's head, so Phaedra went to talk to Hunter instead. He was resting in his room after dinner, staring at the ceiling. "Am I disturbing you?" she asked.

"No," Hunter said, sitting up hurriedly. "I was just thinking about you, actually."

"Really?"

Hunter nodded and stood, looking self-conscious. "I was going to ask if you'd… like to marry me."

Phaedra gawked at him. She opened her mouth, and closed it again. She was dimly aware that she must look like an idiot, but she couldn't so quickly adjust from the conversation she had expected to have, to… to this.

"We're finally here," Hunter continued nervously, "and you're learning magic just like you meant to, and as bad as it is in this world, I think we could make a life together if we wanted to. *Do* you want to?"

Phaedra was still staring, but she forced herself to speak. "This is so sudden," she said.

"I'm sorry," he said. "I didn't mean for it to be sudden. I thought you might already know how I feel, but I guess I'm not that good at expressing…"

"It's all right," she said, awkwardly.

"So… do you want to…?"

"No," Phaedra said, and responded to his wince with one of her own. "I can't, Hunter. Not right now, anyway. There's no telling if we'd conceive as quickly as Bandu and Criton did, but I can't afford the risk. None of us can afford it, really."

"We can't?"

"We can't."

She told him then what Psander had told her about the skyquakes, and of the mission she would soon be leaving on. Additional complications were decidedly unwelcome.

"Oh," Hunter said, and his disappointment was painful to behold. "No, I guess that makes sense."

They stood there in silence, the pain between them growing. Hunter opened his mouth to say something, but Phaedra interjected, "I don't know," and he closed his mouth again. She had imagined him about to ask whether she might marry him sometime in the future, assuming Psander's plan succeeded. Now, regardless of whether this had indeed been his intended question, they both knew it was the question she had answered.

"I see," Hunter said.

"I'm sorry," she said, and left him alone in his room.

She felt terrible. She loved Hunter like family, and she had always been attracted to him. He was such a sweet, gentle man, and he *was* good looking. In another life, under different circumstances, she thought she might have married him without a moment's hesitation.

But the more she thought about it, the more Phaedra realized she had made the right choice. It wasn't just the current circumstances: she didn't think she'd *ever* be ready to leave her studies behind and devote herself to raising children. As terrible as it felt to admit it, she would rather live Psander's life than Bandu's.

She had always assumed that she would have children one day. But that assumption was now a relic of her old life on Tarphae, of the days when her options had been limited by her parents' imagination. Had things gone as they'd been supposed to, had Tarphae never been cursed, Phaedra would have returned home after last year's pilgrimage, married whomever her parents had chosen for her, and had however many children the Gods chose to give her. But that wasn't her life anymore. What's more, she didn't *want* it to be her life.

Now her life was magic. It was full of questions she had never thought to ask as a girl, and answers to the ones she had. Let others marry and have children – there was no lack of children in the world, but there was a distinct lack of wizards. There would be no time for babies during her mission, and there would be no time for them afterward either. How could she ever go from a quest to save all of humanity to a normal life of marriage and pregnancies and childrearing?

And if she did, how could she do it without growing to hate the man who had asked it of her?

She lay awake that night, too overwhelmed to sleep. She ought to talk to Hunter again. She ought to explain that her inability to settle down with him was not only for now, but forever. But he would be asleep by now, and she could not go and wake him. It would give him false hope for a moment, and in the most vulgar possible way. She couldn't do it.

But she couldn't sleep either.

Instead she rose, conjured a ghostly candle in her hand, and stumbled to the library again. This time she didn't make any attempt at rational strategy, but pulled scrolls and codices off the shelf at random and read each one only until she tired of it.

It was in a book about trees that she finally found what she was looking for. It wasn't even a magical text, but an agricultural one – in one section, the author discussed trees' ability to heal and grow, telling the story of a woodcutter who had come across an iron nail fully embedded in the bole of an oak, invisible until the tree had been cut down.

The mesh, Salemis had once said, repaired itself. Why, then, was it thinner in some places than in others? At the gateways it was thin enough that at certain times the elves could tear at its fabric and use it for their nets – at least until the healing mesh drew those nets back into itself. There must be something in those places keeping

it thinner, continually wearing it down. There were nails
hidden somewhere in the wood.

Phaedra put her book down. The mesh was nothing
like a tree, and so this book could teach her nothing
about it – all it had done was to trigger the right thought.

When she made her report to Psander after breakfast,
the wizard frowned. "I'm not sure I follow you," Psander
said. "We already knew that the mesh was thinner at
the gateways than in other places. How has this changed
anything?"

"It's changed everything!" Phaedra cried. How could
Psander not see it? "What I'm saying is that if the mesh
naturally heals, any section that's thinner than the
others must be a place where there's a hidden irritant
continually wearing away at it. If we could find that
irritant and remove it, the mesh would close the wound
on its own!"

"But what would such an irritant look like?"

"It's probably something different at each gate. For
the new one, it could be Silent Hall or the whole island
of Tarphae, or even the Yarek itself. I can't remove any
of those, but I think I can break some of the other ones
if I know what I'm looking for. You said once that the
wizards' tower at Gateway was built around an old elven
gateway that already existed – what did *that* gateway
look like? How did they know it belonged to the elves?"

"There was a pattern there," Psander answered,
leaning against a lectern. "A sort of echo of the fairies'
world, as I recall people saying. It manifested sometimes
in dreams and sometimes in physical phenomena. I was
once instructed to count the leaves that had fallen in the
clearing, and found there to be a hundred and twenty-
one of them – eleven times eleven. It wasn't any single
structure, like a circle of stones or anything of that nature."

"I'll bet there was still something more specific causing it all," Phaedra said. "I might be able to find it if I went back there."

Psander's mouth twisted, but then she nodded. "We might not do any better than that as far as theory goes, not without experimentation. I'll show you how I open the gate in the courtyard, and we can plan for you to leave tomorrow."

"One more thing, please." Phaedra raised the scroll she had taken from the side table, the list of failed attempts to breach the underworld. "This list only has two women on it, and thirty-two men. I thought you said there had been many female academic wizards before you, but if there were, then why didn't they–"

"I said no such thing," Psander answered, cutting her off. "I said only that there had been female wizards before me, which indeed there had been. But it was not a large number, even in the best of times. The community of academics was never welcoming to us – it was a fight for every book and every apprenticeship. When I told you there had been others, I did not mean to imply that I was unexceptional."

"Oh," said Phaedra. "I see. And now there's just you and me."

"Yes," Psander said with a slight smile. "If we survive the coming crisis, I'm sure much will be written about that fact. If others do not write it, we shall have to write it ourselves."

She looked cheerful enough that Phaedra risked asking her about Olimande – and regretted it immediately.

"I may yet eat his brain," the wizard answered. "He seems to have run out of useful things to tell me."

Phaedra shuddered. "Do you think that would actually help?"

"It might," Psander said. "Power is power, and if the elves mean to gain it by feeding on us, we may as well return the favor."

"Has he taught you anything about how to fight the elves off?"

"Yes. It seems that if an elf is not decapitated but pierced through the heart, the magic will bleed out into the world, killing him and returning that magic to the plant-beast this world is made of. The elves have a tradition of decapitating their enemies in battle in order to humiliate them, but only slay each other under very rare circumstances. Battle is a kind of sport to them most of the time."

"But not against us."

"No," Psander said, "of course not against us. They see us as lesser beings, and they envy us for the attention the Gods have shown our world, short-sighted as that makes them. They think we deserve death more than they do."

"Auntie Gava called them demons," Phaedra said. "I think she's right."

"Knowing what we do now? Undoubtedly. If you are successful in closing all the other gates, it will save countless lives not only from our colliding worlds but from the elves as well."

"There's a lot I still don't understand," Phaedra confessed. "I've been assuming so far that the gateways are like tunnels, but do you think they might open in more than one place in our world?"

"Not as far as I know," Psander said, "though I have hardly had the time to verify that. The gate to Tarphae is the only one I have been able to open so far. I frankly would have expected to be more closely connected to the Yarek and my home's previous location, but I suppose one can also see why the new thread connecting us to our world might attach itself to Tarphae instead. Much of the power that brought me here came from Tarphae one way or another: there were the five of you, of course, who performed the final magic, and it was Karassa's unwilling contribution – as harvested through the tears of your king – that pushed us over the threshold into this world.

"I know what you're thinking," she went on, and Phaedra made a frantic sweep of her mind before realizing that it was just a figure of speech. "When I send you back to our world, I will have to send you right back to Tarphae, where you will have to evade the pirates and find your way safely off the island. I wish there was another way."

"There is," Phaedra said, "but it's going to take a lot more power since I won't be using the stronger gate here. I'll need Olimande too, I think. Illweather and Goodweather obey the elves."

Psander lifted an eyebrow. "If you plan to journey to one of their castles, I cannot condone that. I cannot afford for you to get yourself killed."

"I'm not going to the castles," Phaedra said. "I'm going underground. There's a gate down there, among the roots of the world, that leads straight to the Dragon Knight's Tomb."

42

BANDU

Bandu had never been so happy. In all the ways that her relationship with Criton had been bad, the one with Vella was good. Bandu was beginning to realize how lucky she was that Vella loved her.

Goodweather was thriving too. She was learning to crawl on her own, dragging herself along with her arms since she had not yet mastered the use of her legs. She sometimes tried to stand too, pulling herself up to her feet while holding onto Bandu or Vella or a table leg, but such efforts usually ended with a fall and a wail. Then Bandu would scoop her up, or Vella would, and within a minute she would be back to smiling and babbling.

She was babbling a lot now. At this rate, Vella said teasingly, she'd be talking better than Bandu soon. Bandu didn't like that joke, but she knew Vella hadn't said it to make her angry, so she decided that it was all right.

The babble didn't mean anything yet – Goodweather was only experimenting with the sounds she could make. Her cries, on the other hand, were distinct and meaningful. Bandu could tell hunger cries from sleepy cries, lonely cries from hurt cries. Vella couldn't quite, but she would look to Bandu for her cues and it would generally turn out all right.

They were not always happy, of course. Vella still missed her family, for all that her feelings about them were complicated. She talked of them sometimes, telling Bandu stories of the way they had raised her, and especially of how tender her father had been. Bandu hadn't had much of an opinion of Kilion, who had never given her more than the occasional sympathetic glance, but apparently he was a kind and thoughtful man. He was with his children, anyway.

Bandu avoided talking about her childhood, or about Criton. Instead she told Vella about the others, Phaedra and Narky and Hunter. Vella said they sounded like Bandu's real family, which was right. Bandu might have no parents, but she *did* have a family.

Vella was horrified to learn that Bandu did not know how to read. "How could Phaedra not have taught you?" she asked, and when Bandu told her that she didn't want to learn, Vella would not take that for an answer.

"All the Dragon Touched teach their children to read," she insisted. "We were advisors to the king once. Everyone has to learn."

"I don't," Bandu said. "Dead people shouldn't talk."

Vella clearly found that statement confusing, so Bandu had to explain how Psander had had animal skins full of the words of dead people. Bandu did not think it was right for dead people's words to remain after they were gone.

Vella didn't care. "I'll teach you," she said. "I'm sorry, but not being able to read – it's like being a child, for us. You have to at least try."

So Bandu tried. She hated it. A week of lessons

yielded no progress whatsoever. She couldn't tell the symbols apart – they were just meaningless shapes that didn't look anything like what they were supposed to: a camel, a fish, an ox, an eye, and so on. Each made a sound related to its shape, but it was hard to remember what those sounds were when it took such creativity to recognize the pictures.

"Why I do this for you?" she complained. "I never use this."

Vella looked at her sternly. "Of course you'll never use it if you don't learn it. That doesn't mean it isn't useful."

Bandu tried kissing her, but Vella pulled away. "You can't get out of learning to read that easily."

Sometimes Bandu missed Criton.

"How it helps later?" she demanded, not bothering to hide her skepticism. "I never read from dead animal skin, history and lies and bad things. Phaedra reads those, and she can tell me things if I need them. You can do that too – you don't need me to read also."

"And what if I have to go somewhere, and I want to leave you a note to tell you where I've gone? You can't always rely on other people, Bandu. If you don't learn how to read, someday you'll wish you did."

Bandu doubted she was right about that, but there was no dissuading her, so she did her best. Her best wasn't very good, but as long as she was trying, Vella showered her with praise and affection. That made the struggle easier, at least.

She did sometimes resent Vella for forcing her to tire her eyes and her mind; for torturing her with the symbols even when she wanted to relax; for taking even the moments when Bandu was nursing her daughter to test her knowledge. Vella scratched the letters into the wall beside their bed, formed them out of rocks in the garden, used them to count the days. The letters didn't only make sounds, they also represented numbers, and Vella drilled Bandu in those too. She began dreaming at night that the symbols were chasing her through the forest, shouting their names at her. The whole thing was exhausting.

They fought about it sometimes. Bandu didn't like being forced to do anything, and the fact that Vella did it in order to help her was no consolation. Bandu couldn't imagine ever needing to know how to read, and it felt sometimes as if Vella was trying to punish her for not having had parents who taught her such things. She didn't mean it as a punishment, of course, and that was important... but it wasn't everything.

Still, despite the pressure from Vella and the inevitable arguments that resulted, Bandu couldn't help but notice how much happier she was here than she had ever been with Criton. Vella never stopped engaging with Bandu's feelings, never refused to explain herself, and never, never turned violent. They would come out of each fight happier with each other than they'd been before, and that was more precious than anything. When Goodweather grew older, Bandu would teach her to look for that in a mate.

And over time, Bandu had to admit that Vella's lessons were working. When she forced herself to, she could sound out most of the words Vella scratched into the ground for practice, and she nearly cried when she discovered one day that one of the phrases Vella had carved beside their bed the week before was "I love you, Bandu." Vella did not stop teaching her after that, and the lessons didn't get any easier, but Bandu stopped resenting her for it. If it hadn't been for Vella's persistence, Bandu would never have discovered the joy that old words could bring.

Then one morning, Bandu awoke to Vella shaking her. "What's wrong?" she asked.

"I had a nightmare," Vella said. "Could you tell me if you think it means something?"

Bandu nodded, feeling suddenly afraid. She had had a prophetic nightmare once. She had misunderstood it at the time, and it had cost Four-foot his life.

"It started like one of my regular bad dreams," Vella confessed. "You told me you were leaving me and going to find Criton. I have dreams like that sometimes. But this time, you left me holding Goodweather, and she looked up and asked me if you were ever coming back. And I wanted desperately to say 'Yes,' but somehow I couldn't. And she said, 'We never should have left.'

"Then my grandmother was sitting alone in a room, crying. I wasn't holding Goodweather anymore, and I went to try to reassure my grandma, and put a hand on her back, and she turned to me and said, 'I feel sick.' Then she started heaving, and she opened her mouth and black feathers came pouring out. There was blood in the feathers too, it was really frightening and disgusting. I could still see it happening even after I turned away from her, because you don't see things with your eyes in dreams. I think there was more, but I can't remember it now. What does it mean, Bandu?"

Bandu shook her head. "Hessina is all the Dragon Touched. Black feathers are Ravennis, or maybe Narky. Narky is from Tarphae like me, he goes to Ardis before we meet your kind. Maybe Narky is Ardis? Your people try to eat Narky, and that is bad for them. I don't know why Hessina is crying before the feathers."

"And the first part?" Vella asked. "Where you left me with Goodweather and went back to Criton?"

"That never happens," Bandu said firmly. "I don't want him, I want you."

Vella looked dissatisfied, as well she might. In her dream, Goodweather had said that they shouldn't have ever left. They shouldn't have left, and now the Dragon Touched were about to do something foolish. Was it too late to stop them?

"Bandu. Tell me what you're thinking."

Bandu didn't want to say it. Vella was happy here. *She* was happy here. She would have been glad for Vella and Goodweather to be the only Dragon Touched, the only people she saw for the rest of her life. But she did not want Goodweather to grow up as Criton had, believing herself and one parent to be the only two Dragon Touched in the world.

"I think if we don't go back, they try to take Ardis and it is very bad for them. I think if they lose their war, then we are never safe. You are not safe, Goodweather is not safe. Maybe I am looking for Criton in your dream because I want to say don't try to take Ardis. Sometimes Criton listens to me."

Vella looked horrified. "Don't go," she said. "I can't live out here without you, hoping and praying that you'll come back. Don't do that to me."

"I don't go without you," Bandu answered. "Your dream is wrong. You come with me."

"I can't, Bandu! You don't understand! My people don't take kindly to adultery – there's no telling what they'll do to us if we go back together!"

"What is adultery?"

"It's what we've been doing, Bandu. Making love together when we're married to other people. My husband could kill us in front of everyone and no one would stop him!"

"I stop him," Bandu reassured her. "They don't know what we are doing together, because they are not here with us. We tell them we leave together because you love Goodweather, and they don't know anything else. Criton is angry, but he doesn't hate us, and if Pilos hates you and wants to kill you, I stop him. Don't be afraid."

There were tears in Vella's eyes. "I *am* afraid, Bandu. Let's stay here. *Please*."

Bandu looked at her new mate, so beautiful and so frightened, and relented. "You don't want to go," she said, "even if all your people die?"

"We don't know that that's what it means," Vella insisted. "All I know is that if I go back, they'll kill me. They'll kill us both, Bandu. Don't go."

Bandu kissed her and stroked her hair, loving the way it flowed so smoothly down from her head, straight and silky. "If you stay," she said, "I stay. Criton can save your people by himself."

43

PHAEDRA

Now that Phaedra had learned the basics of magical composition, learning how to open a gate turned out to be fairly simple. In many ways it was like tugging on one of the invisible threads that summoned the books in Psander's library down from the shelves. The difficulty was in finding the weak spot and gathering the strength to pull on it. That would be harder at one of the older gates than it was in Psander's courtyard, so Phaedra would need a source of external power. But Psander assured her that that would be no obstacle – she planned to cremate Olimande's body, and between that and the elf's head there would be plenty of fuel for the spell.

To be truthful, Phaedra was extremely uncomfortable with that fuel source. Psander might have no qualms with killing a captured elf for the sake of a spell, but Phaedra did. As odious as the elves were, they were sentient beings – they were essentially *people*. The thought of harvesting a prisoner's life for magic horrified her.

It was worth doing anyway: her mission was to save two worlds, after all. It also helped a little that the elves were mortal enemies, and there was no doubt that

Olimande would have done the same to Phaedra had their situations been reversed. But while that might be enough to convince Phaedra that the deed had to be done, she couldn't bring herself to view it with the same utilitarian coldness that seemed to be Psander's default emotional state.

She wished she could consult with Hunter, who had struggled with his own moral questions and seemed to have found some happy equilibrium in training the villagers to defend themselves. But if she spoke to him about that, she would have to have that other conversation with him too, the one where she dashed his last remaining hopes of marrying her. She had put it off for too long already, and now that she was leaving, could put it off no further.

Well, it had to be done. She could start with the easier part, at least, so that was what she did, telling him of her qualms with using the elf's body and life as ingredients.

"Am I being unreasonable?" she asked. "Should I just learn to live with this?"

Hunter answered, "It sounds like you'll have to live with it, if you're going to do it at all. But that doesn't mean you can't hate it, and never use someone's life that way again unless you're forced to. Don't become like Psander. Don't stop hating it, or start taking it casually. Feeling every death is a good thing, I think."

"It really is horrible," Phaedra said. "I know it's necessary for me to get back to our world and save it from colliding with this one, but that doesn't make the killing any better. It just makes it all more miserable somehow."

Hunter nodded. "Now you know how I've felt."

"But you don't feel that way anymore?"

He frowned. "I didn't say that. Psander is using the

elf about as cruelly as I imagined, and I feel complicit in
that. It's training the others that makes me feel better.
Teaching them how to defend themselves is a worthy
goal – I can throw myself into it without feeling guilty.
We all deserve to live just as much as the elves do."

He said it with a passion she had rarely heard from
him. "You're not coming with me," she said. Hunter
only quietly shook his head. Phaedra had known it all
along in the back of her mind, had even conceived of her
mission as a lone one, but only now that it had been said
could she really acknowledge it. There was no reason for
him to come with her anymore – he had found the life
he wanted, and she had already refused to join it.

He saw the look on her face. "It's not because of that,"
he said. "I promise. I still love you – I wish you could
stay. But even if your work is more important than mine,
these people still have to be defended. They need me."

Phaedra sighed. "You're right, you're right. Oh
Hunter, I'm going to miss you."

He smiled sadly. "I hope so. Will you come back to me,
when this is all over?"

"I…"

It was too painful, what she had to say. He clearly
meant to wait for her, however many years it took. And
she did love him, she realized. She loved him deeply –
just not as deeply as she loved the life she had found. She
would not sacrifice it to him, even if she might someday
be tempted to. He had to know.

"Hunter," she said, trying again, "I love you. I do. But
I can't marry you, not now and not later. We couldn't
consummate it – I don't want any children, ever. I
don't want anything that would keep me from studying
wizardry, or theology, or anything I set my mind to. I
shouldn't have to hate you for doing that to me, and if

we had any children, I would. You deserve better."

Hunter looked devastated, but he was as stoic about it as ever. He had never been one to rage or argue, and that did not change now. All he did was to nod dejectedly and nearly whisper, "I understand. Please come back anyway, if you can. I'll miss you."

She gave him a hug and went to pack.

The next morning, as Phaedra was filling a satchel with dry food, Psander came to her with the urn of ashes from Olimande's body, his head resting on top. She had replaced the top of his skull, but Phaedra knew that if she pulled on his hair it would come off like a lid, and the thought nearly caused her to vomit. She took the urn gingerly and tried to think of something else.

Olimande's head was asleep, or at least pretending to be. Phaedra closed her own eyes and checked to make sure he wasn't reading her mind. He wasn't. The elf must really have been asleep, then. Maybe Psander's interrogations had tired him out.

"Before you go," Psander said, and hurried back upstairs to fetch something. She returned a short while later with the bag of objects they had helped Atella to collect.

"You were right about these," she said. "They will be more useful to you than they are to me. They will not be needed for my wards, in any case. With the information I have extracted from Olimande, and with Hunter's continued assistance in defending the fortress, I believe we will be safe for the time being."

Phaedra took the bag from her. If she was to give Bandu her report on the underworld, she would have to find her somehow. The dirt inside would help with that. The broken arrow and bucket would be useful too, if she ever had to find Narky or Criton. The latter was unlikely to be a problem, since Criton and Bandu were bound to be in the same place, but she supposed one could never be sure.

Every soul in Silent Hall came to see her off. Phaedra bid farewell to them all, saving Hunter for last since she had all but parted with him already. What more was there to say? There was so much pain in his eyes.

She pulled him close and gave him a kiss. "I'm sorry," she said.

"Good luck," he replied.

She left him there and struck out into the forest with Olimande's urn in her left hand and a knife in her right. Every ten steps she stopped to carve a sigil onto a tree trunk. It was a simple sigil of her own design, a lit candle to symbolize her line in the Dragon Knight's prophecy: *let she who is dark bring light to the people.* Ten steps were to avoid the elves, who counted in elevens, while she worked her magic to draw the attention of the plant life. This world was built on the roots of the original Yarek, and it was the plants that would have to come to her aid if she was to find the gateway she was looking for.

When she reached the eleventh tree, she carved two sigils instead of one so that the total number would skip to twelve. She wasn't sure how effective an evasion it was – Olimande woke up while she was carving the twelfth sigil.

"What are you doing?" he asked. Phaedra could feel him trying to probe her mind, but she was ready this time, and he found himself locked out.

"Tell me what Psander has done to you," she deflected.

"She has sawed me open and broken that of me which lies and deceives. She has made me more obedient. And she has hurt me, more than anything I could imagine. She has made me welcome death."

"I'm sorry," Phaedra said. "That's horrible."

"But you benefit nonetheless," Olimande said. "You may be sorry for me, but you still enjoy the rewards of my subjugation. I have been hurt and humiliated and damaged beyond repair, and it only makes me a more useful tool for you."

Phaedra winced. "That's true. Does it help to know that I'm trying to save both our worlds from colliding?"

"It does not," he answered. "I would just as soon see all the worlds destroyed, mine and yours and the Gods' world too. There is no merit in any of them."

Phaedra finished carving her sigil and walked on, counting steps. "You can feel that way, just so long as you help me save them anyway."

"I have no choice in the matter."

At the eighteenth sigil, Phaedra began to notice the trees and undergrowth subtly reaching for her – whether out of attraction or malice, she didn't know. Either way, she was starting to get the attention she wanted, and she stepped up her pace. The effect grew stronger, and by the thirty-fifth sigil, the roots and branches of the forest were actively – if, thankfully, slowly – trying to wrap themselves around her. At the thirty-sixth sigil, the ground shook and split, and a gigantic elder root rose out of it toward her.

"Tell it to stop!" she cried, and Olimande obeyed. The root paused, already halfway around Phaedra's body. "We need to get down to the heart of the world," she told it, though she was not sure it understood. "Ask for me, Olimande."

When he did, the root snapped back into action, wrapping itself around her with a strength that threatened to shatter her ribs. "Safely!" Phaedra shouted, but though the root did not squeeze any harder, neither did it loosen its hold. It lifted her into the air, and with a sudden, gut-wrenching force, plunged back into the ground. It was all Phaedra could do to keep from dropping Olimande and his urn – she let go of her knife and slapped her hand down on his head to keep it from being lost. The top of his skull shifted beneath her fingers. Still she held on, and the Yarek's limb dragged her down into the heart of the world.

The world of the elves was built upon the carcass of the plant-beast that had once threatened the Gods. Its heart was a mass of tangled roots, where the opposing goals and personalities of the elves' living castles came together and intermingled in a sad mimicry of their former unity. It was musty and dark, and Phaedra felt very much entombed. When the plunging and plummeting ceased and the root let her go, she struggled to keep her balance on the uneven roots. "Thank you," she said, to Olimande and the Yarek both.

"Muh ouh," Olimande replied.

Phaedra summoned a light, and groaned. The top of Olimande's skull had slid partway into his brain, which had scratches and scorch marks on it already from Psander's various manipulations. "Can you speak?" she asked.

"Ubbib," Olimande said, and Phaedra cursed. There was such pain in his eyes, so much that it crowded out even the hatred.

"I'm so sorry," she said.

She placed him down on a root and went about her work, sprinkling the elf's ashes here and there in the sequence she and Psander had developed to wring the most power out of the poor elf's body. One pinch here, one there, two here, three there, five here, then eight, and then back down to five and so on. It was a sequence with power of its own, mimicking the shapes of ferns and plants of all kind, and when she was done counting down, she had thrown pinches of the elf's ashes in eleven different directions. The air was growing hazy, and Phaedra concentrated her newly acquired wizard's sight until she could see the threads of mesh glowing before her. She caught one and pulled, calling on the magic of the fallen elf as the hole widened and a mist rose from within it, glowing with the daylight that lay beyond.

She was about to step through when a root sprang into her path. The Yarek wanted its tribute.

"I thought you would take it yourself," Phaedra whined, but the Yarek only responded by putting a second root in her way. So Phaedra turned back to Olimande's poor miserable head. "The Yarek wants me to feed you to it," she told him. "I'm so sorry."

"Muh bub," Olimande replied, and his presence at the edge of her mind was pure in its hatred.

She lifted the head and presented it to the Yarek formally. "Take this elf, his power and his soul, back into you," she said, "and let me pass into the world the Gods built for my kind."

The roots that had impeded her took the head gently from her hands. Then they curled around it and crushed it. Phaedra winced and shut her eyes. When she opened them, her way was clear.

She limped through the mists and stepped into the light beyond.

44
NARKY

"Tribute!" Magerion snarled. "Ardis does not pay tribute."

"You're right," Narky said. "Getting killed is much more dignified."

The king's retainers made angry noises and looked to Magerion for an order, but after a meaningful pause, Magerion waved them off. "Don't take our enemies' side, Narky," the king warned. "High priest or no, I can have you executed as a traitor."

"At which point," Narky said, "you'd be an enemy to Magor, Ravennis, *and* God Most High, and you'd be damned no matter who won the divine struggle."

Magerion's eyes flashed, but he didn't make any more threats. "You counsel me to choose safety over dignity," he said. "That strikes me as going very much against the spirit of Ravennis' teachings. Are you not ashamed? You may wish to resign and let someone more capable take your place."

Narky didn't think much of these rhetorical traps. He answered: "Our church used to have a more capable leader, a truly great one who prized victory and glory over life. You killed her, and now you're stuck with me.

Don't try to wriggle out of it. Ravennis knows you well. He gave you a priest who understands you and shares your motivations. I think you ought to make the most of that."

The king narrowed his eyes, but Narky could tell that he was pleased with his answer. He was getting to know Magerion better, and the king was, at least, *slightly* less intimidating now that Narky knew how to gauge his reactions. Less intimidating, but no less terrifying. He could still order Narky's death any time it suited him.

"You think your God is incapable of defending us," he said.

"I think Ravennis cares more for the reality of winning than for its appearance. Laarna's martyrs are now celebrating their God's victory while Magor's worshippers suffer endless humiliation in the underworld. Look past the obvious victories and losses – half of them aren't real. As long as the city stands, Ardis hasn't lost. If Ravennis wants us to keep fighting this war, He'll give us an omen. Otherwise, take what peace you can get from the Dragon Touched. It didn't turn out well for you the last time you ignored my advice."

Magerion sat in quiet contemplation for a time. "You may be right," he said at last. "Tribute is not death, and we may not have the strength to win this war. Since Bestillos died at your hands, Ardis has suffered defeat after defeat – it is no wonder that we are too weak to stand against the Dragon Touched. A few years' respite would give us a chance to recover. How long do you suppose we'll have to pay this tribute before we are strong enough to resist them?"

Narky shrugged. "As long as it takes for them to displease their God. It'll happen eventually, and when it does we should strike with all the force we have before they have the chance to get in His good graces again. The dragons fought a war without God Most High at their backs, and that's why there's only one left."

"And what of that one? Will it come back?"

"I don't know – from what I hear, he came down to talk to the Dragon Touched and then left again. It would be useful to know what he said."

"Tribute it is, then," Magerion said. "We will put off this war until we have greater strength and more information. It should not be hard to find spies who will pose as deserters and followers of the dragons' God, and we will be prepared should the Dragon Touched falter in their worship. Tell me, then, of your friend's terms."

Narky told him everything, including the requirement that he go before the people and announce God Most High's supremacy. The king frowned. "And you think Ravennis would permit His high priest to call Him a servant? You told me Ravennis and God Most High were allies."

"I don't think the difference matters as much as you think it does," Narky said. "I'll tell you what the Graceful Servant told me: it's been centuries since the last time God Most High was active. He's active again now, but who knows how long that'll last? The Graceful Servant said that there'll come a time when the world has forgotten God Most High, when people might even believe that Ravennis *is* God Most High. I don't think He'll mind if I call Him a servant to God Most High this year, or this decade, or this century. His scope is long."

Magerion looked disgusted. "You would live as a slave your whole life, content because your descendants might one day conquer."

"I'm already a slave to Ravennis," Narky said. "This hardly changes anything."

Magerion nodded. "That may be true. But I am no slave, and my children and grandchildren will not live as slaves. Even so, we will accept this tribute as a temporary solution to our problems. If the Dragon Touched cease their hostilities and leave to settle in the north, we will accept their terms for now. Let us hope that they displease their God soon."

Narky breathed a sigh of relief. "You'll let me tell Criton that we'll take his deal?"

"Yes," Magerion said. "But we must watch for those omens you spoke of. If the Dragon Touched displease their God, we strike. And if you learn that Ravennis means for us to fight this war now after all, do not dare conceal it from me. Ardis has taken Ravennis as its God – if I learned that you have deceived me about your God's wishes just to aid your countrymen among the Dragon Touched, your life will be forfeit, as will your wife's and any children or even friends that you may possess. Your countrymen are enemies to this city, Narky, and though that may yet save Ardis during this time of the Dragon Touched conquest, I will not pretend that I trust you for it."

"I understand," Narky said. "You've got nothing to worry about. If Ravennis wants a war, I won't hesitate to say so. He owns me."

He went back to his new temple, where Ptera was just finishing a communal service. When he told her that Magerion had accepted Criton's peace terms, she nearly shouted for joy. "Thank Ravennis, Narky, you did it! After that night raid, I was sure Ardis would fall."

Two of Ptera's cousins had died in the raid on the Dragon Knight's Tomb, and though Narky hadn't really known either of them, their deaths had been devastating to her. She came from a large family, it seemed, and she was close even with her cousins in a way that Narky couldn't quite fathom. He hadn't even been that close with his father.

The family was proud of Ptera for marrying him, but Narky got the sense that they didn't really see him beyond his role as high priest. Maybe that was for the best – not everybody who knew him liked him.

Sometimes he thought that only Ptera and Magerion realized how young he was. It was as if everyone assumed he was Ptera's age or something. Or maybe it was just that they respected him, and nobody at home ever had. Whatever the reason, all that respect felt wrong to him.

Ptera frowned when he told her about the teachings he would have to adopt to be in keeping with the terms of the peace, but unlike Magerion, she had no problem understanding Narky's reasons for agreeing to those terms.

"You're right," she said, "it doesn't matter if you have to tell people that Ravennis is subservient to God Most High. The dragons' God has no image and only the monstrous Dragon Touched as His representatives – even those who believe Ravennis to be His servant will choose to worship the servant and not the master."

"That may be true," Narky said. "In any case, I doubt Ravennis will be the servant forever, no matter what the Dragon Touched want me to say. It may sound ridiculous, but I think the Graceful Servant might have been too cautious when she talked about the future. It looks like we're going to last the year, and that means Elkinar's priests will have to admit I was right: whether They started that way or not, Ravennis and Elkinar are the same God now. It's possible that Ravennis will even absorb God Most High one day, especially if we can spread His worship beyond Hagardis to the rest of the world. You never know."

Ptera smiled. "You're so ambitious, Narky. I love that in you. Ravennis chose well."

"He's the God of Fate," Narky said, smiling back. "He knows what He's doing. Besides, does it count as ambition if I don't expect to be here to see it happen? It's not like I'll still be high priest then – I'll be long dead."

"That's a comforting thought," Ptera said. "So when do you leave?"

"Tomorrow," Narky said. "We'll tell Criton that Magerion accepts his terms, and then it'll just be a matter of figuring out what order things happen in. Magerion wants to wait until after the Dragon Touched have withdrawn before he sends the first tribute payment. The Dragon Touched will probably demand that we send the payment first. But at that point, the details don't really matter so much. It'll be over."

"You've done well," Ptera said. "Get some rest."

"Don't I get some sort of reward?" Narky whined. "Besides rest?"

Ptera laughed. "Oh definitely, either before you leave or after you come back. I haven't decided which yet, but at this point the details don't matter that much."

She was only teasing – their sex that night was never in doubt. It was wonderful to think that as long as Ardis stood and no further disasters interrupted them, he'd have a full lifetime of this. That happy thought sustained him until he reached the Dragon Knight's Tomb, at which point he was forced to stop thinking about his wife and concentrate on the task at hand.

Magerion had sent his son Mageris to watch over Narky during the proceedings, which was an annoying reminder that the king didn't trust him. But besides that, all seemed to go well at first. Narky had consciously left his spear behind for this journey, calculating that the gesture of trust would put the Dragon Touched more at ease. It seemed to work. They welcomed him and Mageris at the base of the mountain, and four guards climbed alongside them to the cave where the Dragon Knight had been buried. Narky wondered if the Dragon Touched had ever looked inside the great stone sarcophagus – if they had, they'd have seen that the knight's journal was missing, and that the hand that had rested on it was all out of order where the islanders had scattered its bones in their hurry to read the knight's writings. Not that they would know who had committed this act of desecration, unless Criton told them.

Criton and his council were waiting for them, and Criton was already arguing with that idiot cousin of his. "My mind is made up," he was saying as Narky and Mageris entered. "God Most High chose me to lead our people, and as long as I have that authority, this is the path we'll follow. Hello, Narky."

"Don't let me interrupt," Narky said. "I'm sure my news can wait."

Criton regarded him coolly. "Speak, Narky. For God's sake."

"Magerion has accepted your terms," Narky said, "as have I. He stands ready to begin sending his tribute once you've moved back north and chosen a site for your new city."

Criton looked to the members of his council. "That won't do," the old lady said. "He thinks he can trick us into leaving with no more than a promise."

"You've asked for stone, among other things," Narky pointed out. "I don't know what good that would do you here if you mean to build a city elsewhere."

"And you?" the woman asked. There was some

commotion outside, so she spoke loudly to be heard over the noise. It made her voice sound even harsher as she said, "Have you already told your followers of your God's servitude?"

"Not yet," Narky admitted. "But if you'll give me your assurance that the Dragon Touched will make peace with us, I'll make that announcement as soon as I get back. I've only had just enough time to act as a messenger between you and my king. He accepts your terms. Will you hold by them?"

"Yes," Criton said. He turned to one of the guards. "Pilos, you'll go back with Narky to verify that everything happens as he's said, and to collect the gold part of the tribute. The stone can be sent later, as you say, once we've chosen a site for our new city. Does anyone object to this arrangement?"

He said it while looking at his cousin. Before anyone could answer, a voice said, "Excuse me, everyone," and they turned to see another Dragon Touched man step in with Phaedra at his side.

"Phaedra!" Criton called joyously. "You're back! Where's Huh-guhhhh…"

Narky saw the expressions on the faces in front of him change to horror, and he spun back around to see Criton standing with his cousin's claws lodged in his throat, gurgling as the blood dripped down his neck. Phaedra screamed.

"There will be no demon's bargain," Belkos said, his face contorted with hate. "Ardis will fall!"

With that he yanked his hand back, leaving Criton to collapse, throat torn open.

Narky's instincts were all wrong. He ran toward Criton, as if there was something he could do to save him, while Mageris took advantage of the confusion to stab one of their guards and flee. Narky had definitely made the wrong choice – he couldn't save his friend, and the other Dragon Touched were faster than him anyway. Some pounced on Belkos and subdued him while others crowded around Criton, staring down at what their kinsman had done.

He was dying. There was nothing they could do. Soon one of the remaining guards was on top of Narky, pushing him to the ground and tying his hands behind his back.

"Did you catch Mageris?" Narky asked, his head in a blur.

"Your companion?" the guard said. "Not yet."

"Then you'd better," Narky told him. "Holding me hostage won't do you any good. If you want a chance at peace, you have to keep Magerion from finding out what's happened."

The guard shouted something, and his fellows gave chase. But even if they did catch him, Narky thought, it didn't much matter. Their one chance to avoid catastrophe already lay dying on the cavern floor.

45

PARTHA

Belkos went to his death defiantly, spitting and ridiculing those who had condemned him. "I saved you from lives of slavery!" he yelled at the crowd, a disbelieving smile on his face. "I did what no one else was willing to do, and you're executing me for it! Have you all turned upside-down? When the Ardismen come to enslave your children, will you throw flowers at them? Will you give them a welcoming feast? What's the matter with you all?"

"Our God gave us a leader," the old priestess answered him, "and you murdered him. Do not pretend that you have done some holy thing."

She sounded so familiar, that priestess. Did Partha know her from somewhere?

Someone threw a rock at Belkos, and then suddenly everyone was doing it. Iona wailed and held her daughter back as the people stoned her husband and left him buried there under the rocks that had killed him. Partha watched too, horrified and yet relieved, suddenly emptied of the anxiety that had been pressing on her since that first awful vision. If Belkos was dead, that meant it was almost over. Almost over.

She couldn't spot the Black Dragon among the crowd, but she knew this was his fault. He had connived and tricked them all into doing it, and now any minute he would appear and give Iona his mealy-mouthed apology. Partha was so sure of it that even when the stoning was long over and she was alone with her grieving daughter and granddaughter, she couldn't remember if it had already happened or not.

"Grandma was right," the young girl sobbed into Iona's chest. "It's Criton's fault they killed him."

Iona just shook her head and wept.

"It's the She-wolf too," Partha told them, but her daughter turned on her. Wait, no. Not her daughter – Iona was her daughter. What was the word she was looking for? It wasn't "niece," she didn't think.

In any case, the girl pulled away from Iona and glared at her. "Bandu's not even here! She hasn't been here in weeks, remember? She took Vella and she disappeared."

"Vella?" Partha asked. "Who's Vella?"

That made the young one so angry that she screamed and ran from the tent. Oh – Dessa! That was her name! Dessa was furious for some reason.

"Don't worry about her, Mother," Iona said, her voice as dead as her husband. "She'll come back."

"If you say so, dear."

Iona was always trustworthy, and this Iona was clearly the real one. Thank goodness she had returned! If only her husband hadn't been killed by that horrible man and his horrible black wife. Iona deserved happiness, poor thing.

She was staring straight ahead, her eyes fixed on the tent pole. "I can't believe he did it," she said. "I can't believe they took him from us."

"They always wanted to take him," Partha told her. "That Black Dragon—"

"The Black Dragon is dead," Iona snapped. "Belkos murdered him, Mother, that's why they stoned him. None of this is Criton's fault."

Her words baffled Partha – why would Iona lie about this, of all things? Belkos couldn't have killed the Black Dragon, because the Black Dragon was supposed to apologize for all this! Or had he done it already, somehow? She was confused, far too confused. Just like that, all the anxiety came rushing back. Something was very wrong here, and she couldn't see where she'd made the mistake. Were her visions lies too? Why would her God do that to her?

Tears sprung to Partha's eyes. "I don't know what's happening to me," she confessed, and the shame of it swept over her like a flood. "Help me, Iona. I don't understand it. What's happening to me?"

Iona's eyes finally met hers, and they were full of knowledge and pain. "The same as with everyone," she said, and nearly choked. "The whole world is going mad."

"But I don't want this! I hate this!"

"I know," Iona said, and she put both arms around Partha and held her close. "Me too."

46
PHAEDRA

It was like a bad dream: she had returned from the world of the elves just in time to watch her friend die. Criton was gone by the time they'd even bandaged his neck, slipping away into the world beyond. Moments ago she had thought that Olimande's demise was the worst thing she would experience in her life, and it wasn't even the worst thing she was experiencing *today*.

They buried Criton outside the cave, in a grave as deep as the rocky ground would allow. His kin and a huge crowd of human plainsmen all gathered to mourn the man they called the Black Dragon, piling stones atop his grave until the mound was nearly as tall as Criton had been. Little Delika was there, much to Phaedra's surprise, and she threw herself weeping on the stones until one of the Dragon Touched men gently pulled her away. But still Bandu did not come.

Over the next few hours, the situation became clearer. Bandu was gone, having left Criton for reasons nobody knew or was willing to tell her. Goodweather was with her, as was the wife of another Dragon Touched man. Belkos, the cousin who had murdered Criton, was sentenced by his kinsman and stoned to death, after which a much smaller funeral was held. The murderer's family cried and could not be comforted – they had lost two beloved family members in one day, and there was nobody close to them who hadn't taken a hand in the second death.

Narky, now a prisoner, explained the situation that Phaedra's arrival and Criton's assassination had disrupted. Criton had died at a crucial moment, just as he was about to end the war the Dragon Touched had waged against Ardis. Magerion, the new king of Ardis, would take that murder as an omen from Ravennis, proving that their God wanted the war to go on until the Dragon Touched had been annihilated.

"Criton's bastard cousin thought the Dragon Touched should burn Ardis down and build themselves a new city on its ruins," Narky said. "If Magerion attacks them now, it'll give them an excuse to try. This is going to end really badly."

"Bandu needs to be told," Phaedra said. "I don't know what went on between her and Criton, but she's the only one who can bring him back."

"Bring him back?" Narky repeated. "That's possible?"

"It's possible," Phaedra answered. "It's also incredibly dangerous. We'd have to find an entrance to the underworld, which I don't know how to do; then the journey down is its own trial, and beyond that, no one knows. There'll almost certainly be a price for bringing him back, but I haven't the faintest idea what it might be. As far as I know only one person has ever brought someone back from the underworld, and his story of how he did it changed depending on who asked. The nature of the place may even have changed since then, for all I know."

"It has," Narky said. "Ravennis has taken the underworld as His domain, where His worshippers are rewarded and His enemies punished. That's the good news. If my God wants this peace as much as I thought He did, He'll be very supportive of a quest to bring Criton back."

"You don't think this really is an omen then?"

"If it's an omen, it'll be from God Most High and not Ravennis. I could see the point of sacrificing Laarna, and then the Graceful Servant, but Ardis? I can't see how that would benefit Ravennis at this point, and I think we can all agree that He's not planning on beating God Most High in battle."

Phaedra stopped him there. "The Graceful Servant is dead?"

Narky nodded. "I'm the high priest of Ravennis now. What did you *think* I was doing here?"

They had plenty of time to talk and catch up on each other's news: the Dragon Touched had no intention of letting Narky escape back to Ardis, but they clearly didn't know what to do with him otherwise. For now, they seemed to have settled uneasily on the notion that he was an important guest whom nobody had anything to say to, and who for some reason could not be allowed to leave. There had already been some talk of executing him instead, but that seemed to be on hold for now. Hopefully the side of mercy would prevail.

Phaedra learned from Narky about all that had happened in Ardis and Anardis, about the fall of Magor and the rise of Magerion and Ravennis, about Narky's marriage to Ptera and his acclimation to the role of high priest. In return, she told him of her travels with Hunter, and of all that had happened since they had last seen each other.

The Dragon Touched had no idea what to do with Phaedra, and did not seem particularly interested in detaining her, so it would be up to her to find Bandu when the time came. She conferred with Narky about how best to prepare Bandu for the underworld, should she choose to go. Narky kept wishing aloud that he could be more helpful – it seemed wrong that the high priest of Ravennis should have so little to contribute.

"Would you bless a token?" Phaedra asked. "For Bandu to take with her, as a symbol of your support?"

"I have this," Narky said, reaching for the silver chain around his neck, but Phaedra stopped him.

"Not symbolizing Ravennis," she said. "It's Ravennis we're trying to influence. I meant a token symbolizing you."

She opened the bag that Psander had given her, and took out the two thin pieces of wood that had once been a crossbow bolt. Narky gasped when he saw them.

"I can't bless that," he said. "Where did you get that?"

"It's what made you who you are," Phaedra countered. "You wouldn't be here without it. You wouldn't even have worshipped Ravennis, and now you're His high priest."

Narky stared at the broken bolt for a long moment. Then he took it in his two hands and said, "Ravennis, as You know me, let this relic from my past stand for my presence as my friend journeys to meet You. Guide Bandu safely to You as if I were at her side, and return her safely to us, with Criton by her side. I ask this of You as Your servant, knowing that You are a God of Mercy as well as Fate, and that the Fates can bend if You so desire it. As I have asked, let it be so."

When he handed the pieces back to Phaedra she took them reverently. "That was beautiful, Narky," she said. "I had no idea you could compose such a prayer."

"Well," Narky said with a wry smile, "I've had practice."

Phaedra smiled back. She had always had a soft spot for Narky. He wasn't a fundamentally nice or decent person, but he wished he was, and so every gesture of kindness and generosity was a hard-earned victory, a triumph of intent over instinct. He had improved since she'd last seen him, and not just because he seemed more comfortable with himself. It was also good to see him more concerned about his wife in Ardis than about his own survival among the Dragon Touched. The craven boy she knew was outgrowing his past.

She had never asked him about the man he had killed with that crossbow bolt. As long as she didn't know the details, she could relate to Narky as he was in the present, without burying who he was now underneath that sordid history. All she knew was that it had been murder.

She parted with Narky late in the afternoon and set out to find Bandu. She did not take directions from the Dragon Touched, but set out northward so as not to be caught between opposing armies should Narky's assumptions turn out to be correct. She lay down to rest that night under a spell Psander had taught her to ward against rain, but the weather stayed thankfully dry, so she did not have to test it. In the morning, she set her tracing spell.

The major ingredient in the spell was the dirt that she and Hunter had collected with Atella in the area her map had indicated as somehow significant to Bandu. Phaedra wished she knew what that significance was, but the spell ought to function either way. She knelt, pulling dirt out of the bag by the handful. Thankfully, the soil quality was different here, and Bandu's rich black dirt stood out against the ground as Phaedra formed the intricate design that her academic forbears had developed. The design was meant to represent a world crisscrossed by roads, and its purpose was to draw on the Traveler God's power without alerting Him to the fact. The use of Bandu's dirt to draw the design itself was a forced modification, since the classic spell would have required Phaedra to destroy an item belonging to the individual she wanted to track. Phaedra knew of no way to destroy dirt, and she hoped this would do. When she had finished the design, she removed her right shoe and stepped barefoot in the center.

The spell worked beautifully. Almost as soon as Phaedra's toes had touched the ground, a second footprint, a left one, appeared on the ground in front of her. It was smaller than Phaedra's print, and it was dark like the Tarphaean soil. Phaedra slipped her shoe back on and began to follow Bandu's tracks.

The tracks went on and on, and it was hard not to worry about what awaited her at the end. What if Bandu refused to retrieve Criton? It worried Phaedra that they didn't know why Bandu had left him. She and Narky had acted as if Bandu's willingness to undertake the journey was a given, but was it? What if Criton had hurt her, or harmed their child? There were so many possibilities, so many potential reasons for Bandu to decide to let her husband stay dead.

And if she did refuse the journey that Phaedra suggested, did Phaedra dare to attempt it herself, given the risk that her failure and death might doom the entire world? If not, what right had she to ask Bandu to risk her own life?

There were other worries too – plenty of them. She

worried that she hadn't studied enough to prepare
Bandu – or herself for that matter – for the trials that
awaited below. She had let that list of failures dissuade
her from reading any more of Psander's materials on the
subject – what if one of the scrolls she hadn't read held
some essential piece of knowledge, without which any
attempt to breach the underworld was doomed?

For one thing, Phaedra didn't even know how to find
an entrance to the world below. The spell that Maira
the wizard-king had used to reach his wife had clearly
been much celebrated and publicized in wizarding
circles in the years after his journey, but after so many
had died using it, the wizarding council known as the
Blasphemous Clairvoyants had restricted all access to it.
The Clairvoyants had had their own seal, and Phaedra
had dug through all of Psander's books that bore it, but
none had included Maira's spell. She had *some* idea of
how to develop a new spell, but that would carry its own
risks.

After the second day of walking, Phaedra began
rationing her food. It would have been easy to stop at one
of the villages now allied with the Dragon Touched, but
she did not know if her tracking spell could accommodate
a detour. The footprints behind her always disappeared
as soon as she had passed them, and she was afraid that
straying from the path might cause the entire spell to
dissipate.

Three days later, hungry and tired, she came to a
woodcutter's cottage. Outside it, a Dragon Touched
woman about her age was busily clearing space for
a garden, with an infant on the ground beside her
contentedly eating dirt. The infant was Goodweather –
no doubt about it. She had dark skin and tight curly hair,
and her face, though much developed since the last time

Phaedra had seen her, was unmistakable.

"Hello," Phaedra said, and the woman jumped to her feet startled. "I'm looking for Bandu."

"Why?"

"I need to speak with her," Phaedra said. She felt she ought to save her news for when Bandu was present, and she wished the woman wouldn't eye her so suspiciously. "I'm a friend," she said.

"Yes, I see that," the woman said, wiping the dirt off her hands. Of course she'd know Phaedra was a friend: she was clearly an islander, and she had asked for Bandu by name – Bandu didn't have any enemies like that.

"Stay here," the woman added, "I'll bring out some food." She scooped Goodweather up and went inside, and Phaedra was left outside to wonder. When she came back with a bowl of vegetable soup in one hand and Goodweather in the other, Phaedra said, "I could have watched Goodweather out here, you know."

"Oh, no need," the young woman said, but she smiled tentatively and Phaedra could tell she was embarrassed about giving one of Bandu's friends such a cool reception.

Phaedra took the soup gratefully. "Is Bandu out foraging?" she asked.

A nod.

Goodweather, oblivious to the tension between the adults, gave Phaedra a big smile. "Is that a tooth?" Phaedra asked.

"It broke through the gums a week ago. I'm sorry – I'm Vella."

"Vella," Phaedra repeated. "I'm Phaedra. Did you come here with Bandu to be Goodweather's…?"

She had been about to say "nursemaid," but she broke off. She had seen Bandu feed the baby herself without any trouble, and Vella was too young and thin to have recently had a baby and lost it, as Kelina once had. Yet she was acting just as possessive of Goodweather as Kelina had been of Phaedra, almost like a second mother.

She ate her soup in silence.

As she was finishing with it, Vella looked up past her shoulder and said, "Your friend Phaedra is here," and Phaedra turned to see Bandu coming toward them, a pile of mushrooms in her skirt. She dropped these and ran to Phaedra, who rose to embrace her.

"I have bad news," Phaedra said. "Criton is dead."

Bandu let out a cry, looking horror-stricken. "He is dead?"

"His cousin Belkos killed him."

"No," Bandu said, "they are friends!"

"I know," Phaedra said. "But listen, it's worse than that. Criton was about to make peace with Ardis, to end their war. Belkos killed him before that could happen."

Bandu did not weep; she only shook her head and looked sick. "They want to eat Narky," she said nonsensically. "Vella, they kill him because they want to eat Narky, and Narky is Ardis."

"Narky is the high priest of Ravennis now," Phaedra corrected her. "The Dragon Touched have captured him. He's afraid the king of Ardis will take Criton's death as an omen and resume the war."

"Oh God," Vella said.

"If the king of Ardis sends his army against them again," Phaedra said, "the war won't end until one side or the other has been completely annihilated. Criton was the only one insisting that the Dragon Touched make peace with their enemies – the only one with enough authority, anyway."

Bandu and Vella looked meaningfully at each other. "This won't end well for my people," Vella said. "This won't end well for anyone. Bandu, we should have gone. We should have gone while there was something we could have done about it."

Bandu nodded, and she looked down at Goodweather with tears in her eyes. Goodweather had gone back to raking at the ground with her claws and bringing handfuls of turf to her mouth.

"There still is," Phaedra said. "That's why I'm here."

She told them about her studies with Psander, and of the research she had conducted on Bandu's behalf. The girl looked back at her and shook her head. "Criton is not my mate now," she said. "I don't want him. I want Vella."

Phaedra and Vella both winced. "Bandu," Vella said, "you didn't have to…"

"If Ardis is destroyed," Phaedra said, "Narky's wife will be killed, as likely will Narky, and thousands of others besides. If Ardis triumphs, their army will come here too. You won't be safe."

Bandu nodded and wiped her eyes. "You want me to bring back Criton. He is not my mate and I don't want him, but you want me to bring him back."

"You don't have to go," Vella said. "Bandu, you don't have to go."

Bandu turned to her. "In your dream," she said, "your grandmother is sick. Even if your kind win, is still not good. This war is bad for them, is bad for Goodweather. In your dream I go to find Criton."

"And leave me with Goodweather!" Vella cried. "You never came back in my dream, Bandu!"

Bandu nodded, contemplating the situation in silence. "Tell me about the dream," Phaedra said.

When they had done so, Vella repeated, "You never came back."

"But she wasn't lost yet," Phaedra said. "You didn't say she felt lost, only that you couldn't tell Goodweather for sure one way or another."

"That's one way to look at it," Vella said curtly. "Or you could say that she won't come back, and I wasn't able to tell our daughter a lie."

Our daughter. Phaedra looked to Bandu, but Bandu said nothing.

"Bandu," Vella said, "Don't go."

"So many lives will be lost," Phaedra countered. "So many people will die."

Goodweather began coughing, and Vella lifted her and scooped the grass and dirt out of her hands and mouth. Bandu looked at them, and then back to Phaedra. She sighed.

"How do I go?" she asked.

Phaedra explained what she knew, while Vella wept and intermittently pleaded with Bandu not to leave her for this foolish mission. "We can leave this place and go into the mountains," she said, "or up into the far north where no Ardisman will find us."

"Then your parents die?" Bandu asked her. "And your grandmother, and Dessa and Iona? If your kind make peace with Ardis, Goodweather has family and many places to go and nobody hates her. She can find mates who love her and not be like Criton's mother, always hiding. Vella, if I bring back Criton, I don't stay with him. He goes back to your people and has other women and I come back to you."

Vella passed Goodweather over to her and buried her head in her claws. Bandu took the baby and turned back to Phaedra. "There are animals you say that want to eat me when I go to find him. What else?"

"Well, for one thing," Phaedra said, "we'll have to find

a way to get you down there at all. I have a suspicion that the Yarek could help if it chose to. Its branches breached the sky-mesh when it bore Silent Hall off into the fairies' world; it seems likely to me that its roots pierced the barrier into the underworld. If we could somehow convince the Yarek to help..."

"It helps me," Bandu said with confidence. "It already says so before."

Phaedra nodded and handed her the bag that contained Narky's bolt and Criton's bucket. "In that case," she said, "the rest is up to you."

47

BANDU

The Yarek was there when she reached for it. *Come to me where my trunk rises*, it said, *and I will let you into the depths where you wish to go.* When Bandu told Vella and Phaedra of that condition, Phaedra looked worried.

"That journey will take you weeks! Let's hope the war isn't over by the time you get back."

"*If* you get back," Vella corrected her. "Are you sure you want to do this, Bandu?"

"I am sure," Bandu told her. "Phaedra, you stay here with Vella until I am home. Help with Goodweather."

"I can't," Phaedra said. "I need to find and seal the fairy gates as quickly as I can. We may have decades or we may only have weeks, but I can't afford to–"

"Then I don't go," Bandu interrupted.

Phaedra sighed. "All right. But if you're not back in two months, I'll have to assume you're gone. And if Ardis wins and their army marches north, we're leaving and heading for Atuna."

Bandu left then, taking only the satchel that held Phaedra's relics and the food in her belly. In Dragon Touched lands she could rely on the northern plainsmen

417

to feed her, and in the southern plains she could tell people that she was a friend of Narky's. Everyone had heard of Narky the Black Priest, and when people asked her where she was headed, she told them she was going to meet Narky's God and nobody questioned her.

The hardest part of the journey wasn't the travel or the wet weather, but the lack of Goodweather. Bandu's breasts grew hard and swollen after two days without nursing her daughter, and she had to painfully squeeze out some of her milk just to keep them from hurting all day long. She worried about how Goodweather was faring without her. At least she was old enough that she had started eating soft person-food.

It had been years since Bandu had been truly alone, at least for more than a few hours. It was freeing, but it was not pleasant. She missed Vella and Goodweather, she missed Criton, she missed Phaedra and Hunter and Narky. Most of all, she missed Four-foot. The wolf had been her companion since the time she was a little girl afraid in the woods, and it was wrong to travel without him or even the poor substitute of her own kind.

Would she see Four-foot in the world below? She hoped so, if only so that she could apologize. His death had been her fault, even if only indirectly. She wondered if Narky's God would let her bring Four-foot back with her too. It hurt that she had to prioritize Criton over him.

As the days went by and Bandu came ever closer, the trunk and branches of the great tree took up more and more of the horizon. It had grown markedly since the last time Bandu had been this close – how long before it stretched over the entire world? Its parent-self Goodweather had been her friend and ally, but she had no illusions that the Yarek's presence in this world was benign. The plant-beast was a weed that would worm its way into the foundations of this world and someday destroy it – at least, unless God Most High uprooted it again. It was strange how ambivalent she felt about the matter.

At last she neared the Yarek's base and stood among the burnt trees and burnt bodies where Salemis had routed two armies. The Yarek's trunk was wider now than Psander's fortress had ever been, towering before her like the affront to the Gods that its presence truly was. She felt its power, even here among the scorched and skeletal lesser trees, bursting like strong new shoots out of the ground all around her. The Yarek's magical presence was even vaster than its physical one.

When she reached its trunk, she found that the ground in contact with it had fallen away entirely, revealing a massive stairway of tangled roots that spiraled all the way around the trunk and sank deep into the earth.

Bandu took a deep breath and picked her way to the trunk across the uneven walkway that remained. She touched the live wood with her fingertips and said to it, *I am here. Will you help me?*

Of course I will, the Yarek responded. *Have I not told you that I mean to repay you for your efforts to bring me here, to your fertile new world?*

Then bring me to the land of the dead, she said, *and after that, bring me and whoever is with me back again.*

The great tree breathed its assent, a waft of sweet air falling upon her out of the branches above. *Descend,* the tree said. *You are safe with me.*

Down and down she climbed, round and around the tree until the sunlight disappeared and she lost track of the number of times she had circled the trunk. She lit no fire to disturb the mother of all plants, but kept her hand always on the bark, feeling her way down in the dark.

After a time, she became aware of a sound beside her own, the creaking of massive roots growing further and further into the depths of the earth. And then another sound, a dissonant scratching as something large and multi-clawed scrabbled up the root stair toward her.

Show me what I can't see, Bandu asked of the Yarek, and she reached forward with her mind until it showed her what her eyes could not: an eight-legged badger the size of a bear, moving up the staircase toward her with horrifying speed. Bandu thought back to the guardians Phaedra had described for her, but none of them were anything like this beast. When it reached her it reared up on its hind-claws and said in the language of magical thought: *You are not permitted here. Go back or I will devour you.*

The creature had a steel collar around its neck. *Ravennis tames you,* Bandu said. *You don't stop me. I have His highest servant's blessing.*

A servant is still a servant, the badger said, licking its lips. *Speak my name and tame me too, or go back, else you will be eaten.*

Bandu stood her ground. *I give myself two names,* she said, *and they are both better than the name my father gives me. I don't need to know your old name – my name for you is stronger and truer: you are Eight-Claw the Coward, the First Who Runs. You do not stand in my way.*

The badger shrank away from her in fright. *That is not my real name.*

Go back where you come from, Bandu said, *or I call your real name Dust.*

Eight-Claw shuddered and obeyed, retreating until he had disappeared from her mind's vision. Soon he had disappeared from her imagination as well, shifting and fading in memory as if he had been only a dream.

Maybe he *was* a dream, but on this endless stairway, such distinctions were essentially meaningless. Down here, a dream could kill just as easily as flesh could.

Now she heard voices from behind, calling to her from the world of the living. The first voice was Phaedra's. "Bandu!" it cried. "I forgot to tell you the most important part of what I learned! Come back – you're not ready for what's down there!"

Bandu ignored it. It was not plausible. Phaedra did not simply *forget* to give Bandu information. If anything, she sometimes forgot to stop.

"Come back!" Phaedra's voice called again. "It's new information really, I only just put it together from something Narky told me. Please, if you don't come back you won't know how to get past the final gate, and your soul will be trapped forever! At least wait for me to catch up!"

Bandu didn't even slow her pace. Did this new monster think she was that weak, that doubtful of herself? It would learn otherwise.

Voice after voice called down after her, begging her to turn around, and Bandu ignored them all. When even Criton's voice cried that she had overshot her goal and that he was trapped on the level above her, she laughed scornfully at the second guardian's cowardly tactics and willed it to appear before her, which it promptly did.

It was a small creature, half Bandu's size and fragile like a doll made of reeds, which is what it might have been. Its figure solidified as she identified it, taking the form she had named: a wispy little reed-doll carrying a wicked inwardly-curved knife.

Why won't you turn? it squeaked. *I have slain more men than that badger ever did.*

Bandu laughed at its indignation. *Go away,* she said,

but the reed-doll did not obey. Instead it lunged at her.

She stopped it with a kick that bent its upper half backward so far that it nearly folded in two. When it sprang upright again, she caught its knife and tried to wrench it away, but the weightless creature only rose along with the blade, clinging to it. *You cannot destroy me,* it hissed.

I don't care, Bandu told it. *Go away.* She wound her arm back and hurled the blade and the creature into the darkness. She never heard it fall.

She shook her head and kept walking, though at this point her descent was less physical than spiritual. Her callused feet no longer felt the roots beneath her so much as she *knew* that she was still descending. The physical world was receding behind her, a sign that she was nearing her goal.

Then, from her right, she heard a bark of greeting. It was Four-foot's voice, she recognised it in an instant. Going to meet him would take her away from the trunk, though – dare she lose contact with the Yarek? It was best to wait for Four-foot to come to her, if he could.

He could not – as the barks of greeting came closer, so did the sound of a chain being dragged. She felt the moment when he came to the end of his chain more than she heard it – it may as well have been *her* neck jerked backward by the unforgiving steel. Four-foot yelped, then growled, then whined. He could not reach her, and now she even saw him dimly, held by a chain that seemed to stretch back into eternity. There was a lock on his collar that kept it clasped around his neck. There was a key in it already, but without hands like hers, Four-foot could not turn it by himself.

Could she go to him? If it hadn't been for that key, if there had been nothing she could obviously do for her friend except comfort him, she would have done it without a second thought. But that key, it was wrong. It was a detail designed to tempt her, to trick her into thinking that she could free him without a fight. It was a lie.

But Four-foot was no lie, she was sure of that. She'd have known if he were a demon in disguise. She knew the wolf's voice, his *essence* too well to be fooled by some demon who had taken his form. He was really here, and he was really trapped, and he was really whining for her to come to him.

But if she stepped away from the Yarek now, her quest would be over. Maybe she would free Four-foot and maybe she wouldn't, but there was no doubt that the underworld would have won. It might swallow her as it had swallowed so many others. And even if it didn't, even if she survived, it would have managed to keep her away from Criton forever. The key proved it.

The trouble was that she did not *want* Criton, not like she wanted Four-foot. Rescuing him would not bring her the pure joy she would have felt with Four-foot alive once more. He was no longer her mate, no longer her companion; seeing Criton again could only complicate her feelings about him, and about Vella too. For Vella was right: Criton may have spoken of taking other women, but it was Bandu who had actually done so. If she rescued him from this dark place, she would have to face him again.

Four-foot barked again, to get her attention. She shut her eyes tight, so tight that it squeezed tears from the corners. It made no difference – she could see him just as easily through closed eyes as through open ones. She wanted to go to him, wanted it desperately. How many months had she spent among the Dragon Touched,

wishing she could have Four-foot beside her instead of
Criton and his kin? This might be her only chance to
make that happen.

But she couldn't go to him. She could not afford to
save Four-foot and give up on Criton. The wolf could
end no wars. He might have protected her against
the dangers of Tarphae's woods, and even saved her
friends from bandits once, but he could never protect
Goodweather and Vella the way that peace would.

She opened her eyes again, for all that it didn't matter.
I come back for you, she told Four-foot, but what if she was
lying? She stumbled away down the stairway, weeping
as Four-foot howled and whined behind her. His voice
echoed in the darkness, on and on, no matter how far
she went.

And then at last she came to the end, her path blocked
by a wall of solid rock. There was a door in it, and in
the door was a face. It could have been a man's face or
a woman's, or then again, it might have been a dog's or
a jackal's. The dream was growing less and less definite.

Whatever it was, it was looking at her through eyes
of stone, waiting for her to say something. She could tell
somehow that her first words would be very important,
but she didn't know what they ought to be, so instead
she waited, hoping that the door would speak first. It
didn't.

Let me in, she said at last.

The jackal-person grinned at her. *I don't open for the
living, unless they give me blood. Put your hand in my mouth
and I will open for you.*

No.

*Then I will not open. Turn back, girl-whose-pulse-beats-on.
Go home.*

Bandu stood, staring at the door while it stared back

at her. Then she reached into the satchel at her side and pulled out the two halves of Narky's bolt. *If you don't open for me*, she said, *open for your God. His priest blesses my journey.*

The door licked its lips with a great scraping sound. *That relic carries memories of a heart pierced and a life taken. Feed me the arrow and its memory, and I will let you pass.*

Bandu put both halves in the jackal's mouth, and gasped as the memory they held sprang to life in her mind. She got a sudden image of Narky releasing the catch on his crossbow, and of a big Tarphaean boy reeling and falling with the bolt lodged deep in his chest. She felt the wound as if the bolt had struck her chest too, and she collapsed to her knees, gasping for breath. Then the vision dissipated, leaving her to wonder about the circumstances that had led to Narky killing that boy.

Delicious, the door said, and swung backwards to let her through. Both halves of the bolt had vanished. Bandu took a deep breath, and stepped past the doorway into the underworld.

48

PTERA

Narky never came back. Instead, the king's son returned covered in the blood of other men, with the news that the Black Dragon had been slain by his own kinsman.

The first thing Ptera did was to suppress a scream. Being widowed had been nothing the first time, but to lose her second husband, her young Narky, was unthinkable. Had he been killed, or only captured? Would it make any difference? If Ardis won the war, the Dragon Touched would surely slay Narky out of spite. If the Dragon Touched won, they would slay him then too – him, and anyone else they caught.

The second thing Ptera did was to spread the word that Ravennis' temple was buying food. Magerion was probably mere hours away from ordering another assault on the Dragon Touched, and if that gambit turned out to be as disastrous as the last one, the city would soon come under siege.

Ptera did not go to talk to King Magerion. She knew that he would never listen to her, no matter her authority within the church – he had barely listened to Narky, and Narky was both a man and a prophet. It didn't matter what Ptera might say; Magerion would believe that the Black Dragon's death was an omen from Ravennis, proving that He favored war.

This, Ptera knew, was nonsense. If Ravennis had favored war, He would have told Narky so. At the very least, He would have brought Narky safely home to her, and allowed *him* to deliver the news of the Black Dragon's assassination. He would not, in His wisdom, have allowed Narky to be captured like this.

This was what Ptera thought: either the Dragon Touched assassin had been acting alone, without divine favor, or God Most High had decided to lure Magerion in so that He could condemn Ravennis and the people of Ardis to complete destruction. Under the first scenario, Magerion would be making a mistake. Under the second, he would be dooming his people.

Even so, Ptera had no intention of leaving the city. Ravennis could surely survive losing a second city if He had survived the loss of the first, and as long as Ravennis remained Lord Among the Fallen, Ptera must not fear death. Better to be a martyr in Ardis than to make her God think she did not trust Him.

So she had the church buy grain with the money that Magerion and his terrified fellow nobles had donated, and she gave sermons about the delights that awaited Ravennis' followers in the world below. People whispered about the grain, of course, but Ptera only smiled and carried on as if nothing was the matter. Either the king would order her to stop stockpiling food, or he wouldn't.

Within a week, the men of Ardis were marching off to war again, assured by their king that victory would be swift. Ptera hoped he was right – though if he was, what would happen to Narky? There had been no contact from the Dragon Touched regarding his release, but that was probably because they were in disarray after the slaying of their leader. Would their disarray be enough to give Magerion the victory he sought?

The people of Ardis were hopeful, but it took no special insight to sense their wariness. More than two thousand men had died since the day Bestillos marched south to punish a wizard, and the city was feeling their loss. When word came of a standoff on the mountainside, the relief in the city was palpable – yet how low had Ardis sunk, that simply failing to lose their army in its first week of combat should be considered a good sign?

The campaign dragged through another week, and another, as the army of Ardis proved unable to dislodge the Dragon Touched from their mountain. The swift victory that Magerion had promised was proving to be just as illusory as Ptera had expected: Ravennis did not truly support this war. Or if He did, He was opposed by an equally powerful force.

Then at last the word came. The Ardisian army had been routed again, and Magerion's son Atlon, who had been given its command, had died in battle.

The news destroyed the fragile equilibrium of the city, and the people came to Ptera in droves, hoping for words of comfort, at least, before their city went the way of Laarna. She gave them that comfort as best she could, and at every service, the crowd grew. Even Mageris, the king's second son, came to her to learn about his brother's fate in the world below – and, it went unsaid, about the fate they were all likely to face in the near future.

She spoke to him and to the others of the glories of Ravennis, and of the marvelous second lives that awaited them in His kingdom. But of course, that didn't change the fact that nobody *wanted* to die. Ptera certainly didn't, and it gave her great comfort to know that Narky hadn't either. If even the high priest of Ravennis didn't look forward to death, there was nothing wrong with her or with anyone for feeling the same way.

The Dragon Touched reached the city two days later, and Magerion ordered the gate closed. Those farmers who had not found their way within the walls were stranded outside, presumably begging for their lives. The Dragon Touched showed them little mercy.

The first assault on the city shook Ardis to its foundations. How many years had it been since these city walls had been tested? Over a hundred, probably; Ptera did not even know of a time when it had happened. Now they ran with blood and fire, and the sounds of war horns and clanging weaponry echoed into the night. Some of the city's women took up arms and joined their husbands and brothers on the wall, while the rest crowded into the Temple of Ravennis with their children. Ptera led them all in prayers until word came that the Dragon Touched had been repelled, at which point the women looked at each other in dubious relief, and she turned to prayers of thanksgiving.

The thanksgiving prayers were ones of Ptera's own invention. It was a sad fact that much of the Ravennian liturgy had been lost when the Graceful Servant was martyred. Though refugees from Laarna had no doubt settled in Atuna and elsewhere, Ptera and Narky had yet to meet any of them, and so they had been forced to develop prayers of their own. In some ways, though, it was not as great a loss as it seemed: the old prayers had been developed at a time when Ravennis was not yet God of the Dead, so the break from the past was perfectly excusable.

The Dragon Touched did not renew their assault the

next day, so on Magerion's invitation Ptera spent the
morning blessing the walls that had held them back.
From her vantage point atop the gates, she was able to
view the opposing army as it camped outside, nursing
its wounds.

The army was small. If they had not humbled the men
of Ardis so completely and repeatedly, Ptera would have
thought the Dragon Touched too few to pose the city any
threat. And yet, Ardis no longer had the kind of force to
drive them away. The walls might hold or they might
not, but no army of Ardismen would be leaving through
these gates to break the siege. If Magerion could not buy
the Dragon Touched off, the city would starve.

The king sent messengers suggesting an end to the war
under new terms, but no peace could be brokered. The
Dragon Touched were now led by their high priestess,
Hessina, and she was less invested in the notion of peace
than the young Black Dragon had been. The messengers
told of how she had ridiculed their king for suggesting
peace now, after he had so quickly withdrawn Narky's
offer when he thought the Dragon Touched were too
weak to defend themselves. She would no longer trust
Magerion's offers, she said – the war could only end with
Ardis' destruction.

There was no word of Narky.

For the next few days, a double contingent of men
patrolled the walls day and night. Yet for now, the
Dragon Touched seemed content to starve them out.
Two weeks passed without a second assault on the walls,
even as the food supplies within them dwindled. After
another two weeks, Ptera opened up the temple's food
stores. But soon enough, her stockpile too was gone.

The king sent for Ptera now, for the first time since
Narky's capture. Despite everything, the summons made

her nervous. Ptera's family had been minor members of the king's clan, and they had always worshipped and feared their representative on the Council of Generals. Magerion was a powerful man, and a dangerous one.

She had thought, somehow, that he would never call for her, despite the prominence she had gained in Narky's absence. But, of course, she was the only representative Ravennis had in the city now. She would have to stand for the entire church. That meant she could not afford to be intimidated.

She saw now how much of an asset Narky's bluntness had been to their God. Her young husband was impudent and imprudent, but another man's power and stature could never prevent him from speaking. The Graceful Servant's power had been in her fearlessness; Narky's was in his bluntness. Where did Ptera's power lie?

She met the king on the walkway above the city gate, where he had been surveying the army that threatened to starve them all to death. He waved his retainers off as she approached, and the two of them made their own patrol of the city wall, alone.

"Our people have begun slaughtering their mules rather than feed them precious grain," the king said. "When the grain is gone too, it will be cats next, and dogs, and rats."

Ptera said nothing. She had prided herself once on her strength of character and her quick wit, but now she was standing next to the man whose very name had made her parents quake. He hulked above her, his shoulders wide and his voice gravelly and deep. Though she was a strong woman herself, though she was here to represent her God and His church, she still could not speak.

"We are going to have to break this siege," the king said. "We have no choice. The Dragon Touched have

defeated us every time we've met on the open field, but
that is no excuse to hide behind our walls. I would rather
our people died in battle than in starvation – I will not
leave this world without bringing some of the Dragon
Touched with me."

This time, Ptera found her voice. "They'll outnumber
our army for the first time," she said.

Magerion shook his head. "Widows will have to take
up their husbands' weapons for this final battle, and
orphans their parents' tools of war. Everyone with legs
to charge and hands to hold a spear must join us. That
is why I called for you. What blessing can you give our
people so that they will not fear the army they face?"

Ptera pulled her eyes away from his bulk and thought
on this. Was there *anything* that could keep their people
from fearing this calamitous final battle? What could
Ptera possibly say to them that she hadn't said already?

Part of the trouble was that the people of Ardis were
so new to the worship of Ravennis. They trusted Him, or
at least, they trusted her, but Ravennis could not recover
for them the feeling that they were *Ardismen*, the fiercest
and most feared warriors in the known world. How
could a God who had come upon them only in their
weakness ever hope to remind them of their strength?

"Speak, girl."

The words hit her like a blow. Calling her "girl" was
an attack on her, but it was more than that – it was an
attack on Ravennis too. Blast her parents for teaching
her to be intimidated by this man, and blast her own
sudden shyness – she could not let him speak like that to
a priestess. Afraid as she might be of Magerion, her faith
demanded that he be chastised.

She could not be Ptera anymore, not right now. No.
She was the Graceful Servant.

She stopped walking. "You can't call a priestess of Ravennis 'girl,' and expect our God to serve you. Do you think that Ravennis is so weak or so forgiving that He will ignore your disrespect, *old man*?"

Magerion was not accustomed to hearing such words from women. His first instinct was to raise his hand. But Ptera was ready, and she did not flinch. Instead she took a step closer to him.

"Ravennis does not fear you," she said, "and He does not serve you. Whether we drive the Dragon Touched away or whether we perish in hunger or in flames, your soul will soon pass into His halls, and you can expect to be judged according to your worth. Are you prepared for that?"

The king's hand was still up by his shoulder, but she was so close now that he could hardly have hit her with it if he'd tried. There was fear in his eyes.

"There is no time for you to switch sides," Ptera said, and the king himself flinched at her tone. She really was the Graceful Servant now, back in the flesh. "You have given Ardis to Ravennis," she said, "and He will not give it back."

"I... apologize," the king said at last, and when she would not step away, he did so himself. "But is your God – is our God content to let His second home on this earth fall, and His people starve, or will He help us? Will you do nothing to bless your city's cause?"

Ptera turned and walked on, forcing the king to follow. This game of imagining herself as the Graceful Servant really *worked.* An answer to his question presented itself quite suddenly, but she acted as if she had known of it all along and said confidently: "Our people need to know that it wasn't Magor that gave them strength. We should have a spear dance tonight."

"But spear dances were a sacred rite of His!"

"Magor is defeated," Ptera countered. "His people have turned to Ravennis. Why shouldn't Ravennis take His rituals too, if it suits Him?"

Magerion considered this. "A spear dance would hearten our people. Thank you, priestess. Consider it done."

That night, as the flames of a bonfire rose between the armory and the Temple of Ravennis, the men of Ardis displayed their prowess in sacred dance, spinning and leaping as if the Dragon Touched had never broken their confidence, never sent their brothers fleeing across the countryside. They danced and forgot the Dragon Touched – danced, and remembered Ardis.

The next day Ptera took up Narky's spear and joined Magerion at the gate, alongside every able-bodied man and woman in the city, and a few who were less than able-bodied. In size, their force would easily dwarf the Dragon Touched army, or any other army for that matter. It was enough to help them pretend that they would not break upon first contact with their enemies.

Magerion stood before them, dressed in scales of interlaced bronze and steel, polished to a magnificent shine. "The Dragon Touched think they can starve us to death," he said. "Today we show them what Ardis is, what the men and women of this great city can do to their puny little army. Today, this war ends."

Ptera cheered along with the rest, knowing that few of them truly expected to win, but willing to indulge in the fantasy. *Ravennis,* she prayed silently, *bring us to victory today. If You can do anything, bring these people home safely. Let us come to you another day.*

Perhaps Ravennis heard her. Perhaps He didn't.

The gates were opened.

49

Bandu

The first thing Bandu noticed when she stepped through the door was that the floor was made of stone, not roots. The Yarek's strength was enough to touch the underworld, but not enough to breach it. Beyond the door, she was on her own.

On this stone floor, bodies were piled. Hundreds of bodies, their skin a dark gray, were stacked one on top of the other all across the room, with only a narrow path leading between them. Now and then, one would mumble something or try to turn in its sleep, unsuccessfully. The bodies reminded Bandu of the ghosts she had seen on Tarphae a year ago, with no faces and no features. But they were solid. She accidentally brushed against one as she walked past, and there was no mistaking it.

There was an open archway in the wall ahead, and she passed from one chamber of bodies into another. There was no ceiling that she could see – the walls rose up into darkness. The second chamber was identical to the first, and when she came to a third, the only difference there was that the bodies here were not piled quite as high – they only came up to Bandu's waist and not her shoulder.

It was warmer than she had expected in the land of the dead – the kind of warmth that fogged the mind and made her eyes keep trying to close. But she forced herself to keep them open. She knew better than to fall asleep among the dead.

A screech from above made Bandu duck as a pale monster flew past her on raven wings, carrying another body in its arms. Bandu had seen these monsters before, with their bald heads and spiked teeth. Phaedra had called them angels, messengers from Ravennis. Two of these had attacked Bandu and her friends once. She knew how easily those talons could tear flesh, and that when these creatures died, they would turn back into crows.

But this one did not attack her. It only put its cargo down, almost lovingly, atop the other sleepers, and flew off into the darkness. Bandu stayed crouched for some time, until her body cried for her to stretch out, preferably on the ground, and her eyes began to shut themselves again. She rose, and pinched herself until a trickle of blood ran between her fingernails. The sting was enough to jolt her eyes open. For now.

She walked on, but before she could reach the next chamber two more angels swooped out of the darkness and stood before her on either side of the path. She was cautious in her approach, but the angels were faster than she expected. They caught her each under an arm and immediately lifted her into the air. Bandu wriggled in their grip, but it did no good. Higher and higher they rose until the chamber's walls came to an end and they flew over them through the darkness, sometimes veering left or right to avoid a collision with another body carrier. Bandu barely had the chance to catch her breath before they took a final turn over a high wall and lowered her to the floor. Then they screeched and flew away.

The new room was well-lit, with a rich carpet of woven feathers on the floor leading up to a majestic throne. On this throne sat the God Ravennis.

His body was like a man's, though easily three times too large, with the head of a crow. In His right palm He held an eye the size of a fist, a trophy she recognized. It was the eye of the Boar of Hagardis, which the Tarphaeans had given to Ravennis in the hopes that He might protect them from Magor. They had given other parts to other Gods, but apparently Narky's God cherished the gift nonetheless.

He nodded at her as she approached, and turned His head slightly to watch her. *I am glad you've come,* He said.

She knew His voice instantly. It was the voice that had whispered to her of Tarphae's drowning, the voice that had told her which water-leaf to hide in when she was a little girl trying to escape the fairies. It had always spoken to her through the wind, but she did not think Ravennis was the wind itself. He couldn't be. Could He?

Maybe He just wanted her to *think* He was the wind – He was tricky, Narky's God. Even now, He was lying to her with His presence.

Why are you showing me this body? Bandu asked. *It isn't real.*

Of course it is not real, Ravennis said. *We are not contained in bodies in Our world – that is why the Yarek's physicality was such a danger to Us. But the lower worlds are different. Yours* requires *physical manifestations. This lowest world is a place of dreams, and so I have fashioned this dream body to meet with you. I wanted to be prepared for your arrival.*

I am here for Criton, Bandu said, though He seemed to already know. *Give him to me.*

Ravennis laughed with a horrible cawing sound that

grated at the soul as much as at her nerves. *You don't sound like you want him.*

I don't, Bandu answered. *But I need him back anyway.*

Ravennis turned His head all the way to the side to get a better look at her. *You don't want him? That will be a problem. Are you ready to pay the price for bringing him back with you?*

Yes, Bandu said, though she was very aware that she didn't know what that price would be. Phaedra had convinced her that this journey was necessary and that only she could make it, but she hadn't known what Ravennis would ask of Bandu, and so she had spent most of her time discussing the risks of the journey instead. What would Ravennis demand of her, now that Bandu was finally here?

I am glad you have come, Ravennis said. *You can help Me find him.*

His words confused Bandu. Did the God of the Underworld not know where Criton was? How was such a thing possible?

Ravennis answered her question without her speaking it. *I have been here less than a year,* He said, *turning the chaos that was here before Me into order. You will soon see how much work there remains.*

The God rose, towering above her. *Come,* He said.

His enormous strides took Him to the other side of the room within seconds, and Bandu found that she was with Him already, as if she had somehow been sucked into His wake. The wall parted as Ravennis approached it and they passed through onto a sort of balcony that jutted out into the chamber beyond.

It was not a room, this chamber, and it was not filled with air. The substance in which they stood was too thick, halfway between liquid and gas, and the bodies of sleepers were suspended in it as far as the eye could see, above and below for what must have been hundreds of miles. The bodies were surrounded in globes of faint light that changed colors and rippled outward in all directions, and where they met each other a light flashed or a sound boomed, or a sudden landscape appeared and vanished again. Raven-angels flew among them, moving them this way and that with some logic that Bandu could not discern.

What they are doing? she asked. She could not decide if the bodies were floating in a sky or in a sea, or if they were even floating at all. They all looked like they were lying down, regardless of whether they were upright or horizontal or upside-down. Sometimes they turned over.

They are dreaming, Ravennis answered. *The dead that you saw when you first came here are only the harmless ones, those who are safe to pile together as they sleep. My servants have been piling them up to make more room for these, the active dreamers.*

Bandu couldn't help but notice that some of the bodies were much smaller than the others. *There are children here,* she said. *There aren't in the piles.*

Yes, Ravennis said. *The dreams of children are too strong for the piles. Even in life, their dreams are more visceral. In death, they are dangerous. I have seen their nightmares come to life and devour the souls of other sleepers – those souls are now gone forever.*

As they watched, the ripples of three dreamers came together with a flash, and at their intersection a monster bubbled into existence. It rose from the mud, a patch of mud that hadn't even existed until it suddenly had. The monster had the head and body of a goat, but with three tails that looked like snakes, thrashing this way and that. It was brown and wet as clay, and it quickly turned on one of the dreamers above it and charged. Before it could get there, two raven-angels fell upon it and tore it to shreds. Then they took the dreamer's body and pushed it upward, away from the others.

The guardians of the underworld are some of the oldest dreams, Ravennis said. *They devoured their creators in days of old and broke free of their prison, but were too afraid to emerge into the light of the Gods. There are hundreds of them, patrolling the many entrances to this place. They see the dreamers as a treasure to be hoarded. I see them as children to be protected.*

A naked baby floated past them, giggling, its face a vision of pure joy. Its skin was the pale tone of the mountain clans, its cheeks rosy. One of the angels who had fought the goat-monster turned and flew toward it at a furious pace, its claws outstretched.

Your angels kill the good dreams too?

When they can, Ravennis said. *Sometimes a good dream turns bad, and that can be even worse than those that start that way.*

Bandu watched in horror as the angel approached the baby, screeching. They reached toward each other, baby and angel, and then the baby grabbed the angel's claws in its little fingers and pulled them off. The angel screeched again, trying to back away, but the baby floated forward excitedly and pulled its head off. The head and body shrank back into those of a crow, a transformation the infant watched in fascination. Then the baby lifted the crow's head to its mouth and gummed at its beak, cooing.

Do the dreamers know this is happening? Bandu asked.

They do not, Ravennis said. *They live immersed in their dreams, at least until one swallows them. Thankfully, that happens rarely. We are working to make it rarer still. With increased power in the world above, I will one day bring peace and justice to the world below.*

Justice?

Ravennis gazed down at her with His crow's eye. *There is no justice in death. Not yet. Whether the dead dream well or terribly is a matter of their own haunting, not their virtue. The anxious dream anxiously, the unrepentant proudly. I would have the virtuous dream well and grant nightmares only to the unworthy.*

Bandu wasn't fooled. *You want to punish Your enemies.*

Ravennis showed no outward sign of embarrassment. *Yes, so long as I am allowed to. If My Master wills otherwise, I know better than to disobey. The Gods above are only just learning the dangers of opposing God Most High.*

Bandu looked around. *Why there aren't any animals?* she asked. *These bodies are all of my kind.*

Your wolf is not trapped outside, Ravennis said, answering the question she hadn't asked. *The monster that appeared to you in his guise was preying on your desires. But he is not likely to be in this chamber either. The souls down here mostly segregate themselves, fortunately for all. Fewer are lost that way. There have been a few animal souls that appeared here, but We have moved them elsewhere. Human dreams are not kind to them.*

But let Me be clear, Ravennis continued. *I do not know where every animal dwells, just as I do not know where precisely Criton's soul has come to rest. There are whole realms in the underworld that My servants and I have yet to explore. The dragon souls, for instance, lie somewhere beyond this sea, and even I hesitate to seek them out.*

Bandu's estimation of Narky's God kept falling. For all that He was bigger and stronger than Bandu, bigger and stronger than Psander, or Salemis, or the queen of the elves, He was still so much smaller and weaker than she had expected. He didn't know where Criton was, He didn't know where Four-foot was – what *did* He know? He wasn't even one of the weaker ones – that was the worst of it. She could see now why the Gods had been forced to cut Themselves off from the elves' world, why the dragons hadn't been afraid to fight Them, and why They had relied on Their own God Most High to defeat the Yarek. She was glad she had never worshipped these beings.

Bring me to Criton now, she said. *I don't like this place.*

We can search for him together, Ravennis answered. *As I have told you, I don't know where he is. Trust Me in this: I want peace in Ardis as much as you do.*

She looked up at Him skeptically. *Peace is good for the Dragon Touched too, and Criton's God is bigger and stronger than You. He doesn't tell you where to find him?*

He sent you.

Ravennis took her by the hand and pulled her off the balcony with Him. They navigated the sea of the dead together, inspecting the bodies they passed. None of them looked like Criton. They had no features any of them, and it was only by coming close enough to feel their dreams that Bandu was able to identify them as not-Criton.

There has to be a better way, Ravennis said. *Did you bring nothing that can help us?*

Bandu let go of the God's hand and reached into her satchel. The bucket was still there. When she pulled it out she found that it had mended itself. It was pulsing with power here in the sea of the dead, where dreams came to life. Its power drew the nearest sleeper toward her.

Is that him? Ravennis asked.

The body didn't feel especially like a not-Criton, but Bandu shook her head. *No. This is wrong.*

The God took her hand again and they flew off, or maybe swam. It soon became clear that the bucket's power was drawing all the sleepers toward it, and the monsters too. One terrifying white dog-thing came charging at them, roaring, "MOGAWOR!" – but the God of the Underworld only motioned it aside with the hand that held the boar's eye. The Mogawor creature retreated as if struck, and they moved on.

They seemed to drift forever through the sea of the dead, passing through varied dream-landscapes and waving away their more dangerous inhabitants until Bandu finally lifted the bucket and pointed. *That one.*

Among all those floating in the sea, one body in the distance was drifting slowly away from them. *How do you know?* Narky's God asked, sounding for a moment just like Narky himself.

Phaedra finds this in Criton's house, Bandu said. *Only bad things happen to him there. He doesn't want this bucket; he wants to get away from it.*

They sped toward the body. *You will have to catch him yourself,* Ravennis warned. *The souls of the dead are too delicate for Me to touch without destroying them. That is why I have these angels.*

Bandu and Ravennis were not the only ones who quickened their pace. By the time they reached Criton's soul, it was actively trying to escape them. Even in its sleep, it was kicking and thrashing and trying to swim away. Bandu released her hold on the bucket and caught one of the body's arms. It was cold and vaguely wet, and she nearly lost her grip as it tried to shake her off, but the arm was thinner than Criton's arms had been in life, and she was able to close her fingers around it. Then Ravennis was pulling them away, through drifting souls and nightmares, back onto the balcony and into His throne room. When they arrived, Criton's soul stopped struggling and stood somewhat limply at her side.

Ravennis let go of her hand and sat back down on His throne. *You have done well. But Criton's soul cannot survive leaving this place unless you pay for it.*

Bandu nodded to show she understood. *What do I pay?*

Criton's years among the living have run out. To bring him back, you must bind his soul to yours and let him feed off of you, taking a year of your life for each year he lives. Practically speaking, you will age at double the rate until he dies again, and if you die first, he will wither before his people's eyes and join you here before the day is through.

Bandu blinked, standing before Narky's God in shock. Criton did not deserve her years – he was not even her mate anymore! He had never been right for her, had never made her feel safe – why should she give half her life for him?

What would Vella say if she learned of this bargain? It was so wrong. It was unfair. Why should peace between Ardis and the Dragon Touched require this sacrifice of *her?*

Psander's words came back to her, from so long ago: "There was once a great warrior mage, whose wife died while she was still young. By magic, he tore his way into the underworld and retrieved her, and she lived with him another fifty years."

Fifty years! Those could not have come entirely from the wizard, could they?

Psander says there is a man who brings his wife back for fifty years, she said. *Does he give those years from his life?*

No, Ravennis admitted. *That man had an infant son whom he'd left behind when he took his journey. He traded the boy's years for his wife's. She never forgave him. Will you give Criton Goodweather's years instead of your own?*

Bandu recoiled. *Never.*

Then I am afraid this is how it must be. I do not have the power to grant him extra years Myself, much though I might like to. For as long as Criton lives, he will feed off you. Will you bind yourself to him like this?

Bandu stood for a moment in uncertainty. How much did she want this? Goodweather might live a long and happy life even without the peace Narky and Criton wanted. The Dragon Touched might win their war, for all that Vella's dream suggested otherwise, and even if they didn't, Bandu and Vella could flee into the mountains or further into the forest and raise Goodweather without any fear of being tracked. Many would die that way, but that was not Bandu's fault, for all that her sacrifice might prevent it.

Or, she could accept the injustice of the underworld's price, and save Criton's people. Vella would curse her decision, but she would be secretly grateful for the results – she did not want her people to die. And Goodweather would grow and flourish in a world at peace, and might even meet her father again if Bandu chose to let her. Was she willing to make this sacrifice for Goodweather's sake?

She was. Bandu sighed. *I do it,* she said. *Show me how.*

You know how to already.

Bandu nodded. She felt the flexibility of this place. She took Criton's hand and plunged it into her chest, through meat and bone, until it touched her heart. When she drew it out, her body closed itself up again and only the blood on Criton's fingertips remained.

"Come with me," she said aloud.

Ravennis opened a doorway through the wall for her. *Lead him up the stairway without letting go of his hand. He will grow more substantial as you go, but do not turn to see him*

until you are both standing in the sunlight. If God Most High
wills it, it will be many years before I see you in My chambers
again. By that time, I hope to be ready to receive you.

50

CRITON

Criton groaned, trying to focus his eyes. His vision was blurry, and the light ahead was blinding. Where was he? Was that the entrance of the Dragon Knight's Tomb up ahead?

Bandu was holding his hand, pulling him along. That was nice. She was pulling him toward the light, though, and he would have liked to spend a little longer in the darkness, at least to let his eyes adjust. He tried to pull back, but her grip only tightened, and she dragged him harder up the stairway.

A stairway. That was odd. There weren't any stairs in the Dragon Knight's Tomb.

"Bandu," he said, "where are we?"

Bandu didn't speak, didn't even turn her head to look at him. She was still angry, then. He remembered the argument now: he had said he wanted to take another wife or two, and the results had been... predictable. So what was she doing back here? Had she forgiven him?

Slowly, slowly, his surroundings came into focus. They had almost reached the light by now, at the base of the tree. It must have been the Yarek, then, because it was far, far too massive to be anything else. These stairs were not stairs at all, but roots. He turned his head to try to see where he had come from, but there was nothing but darkness behind him.

"Bandu," he said, "what are we doing here? The last thing I remember, I..."

It came back to him then. Narky, the Dragon Knight's Tomb, the sight of Phaedra and the feeling of Belkos' claws digging into his throat, breaking through skin and muscle, tearing into his windpipe. He had been dying not too long ago. Dying. And now he was here.

They reached the light, then the top of the stairway of roots, and finally the sweet dirt of the southern plains. It made no sense for him to be here; or rather, it made perfect sense, but it was impossible for him to believe it anyway. He *couldn't* have been.

"Bandu?" he asked. "Was I dead?"

Finally she turned to look at him. "Yes," she said, letting go of his hand. "I bring you back."

"Does that mean... that you forgive me?"

"No."

He had been trying to brace himself for a response like that, but it wasn't enough. He had allowed himself to hope.

"You are not my mate now," Bandu said. "You can take other women and do what you want. I don't care. I'm not yours and you're not mine. But now you go and make peace between Ardis and your kind."

She turned from him and walked back the way they had come, just until she could touch the Yarek's trunk. "Thank you," she said to the great tree.

He stood, watching her. "I still love you," he said.

She looked back at him coldly, so coldly. "That is sad for you."

They walked away from the Yarek in silence, together and yet not. "How long was I gone?" he asked her at last.

"A long time. I walk here to find you."

Over a month then. And in that time, how many had died? It was too much to hope that there had been no bloodshed in his absence – without his influence, his people might easily have decided to sack Ardis after all. But Bandu wouldn't have any useful news for him on that front. She hadn't stayed to find out what the Dragon Touched were up to, she had come after him.

He should have been so grateful for what she'd done. She'd *brought him back from the dead*, for God's sake. Yet her rejection still stung. It hurt more than anything he had ever known, more than having his throat pierced by his cousin's claws. It was hard to be as grateful as he should have been when she'd brought him back to such pain.

It was hot and dry that night, but Bandu didn't remove a single garment as they lay down on the ground across from each other. Criton kept apologizing for what he'd done, but she wouldn't listen. He begged her to forgive him, and she ignored him. She didn't care that he hadn't taken any other wives after she left him. She was unmoved by his tears. Finally, he made the mistake of asking what he could do to change her mind.

"Nothing," she said. "I love Vella. She is a better mate than you."

He sat up and gaped at her. "*What?* You took another man's wife as your, as your… as *your* wife?"

"Yes."

He lay back down with an angry thump. It was more than he could even process. Here he'd been, begging this woman to forgive him for *suggesting* that he might marry again, when she'd gone and taken another man's

450 AMONG THE FALLEN

wife for herself! She didn't deserve his love; she didn't deserve his pain.

"How could you?" he said at last. "How could you be angry at me, and then go and do something like *that?*"

Now Bandu sat up. "I don't care what you think, Criton. I am not angry because you want other women. I don't *care* if you take others or don't take others. You are never good for me. Never. You can be angry about Vella if you want to be angry. I don't care. But if you try to hurt her, Criton, then I *kill* you."

"And Goodweather? What about her?"

"What about her?" Bandu repeated. "I take care of Goodweather before. I take care of her now. You have Delika now, and you can have other young with other women. If you make peace with Ardis and you tell your kind to be good to me and to Vella, then maybe you can help with Goodweather sometimes. I don't want her to be like you: she can know who her father is. She can love you. But I don't."

Criton had no response, no answer for her. He wondered what had become of poor Delika during his absence. Had Iona taken her in? Had anybody?

By the time he spoke again, Bandu had lain down and fallen asleep, her soft regular breaths unmistakable.

"I don't want Goodweather to be like me either," he said.

Criton did not count the days of their journey. Traveling with Bandu now, on the same route northward where they had once learned to make love together, was a painful affair. It was uncomfortable too: where once they had traveled this road with friends and a tent, now Criton had neither.

The villages that had once shut their doors against the cursed wanderers of Tarphae now opened those doors when Criton knocked, but he and Bandu always moved on as soon as they were fed. They couldn't trust the inhabitants not to try to kill him in his sleep. He was the Black Dragon now, after all, and what's more, they knew that he was *supposed* to be dead.

When Bandu had left him, it had broken his heart and shattered his confidence, but their relations now were so tense that it was a relief when Bandu finally left him again, striking out on her own sometime after they passed Anardis. It was so much easier to miss the Bandu who had loved him when the one who didn't was gone.

Criton only realized the next day that he hadn't asked her where she and Vella were living. He cursed himself then, because not knowing where she lived meant that he couldn't come to visit Goodweather either. Could he trust Bandu to bring their daughter to visit him instead? He had been a poor husband and an inattentive father, but he still loved the baby more than he could say.

He still loved them both, really. But Bandu would not have him, and her rejection freed him to make his political marriages. The notion no longer appealed to him, but it would have to do. Maybe he could find love again with one of the new wives the elders would choose for him.

He would have to be better to her than he'd been to Bandu.

Criton followed the road straight to Ardis, afraid that he would find a burning ruin there, or else a battlefield littered with the corpses of his kin. He breathed a sigh of relief when the city came into sight and he spotted the Dragon Touched camp outside it. He wasn't too late, then.

He arrived just before sunset, when the Dragon Touched were conducting their rituals to welcome the evening. If he had worried at all about what reception his people would give him, he needn't have. They greeted him with reverence, and brought him directly to Hessina's tent.

The high priestess regarded him with awe. "I prayed to our God for guidance," she said. "I did not expect this."

He soon learned of the losses his people had suffered in his absence, first at the Dragon Knight's Tomb and then during the disastrous assault on the walls of Ardis. Hundreds had died in that assault, not just plainsmen but true Dragon Touched as well. Criton winced at this description. His failure to marry any plainswomen had reinforced the feeling that the Dragon Touched were somehow above their allies, and that was a dangerous thing. He would have to speak to the elders, and marry the women they suggested as soon as possible.

He could not help but ask if Pilos, Vella's husband, was among the fallen. Was Bandu carrying on with another man's wife, or with a widow? It turned out that Vella was a widow – Pilos had died during the assault on Ardis. But upon learning so, Criton discovered that it didn't make him feel any better about Bandu and Vella. It might have made the whole thing worse.

He asked after Delika, and Hessina told him that her son Kilion had taken it upon himself to raise the girl in Criton's absence. Criton was surprised at first that it hadn't been Iona, but then on second thought, of course it hadn't. He resolved to visit Kilion's tent soon and reclaim her as his adopted child... but not yet. He had too many other problems to deal with.

The Dragon Touched did not have enough men to stage another assault on the walls, so they had decided to fortify their position outside and starve the Ardismen out. Hessina had scorned an offer of peace from

Magerion, but now she was having second thoughts. The Dragon Touched had never lost a battle in the open field, but their failure to storm the walls of Ardis raised the worrisome possibility that God Most High might have turned against them after Criton's death. Now even Hessina admitted that complete victory was unlikely, that she ought to have taken the bargain. And yet, Magerion was unlikely to renew his offer.

Criton's resurrection brought the hope of peace back to life. He had become a symbol of that peace in the weeks after his death, and whereas Hessina could no longer offer terms without signaling her army's weakness, Criton was uniquely suited to the task of rekindling the negotiations while still projecting strength. And yet, even this came with a price: where Criton had become a symbol of peace, Belkos' family had grown to represent war and hate, and had become increasingly ostracized within the community.

Criton put an end to that. He visited Iona with the elders in tow, and apologized for her husband's execution. It was ridiculous, on the face of it, to act as if he had killed Belkos and not the other way around, but the fact remained that Criton was alive now and Belkos was dead, and that it was Dessa and not Goodweather who would have to live without a father.

Iona accepted his apology with the grace of a martyr. Her mother and daughter did not – they took it as a vindication of their hatred for him. But there was nothing Criton could do except apologize again and move on.

He was horrified when Hessina asked him what he meant to do with Narky. He hadn't realized his friend was being held captive, and it seemed that even that much was a courtesy Hessina had extended to him as an islander and friend of Criton's, when the more popular option had been to give him a public execution before the walls of Ardis.

Narky shouted for joy when he saw Criton. "I knew it!" he cried. "I kept telling them that you'd be back, that Phaedra and Bandu would come through, but they wouldn't believe me."

"Bandu did bring me back," Criton said.

"So we can make the peace treaty happen now, right? You'll go with me and tell Magerion that you'll accept his tribute?"

Criton nodded. "And you'll tell your people that Ravennis is a servant of God Most High?"

"Gladly," Narky said. "Your coming back sort of proves that, doesn't it?"

Criton turned to Hessina. "You were right not to execute my friend. That decision is probably what saved you while I was away, and it'll make our peace possible now."

"Thank my son," Hessina said. "I was leaning toward execution, but he was very passionate about keeping your friend alive."

Criton's estimation of Kilion grew yet again. He had thought the man timid, but even in that he'd been wrong. Saving Narky, caring for Delika – these were not timid acts. His voice might be quiet, but it was a powerful voice for decency.

"Let's go," Narky said. "Let's go now and end this war."

"At dawn tomorrow," Criton said. "I need sleep."

He didn't get much. He was too anxious about the day ahead. He awoke well before dawn, and finding Narky in the same situation spent an hour in nervous chatter, going over what little they knew about Bandu's journey to rescue him. Narky was surprised that Bandu hadn't told Criton more, but Criton assured him that she hadn't, and when Narky asked him what had gone wrong between the two of them, he spilled his heart and told his friend about Vella.

After that, everything came out: his poor treatment of Bandu, her disappearance, and her final rejection of him, even after rescuing him from the underworld. Narky listened sympathetically, but he asked painful questions. Criton hated having to relive the way he had left Goodweather almost exclusively to Bandu's care, and how he had taken Bandu for granted – not only on the night she had left him, but really all along.

"I was a terrible husband," he admitted. "Just like I thought I'd be."

To his credit, Narky said nothing. Criton knew he agreed, but there had been a time when he would have had no qualms about agreeing much more vocally.

"It's no wonder Bandu hates me."

"She shouldn't," Narky said. "You're a good man. You saved us when we were trapped in Anardis, you saved us when we were trapped in Castle Illweather – you're braver and more loyal than anyone I know. It sounds like Bandu had good reasons to leave you, but that doesn't mean she has to hate you."

"That might be true," Criton admitted. "But it's still hard knowing that she left me because I deserved it. You can't imagine how much I regret it now."

Narky snorted. "I can't imagine how much you regret something? I killed a man, Criton. I shot him with my father's crossbow just a few days before you met me. After that, I stole this symbol of Ravennis from someone who was staying at our inn in Atuna. I hid it in my shoe, and I walked all the way to the Crossroads on it. Trust me, I know all about regret."

So Narky was the murderer from the prophecy. Criton wasn't exactly surprised that that was the case, but he was amazed that Narky felt he could admit it to him. "Who was he?" he asked. "Why did you kill him?"

Narky sighed. "I thought I was in love. He humiliated me for it, and… I was an idiot. When Ravennis spared me, I decided it was my chance to become a better person."

"I'm glad you took it."

"You helped," Narky said earnestly. "You and Phaedra and Hunter, and Bandu too. You all taught me how to be better, and I'm never going to forget that."

Criton smiled. It was good, so good, to talk to Narky again, not as leaders of men but as young men themselves; as people who didn't know. He couldn't think of a time when he'd enjoyed Narky's company more. They moved onto happier topics, and by the time they finished their conversation and left for the city, the sun had risen and was shining brightly in the east.

They took no guard, approaching the city together like brothers. As they walked, Criton rehearsed what he would say in his head, hoping that the guards at the Ardisian gates would listen to him rather than try to shoot him down. But the gates opened well before they arrived and an army came pouring forth, marching toward them ready for battle. It was an army like none Criton had ever seen before, more massive than even the one that had besieged Silent Hall. His first thoughts were panicked – with an army like that, would the Ardismen even care that he was offering them peace?

The closer they came, the more obvious it became that this was no ordinary army. At least two thirds of its soldiers were women, and half of them didn't even have weapons. They were marching on the Dragon Touched in a last act of desperation. But knowing what losses his people had taken, he couldn't have said who would win that final battle.

The army halted as Criton and Narky neared, and a man and a woman stepped forward to meet them. The man must have been Magerion. His armor was polished and majestic, and the crown on his head dispelled any doubts that might have remained about his identity. The woman, Criton soon learned, was Ptera. The looks that Narky and his wife exchanged filled Criton with sudden jealousy, so he willed himself to ignore them and concentrate on the Ardisian king.

"Black Dragon!" King Magerion called to him. "My son told me you were dead."

"I was," Criton answered. "But God Most High, who rules above all, commanded His servant Ravennis to release me so that we could bring an end to this war, which has wearied my people and prompted yours to march against them hopeless, desperate, and unarmed. So will you accept the terms I gave you before my death, and send all these people home in safety?"

All eyes fell on Magerion, the general and the king.

"Yes," he said. "I will."

51

NARKY

Narky made his proclamation that very evening, as the sun set behind the mountains. The square before the temple was so crowded that Narky thought a strong shove on one side might have knocked the whole multitude over, from the armory to the temple walls. With the king on his right side and Ptera on his left, Narky stood on the altar where once an angel had died and told his people that Ravennis, God of Laarna and of Ardis, Keeper of Fates and Lord Among the Fallen, was a servant.

"Ravennis Below interceded with His master above on our behalf," he told the crowd, "and through Him we were all saved. If not for the leadership of the Graceful Servant and the foresight of King Magerion, you worshippers of Magor would have been slaughtered like sheep, and your souls tormented for all eternity. Ardis still stands today because you turned to Ravennis, and He chose to favor you.

"The last time I was here with you, the man you call the Black Dragon had made an offer to our king and was willing to lead his people to peace. But when I went to accept his terms, his cousin killed him before my eyes.

"It was Ravennis who sent him back, Ravennis who took pity on our city and made this peace possible again. I'll say it again: only through Him was Ardis saved. Only through Him can we all be saved."

Narky surveyed the crowd, proud of the speech that he and Ptera had composed, and that he'd spent the last three hours memorizing. Nobody could say that Narky hadn't honored the terms of his agreement with Criton. He had been quite explicit about God Most High's supremacy – and yet, the Ardismen would not be turning from Ravennis to His master over this speech. Ardis still belonged to the God Below.

"And now," Narky said, "Priestess Ptera will lead us all in prayer."

He hopped nimbly off the altar while the men nearby – the king included – helped Ptera climb up it. While she led the crowd in prayer, Narky turned to the old man Criton had left behind to verify that he would be true to his word.

"You'll tell Criton that I kept my promise?"

"I will," the man said. He was an elder among the plainsmen, but Narky couldn't remember his name. Kenda, maybe?

"It's not the speech I'd have given," Kenda-or-whatever-his-name-was said, "but I'm not a priest of Ravennis. You kept your word. So long as your king delivers on his own promises, the peace between our peoples will hold for a generation."

Narky had hopes that it would. The first payment of gold was made the next day, and over the following weeks, shipments of stone were sent north to round out the first year's tribute. The Dragon Touched, in the meantime, withdrew from the gates of Ardis and moved northward as far as the Dragon Knight's Tomb. Per the agreement Criton had struck, the tomb would mark the southernmost point of his people's territory.

The treaty called for yearly tribute to be paid for only fifteen years, after which Ardis could consider its side of the bargain fulfilled. Narky had suggested the provision to Criton and Magerion, pointing out that it was the threat of a cessation of payments that had caused Ardis to make war on Anardis last year. If the treaty called for an end to the tribute payments within a reasonable span of time, there would be less temptation for either side to go to war again over the issue. The idea had appealed to Magerion for obvious reasons, and Criton too had accepted Narky's logic. Between that and his proclamation regarding their Gods, Narky felt personal responsibility for the treaty's success.

Perhaps the best part was how proud Ptera was of him for what he'd done. There was truth to her assertion that he had saved the city, for all that his part had been more minor than Bandu's or Criton's. And it was good, so good to finally settle into this life with her. Without war, capture, threat of execution, or fear of another religious betrayal by Magerion, he could finally exhale and begin enjoying his position as high priest. And in a year's time, Mother Dinendra would be forced to admit that Ravennis and Elkinar were one and the same, and the whole priesthood of Elkinar would be his to command.

To make things even better, Magerion seemed far less sure of his power over Narky than he had once been. Ptera had said something to him, something that had shaken him to his core. Though he clearly didn't like Narky or his wife any better than before, the king no longer viewed the priests of Ravennis as his tools to be used or discarded. What word would Phaedra have used? "Reverent," that was it. The king was reverent now.

There was another word at the back of Narky's mind, a word that would have applied to his situation now but that he was nonetheless afraid to use, afraid to even think about. Its power had haunted him all his life, but these last two years especially. To use it would have been an affront to his father's memory, and, he feared, an affront to the Gods as well.

But as the weeks went by, it was impossible not to feel it. For all his worries, there was no denying that feeling that he could finally breathe, breathe like a man who need never fear drowning. And one day, Ptera looked at him with those off-balance eyes of hers and asked how he felt, and it finally came out, bursting from its hiding place in his mind.

He felt safe.

52

DESSA

Dessa lay in her parents' tent, crying. She had such conflicting emotions, it was overwhelming. Anger at Father for sacrificing himself over something that everyone now agreed had been stupid. Guilt because she hadn't believed Grandma about Criton and Bandu. Guilt because she hadn't been able to stop their people from killing Father, and anger at Criton for being alive again when Father was dead. And above it all, sadness like she'd never known.

Bandu hadn't even come back to visit after rescuing Criton from the underworld. Dessa felt even more alone than before – Father was gone; Vella was gone; Bandu and Goodweather were gone.

If she had been more like Bandu, she could have gone to the underworld and brought Father back, just like Bandu had retrieved Criton. Maybe if she found Bandu, she could make her tell her how she'd done it. It wasn't fair that Criton should have a second chance just because his wife was a powerful witch and Dessa wasn't.

Mother didn't want Dessa to become a powerful witch. She wanted her to marry Malkon while she could, and join his family so that Father's taint wouldn't hang over her as it did his widow. Dessa wanted nothing to do with such plans. She didn't think she *could* live untainted anyway, not around people who knew about Father. Attaching herself to the Highservants would only make things worse.

Could she strike out on her own, and go find Bandu and Vella wherever they were hiding? Mother would have said she was too young, and would have forbidden it regardless, but hadn't Criton's mother left home at just such an age? Dessa didn't want to get married, and she didn't want to stay here and be hated. She had bigger plans for herself.

So she wrote her mother a note and left it where she'd find it, and then slipped away one afternoon while Mother was busy trying to calm Grandma. She took some food and some water and just sort of wandered off, trying to look like she was running an errand of some sort. At least for now, nobody seemed to notice her leave.

She knew that Bandu and Vella had disappeared while the camp was well north of here, but her sense of direction wasn't spectacular. All she knew was that she ought to head away from Ardis.

So she did, and spent her first night alone huddled in an empty barn, its animals already either eaten or carrying supplies for the Dragon Touched. She considered going back home that very night, but she knew that Bandu would have done no such thing. Bandu was always powerful, always confident. Dessa would be like her.

So she woke up the next morning and traveled onward, stopping whenever she needed to and foraging whenever she could. It was hard, but it was also good to be away from all the people who hated her over what her father had done.

She dreamt that Mother had found her and dragged her home to be stoned – she woke up shaking. But she got up, rubbed her eyes, and moved on. She always moved on.

Her legs got tired. Her stomach got empty. But still she traveled on and on, asking everyone she met whether they had seen two women like Bandu and Vella. Nobody had.

Even when she had been gone a week and a half and still turned up no sign of her friends, that little voice inside her would not let her give up. If she couldn't find Bandu, she could at least be independent like her. Maybe it didn't matter if she found her or not – so long as she made sure she was always eating enough and never falling asleep in dangerous places, she could still be *like* Bandu.

By God, she could be like her.

53

PHAEDRA

Phaedra stayed with Vella and Goodweather for over two months, waiting for Bandu to return. The wait was awful, but it could have been a good deal worse. Her relationship with Vella had grown more cordial, though Phaedra still sometimes caught her hostess looking at her with eyes that blamed her for the danger Bandu was in.

It was the words on the walls that softened their stances toward each other and turned them into tentative friends. Vella had been teaching Bandu to read, a feat that Phaedra had believed impossible until she saw the row of letters that Bandu herself had carved under Vella's set. Phaedra hadn't been able to hold in her respect and admiration for that – not that she would have wanted to. It was the first real smile Vella gave her, the one that lit up her face when Phaedra expressed such admiration and wonder at her work.

Phaedra couldn't have missed the *I love you, Bandu* that was carved above the bed, but she pretended to anyway, though she knew it didn't fool Vella. It was such an intimate message that she felt guilty for having read it at all, even though it was carved quite prominently on the wall. It showed the confidence with which Vella had written it – and the confidence with which she had assumed that the two of them would be entertaining no guests.

It was hard to escape the feeling that Phaedra was intruding on someone else's life. Particularly with Goodweather, who knew Vella but had no memory of Phaedra, it was clear that Phaedra didn't belong here – that her presence only made Bandu's absence worse.

Except, of course, on a practical level. Vella needed all her support just to keep Goodweather alive and healthy. The forced weaning that had taken place at Bandu's departure was a terrible transition, but they got through it together, taking turns consoling an inconsolable baby and trying to sneak another mouthful past her trembling lips. Phaedra had never realized an infant could give a person such a murderous look.

But she took to it in the end, and by the third week she was chomping happily on mashed chickpeas. All was apparently forgiven after that, and Phaedra even came to enjoy feeding her. The memory of an infant was short.

Phaedra's memory wasn't, though. Even in the midst of caring for Goodweather, she could not help but remember the mission Psander had sent her on, and worry about the length of this diversion. It was practically springtime already – just this week, Vella had planted the seeds for her garden! Could the world afford for Phaedra to spend another month waiting for Bandu, when she might have been sealing fairy gateways already?

And what if Bandu never came back? What if Phaedra had sent her to her death? Judging from the looks Vella gave her now and again, Phaedra wasn't the only one thinking about such questions. As much as Phaedra might blame herself if Bandu did not return,

Vella would blame her more.

But Bandu did return in the end, looking so grim that Phaedra was afraid she might have failed after all. But no, she had succeeded. Criton was alive, and the region would know peace once more. It was the price of his return that had her looking that way, and when she explained it in her halting manner, Phaedra couldn't help but feel that Bandu blamed her for not having known. Phaedra had to beg her for details about her journey, which Bandu gave, incompletely. There were details that she claimed not to remember, and others that she gave only begrudgingly.

Phaedra recorded all she could, wary of forgetting anything that Bandu would supply. She was also wary of losing her work as she had lost her father's scrolls in Hession's cavern, so she found a sturdy branch in the woods to use for a walking stick and scratched Bandu's narrative in a spiral on its surface. Her story of the underworld and its sea of sleeping dead might well be the greatest revelation of the century, and Phaedra meant to carry it everywhere.

As soon as the staff was complete, she left Bandu and Vella to their life together. Bandu didn't want her to go at first. She had missed Phaedra as much as Phaedra missed her – couldn't she stay awhile longer?

But Phaedra could not. "I'll come back," she promised. "There are things I have to do first, but I promise I'll come back. All right?"

Bandu was reluctant to accept that. But Vella was not, and whatever Bandu's thoughts on privacy, Phaedra preferred to let them have their moments alone. So she gave Goodweather a final kiss goodbye and left them all to their reunion.

She walked first southward, the way that Bandu had

come. There was a passage to the elves' world at the
Dragon Knight's Tomb, which she ought to try and close,
but that one might be best kept open until she had found
a way to clear Mura and his pirates off Tarphae. Until
then, the Dragon Knight's Tomb was her best and safest
connection back to Psander.

So she made Gateway her destination instead. Her first
exposure to the fairies had come by wandering through
that passage, and it had been a terrible awakening to the
dangers that lay beyond the mesh. It was fitting that she
should try to close that gate first.

Phaedra had always been a social person. She made
friends easily, had loved the dances and parties of pre-
curse Tarphae, and would never embrace solitude as
Psander had. But to her surprise, she found that she
liked traveling alone. It was good to walk at her own
pace, with no need to be self-conscious about her limp
or her need to stop now and then to rest her legs, hips,
and back. Perhaps she would learn one day how to fix
that ankle of hers properly, and then she would walk
and run and dance however she pleased. But until
then, she still had magic. She still had learning. She still
had power.

So she walked southward at her own pace, and when
night came, she set a ward to protect herself from the
rain and lay down on the ground to sleep. It was not
such a bad life for her, the life of a wandering academic
wizard.

It wasn't the life her parents had meant for her, of
course. How they would have thrilled to hear that
Hunter wanted to marry her! What would they have
said, had they learned that she had turned him down?
What would her friends on Tarphae have said? They
would have thought her insane.

But marriage carried too great a risk of children, and she did not want children. If she hadn't been convinced of that already, Goodweather had confirmed it. The girl was delightful, but caring for her was incredibly taxing. Even without a pair of worlds to save, Phaedra doubted she would ever want such a responsibility for herself.

And she did have a pair of worlds to save. Gods help them all.

54
VELLA

Bandu was back, that was all that mattered. Yes, Vella
wanted to pick at these wounds – she hated the sacrifice
Bandu had made for Criton to live. The sacrifice they
had both made, in a way. For peace, for safety, they had
traded away years that might otherwise have been spent
together. But there was no sense in bringing it up over
and over, much though she kept wanting to. There was
certainly no sense in bringing it up now.

Anyway, what was there to complain about when
Bandu was back? Bandu was back! They would live
together in peace and happiness for however many years
they had left, and that was more than enough. It was
more than Vella had any right to hope for.

So short a time ago, Vella had thought that she would
never be happy. Now her heart was filled to overflowing.
She had Bandu, and surely her people wouldn't dare to
give them trouble when it was Bandu who had saved
their nation. What more could Vella want?

Besides, it had been for Vella and her people that
Bandu had made her sacrifice, and it would have been
profoundly ungrateful to complain about it.

If only she could let these things go.

Bandu helped. Her grim mood vanished at their first kiss, and her high spirits seemed immune to thoughts of the future.

"You are so good," she kept saying. "So good all the time. I wish I have you sooner. Criton is never so good for me."

If Bandu could live in the present, by God, so could Vella.

Goodweather delighted at Bandu's presence, and spent the rest of the day squealing and waving her arms in excitement whenever her mother looked at her. It was a joy to behold.

"Now that she's weaned," Vella said, "we can make her a straw mattress on the floor and keep the bed to ourselves. She's sleeping better now."

Bandu nodded happily and said, "Tomorrow. I want everyone with me now."

So they didn't make love that night, but Vella didn't mind. Life was too good for her to mind much of anything. She lay in the bed, smiling to herself even as Goodweather wriggled and kicked in her sleep. What a beautiful world this was. She hoped it would never end.

ACKNOWLEDGMENTS

This was a much more tumultuous experience than the last time around. It was my first time writing a sequel, my first time writing on a deadline, and my first time submitting a draft I wasn't completely satisfied with. It took all manner of support to whip this novel into shape, and I'm profoundly grateful to those who gave me that support.

First and foremost, I need to thank my parents Claudette and Jonathan Beit-Aharon, and my in-laws, Vivian and Ken Dolkart, whose extensive babysitting gave me a lot more time to write without too severely increasing the burden on my wife. We both owe them a debt of gratitude, as does anyone who enjoyed this book. It might not have been written at all without their support, and certainly not on time!

I played my cards closer to the chest with this novel, but I also need to thank my family for their input into the book's contents. So thank you again to my parents and in-laws, to my sister Miriam and my brother Nathan and sister-in-law Becca, who were always willing to read multiple drafts, brainstorm improvements, and tell me honestly when they found a development disappointing. I can't stress enough how valuable it was to have readers like them in my corner.

I'd like to thank Paul Simpson for stepping into the role of my editor while Phil Jourdan was on sabbatical. His notes were detailed and excellent, and helped this book become what it is.

Lastly and most importantly, I want to thank my wife, Becky Jill Dolkart Beit-Aharon, whose support has been constant. She was the only person who read my first draft as I was writing it, gave me advice and encouragement every step of the way, and who would prompt me to talk my way through whatever problems I was having. When the deadlines grew short and the work stretched itself out before me, she gave me love and patience and even the occasional evening off from parenting. To say that I couldn't have done this without her feels like a ridiculous understatement – I couldn't have written the *first* book without her, let alone this one. And, true to form, she's reading this acknowledgments page as I write it, encouraging me to finish it with a perfect flourish and send it in already. So I will.

~ THE TIDES OF WAR ~

JAMES A. MOORE

THE LAST SACRIFICE

"The prose is sharp, the pace wonderfully timed with great action. Cracking!" — FALCATA TIMES

COME WITH US *to a thrilling new world of war-torn fantasy, with the new series from* JAMES A MOORE, *author of the popular* SEVEN FORGES *saga.*

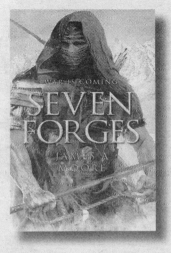

I: SEVEN FORGES

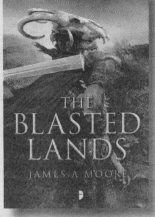

II: THE BLASTED LANDS

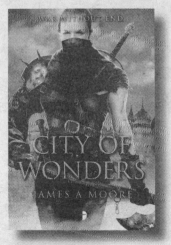

III: CITY OF WONDERS

IV: THE SILENT ARMY

Silent Hall
N. S. DOLKART

Refugees from a cursed island must face their pasts
if they are to defy their gods

"This was crazy good!"
KOEUR'S BOOK REVIEWS